JANE

I love writing authentic, passionate and emotional love stories. I began my first novel, a historical, when I was sixteen, but life derailed me a bit when I started suffering with Ankylosing Spondylitis, so I didn't complete a novel until after I was thirty when I put it on my to do before I'm forty list. Now I love getting caught up in the lives and traumas of my characters, and I'm so thrilled to be giving my characters life in others' imaginations, especially when readers tell me they've read the characters just as I've tried to portray them.

You can follow me on Twitter @JaneLark.

The Passionate Love of a Rake

JANE LARK

Harper*Impulse* an imprint of
HarperCollins*Publishers Ltd*
77–85 Fulham Palace Road
Hammersmith, London W6 8JB

www.harpercollins.co.uk

A Paperback Original 2013

First published in Great Britain in ebook format by HarperImpulse 2013

Copyright © Jane Lark 2013

Cover Images © Shutterstock.com

Jane Lark asserts the moral right to
be identified as the author of this work

A catalogue record for this book
is available from the British Library

ISBN: 978-0-00-757777-4

Automatically produced by Atomik ePublisher from Easypress

Chapter One

"If you think I shall allow you to rob me of my inheritance, then you may think again!" Hector had given his fortune to her freely. Had she not been through enough? She'd earned every penny of it, spending her life closeted away, body and soul, trapped in her dead husband's private form of hell. She had earned her independence, and Hector had given it to her. She would not let his son take it away again!

Jane Grey, the young Dowager Duchess of Sutton, leaned backward, inwardly cursing herself for even this outward sign that her stepson's intimidation was succeeding. The tenth Duke of Sutton, a man over twenty years her senior, loomed over her, applying the threat of his greater height and physical strength.

His eyes fixed on hers with a clear intent to intimidate and his hands gripped the arms of the delicate Chesterfield chair in which she sat. A chair in which she had been sitting, taking her afternoon tea in peace and solitude until his rude and uninvited intrusion.

"I am not afraid of you, Your Grace," she hissed into his face, which was barely two inches from her own, lying through her teeth. Of course, she was, she was terrified, but she refused to let him have the upper hand. In answer, he merely growled, making her flinch and proving how fraudulent her brave words were.

1

He'd never actually raised a hand to her *yet*. However, that he was capable of it and willing to be physically violent she did not doubt. Until now, Hector had always been there. Hector had liked to play his little mind games and cared not a jot for her happiness or well-being, but out of sheer spite, he would not have let Joshua harm her. Now, there was no Hector, and no one to protect her from his arrogant, evil son.

"No, Jane?" Joshua mocked, laughing at her as he suddenly pulled away to stand before her, his hands sweeping back and opening his blue, superfine redingote to display the robin-redbreast colour of his waistcoat beneath. He rested his hands on his waist. She wished to stand, but his legs were still on either side of one of her knees; it would bring her body up against his, and he hardly needed that incitement. Instead, she was forced to tilt her head back to hold his gaze.

"Your father left me his fortune by choice. You have all that is entailed. If you had shown Hector this much interest during his life, I am sure he would have left it all to you. But as it is, Your Grace, he did not."

Joshua stepped back, his hands falling to his sides and curling into fists.

Instantly, she stood, glad to be in a position to escape, if she had to. But whatever he did, she had no intention of bowing to his demands.

Tipping her chin up another notch, she glared at the man, her fingers curling into fists, too. "I will not give you what has been legally left to me." She could not fight him physically but she would fight him in court, if she must, and with every ounce of blood flowing in her veins. It was not her fault his father had lusted after a young bride, and it was not her fault Hector had chosen to leave her the vast majority of his unentailed wealth. But now, she was not about to let his bully boy of a son take it away.

"Your Grace, did you call?"

Jane swiftly turned her gaze to her butler, knowing her discomfort must be visible. She was surely flushed, and a thundercloud probably flashed in her eyes. Undoubtedly, Garnett had heard their raised voices from the hall and had come to her rescue. Thank God.

"The Duke is just leaving, Garnett. Perhaps you could show him out."

She met Joshua's gaze again. His eyes were as Hector's would have been in his youth, clear and dark brown. His tall stature was magnificent, imposing, and although she hated to admit it, he was handsome in his way. But there was nothing handsome in his character.

For nine years, she had suffered life as Hector's wife and this man had helped make those years miserable. So while part of her could not blame Joshua for his anger over the money, another part could. It was not her fault, so why should she be the one to pay?

He did not move, didn't budge an inch except for a muscle twitching at the edge of his mouth. His eyes told her he was assessing the situation and deciding his next move. After all, he could not force her to comply unless he was also prepared to force all of her staff, who would undoubtedly testify on her behalf that she had been coerced.

He must have drawn the same conclusion, for his brow furrowed, and he virtually spat his final words on the subject in her direction. "Very well, Jane, I shall leave, but I warn you, this is not the end. *I shall have my father's fortune.*"

It was not even a statement; it was a decree.

Watching, she waited, still stiff with fear and irritation.

He spun about and strode from the room, the tension of his anger visible in every taut, muscular line of his body.

She held her erect stance, not even daring to breathe, while Garnett followed in Joshua's wake; her fists were curled so tight against her sides, her fingernails pressed into her palms.

When she heard the front door open and close, she crumpled, dropping back into the chair.

Her shoulders were shaking in response to her retreating fear, and she covered her face with her hands. A sob escaped her throat before she could control it, even though her eyes were dry.

"Your Grace?"

Garnett.

She sensed him moving closer and drew in a deep breath, fighting for composure as she let her hands fall to her lap and straightened up.

"Madam, is there anything I may fetch you?"

The young butler bowed to her as she looked up. It was not his place to ask if she was well or needed help, but his expression admitted his concern.

Her life was unravelling at the seams. Unfortunately, she did not think a cup of tea would fix it. A raucous, disturbing laugh rang in her thoughts, a sound she knew bordered on insanity.

It was ridiculous.

She was now completely alone, apart from her servants.

There was no way out. No going back. She could only seek a path forward, and she could not do that if she became a simpering wreck or lost her marbles. No, she had to think, and get away from Joshua. She needed somewhere else to go.

She sucked all her courage back into her lungs on a long, deep breath. "No, thank you, Garnett." Her eyes looked past the butler, her mind reaching for ideas. Then she remembered Garnett's timely interruption. "Thank you for your intervention. I am grateful."

"Your Grace," he accepted, his voice full of compassion. "If you have need of anything, you will ring?" Then he bowed once more and left.

Jane stood. Her body was tense and her thoughts raced. She began pacing the hearth rug, crossing back and forth, her hands clasped at her waist. The sound of Joshua's carriage pulling away permeated the windows.

She had thought this property secure, a place which would be a home at last. She had rented it only last week and moved in but two days ago, and Number Three, The Circle, Bath, was the answer to her prayers, the supposed beginning of a new and independent life. Joshua had proved her wrong. No doubt Messrs Brampton and Bailey, Hector's solicitors, who had arranged her tenancy, had passed on her forwarding address. It had never occurred to her Joshua would follow.

She'd vacated the entailed property, which had become Joshua's, within a week, allowing the new Duke, his wife, and eight children to take up residence. But it seemed having his father's sprawling country estate and his town mansion, as well as a number of other smaller holdings and all the tenancies and income which went with them, was not enough.

Of course, a man in his father's mould completely, Joshua wanted it all, and he wanted her to have nothing. But let him bully her as much as he wished. "I will not give in."

Stopping before the mirror over the mantelpiece, she looked at her sad, pathetic reflection. She was gaunt, her skin sallow and grey, large dark circles rimmed her eyes, but then she had slept very little since Hector's sudden death four weeks ago. She had arranged the funeral and played sorrowful widow at his wake, while neither Joshua nor his wife had made any effort to attend.

Joshua had severed all ties with his father the day the old Duke had married Jane. Since then, her stepson had taken the greatest pleasure in victimising her, including making several indecent propositions.

Yet when Hector was alive, Joshua had never entered their home.

Her eyes faced her reflection, Jane Grey, the Dowager Duchess of Sutton. A dowager at the ripe old age of six and twenty. It was ludicrous. It had always been ludicrous marrying a man more than four times her age with a son over twenty years her senior. But her parents had thought only of the title and their financial security. They hadn't given a fig for her happiness. She had been bartered off for profit.

Finally, happiness was in reach. But Joshua was snatching it from her grasp once more. She was in equal measure angry and afraid.

He had the estates. They would make another fortune in time and plenty to live on. Why could he not leave her alone?

Oh, she wished her parents were alive. She would have run to them and let them share the hell they'd crafted.

Pressing her fingers to her forehead, she caught her sharp emerald gaze reflected in the mirror. Her almond-shaped eyes shone. She frowned in self-deprecation. Despite her current worn and sickly look, she was still beautiful. She did not feel in the least vain to recognise it. To her, it had been a simple and sorrowful fact for years, no blessing. Her unusual colouring, her jet-black, spiralling hair, her honeyed skin tone and, most of all, her vivid green eyes, were all at fault.

As Sutton's wife, her beauty had drawn constant attention. It was a gift from her ancestors – so her mother had once told Jane, glowing with pride. She came from a distant line of Spanish nobility.

Jane saw little to be proud of today. Beauty was a curse. It attracted men like Hector. Men who wanted to acquire it.

He'd sought eternal youth through an innocent, young woman in her sixteenth year and he'd drained Jane's life from her. She was an empty shell now. That blind, ignorant girl died the night her seventeenth year commenced. The woman who faced her now was born when she'd stood before an altar and promised herself to a man four times her age.

But it was useless thinking of the past; she could not change it. The only thing she was certain of was her future would not be under her stepson's rule.

Jane turned and paced back across the rug. She thought of Lady Rimes, Violet. The woman Jane had lovingly named the wicked widow. Last winter in Bath, when Hector had visited the spa to take the waters, Jane had snatched moments to escape and formed an unlikely and rare friendship with Violet. Violet was everything Jane was not, and the reason Jane had come to Bath. She'd hoped Violet would be here. It had taken one look in the register book at the pump room to realise her hopes were naïve.

This was not winter. The month of May meant the *ton*, England's elite society, were in London; of course Violet was there.

But Jane knew Violet would help her. They'd sought each other out numerous times last winter. Violet had made Jane laugh for the first time in years, and when Jane had left Bath, her friend had begged Jane to visit whenever she wished.

Then this is my answer.

If she lived with Violet, surely Joshua would not dare barge into the house. Every insult he'd thrown had been out of the earshot of society. He picked his moments carefully. Violet's presence would hold him at bay until Jane could find a pathway forward.

Impatient suddenly, she strode to the door, the black muslin skirt of her high-waist gown with its fashionable empire line, slashing against her legs, restricting her hurried and determined steps. When she reached the door, she looked out into the hall.

Garnett stood beside the front door. "Garnett, would you have Meg fetch my pelisse and bonnet? I am going out, and while I am out, please hire a post-chaise and team to transport me to London, and have Meg pack. I will be leaving tomorrow."

The Pump Room's director would know Violet's address.

The butler bowed stiffly.

Chapter Two

Jane's gaze swept the spectacle of the Duchess of Weldon's spring Ball. The room was flooded with shimmering, spinning colours as she watched the dancers, the debutantes in white muslins, and their mamas and chaperones wearing every shade of the rainbow and beyond. Gentlemen punctuated the spectacle in formal black, crisply starched white cravats and silk stockings; their only show of frivolity, the glinting embroidery on their waistcoats.

It was a beautiful sight, and all the glamour was reflected in shards of light, spinning and flickering from the crystal prisms of glass dangling from the chandeliers above, and from mirrors which lined the ballroom above head height. The orchestra played a merry country tune, and the dancers bounced and stepped in time, skirts swaying. Laughter, chatter, and the sound of their footsteps filled the stifling air.

Jane had never been to a ball in London until recently. Access to the splendour of this society ritual should have been hers by right as a duchess, but Hector had preferred small, crude affairs for entertainment. He had not held balls, nor attended them, and so, nor had she.

It all appeared surreal to her now, a place of dreams. Yet she'd existed in this world of illusion for over two weeks. It was Violet's everyday life. Jane was still overawed by it. She wished for her friend's air of confidence.

For the past two weeks, Jane had studied Violet's every movement, longing to gain both town polish and society's approval. To date, they had eluded her. Of course, wearing black did not help. She should not even be on the social round. She ought to be at home, tucked up in bed and reading a book, acting out the role of deepest mourning. But if she obeyed that unwritten law, then she would be at the mercy of Joshua.

Besides, Violet, the model on whom Jane was moulding her own image, did not give a whit for society's conventions, and no one seemed to pay any attention to Violet's blatant misdemeanours. Violet's favourite saying was, "Society's rules are only there to be broken." She put no store at all by them and persistently urged Jane to just put off her blacks and face the indignation, weighting her argument by pointing out Jane was now a wealthy widow and she need not pander to the *ton*'s condescension. Violet also said it was only the women who'd care. The men would not give a damn. They would be too busy being intrigued by another merry widow entering the fray.

Jane was not that brave. Yet she did not doubt Violet's perception. Everywhere they went, men glanced sideways, implying their interest.

Jane had not come to town to become embroiled with another man though. She had come to town to escape one. At least that, to date, *had* been successful.

"Jane, dear, I know you do not wish to dance while in mourning; would you care for cards?"

Violet's words stirred Jane from her reverie. She turned to her friend and smiled. "Truly, Violet, I do not mind at all if you wish to dance. I am quite happy to sit it out alone."

Violet's sole purpose in life was bringing men to her heel; she kept them on an invisible leash. She'd had numerous affairs, and

9

made no secret of them. Jane thought such things too *risqué*.

Yet observing Violet's intrigues had stirred new emotions in Jane. She noticed the muscular turn of a man's calf and his broad shoulders and slender hips far more than she had before.

"Lady Rimes, you will, of course, allow me to take your hand for the waltz." Lord Sparks, a third son, a very attractive man, a little older than Jane, bowed over Violet's hand.

Jane turned to gaze at the gathering dancers, ignoring the caressing forefinger she had seen him slip inside her friend's glove beneath her wrist. Jane knew Lord Sparks. He was one of Violet's long-standing flirts and a man of excessive qualities according to her friend's indiscreet descriptions.

His attention turned to Jane.

He had an unabashed beauty and an impressive figure. The dancing glimmer in his eyes made Jane blush. She dropped a slight curtsy. He took her hand, but his grip was formal, not testing any of convention's boundaries. "Your Grace, it is a pleasure to see you again. I hope you do not mind if I steal your friend away for a while?"

Matching his broad smile, Jane answered, "How could I possibly deny either of you? Of course I do not mind."

"You are very kind, Your Grace." He bowed, then turned to Violet and extended his hand. "Lady Rimes?"

Violet took it and let him draw her away, sending Jane a jovial smile over her shoulder, as if to say she would not be long.

To give her fingers something to do, Jane applied her black lace fan in a swift sweep beneath her chin and looked up at the call of a new arrival. The footman positioned at the head of the stairs, rapped his staff on the wooden floor and announced the guest whose name was swept away by the tune of the Venetian waltz flooding the room. Yet when the imposing male stepped forward, Jane's heart stopped, as did the movement of her fan.

Lord Robert Marlow, the eleventh Earl of Barrington, was the last person on earth she wished to meet. Or perhaps – her heart set up a wild and anxious rhythm – he was the person she most wished to. But not like this, not in her blacks, when she did not look her best.

Blushing and lifting her fan a little, hiding the lower half of her face, Jane set it back into motion, cooling her hot skin and peering over its top, unable to tear her eyes away from him. She had not seen him for years, not since they had both been young, innocent and naïve. He looked different, more confident, stronger, more handsome too, and taller, and broader.

He surveyed the gathering from his vantage point at the top of the stairs as though he assessed and judged everyone.

She'd considered this meeting thousands of times in the years since their last and she'd pictured herself armoured in sophistication, someone he would respect and admire. Yet, now, she felt completely the opposite: unworthy and unsure.

The gulf he'd left in her life ripped open wider. He was magnificent – she insignificant. If he'd been attractive as a nineteen-year-old youth, he was a demigod as a man in his late twenties. His physique was muscular, yet lean and athletic.

His hand rose and swept long fingers through his chestnut-coloured hair, swiping a loose lock from his brow. A gesture she had seen him do a hundred times as a child.

Still, he did not move, just looked, watching, appearing self-absorbed.

His confidence had not been there in the zealous youth, full of adventure and expectation.

She felt tears in her eyes and an ache in her chest, inspired by the *could-have-beens* and *if-onlys* which had haunted her throughout her married life.

It was a long time since Robert Marlow held her dear. In the

11

intervening years, he'd toured the continent, establishing a reputation in the vices of a gentleman. His prowess in the sexual arts was renowned. He was no longer the young man she'd adored. He was a very different beast, one whom she'd no experience or knowledge to understand.

When he'd returned to claim his father's estate a few years ago, his reputation had endured. He was one of, if not *the most*, profligate rakes in the *ton*.

She'd never been able to stop herself seeking his name in the gossip columns of the papers Hector left lying on the breakfast table.

Robert's gaze passed across the dancers and reached towardss her. Jane turned, covering her face with the fan, hiding. She needed to regain command of her wits.

Her feet led to the refreshment room, where groups and couples stood with glasses in their hands, and servants hovered around the tables bearing the giant bowls of punch and orgeat. The sweet scent of almond and orange blossom permeated her senses as a footman held out a silver tray and offered her a glass. She refused, waving a hand and walking on towardss a door in the far wall.

She knew it opened into the hall. She would go to the ladies' retiring room. She was in no state to face the ghost of her past when she had yet to master the demon of her present.

"Oh!"

As if summoned, when she stepped through into the hall, the very man she had come to the capital to escape was there, blocking her path.

"Jane, are you going somewhere? Perhaps I could accompany you?" He posed it as a question, but she knew he meant to give her no choice, as the oppressive size of the current Duke of Sutton, Joshua Grey, her stepson, presented a solid barrier.

She stepped back so she could look him in the eye, rather than face his cravat, and used the moment to assess her situation. Two footmen stood by the front door, and the hall was a thoroughfare for a number of gossiping women, passing to and from the retiring room.

She met the silent, venomous anger in Joshua's eyes and swallowed her inner panic. "I do not recall giving you permission to use my given name, Your Grace."

"I did not ask your permission, Jane." His fingers gripped her elbow, and although she discreetly tried to pull away, his strength was beyond hers. There was nothing she could do but follow his lead, unless she kicked and screamed, and she did not wish to make a fuss; it was better for appearance's sake that her fear went unnoticed. Joshua would not attempt violence in a public place.

Would he?

He drew her through an open door beside them, into the shadows of the Duke of Weldon's library. Then he shut the door and pressed her back against it, his hands gripping her shoulders, his thumbs and fingers incredibly close to her neck.

"Did you think you'd escaped me, Jane?"

No, she'd known it was only a reprieve. "I have no need to escape you, Your Grace. I am merely visiting a friend." The defiance in her voice was entirely at odds with her racing heartbeat, and he knew it; the pad of his thumb caressed the pulsing vein in her neck. But she refused to let fear paralyse her. She had endured enough years of this. She would not suffer any more. She would not give in.

His gaze dropped, descending to her cleavage.

She felt her breasts press against the low neckline of her gown as she snatched a sharp, deep breath. But before he had the opportunity to react, she stole the chance of his distraction and twisted free, slipping beneath his arm.

She could not escape the room; he stood before the door. Instead, she backed away, watching him all the time, setting about

13

ten feet between them.

"Jane." His voice was conciliatory and coaxing. "When will you accept you shall never win, and give me my inheritance?"

"Never. And *you* must accept *that*, and leave me alone!" she hissed.

"No, Jane?" His white smile breached the low light of the dark room. "Perhaps there are ways I could persuade you."

Her heart stopped and her mouth dried.

"I have always found you attractive, you know. I understand a little of my father's obsession. Perhaps I will let you keep some of his fortune if you are good to me. Would you be good to me, Jane?"

No. Bile rose in her throat. She swallowed it back as cold sweat dampened her palms. "I would die before I let you touch me."

"Do not give me ideas, Jane."

A shiver ran up her spine. "I would rather sleep with a hundred men than you!"

She had gone too far. Like a whiplash, he moved forward, snatching for her as she tried to dodge his grasp and run about him. She failed. He caught her upper arm in a vice-like grip and drew her body hard against his chest. His arm was like an iron bar as it wrapped about her waist, and his other hand grasped her jaw, anchoring it, forcing her face to turn to him. His teeth nipped her lower lip, then her neck.

"If I want you, you will not deny me," he whispered in a threat by her ear.

She tried to hide the shiver which ran across her skin, but she knew she failed, and fear constricted her chest, trapping the air so her breaths were shallow.

He pulled away a little, the white of his eyes glimmering in the darkness as his glare reiterated the threat. "And even if I do not want you, I'll not let another have you. So, if you have come to London to seek a protector, you'll find none. I will make that

14

certain."

He thrust her away, his grip releasing her so fiercely she fell to the floor, landing on her derriere with her hands at her sides. She looked up, hating to be so disadvantaged. He leaned over her. "Do you understand me, Jane?"

Oh yes, she understood. She understood she had never wanted anything more than to take every man in town to her bed except for him. Impotent and unable to find a single word in retort, she was left to watch as he turned away and strode out the door without looking back.

Her limbs trembled, and her heart still thumped a tattoo in her chest as she stood up. She brushed the creases from her skirt and fought for calm, then touched her hair, checking for loose pins. It did not feel too disturbed; she could fix it upstairs. At the door, she held still a moment, regaining her poise and catching her breath before she left the library. When she stepped out, she let herself show nothing but fashionable disinterest, denying that anything had occurred.

She crossed the hall and climbed the stairs, refusing to look for any reaction in the faces of the footmen who must have speculated on what had gone on in their lordship's library.

In the haven of the ladies' retiring room, Jane took a deep breath. Luck was still not on her side. She had prayed it would be empty; it was not. Three women sat under the attendance of their maids, and Jane needed to maintain the illusion of self-control.

"Your Grace?" Violet's ever attentive and highly skilled lady's maid stepped forward.

"Gail, please check my hair. I lost a pin or two I think."

"Sit here, Your Grace. No need to worry, it is easily fixed."

No need to worry? Jane had not hidden her distress as well as she'd thought then. In the mirror, she saw her skin was excessively pale, and her eyes were bright and still dilated with shock. The maid unwound the curls then reset and re-pinned them.

"Did you see the Earl of Barrington?" the woman next to Jane whispered to her friend. "He's such a stallion. I heard Verity took him to her bed. I wish he would ask me."

The woman's friend laughed and her fair skin coloured. She flicked open her fan and wafted air across her face. "Last summer, he made me an offer at Vauxhall. Unfortunately, before I could agree, my Charles arrived to drag me away. Even I would consider adultery for a man like that."

"He has every woman dangling from his hook," the third woman chimed up across the room, "with his insufferable refusal to let any affair stretch beyond a single night. He is playing with us. It is his little game. He knows he entices us all to win him for more. He sets us one against another, challenging us to break his nomadic ways. Barrington is a wicked taunt, and yet, such a handsome and skilled one none of us can refuse."

Another round of laughter, then the women began to rise, preparing to return to the ball.

"That will do, Gail," Jane dismissed the maid, rising too, eager to accompany the women rather than walk alone. "Thank you," she said in apology for her haste to the maid's lowered head as the woman bobbed a curtsy. Then Jane turned and followed the other women from the room, two steps behind.

"I know if I had captured his attention, I would not have lost it for the world, and your Charles would do nothing even if you succumbed to Lord Barrington's attentions. All the men are afraid of him. Rumour has it he killed someone," the first woman confided to her friend, with a tap of her fan on her companion's arm.

The third woman leaned closer, whispering conspiratorially, "I heard he currently favours Lady Baxter. He has been following her for nights."

At the foot of the stairs, Jane left their trail to re-enter the ballroom via the route she'd used to leave it. A few moments later, she was weaving through the crush and glancing about, looking for Violet. When Jane reached the front of the crowd, her eyes scanned the dancers and the people at the edge watching. She did not spot Violet. Instead, her gaze struck the tall man who she'd sought to avoid before confronting Joshua. He leaned forward to speak into the ear of his partner, and his hair fell across his brow. The action was so familiar.

Robert.

Yet the hungry look he bestowed on the slim blonde as his head rose was foreign. His hand slipped from her waist to discreetly brush the curve of her breast.

He was so familiar, and yet, in other ways, it was like looking at a stranger.

"You set your mark high, Jane, if you aim for the Earl of Barrington as your first conquest."

Jane's cheeks heated with embarrassment as she spun about and faced Violet.

"I was not..." Jane began then realised her denial probably made her appear guilty and halted. "I was looking for you."

"While enjoying the view?" Violet's eyebrows lifted as she laughed.

Despite their friendship, Jane had not shared her current, or former, woes. She did not wish to burden Violet with her problems. No one in the *ton* was aware of the history between the Dowager Duchess of Sutton and the Earl of Barrington, and it was far better left that way. What little had passed between them had been long ago, and only Robert's younger brother was left to comment on their friendship. Their parents were long deceased, and Edward, Robert's brother, had known nothing of their short affair.

"Jane, I have never seen you look so intently at a man before,"

17

Violet said, her eyes turning to Robert. "But heavens, do not look now, for I think the feeling is mutual."

Instinctively, Jane's gaze swung back and met his. It was locked on her, reaching through the scores of dancers, capturing her in a steady observation which seemed to question her existence.

"I said, *do not look*," Violet whispered in Jane's ear as Jane found herself transfixed.

He was so astonishingly handsome. It was in the strong line of his jaw, the curve of his brow and his nose. He made her knees feel weak just as he'd done when she was younger. At fifteen, she'd followed him as though he was the sun to her flowering woman-hood, but she had not realised his full potential then. Now, it was blatant.

She could not tell what he thought of her. There was no hint of emotion in the dark eyes holding hers. His face was blank and unsmiling, yet his gaze did not leave hers as he followed the steps of the dance, crossing with his partner.

"My, my," Violet whispered. "There is quite a spark between the two of you, isn't there?"

Jane tore her gaze away and looked at Violet. "Do not be ridiculous. He is merely staring because I am the only woman in the room wearing black. He probably thinks me improper."

"The Earl of Barrington?" A short bark of laughter left Violet's throat. "He is not shockable. He is scandalous. A titled gentleman can get away with murder, and *he* often does." Violet's brows lifted again, and Jane understood the implication. After all, she had read the frequent rumours of illicit affairs and forbidden duels which constantly surrounded him.

Remembering Joshua's earlier threat though, the thought of a gentleman being beyond the law was no comfort.

With his usual skill for timely appearance, she saw Joshua in the crowd behind Violet. He stood in the corner, arms folded over his chest, observing Jane with a scowl.

Wicked, indecent ideas began forming in Jane's head. Joshua would hate it if she took a rake like Robert to her bed, and she would so love to rub it in Joshua's face and prove his threats could not restrain her.

"Please, tell me you are not contemplating it?" Violet whispered, her voice dropping to a shocked tone. "I know he is rumoured to be quite brilliant in bed, but he is not a man to toy with. He has a reputation for being callous. I prefer a man who will at least pretend to pamper me a little, like Sparks. Your Earl goes out with an aim for seduction, takes what he wishes and walks away."

"He is hardly my Earl, Violet. All I have done is look at him, and all he has done is look at me."

Jane glanced back at the dancers and found the man in question still looking.

He was watching her intently with complete disregard for his dancing partner who, a moment before, had held all his attention. His actions certainly bore out Violet's words.

Yet the Robert of old had been a kind and tender-hearted youth. Surely he could not be *so* changed? If she were to take up with anyone, Robert would be her obvious choice. Despite Violet's warning, Jane still felt she could trust him. But his fixed stare was predatory. It stole her breath away and sent her heart kicking into a sharp beat.

"I think he is more than looking, Jane. He is busy eyeing up his next course. And *you*, my dear, should armour yourself, for if I am not mistaken, that man shall soon be on the prowl and at your door."

Violet's words should have scared Jane, but instead, she felt an unfamiliar stir of excitement and expectation.

"Come, I am of a mind to save you. Let us seek a glass of punch."

Jane complied with Violet's proposal, but as Jane turned away, she took one last look across her shoulder and faced that powerful gaze again. His eyes followed her movement like a hunting wolf.

She turned away, a shiver of anticipation running down her spine.

Robert's gaze tracked Her Grace, Jane Grey, as she disappeared amongst the crowd. The only woman who had the power to disturb his equilibrium had just appeared from nowhere and was now walking away from him, *again*. He'd been on the path of Lady Baxter for days, and he'd been winning, but now, he'd probably need to regroup and start again, having ignored her for nearly the entire dance. Yet he simply could not draw his attention back to the luscious blonde with whom he danced. His thoughts had been captured by the singular, familiar beauty of the brunette across the room. Jane.

Lady Baxter had given him a rare opportunity for diversion by persistently refusing his attempts to persuade her. He'd been enjoying the chase. Yet now he'd seen Jane, it was like holding up a rock to a diamond. Jane's superior beauty had always outshone every other woman in his head, and now he'd seen the reality again, he doubted any woman could ever appease the constant need in him for her, *for Jane*.

The melody of the dance ceased. Robert turned to Lady Baxter and bowed over her hand. "Forgive me." He suddenly felt angry and frustrated. With no further explanation, he let her hand fall, then walked past her in the direction Jane had gone. If he was being obvious, he did not care.

He'd heard Sutton had died and realised the implication – Jane was free. Yet he'd not expected to see her in town so soon, not mere weeks after the man was buried, and he'd had no intention of denting his pride by seeking her out.

In fact, when he'd thought of her, and he would not even admit to himself how many times he had, he had always imagined his desire would be for revenge, not her. Yet here he was, acting like a dog, chasing after her bloody bones.

His superior height gave him an advantage when he reached the open double doors of the refreshment room. He spotted Jane easily. She stood at the edge of a table, holding a glass which she sipped from in between speaking. While he watched, Lord Sparks approached and bowed to Jane, but his attention seemed focused on the woman Jane was with, Lady Violet Rimes.

Violet was not to Robert's taste, nor did he think he was hers. They had rarely shared more than two words. Yet a renowned flirt was not the sort of woman he'd expected to see the Jane he'd once thought he'd known and loved, with. Yet *that* Jane was not the Jane who'd married Sutton. *That* Jane had merely been his fiction.

Did I ever know her? He would not have thought for one moment the woman... Woman? In honesty, now, when he looked back, she'd been little more than a girl. But still, that girl had callously tossed him aside for a man more than four times her age. How she'd lived her life since, Robert had no idea. For all he knew, she'd slept with every man in Suffolk.

What would he make of that? So many emotions seemed to be vying for control within him, he could not say whether the idea was gratifying, arousing, or disgusting.

Jane's eyes turned towards him as her companion engaged Sparks in conversation.

He had forgotten how the ground could shift beneath his feet at just a simple look from Jane. He'd always thought her exceptionally pretty, even outstanding, with her unfashionably dark and sensual look. Yet now, she seemed to have truly grown into her beauty, her features were more mature, defined. The aura of it hung about her.

Holding her gaze, he gave her a lilting smile, not moving from

21

his position at the open door. Would she come to him, or would she wait to see if he would go to her? He was an expert at this game of cat and mouse with women.

Unmoving, he waited for the next steps to play out as they would. It was her turn. He'd followed, and now she had to decide how she would react. His gaze lowered, following the line of her dress. She was slimmer than he remembered. The high bodice tucked beneath her breasts presented a clear definition of her smallish but beautifully lush bosom. There was ample to cup in his palm with little unneeded excess. A memory of his hands at her waist, her lips meeting his, sent a shaft of painful arousal to his groin. He had been almost as innocent as her in those days, even though he was the elder by three years.

His eyes met hers again. They were distinctly green, the colour of emeralds. He'd particularly revered their unusual shade in his youth as something individual to Jane. He'd seen no one else with eyes like hers then. Though now he'd travelled widely, he'd seen the same a few times in other women, but even so, when visions of Jane disturbed his sleep or threatened his waking thoughts, it was always those green, almond-shaped eyes which haunted him. Her broad, genuine smile had charmed him as a boy, too, and brought him to his knees at her feet when he was a youth. Well, he had learned his lesson there. He'd never made the same mistake again, never trusted another woman so openly.

She'd made no move towards him, and suddenly, he was in a mood to drag this out and not bend. He did not doubt for a moment that eventually she would be too intrigued not to seek him out. Disengaging his gaze, he turned away. He had lived without her for years; what did he care if she chose not to rush?

His feet carried him back into the ballroom, and his gaze searched for Lady Baxter.

"Robert." Light fingers caught the sleeve of his black evening coat.

So she did intend to rush after all.

He turned back with a lazy smile, feeling incredibly smug to realise his skills had even worked on the ice maiden. When they'd parted, she'd held all the aces. Well now, the whole pack of cards was in his hands.

"Jane?"

When Robert turned to face her, Jane felt the floor drop away beneath her. If she had found his looks imposing from a distance, close to him, with that rakish smile lifting his lips, his handsomeness was devastating. It took her breath away. She sought to speak, but no sound came out. In his shadow, she was gauche.

"You had something to say to me, I presume?"

"Yes, I..." Words erupted and then dried up. She shut her mouth and drew herself together. What had she come to say to him? She had just seen him turn away and knew she could not let him go without speaking. *Say something.* "I – I..." She stopped again, then suddenly grasped control of her stray wits. "Could we go somewhere to talk?"

"Because you do have something to say to me?" His languid voice, his falling smile, and the suddenly intent look in his eyes implied she could have nothing to say he wished to hear.

She would not apologise to him. What had happened had not been her choice. She'd longed for him to save her even as she had said the words that turned him away. *He* had not come to her defence, and she'd hoped beyond reason he would come back, right up to the moment when she'd stood before the altar in Sutton's small church, feeling bewildered and betrayed, and said, "I will."

Common sense returning, she dropped a slight curtsy in parting. "No, of course not. I was wrong to think we have anything to speak of. Forgive me for interrupting you, my Lord." She turned away.

23

He caught her elbow and stopped her, his grip gentle. "You confound me, Jane. There *was* something you wished to say."

The truth struck her. It was in his expectant tone. He knew of the magnetic tug which had drawn her across the room. "No, I'm sorry. There is nothing we can have to say." She stepped back as he let go of her arm, and then saw Joshua across Robert's shoulder, observing everything.

"*Nothing?*" Robert prompted in a deep burr.

If she left Robert now, she would face Joshua's recrimination. The threat was written on Joshua's face. She needed to get out of the ballroom, out of the house, and away from the reach of her stepson. Her eyes met Robert's dark-brown intense gaze, the central onyx pools glinted in the candlelight and offered more than conversation. Spiralling warmth stirred in Jane's stomach. "But perhaps we could find somewhere private." There, the hint was laid down, and in her mind, Jane thought of Violet at her most flirtatious and tried to act the same. She lowered her eyelids a little, veiling her eyes.

God, that coquettish look heated his blood. Well, the mystery of her intervening years was answered; she knew how to play the game, and she played it fast. Yet there was still a question in his thoughts, a nagging doubt about her. She'd seemed almost as shy as a virgin, at first. But he supposed the cause of that lay at the door of their previous acquaintance, probably guilt or embarrassment, which he'd mistaken for innocence in his pathetic need to see and know his fictional Jane again. But even if he could never have his fictional Jane, it was still satisfying to know he could have *her*. He could take her for one night and finally free his blood of the poison her desertion had injected into his veins years before.

Oh yes, he would enjoy seeing her face in the morning when he was the one to say it has been nice, but goodbye. Was he heartless enough to want vengeance? *Hell, yes! Too right, I am.* He would dine on it for weeks. He could make the woman a laughing stock, if he chose, her husband but weeks dead, and yet, perhaps he was not cruel enough to go that far. He surprised himself. He had thought not an ounce of conscience left in his beleaguered honour.

"Very well, then." His words were blunt, but he smiled, speculating on the pleasure for them both. Bending to her ear, he whispered, "To your house, or mine, sweetheart?" Touching her elbow as he spoke, to add pressure and steer her from the room, he felt her jump and saw pink flood her cheeks.

"I am staying with Lady Rimes..." she faltered, her voice implying an intention to offer an excuse.

He was not about to let her articulate it. He'd set his mind on this now. He was not going to let her balk.

"Then it is mine. We'll take my carriage." He refused to let her deny him.

She shook her head. "I must tell Violet. She will wonder—"

"Leave a message with a footman. He'll pass it on."

He let go of her elbow and splayed his hand on the small of her back, applying an encouraging pressure to move her forward. She shifted and pulled away from his touch, walking a little ahead and separating them in the crowd.

He assumed she did it to conceal their joint exit, which meant she was ashamed to be seen with him. The thought made him irritable again.

Reaching the hall, he drew closer, his wicked and vengeful demons wanting to disconcert her – the part of him that was still hurt and angry at the way she had discarded him so easily years before. He settled his fingers on the curve of her waist in a possessive fashion. Her muscles jumped. Ignoring it, he walked on with his arm about her.

They passed four women returning from the retiring room.

She kept her gaze fixed towards the door.

"The Dowager Duchess of Sutton's cloak." His voice echoed in the space about them. One footman disappeared. "And send for my carriage. Oh, and once we have left, please tell Lady Rimes the Duchess has gone." Robert smiled, telling the man their reason for leaving.

When the footman returned, he held up her cloak, but Robert claimed it and put it on for her, stealing the opportunity to brush the skin at her nape and across her neckline from the back of her gown over her shoulders.

She shivered, and he saw her fingers tremble as she tied it.

It was pleasing to know he could discompose her. In fact, the thought sent his blood thrumming in his veins and a weight into his groin.

How would it feel if she shivered from his touch and his kiss when they lay naked?

The muffled sound of his carriage drawing up outside penetrated the door and his thoughts. A footman opened it and stepped back. Robert splayed his hand across her back again and felt her muscles tighten further. Her head was high and her back straight, apparently ignoring the footman's speculation.

James, Robert's groom, stood before them, holding the carriage door open. The step was already lowered.

Robert nodded up at his driver, Parkin, before taking Jane's hand and helping her ascend. Once she was inside, Robert turned and whispered instructions to James, then followed her in, climbing the step and ducking inside.

He neither lit the internal lamp nor drew the blinds. Instead, he let the gas lamps in the street give them a little light, but there were not many, and the carriage was frequently thrown from light into shadow as it rolled forward.

She'd taken a seat in the opposite corner, her back still stiff, her fingers clasped on her lap, and her eyes turning to the view from the far window.

He did not break the silence, but leaned against the window beside him, propping his shoulder against the pane of glass, his elbow resting on the narrow sill and his chin on his fist. He lifted one foot to the seat on the far side, leaving his knee bent. But he did not look out the window; he looked at Jane.

Lord, she was beautiful. At times, he'd thought her beauty embroidered from his patchy memories, as much of a fiction as her personality had been. Yet she was sitting before him now – it had never been a fabrication.

He'd spent his entire life since Jane honouring the beauty of women, learning to appreciate their every form, and Jane was the pattern card he judged them all by. But when he'd appreciated a woman's body and compared it to Jane's, it *had* only ever been an imagined view. He'd never seen her naked, never touched her beyond a superficial fondle. She'd been innocent, so had he, and he'd treasured it then, and treasured her.

Now, though? Now, they were experienced, mature players of the game. Now, he would know if she was all he'd dreamt.

The thought was disarming. In a way, he almost did not wish to know. He did not want his blissful illusion shattered. No, he'd loved a fictional Jane, and perhaps he had idolised a fictional Jane all through these empty years, too. Did he really want to know the truth?

She neither moved nor spoke, her eyes on the street, but he was certain she was not looking at anything in particular, just away from him.

He remained silent, too. He was in no mood to be conciliatory or ease her path.

If she'd been his intended companion, Lady Baxter, he would have had the woman pressed down upon the seat by now and his hands up her skirt.

A smile pulled at his lips. Sometimes he did not even get a woman as far as Bloomsbury Square before he had taken what he wished and set her down.

But with Jane, he required more than that. He intended to savour each moment, to learn every inch of her body and consign it to memory. It would take hours of slow appreciation to satisfy the thirst which had been in his blood for years.

His mind began crafting images, the ideas, the method of her seduction, and the achievement of their completion. Oh yes, he intended to enjoy this, and he intended to enjoy it in the comfort of a bed, unrestrained by time or space. The weight in his groin grew denser merely at the thought of touching her.

His impatience beginning to build, he reached up and tapped the carriage roof twice, ordering Parkin to stir up the horses.

Chapter Three

The carriage lurched forward a moment after he'd tapped the roof.

Jane grasped the strap.

He watched her with such brooding intensity, she felt as though she'd leapt from the frying pan into the fire. Of course, she'd realised abruptly when he began leading her from the ballroom, he was *not* the man she'd known before. Yet since they'd sat in the carriage, numerous memories of him sulking as a youth had spun through her head.

In childhood, his temper had always shown in this moody disengagement, when he'd not gotten what he wished, or hadn't won, or been unable to have the final say.

But surely, he was getting his way now, wasn't he? Or did he expect her to do more? How on earth would Violet behave in this situation? Should Jane speak? Should she move closer? She had no idea what to do or say. She had never been party to anything more than the light flirtation they'd shared before.

The silence stretched between them. She looked out the window and listened to the low rumble of the iron-wrapped carriage wheels striking the cobble, the horses' hooves hitting the stone, the creak of the wooden shafts beneath the carriage, the encouraging call of their driver, and the crack of his whip.

She couldn't stand it any longer.

Her head spinning to face him, she said, "A penny for them?"

His slouching silhouette was etched against the passing gaslight and silver moonlight that reached into the carriage as bars of light ran across him then disappeared. He was the epitome of all she'd heard and seen of a town rake.

"I'm sure if I spoke them, you'd blush."

"As it is too dark for you to see, why would I care?" Her words were braver than she felt, yet if his thoughts were of her, she wanted to know them.

"I am thinking of how I shall make love to you. What do you like, Jane? What makes you sigh with pleasure? What brings you to conclusion?"

His tall, lean frame unfolded from his slumped contemplative pose, and his foot fell back to the floor. Then he slid closer and leaned forward, taking her hands in his while his elbows rested on his knees. His thumbs began gently stroking across her palms. She felt it all the way to her stomach, and a deep longing, a thirst or hunger, settled in the back of her throat.

"I shall begin by touching you, everywhere." The movement of his thumbs slowed and became more sensual. "Then I wondered how you'll taste."

Her heart hammered, and the ache in her throat descended to her stomach. She wanted all of that. Did it make her wicked? She wanted to share it with him.

"Jane." He brought her to her senses. "What do *you* want?"

She wanted to reach her hands to his face and draw his mouth to hers, to kiss away all that had happened before, to go back to him and the hopes they'd once shared. To be in his arms forever. For the rest of the world and her past to simply melt away and become a forgotten history. Could he give her that? Perhaps for an hour or two, if she accepted what he was offering, but not forever. She'd lost forever with him. Yet she could take what he was willing to give. She could have now.

What would Violet say? She wondered. How would Violet respond to this?

Violet would not merely sit here waiting to be done to. Violet would take the lead. Jane leaned forward, too, and pressed her lips to his. She felt his lift into a smile.

She pulled away, but he whispered, "Show me then, if you wish. Do not stop." His grip on her hands pulled her back.

Her heart raced like a hammer ringing on an anvil as she freed her hands and curved one about his nape while the other rested against his cheek before sliding into his hair. She licked her lips as she leaned forward to kiss him again, and her tongue touched his mouth. He groaned, and the sound emboldened her. She touched the tip of her tongue against his lips as she kissed him, and, as if he could not resist it, his mouth opened, and his tongue touched hers, sweeping into her mouth as his hands rested on her back. Then his mouth pressed more firmly against hers, their lips open and their tongues fencing as he tasted her, just as he'd promised.

She had not known people kissed like this. He'd never kissed her like this before.

She felt the magnetic tug which had pulled her from the moment she had seen him standing at the head of the stairs in the ballroom, and moved to cross the carriage, her body arching towards him, but he gripped her arms and held her back.

"Not so fast, Jane, I don't want to rush this. We have all night, as long as you like."

A long breath slipped from her lungs, and her heart beat erratically as she dropped back into her seat. Had she made a mistake? She thanked God it was too dark for him to see her embarrassment.

"We've waited long enough for this. I'd rather savour it." His harsh whisper filled the small space of the carriage.

He sounded frustrated with her, angry.

I did do something wrong.

Robert's body strained against the confines of his breeches. He wanted her now, to strip her clothes away, taste and touch her, feel himself inside her, and know her body surrendered to his. He looked out the window and fought his impatience. They'd be home in fifteen minutes. She was silent again, too.

Did she want him as much as he wanted her?

Was she hungry for *him*, or was he just another man to her, a sexual acquaintance?

Was she just pleasure seeking, or was this *about them*, as it was for him?

She'd cast him aside before, stung his pride, more, given it a permanent dent. God, this was folly, tearing open this old wound, which had taken years to heal and left a scar running deep into his head and heart.

If... if? No, he'd not face the thought of a second rejection. What did he care now? He had four dozen other women who wanted him if she did not.

But here was the rub of it. Here was why he'd never truly dispelled her from his blood, because Jane was the one woman who'd turned him away. He'd spent his life since, proving no other woman could. His whole life was testament to the fact that the error had not been his. The fault lay with her.

He would make *sure* she did not reject him. His charm was an art form women could not refuse, wasn't it? He'd spent bloody long enough making it so, making himself a master at this, so *Jane* would not refuse him again. If she did, he dare not contemplate the pain.

The carriage rolled to a halt before his home, and in a moment, James opened the door and set down the steps. Robert climbed down first and lifted his hand to take hers. Her fingers were delicate and slender. They stirred something deep inside him. He did not wish to explore the feeling. No other woman had stirred it.

He retained her fingers and led her up the steps. His butler, Jenkins, opened the door before them. Robert encouraged her to enter first and let go of her hand. She stopped, her eyes following the square rise of the staircase about the edge of the hall. It was one of those which seemed to hang in the air, without a single pillar to support it.

He pulled the bow of her cloak loose, slid the garment from her shoulders, and passed it to Jenkins. "Thank you. That will be all."

Jenkins did not speak. He knew the protocol, as did all Robert's household. They were to ensure his women felt secure in their discretion.

Robert bent and whispered to Jane as Jenkins walked away, "Shall we go upstairs, or would you rather seek refreshment in the drawing room first?"

Her perfume filled his nostrils, vanilla.

Robert touched her waist, felt her shiver, remembered his earlier expectation, and made the choice for her as she'd voiced no opinion. "Champagne in my chamber it is then, Jenkins."

The butler merely nodded from across the room.

Feeling satisfied, Robert smiled and drew her towards the oak staircase.

Her eyes lifted again, apparently exploring the vast entrance hall as if awed. But he knew it could not be awe. Sutton's must have been grander.

"Come, Jane," he urged her on, catching up her hand.

When they reached the first floor, she was breathless.

He slowed his pace a little and squeezed the fingers gripped in his. The action stirred up a memory of being with her in the woods, where the border of his lands had joined her father's, the two of them eagerly running through the trees, heading for their secret meeting place, then falling onto a pile of straw in a stable by the woodman's hut. She'd been laughing.

The youth who'd been with her was not a person he knew any more, but what of that girl? She seemed different, too.

He opened the door to his chamber and let her enter first. His usual frippery greeted him, laid out just as he'd ordered. He'd forgotten all of that, all the ceremony he enlisted to aid a woman's seduction.

Vases of white roses were spread about the room, filling the air with a heady floral perfume, and the fire had been lit to ward off a chill. It now glowed in the hearth, nearly burned out.

He smiled as he watched her absorb the scene. Her eyes were wide as they passed over the pale cream and light gold colours, the satinwood dresser and chest, the two soft leather armchairs before the hearth, the three burning candelabras on the mantel, and the fourth by his bed. Her perusal stopped as her gaze rested on the tall, wide, four-poster bed. The rich orange walnut wood shone, polished like glass. The cream covers and sheets were turned back a little.

It was the temple he worshipped at – the bliss that could be found in a bed with a woman.

He sensed she was about to turn and flee, and rested his hands on her narrow waist. He looked towards her lips, deliberately denying her the opportunity to offer any excuse to leave by not meeting her gaze, and lowered his head, whispering, "Where were we?"

His lips touched hers, and he felt them stir into movement as her hands slipped to his back then up across his shoulders and into his hair.

Her mouth was soft against his. She kissed with uncertainty and hesitation.

Because it was *him*, he supposed. Because it was *them*. But even so, she set his blood on fire, as she had done in the carriage.

He broke the kiss and left some space between them to watch

his gloved hand slide up across her stomach, over her ribs and her bosom, to her neck, and then he touched her mouth. She sighed. He stripped off his gloves and threw them aside, knowing an expectant smile played on his lips.

Her gaze dropped as his hand touched her shoulder, his thumb resting on the bare flesh covering her collarbone, and he felt her shiver again when his fingers moved swiftly to release the four little buttons on her bodice.

Her breath pulled into her lungs, lifting her breasts a little.

Beneath her bodice, he tugged loose the ribbon securing the neck of her chemise, then slid his fingers inside, touching flesh. The circle of black at the centre of her eyes was a deep, inky pool, narrowing the emerald to only a slender rim.

Her eyelids fell, and a fan of long dark lashes rested on her cheek.

Her flesh was warm, and the sharp peak of her nipple pressed into his palm.

Her eyebrows had been plucked and were narrow and shapely, defining her forehead and the elegant bridge of her slim nose. Her cheekbones were high and her jawline beautifully crafted. Her appearance tilted an axis deep within him, flooding him with warmth, like hot glowing coals in his stomach. *Jane. God. This was Jane.*

He kissed her again, the delicate weight of her breast burning into his palm, its soft texture fluid in his fingers.

Another sigh escaped her lips, passing through their kiss.

He rained kisses along her jaw and down her neck. Then, as her head tilted sideward, he captured her nipple between finger and thumb and pinched it gently. She jumped and gasped, but it was not a displeased sound.

With his other palm at the small of her back, he bent and claimed her nipple with his mouth.

In his youth, he'd longed to do this, but then his sense of honour and his respect for her innocence had been too great. Now he would do as he wished and take whatever she gave.

A false cough echoed in the silence about them, then Jenkins said, "My Lord?"

Jane pulled away sharply and turned her back.

Robert smiled. So, the Dowager Duchess of Sutton *was* shy, though, as he looked at his butler, he could toss a coin for who was more embarrassed.

Robert supposed he should have shut the door, but at least Jenkins had the sense to keep his gaze lowered.

"Bring it in," Robert stated, "and set it down beside the bed."

The man nodded, doing Robert's bidding with his eyes still to the floor. When he withdrew, he backed out without ever looking up.

"Will there be anything else, my Lord?" he asked from the door.

"No, Jenkins, that will be all for tonight. You may retire."

Jenkins pointedly shut the door, and, internally, Robert laughed as he turned back to Jane.

She'd pulled her bodice back over her breast, but it still hung open, and it drew his eyes to the colour and texture of her skin. There had always been something exotic about Jane. Her skin was more ivory than cream, her hair so dark. Perhaps he'd stayed abroad because somehow being nearer to Spain, where her ancestors had come from, made him feel closer to her. He'd found many women of her ilk on the continent, but here in London, she was still rare.

He turned away and crossed the room to collect their champagne, and poured them both a drink.

When he returned, holding out a glass, she said, "Thank you," her voice shaky and her eyes on his cravat.

She did not look at all coquettish now. She looked like the bashful, blushing fifteen-year-old bewildered by her first kiss.

He sipped his champagne and watched her do the same.

Champagne was not his preference, but it was what women liked, and as what he liked was women, he drank champagne to please them.

She coughed, clearly choking on the bubbles, and set the glass down. When she straightened, her eyes finally met his again.

He discarded his glass, too, and felt her magnetism draw him closer. His fingers surrounded her chin and tilted her mouth to his.

"Should we not talk first?"

"I didn't invite you here to talk. Your chance to talk was at the ball. You didn't take it," he whispered harshly against her mouth before claiming another kiss. His fingers slid her gown from her shoulders. With her arms hanging limp at her sides, it kept on going and dropped into a pool at her feet.

She wore no corset. But then he'd realised that before, when his hand had touched her back and he'd felt the slight, feminine muscle play about her spine. He would lay his hands beneath her while they made love to feel the curve and flex of her slender form as he drove himself inside her. Lord, she aroused him.

He felt her fingers pull the buttons of his evening coat, shaking.

He smiled against her lips, and, stepping back, took over the task, undoing his coat and shrugging it off before tossing it over the arm of the closest chair. When his fingers moved to the buttons of his waistcoat, her gaze lifted and met his once more, pupils wide and glimmering with desire. Once he was stripped of his waistcoat, too, she stepped forward and touched his arms, her fingers running across his shirt.

Of course, in his youth, his muscles had not been so defined.

She began untying his cravat.

Yet again, she was too slow for his liking, and he took over the task, itching to be free of his clothes and have her delicate skin against his.

She did not appear skilled in undressing men, but then she was nervous, and that probably explained it.

When his neckcloth was loose, that was thrown to the chair, too. He gripped her waist and pulled her hips to his, kissing her as he pressed against her stomach. Her lips trembled a little beneath his, but her fingers began pulling his shirt from his waistband, brushing his skin beneath it.

God he could lay her down now and take her through the slit of her drawers. But he would not. He wanted this to last. He wanted the contact of flesh against flesh.

"Jane," he said on a sigh into her mouth as her fingers lifted his shirt. He took it off while her eyes and her fingertips skimmed over his skin, exploring every contour of his midriff and his chest, pausing to brush over his nipples before sliding to his shoulders.

"You're magnificent," she whispered as he tossed his shirt aside, her eyes shining.

She kissed him.

Robert laughed into her mouth, and Jane slid her fingers from his cheek into his hair. She was being naïve again. But she didn't care. Everything he did was turning her bones to liquid.

His fingers gripped her ribs below her breasts.

She was intensely aware of every move he made. He kissed like a master. It bore no resemblance to the stumbling kisses they'd shared in their youth.

This was her beloved Robert, but Robert was a changed man.

Drugged by his kisses, she didn't care.

Her mouth open wide beneath his; she let him plunder.

The warmth of his palms heated her breasts again, and she ached for him to take her in his mouth as he'd done before. He did not. Instead, his fingers drifted downward, caught the fabric of her chemise, then drew it up.

She lifted her arms and let him strip it off.

He threw it aside.

A sharp rush of desire spun from her stomach and pooled between her legs as his head lowered and his hands lifted her breasts.

When he dropped to his knees, she felt something inside her drop with him, a sharp, sudden spasm of beautiful pain. She felt like a goddess with Robert on his knees before her, savouring her, while her fingers sifted through his dark brown hair.

An ache burned like fire beneath her skin. She had never imagined it would be like this.

"Jane," he whispered as he glanced up and met her gaze, his voice reverential. But then he was kissing her again, his lips pressing against her stomach as his fingertips tugged loose the ribbon of her drawers. The garment fell away. It left her naked, bar her stockings and shoes.

She shivered as his lips drifted lower, pressing against the curve of her pelvic bone while his fingers slid up the sensitive skin of her inner thigh above her garter.

Her leg muscles jolted, surprised by the progression.

But then his touch was within her. "Oh." Her exclamation was half shock, half bliss. She clutched his hair, holding on against the sensual storm he invoked.

She felt so gauche and inept. This was Robert's art – love play, sex – and she hadn't a clue how to take part. He was a master. She was a novice. Yet she was learning, oh how she was learning.

His mouth touched her there, too, and her whole body jolted at the shock of his intimacy. She felt herself redden with embarrassment. *This* was what he'd meant in the carriage. He'd not spoken of the taste of her mouth. He'd spoken of her taste *there*.

She shut her eyes and just felt, letting him touch and taste.

The ache inside was growing, rising in intensity. It was too excruciating to bear this slow caress.

"This is torment," she whispered.

He looked up.

Her fingers gripped his scalp, her fingernails sinking into his skin.

"Give it up, then," he drawled in a deep heavy burr, his dark eyes sparkling. "Let it happen, Jane."

Let it happen? Let what happen?

Oh, Robert, what are you doing? she wanted to scream as she felt heat race across her skin.

He was laughing internally. She could see it in his eyes as they twinkled up at her, laughing at her naïvety. God knows what expression was on her face.

Then his hand took one of hers from his hair, and he pressed a kiss into her palm before letting it go. It was the sweetest gesture, but only a pause in the momentum of his onslaught, though the heat of his kiss continued to burn in her hand.

The crescendo was rising again. She gripped his hair.

Let it happen? What!

"Oh! Robert!" Her voice broke on a sharp, desperate cry, and her nails dug into his scalp. She felt as though she shattered, reeling into a wave of what could only be described as ecstasy. It tore through her senses, swirling into her limbs like a high tide in between the rocks. The muscles in her legs quaked, and she felt weak when it passed. But this must have been what he'd spoken of, because he seemed to know she could no longer stand. He laid her down, the rug beneath her.

"Robert? I..." She could find no words.

It didn't matter. He hadn't brought her here to talk.

His fingers were working a charm over her again, and his kiss did the same to her mouth.

It was coming again.

Her hips pressed upward with an instinct of their own.

40

She lost her breath as the fire broke out on her skin. Her hands gripped his shoulders and merely held on. He had complete control. She had no power at all.

"Oh, Robert." She slipped into a deep pool of pleasure once more. She wanted to feel their joining, to be complete. Her fingers searched for the buttons of his flap.

"Wait. Let's get into bed," he whispered, giving her a lazy, heated smile.

Into bed. Anticipation ripped through her as he took her hand and helped her rise. Walking backward, he pulled her towards the bed. She recalled holding his hand when they were younger, running or walking through the woods.

He bent to lift the covers and threw them back. The sheet beneath was dotted with heads of dried lavender, and the scent lifted into the air.

She suddenly felt intensely cold, and her arm covered her breasts as she pulled her hand free of his. How could she have been such a fool? This was not about her – the flowers, the candles, the bed. He'd planned to seduce Lady Baxter tonight. All this was for Lady Baxter.

Reality came crashing back in. All *she* was to him was another female body. Of course he knew how to make her feel good. He'd done this hundreds of times before, with numerous women. She could not do it, do this, and know it meant nothing to him.

How could she have thought she could?

She met his gaze and stepped back. "I cannot." Then she turned away to collect her clothes, shaking. She felt so foolish.

"Jane? What the hell is this?" His voice was irate and impatient.

Oh yes, she remembered his anger, his instinct to judge and blame, and the cruel accusations he could cast. He'd yelled and railed at her when she'd told him she was promised to the Duke of Sutton. That was the last time she'd seen Robert.

41

Her clothes clutched against her chest, she held a hand out to ward him off as he stepped forward. "Robert, I, I'm sorry. I thought I could, but I cannot."

He stilled, staring at her, and she could see he was seething. God knew what he thought of her after this.

She moved to touch his arm. "Robert, I just—"

He knocked her hand aside. "Do not bother, Jane. I have no desire to hear more of your excuses. I heard enough years ago. You obviously take great pleasure in turning me down. What was this, a game? No, do not answer that. I don't care."

With that, he spun away and strode towards the door, growling as he went.

His anger was in every taut muscle as he moved.

"I'll stir Jenkins from his bed and have him call for the carriage. If you are lucky, he may have not yet retired."

"Robert! Wait! I can walk."

He stopped dead and laughed. It was a horrible, heartless, mocking sound. Then he looked back, and his glare hit her like a blow. It was callous and accusing. He turned, then, and crossed the room with long strides, advancing so fast, she instinctively backed away.

"Jane," he barked to stop her as he neared. Then his eyes dropped to look at her left hand a moment before his fingers gripped it.

It was then before her face, with his finger pressing beneath hers, which still bore Hector's obscenely large, emerald betrothal ring.

"You think you would make it home safely with this on your finger? No, Jane. I will get you a carriage. No one has ever accused me of being inconsiderate. Perhaps that is why you think you can be so cruel to me? Perhaps you believe the rest of us are as heartless as you?" As he glared at her, one eyebrow tilted as though waiting for some response, and his lips twisted in a sneer.

What could she say? This was beyond an apology. It was

not about what had happened just now. It was about what had happened between them years before, and she wouldn't apologise for what had not been her fault.

She lifted her chin and held his gaze, unflinching, just as she had faced Joshua earlier, determined not to bow or bend. She had done enough of that in her life.

He turned away, growling again, then launched into a stream of what she knew must be obscenities, but not in English. He grabbed his shirt before storming from the room.

Her heart hammered as she rushed to dress. Why had she thought she could do this? It did not take her much to find the answer. It was because Joshua had made her angry. That was a part of it. She'd wanted to spite him, yes, but mostly because it was Robert. She would not have even considered it with any other man. But he wasn't *her* Robert. She didn't know this man. He was a stranger in so many ways. Not the youth who'd loved her, but a man who'd mastered seduction and sex, and played with sensual feeling solely to use and discard women.

Tears in her eyes, her fingers shaking, she struggled to secure the buttons of her dress. She'd made a mess of things again. She'd never be like Violet. Perhaps she ought to just stop trying to emulate her friend.

"Let me do it," he barked from across the room, his sudden reappearance making her jump, but his temper seemed to have cooled a little, at least.

Her hands dropped as he crossed the space between them, and her eyes lifted to his face.

His hair fell forward on his brow as his head bent, and he looked at her buttons. They were secure in a moment.

He'd roughly tucked his shirt into his breeches while he'd been away, and now, his back to her, he picked up his evening coat. He

43

did not put on his neckcloth or his waistcoat and left his evening coat undone. He looked back at her.

"Are you ready?"

She nodded, unable to speak past the lump in her throat.

His arm lifted as if to encourage her forward, and it somewhat surrounded her as she passed him, but he did not touch her. They left the room in silence, and when they reached the hall, she saw the butler below. He also looked as though he'd dressed quickly, and he frowned when he passed her cloak to Robert.

She stood still as Robert slipped it on her shoulders, but she could not stop herself from shaking. She made no comment, knowing if she did, the only thing that would erupt would be tears.

Robert did not speak, either, but once her cloak was on, his hand touched her back and slipped to her waist. It only made her wish to cry more.

They left the house and faced his groom, who held the carriage door open, struggling to hide a yawn.

Robert gripped her elbow when she climbed the step, then followed her in.

They sat on opposite sides in the furthest corners as they'd done before.

Once the door had slammed shut, Robert knocked on the roof, and the carriage stirred sharply forward.

She stared out the window again as they raced across town through the dark streets, never looking at Robert.

When they reached Violet's a short time later, Robert shifted quickly, rising, opening the door, and kicking the step down himself before the groom was even on the pavement.

She accepted Robert's hand to descend. There was nothing intimate in his touch now. It seemed cold, and she felt bereft of him.

He let go the moment her feet touched the pavement.

She wished she could thank him for sharing with her the things he'd done. It had felt good in the moment. He'd been gentle and kind, despite her desertion. But, instead, she fought against the lump in her throat, held back her tears and ran up the steps to Violet's front door, expecting him to go.

He did not. He followed her up and stood beside her again.

"Do you have a key?"

She shook her head.

He sighed before lifting the knocker with a resigned air.

It seemed ages before there was any sound. Then, finally, she heard footsteps.

A sigh escaped her throat, but on her inward breath, it became a slight sob as pain welled in her chest, and she bit her lip.

Then, as they heard a bolt draw back with a sharp, metallic scrape, his fingers touched her shoulder, turning her to him, while his other hand tucked beneath her chin and lifted her face. Then his lips touched hers briefly.

"I am sorry I shouted at you," he whispered when he pulled away.

He must think it was that which had upset her.

The door opened.

"Your Grace?" the young night footman questioned.

"Forgive me." It was all she could get out as she stepped inside without a word to Robert. She could not even look at him.

Immediately, once she was in, she swept across the hall and up the stairs in as close to a run as she could discreetly manage. When she reached her bedchamber, she shut the door behind her, and, leaning against it, slid to the floor and wept.

Chapter Four

The next morning, Jane walked into the day room where Violet took breakfast, knowing she did not look her best.

Meg, Jane's maid, had tried to hide the ravages of a late, tearful night, but with little success.

Jane was tired, and her thoughts were a tangled muddle as images of Joshua and Robert tormented her.

Her body was still alive with the sensations Robert had taught her last night, and her heart ached for impossibilities.

She felt exhausted and fragile.

The wonderful aroma of freshly ground coffee and chocolate instantly restored her appetite, though, and a blue sky beyond the windows mocked the unsettling regrets in her thoughts.

Jane liked this bright room. The morning sun always reached in through the bank of windows facing the garden, and its cream and yellow decoration was a cheery choice, distinctly Violet. The mahogany table was laid for breakfast, covered in a starched, cream cloth and laden with coffee, tea, chocolate, hams, cheeses and sweet cinnamon rolls.

"Ah, my dear." Violet smiled and beckoned Jane forward. "You must be starving."

Jane smiled and took the seat that a footman withdrew, facing Violet.

"Coffee, please," Jane ordered. She needed something to get her thoughts in order. The footman poured it.

"And now, Daniels, disappear. I am sure Jane will be happy to serve herself." Violet waved him off with a flick of her hand.

Jane's fingers trembled as she reached for her cup and, yet again, she remembered the things Robert had done last night.

He'd dislodged her sanity. Her tingling senses just kept stirring memories in her head, of his kisses and his touch. The image of his predatory stare in the ballroom hung in her mind, too, and the conversation she'd overheard.

He knew how to capture a woman's interest. He knew how to speak his intention without words. He knew how to make a woman feel special. No wonder he was infamous.

She thought of his room, of the props set out for Lady Baxter, not *her*. Yet, as she pictured it, she heard the apology he'd given as he'd left.

The door clicked shut behind the footman. Jane looked up and met Violet's gaze.

"Well, well, Jane," Violet whispered, her eyes dancing with silent laughter. "And there was I thinking you the shy and retiring type. How wrong I was!"

Jane opened her mouth to answer, but Violet lifted her hand.

"No need for explanations. I am not shocked in the least. But surprised, yes! Your husband is but weeks in the grave and you allow Barrington to take you home. I am sorry, Jane, but you are fooling no one now. You must take off those blacks." Violet laughed.

Jane opened her mouth again, but Violet's butter knife lifted and bobbed up and down, pointing in Jane's direction.

"Do not try to deny it, my dear, you cannot. I saw you return in his carriage in the early hours, with Barrington in dishabille."

"But I did not—"

"Oh Jane, there is no need to explain. I really do not care what

47

you do. You know I am partial to the company of men. But you have outdone me by a mile. It was at least a year after my dear Frederick passed before I took another man.

"However I suppose the former Duke of Sutton can be no comparison to a buck like Barrington. Yet, you strike me as a woman with a tender heart, Jane, and Barrington is likely to break it. As I said last night, he is not known for his constancy. The man is fickle. He's littered Europe with broken hearts."

Jane interrupted then, her coffee cup clicking back down on its saucer. She could not let Violet think Robert was *any* man. "Violet, you misunderstood. He and I are old friends. Last night was not our first meeting, and—"

Violet's knife bobbed again. "*Jane*, have you been keeping secrets? Friends with Barrington, indeed? Why did you not mention it?"

"Because I had no idea he was in London, and it is a lifetime since I last saw him." To Violet's knowing look, Jane added, "It is not what you think, Violet. My father's estate and his bordered one another. We knew each other as children. We were catching up, that is all."

Violet laughed. "And does catching up remove a gentleman's cravat?"

Jane felt a blush rise in her cheeks.

"Well, it is of no concern to me if you were catching up or not, just guard your heart, Jane. Your friend or not, he is not reliable."

That hardly mattered. Jane knew she had no heart to break. He'd shattered it years ago. Then why was there a deep ache lodged in her chest this morning?

"See." Violet pointed her knife again, and her voice rose in pitch, but she smiled. "You are already affected. You cannot take your mind from him. *Beware*."

Jane smiled too, and wondered where she would be without Violet. But she still denied the truth with a blatant lie. "I am not affected. He has simply reminded me of the past, that is all."

Violet's eyebrows lifted.

Jane blushed, but she did not let Violet speak. "We were very young, nothing happened, and please, do not say anything to anyone else, or to him. It would mortify me if it became common knowledge, especially with his reputation as it stands. I would rather keep our former friendship between ourselves."

Violet's colour suddenly heightened, too.

Jane assumed she had caused offence.

"I am not a gossip, Jane. You are my friend. But if you wish to keep it secret, then disappearing with him from an event the size of the Duchess of Weldon's was not the way to do it."

"I know, it was foolish." Jane felt a blush again. "I was just surprised to see him, and when he suggested it, I did not think."

"A symptom which is common for women in Barrington's company, I believe."

"You do not like him?" A memory of the scene in his bedchamber spun through Jane's head. Had Violet?

"I only know him by reputation. But he is not for me, and I have not, Jane, if that is what you are asking." Jane felt her skin turn crimson as Violet continued. "He is polite and indecently good-looking. But just keep your head over the man, Jane. I do not wish to see you hurt."

The thought gave Jane pause. The man who'd apologised before he'd left had been the Robert she remembered and had loved, and the one who'd kissed her palm... But Violet implied he treated women callously and last night, it had seemed he could. The room had been dressed so carefully, and they'd shared such intimacies, yet he'd shared the same with numerous women. It appeared it was the act of sex he was attracted to, not the woman, if he could swap his attentions from Lady Baxter to her so easily.

She'd known he'd changed though. It was no surprise. "I did

49

not have to come to London to hear his reputation. The gossip sheets have been full of tales about him for years, Violet. I know what he's become. You do not need to warn me. But he was like a brother to me as a child." She could not think him callous.

"A brother?" Violet challenged with another laugh.

"And later, a good friend," Jane redefined at Violet's dismissive hand gesture.

"A good friend who is a good kisser, no? You did not look at all like brother and sister from my bedroom window last night. You looked thoroughly kissed, and he looked—"

"I—" Jane again sought to deny it, but Violet stopped her, lifting her hand.

"Never mind, Jane. I am only teasing you. You do not need to justify yourself to me." Then with a smile she asked, "Well, then, what shall we do today? Lord Sparks has invited us to the horse races, if you would like to go?"

Jane smiled and nodded. Most of their days had been spent visiting or shopping. Watching the races would be a novelty. It might even stimulate her mind to think of something other than Robert.

~

Jane wished she'd found an excuse to cry off and stay at Violet's as she walked beside her friend and Lord Sparks. Lord Sparks was naming the horses as they passed them, while Jane's eyes were drawn forward for the umpteenth time to the couple strolling some distance ahead. The Earl of Barrington's broad, muscular back dominated her view, and his arm embraced Lady Baxter, his fingers gripping the woman's waist.

It was torture, watching them. Jane felt a fool.

Robert had not once turned back as they progressed, but Jane would swear he knew she was there.

He leaned and whispered something to his companion.

Jane felt herself blush and looked at Lord Sparks, trying to focus on his explanation. She felt as if she was intruding on Violet and her lover, though. Violet's hands were wrapped about Lord Sparks's forearm as they walked, and her attention was all for her beau.

Jane tipped her head back to see beyond the rim of her black bonnet, and looked up at the blue sky.

A single, wispy, white cloud hung above her. The rest of the sky was clear.

She really did not wish to watch Robert pawing the blonde woman in front of her.

Taking a deep breath, she shut her eyes for a moment, begging for patience and sanity, or, at least, a little common sense. She could not allow Robert to unsettle her. She had enough things to worry about without adding to her woes.

So, last night, he had chosen her over Lady Baxter, and now, he was merely gathering up loose ends. No doubt he was angry because Jane had walked away. Well, she had not come to town for an affair. She'd come to escape Joshua, and certainly not to find Robert.

Her heart clenched. She'd thought she'd conquered this pain long ago. She stubbornly thrust it aside and opened her eyes.

She was a long way behind Violet and Lord Sparks. Instead of following, she turned towards the horses. If she must feel alone in a crowded place, she may as well be alone.

A black mare whinnied in Jane's direction, pitching up her muzzle for attention. A young groom stood beside the horse. Jane walked over, answering the mare's call, and touched its muzzle.

It was a beautiful animal. She kissed its velvet cheek, and the mare's nostrils flared. "You're a beauty, aren't you?" she whispered.

The horse whickered, pushing its head gently against Jane. She gripped the loop of the bit at the edge of the horse's mouth and looked into the animal's large, dark eye. "Now, what did Lord Sparks say they called you?"

"Her name is Minstrel, Ma'am," the young groom acknowledged, bowing briefly. Then he smiled. "I helped to train her."

"And is she a good runner?" Jane's hand fell on the animal's flank.

"Oh aye, Ma'am, she's a real fine, fast runner."

"Then you would recommend I put my stake on her?"

"My Lord said she'll win us a fortune, Ma'am."

Jane smiled, but the boy's gaze had passed across her shoulder. "Billy, get Minstrel walking."

Jane's hands fell, and she turned to face Robert. He looked surprised at first, but then there was pleasure on his face. His hand lifted and removed his hat, and he bowed. Jane looked beyond him for Lady Baxter. She was nowhere near.

"Your Grace," Robert said, straightening up again. "Are you interested in my horse?"

"*Your horse?*" Jane felt the rush of gaucheness, again.

She was no Lady Baxter. Jane was unpolished in comparison and drab in her blacks, like a sparrow to a peacock, and yet, last night, he had chosen to take *her* home.

"Yes." He reached across her and stroked the mare. "Minstrel. We've high hopes for her. Have we not, Billy?"

"Oh aye, my Lord." The young groom glowed, clearly thrilled by Robert's attention. "Her Grace was going to put down a stake. I said Minstrel's a safe bet."

"As safe as ever a bet can be," Robert expanded with a smile, but his brow furrowed then. "How did you get here?"

He had not known she was here then. She was unsure if it made observing his flirtation better or worse. If he had not been lavishing his attention on Lady Baxter to rile Jane, then his attentions had been genuinely bestowed. *Which was worse?*

"Lord Sparks invited Lady Rimes. I came with them." Her heart raced. "I should go back. They'll be looking for me."

"I'll walk with you." His words were a statement, not an offer. He held out his arm. She did not take it. She was too out of charity with him today.

"I can manage alone."

"But you need not." He blocked her path as she moved. "You do not have to take my arm if you don't wish to, but allow me to escort you, Jane."

His behaviour angered her. He acted as though nothing had occurred last night, and as though *nothing* had occurred today, as though Lady Baxter had not recently been acting brazen beside him. Jane brushed past him and strode away, but her pace was hindered by the dense, spongy grass.

"Jane!" He was at her side and speaking in a fast, sharp whisper as he bent towards her. "I am sorry for what happened last night. I realise it was wrong of me to assume..." He stopped speaking as they passed two men, and she glanced up at him, only to feel the full force of his charm as he smiled. "I should not have expected it of you so soon."

She was astonished. Did he think if he'd taken longer, she would have let him progress? Of course, it was nothing to do with her feelings and all to do with his mastery. "Women are not mares to be coaxed across the last fence, my Lord, which is what you seem to think. And may I ask; where is your companion, Lady Baxter?"

He looked dumbstruck for a moment, but only a moment. Almost immediately, he was back in control, and a bark of laughter escaped his throat. "So, that is it, is it, Jane? You're jealous."

She realised, from the sudden bright knowing look in his eyes, he was not just speaking of today. He understood her words too well. He was thinking of last night.

"Well, sorry, Jane. I apologise for having a life after you. What did you expect? That, while you made merry with Sutton's wealth and status, I would twiddle my thumbs and wait for you, counting the days until the old man croaked? No, Jane. I moved on."

She opened her mouth, but had nothing to say. She could not explain to him in a single sentence how she had felt forced to take Sutton. Or how she had stood and watched him, Robert, the man she loved, ride away, and felt her heart leave with him, nor how she had cried herself to sleep for years, longing for him. And anyway, *that* Robert was in the past. This one would not even wish to know.

"I have nothing to say to you," she snapped and turned away. She walked hastily, but her foot caught on an uneven bulge of grass, and her ankle twisted. He caught her arm and stopped her fall.

His touch engendered a memory of the night before. She did not welcome it.

He bent to her ear, just as she had seen him do to Lady Baxter, and whispered, "Then what was last night about?"

"Last night was nothing but nostalgia and an appalling mistake." She pulled her arm free then hurried away, gratefully hearing him delayed by an acquaintance while she was absorbed in the jostling crowd as people moved forward to watch the race.

Jane looked up and saw Violet with Lord Sparks in his box and hoped the crush would deter Robert. But glancing back, she saw him a few feet behind her, still following. She strode the last few yards with unladylike haste and quickly climbed the steps of the box, hoping Robert would give up the chase.

"I was about to send Lord Sparks to look for you," Violet chimed as the footman opened the gate. "Where on earth did you get to? Oh..." She stopped.

"Her Grace was admiring the form of my mare." Robert's slow drawling tone rose from behind Jane. "Did you wish to lay a bet,

Your Grace? I would be happy to take it for you before you miss your chance."

Jane turned and gave him a false smile. "I believe Lady Baxter is waving to you, my Lord. Perhaps you ought to return to your companion?"

He looked amused, while Jane wished for a hole to jump into.

"Lady Baxter is quite able to cope without me for a little while longer. She is with friends. Would you like me to take your bet or not, Your Grace?" She wanted to say not, but before Violet and Lord Sparks it would seem churlish.

Her fingers shaking, blushing again, she lifted the reticule which hung from her wrist, but Robert's hand lay over hers then. "Simply tell me how much. We may settle up later."

"Five pounds, that's all," she acknowledged.

His hand lifted, but as it did, he leaned forward and whispered, "I asked Lady Baxter a week ago. It would have been cruel to withdraw the invitation now. I may have the right to be angry at you, but still, I find I would not wish to see you upset for the world. *Enjoy the race, Your Grace. Minstrel shall not let you down.*" The last words were voiced loudly as he stepped back. Then he turned and walked away.

Disgusted with herself, Jane took her seat on the other side of Lord Sparks to Violet and accepted the opera glasses the footman passed her to enable her to see the horses in more detail as they raced. The animals were already being led into the traces. She looked through the glasses and watched for a moment, but could not resist the urge to turn them on the other boxes. She spotted Lady Baxter, then followed the direction of her gaze to see Robert transferring the bet.

His expression was stiff, masked. He turned back towards the boxes and began walking. He smiled, Jane presumed, at Lady Baxter, and lifted a hand.

Jane turned the glasses onto the group within his box. They were mostly men, but there were three women. They all seemed in high spirits.

What Robert had said was true, of course. He hadn't even known Jane was in London when he'd courted Lady Baxter. Yet the thought of him with another woman made Jane's skin crawl. She hated Lady Baxter for no good reason at all. Well, *that,* Jane had best get used to. If his reputation was true, there were hundreds of other women, and there would be hundreds more. Perhaps coming to London had been a mistake.

"Forgive me for intruding, Your Grace, but you are being a little obvious." Lord Sparks's whispered baritone made her jump, and her hand dropped to her lap, the weight of the glasses resting on her thigh. His eyes were laughing. "If you will permit me?" He pointed towards the course. "The horses are in that direction. But, of course, if you are weighing up the potential of another type of stallion..."

Again, Jane blushed. She had done nothing but blush today, and she was unable to offer any response. Her eyes involuntarily lifted to the box across the green, from which she heard a burst of raucous laughter as the Earl of Barrington climbed up.

Blushing more strongly, she turned her eyes to the race and sought to hide behind the rim of her bonnet. Another laugh rang out. She could not help it, she turned back. She could see enough without the glasses to know Robert was looking in her direction, along with half the men in his group.

A slight, deep laugh erupted beside her. Lord Sparks had followed the direction of her gaze once more. She felt his gloved hand cover hers, which over-tightly gripped the glasses in her lap.

"Barrington is not the sort to kiss and tell, if that is what you are worrying over."

Her gaze spun to Lord Sparks. She surely could not be any

redder. "*You know?*" Her whisper was half question, half accusation, at the thought that Robert had told him.

He let go of her hand. "I was with Violet when you returned."

Jane was mortified, if only the ground would swallow her whole. To think Violet had been – while Jane had refused. "We did not—"

"It is none of my business, if you did. Really, Your Grace, I do not care. I only meant to reassure."

"I have warned her," Violet piped up, leaning across Lord Sparks. "I told you Barrington is an out and out bounder, Jane. He is playing you off against that woman."

"He is not so bad, Vi. If the Dowager Duchess likes him—"

Violet visibly bristled. "I know he is your friend, and I know your sister's silly theory about his broken heart, but that man *has* no heart."

"As you may tell," Lord Sparks laughed, glancing back at Jane, "Violet is very opinionated on the subject of Lord Barrington. She disapproves of our friendship."

"You may have whom you like as your friend. It is what he does to mine I care about. He is callous. Anyway, Jane, you have done what you have done, and that will be an end to it in any case."

A shot rang out, setting the horses underway, and any thought of their conversation was lost as the crowd began to yell for the various horses. Jane lifted her glasses to her eyes and saw the black mare. The jockey was in the colours of the Barrington's livery, maroon and cream, and his short whip tapped regularly at the animal's rump, driving the mare on.

The horse was a dream. She flew through the rest of the field, her head down and focused as though she enjoyed the sheer thrill of the race. When she stretched over the finishing line, Jane could not help but cheer, and turned to see pandemonium break out in Robert's box. Robert was gifting Lady Baxter with a very thorough kiss.

Jane's gaze spun back to the course. Violet was right. It was silly to think of yesterdays. What Jane had longed for in the past could not come true now. She pressed her fingers to her right temple and felt a pounding pain commence in her head.

~

"Enough. Why not go and look over the animals for the next race with Lord Franklin? I am sure he would escort you." Robert slipped Lady Baxter's arms from about his neck and set the woman away gently, ignoring her pout.

Lord Franklin heard his name and glanced over with a knowing smile, then offered the lady his arm.

She conceded and went off with Robert's friend with a flounce and a lifted chin, sidling close to Franklin in an obvious ploy to make Robert jealous.

It was pointless. He'd had his fill of her. He never bent to feminine games unless it suited his own aims. He was not, in general, a man led by his emotions. His desire for women was a mental game. The pumping organ in his chest was a cold and empty thing. Women, in general, did not affect it. He crossed his arms over his chest and watched Lady Baxter walk away.

Yesterday, he would have welcomed her fawning as a mark of his success, but today, it was cloying.

She had not accepted his desertion last night gracefully though. She'd been angry this morning, but despite that, the woman was not to be set off lightly. She was blatantly throwing herself at him now because she'd divined his interest was fading. More fool her. She'd clearly learned nothing about him. It would only put him off. It also convinced him that her previous disinclination had been a foil. She'd taken two weeks to woo, but now, he suspected, she'd never been disinclined, only hoping to snare him for longer than a brief affair. A game he was learning to be wary of.

He did not deliberately avoid long-term relationships. On the continent he'd had several.

A smile pulled at his lips when he remembered the opera singer in Rome. Then there was his widow in Venice. They'd taught him much of women. He'd learned many skills in his dissipated years abroad. It had changed him from a naïve and greedy youth, hungry for everything and anything that filled and fuelled his violently empty soul, to a connoisseur who liked to savour stimulation. Gluttony was no longer to his taste. He enjoyed relishing every morsel. Sadly, he just hadn't found a woman who held his interest in a while. His eyes strayed towards Sparks's box. And no woman had ever truly filled the void. Not since Jane. That damn woman had tainted everything beyond her, and now he'd seen and savoured an appetizer of the original woman he judged all others by, he'd lost his hunger for anything else again. He wanted her.

His stare reached to where she sat and caught her gaze. Instantly, she looked away in an obvious attempt to pretend she had not been watching. Her face now hidden behind the broad rim of her black bonnet, he turned fully in her direction and rested his gloved hands on the rail, making no secret of his contemplation.

Her slender, black-clad figure was tense. She was, perhaps, nervous. She probably knew he was still looking. Well, she deserved a little discomfort. He smiled.

When she'd suggested their assignation, he'd assumed she was fast, and she'd be eager, but in his chamber, she'd seemed hesitant. Yet her responses had been beautiful, real, honest, and open in a way he was unused to.

She'd let her defences fall last night. It had been all he'd anticipated.

He leaned forward onto his elbows and tipped the brim of his hat a little lower, hiding his gaze.

She was peeved because his attentions had been planned for Lady Baxter, yes, but from the way she'd looked at him just a moment ago, he would make a fair guess she *was* jealous, too. Well, jealousy was a useful tool.

She'd changed. But then, so had he. What to make of it? That was the question. All he knew at this moment was she piqued his interest, and he was unwilling to simply let her shrug him off. When he'd first seen her last night, the anger, which had driven his desire for self-destruction in the early years of his life after Jane, had fired up again within his gut. But equally, there had been a deep-seated need for her.

She had been everything to him once. He couldn't say if it made him glad to have her so close, or if he wished to see her suffer by his hand in exchange for the harm she'd done him. Tangled emotions had disturbed his sleep and still tormented him, conflicting tumultuous and dissipated desires.

Jane was the only woman who could make his heart pump harder, and the one thing he knew was she could hurt him. He could not dispel her from his mind now any more easily than he had been able to dispel her from his heart years before.

He stood up again with a self-deprecating sigh, and his fingers touched the betting slip in his pocket. He had an excuse to call on her. Perhaps he would explore what he felt for her. He'd learned to enjoy the pleasure of the wooing as much as the winning, the art of it and the power in persuasion. That was his true vice. He liked very much to feel a woman succumb and submit and mould to his will. Once she was tame, usually his interest waned. But there was still a lot of pleasure to be found in Jane, no matter which direction this led.

Jane knew he was watching her. She could sense his gaze like a dagger piercing between her shoulder blades.

Her fingers pressed to her temple as she tried to quell the ache in her head, and her heart would not cease racing.

She'd seen him pull Lady Baxter loose and the woman walk away with another gentleman. Even from a distance, Jane could tell from Lady Baxter's movements she had not been happy.

Why had Robert cast off Lady Baxter?

Had he done it because he'd known it was upsetting *her*?

Jane tried to watch the next race, but felt too angry to pay attention. She should not care what the villain did. He was not for her. No man was. Her future life was solitary. That was what she longed and prayed for, just some peace. Robert would not even wish to be a part of it.

Still she sensed him staring, and a long breath escaped her lips.

She felt so out of control. She'd held so many hopes for her life after Hector. She'd imagined she could, at last, do as she willed. All she wished for was a simple life, friendships, and mundane pursuits. Normality was a treasure she'd ached for for years. She'd thought Hector's loss would release her from her loneliness, but even in Violet's company, the loneliness had not abated. There was that stupid Robert-shaped hole in her life again. She had enough to worry over, fending off Joshua. She did not need to become embroiled in Robert's games as well. The only thing she was certain of regarding Robert was he was trouble.

Jane endured two more races, refusing to look in Robert's direction again, the ache in her head intensifying with every moment.

Then Violet commented on her silence.

Jane gave up the pretence. The headache was unbearable, and she could not go on.

When she asked if they could leave, Violet was all concern, and Jane felt awful for dragging her friend away.

On the drive home, Lord Sparks and Violet chattered merrily as Violet gripped his arm, and Jane pretended to sleep.

When they reached Violet's, Jane retired immediately and curled up on her bed. She felt so alone. She had been alone for so many years, from the moment she'd watched Robert ride away. But it had never cut her as deeply as now.

Unable to cry because coping was too ingrained, yet unable to sleep either, her thoughts reeled with recent and distant memories of Robert.

The longing in her heart was for a home, somewhere safe and comforting she could retreat to, but nowhere was safe, thanks to Joshua. There was nowhere to hide away from the pain of meeting Robert again. Oh, she just wished she could die, but then that would let Joshua win, and what she wanted most of all was to fight back against the Suttons. The last Duke had stolen half her life. She would not give the other half to his son. She would suffer anything to ensure Joshua did not win. That was the one decision she could make. It was the only control she had. She would not run, and nor would she let him win, which meant she must also keep coming face-to-face with Robert.

~

Looking in the mirror, Robert admired the cravat his valet, Archer, had deftly tied, and smiled, a mocking twist on his lips. His fingers swept back his fringe. He was a handsome devil. The knowledge boosted his confidence.

Women adored him. Well, every bloody woman except the one he'd wished to keep. His smile turned to a sneer for his reflection.

What did his looks count for? In this respect, not a thing.

He slipped his arms into the black evening coat Archer held up.

Edward, Robert's younger brother, would call Robert vain to the point of arrogant. Robert preferred to think of his appreciation of his looks as a desire for perfection. To which Edward would say, "more like perversity".

A self-deprecating laugh escaped Robert's throat as Archer slid Robert's coat onto his shoulders.

Robert slipped each button into place himself, while Archer swept a fleck of dust from the shoulder.

"You are in good humor tonight, my Lord."

Robert smiled again. Archer had been with him through his adolescent and maturing years abroad. The man was a saint, and sinner too, and a godsend. Archer could be counted on for anything. The man was Robert's right arm, his co-conspirator, and, at times, his saviour.

"I am, Archer," he answered, giving the man a wicked grin and patting his shoulder.

He knew what Archer was asking. Would there be a lady returning on his arm tonight? Somehow, Robert doubted it, not unless Jane could be persuaded, but, after last night, he thought it unlikely.

"I believe I am a-wooing, Archer. With a lonely night ahead."

The valet nodded, and the look in his eye told Robert, Archer had his own wooing to do.

"You may have the night off. I'll not need you again." If Robert's luck did come in by some remote chance, he could manage alone. Jane was clearly not a woman who appreciated frills and fuss. He suddenly remembered her excitement over bluebells in the woods at Farnborough when they'd been young. She'd been easily pleased then.

A smile still playing on his lips, Robert left the room.

He felt a sense of purpose he'd not known in ages, and blood pumped into his veins.

Yes, this was what he enjoyed, the invigorating pleasure of the chase.

Chapter Five

Robert strode into the Coleford's soirée with a feeling of expectation and scanned the people gathered in the drawing room.

He was pleased with himself. After a quick trip to White's, he'd discovered Violet's whereabouts, and if Lady Rimes was here, then Jane would be, too.

Standing taller than many of those around him, Robert had the perfect vantage point from which to spot his black-clad quarry, but one swift glance revealed nothing.

"Lord Barrington!" Robert turned and faced a slender blonde, a former conquest, Lady Shaw. She wrapped her fingers about his arm as if claiming him.

Robert unwound them about to give her a polite set down, but the Earl of Coleford chose the same moment to welcome his late arrival.

It was a timely rescue, and Lady Shaw withdrew.

"Barrington, I did not expect you, but you are welcome."

Coleford had been a friend of Robert's father, and the man had a daughter to marry off, so any bachelor within a thousand-mile radius was welcome. Even Robert's rakish ways were no deterrence when weighed in balance to his title and wealth.

"Lord Coleford." He shook the man's hand and offered a slight bow. "I was unexpectedly available and heard my friend Lord

Sparks was attending. I hope you will forgive my intrusion."

"Forgive it." The man laughed. "You forget how close your father and I were, Barrington. You should know you are always welcome here. Have you met my daughter?"

Robert was impatient to see Jane but pinned a smile on his face regardless, and greeted Coleford's girl, an attractive brunette with a bright, wide smile and sparkling blue eyes, but far too shallow and light-headed for Robert's tastes. He did not do young, and he did not do innocent.

After several minutes of making polite conversation, he took the opportunity to ask Coleford if he'd seen Sparks.

Coleford pointed him in the direction of the garden, and Robert excused himself.

His heart kicked into a quicker beat as he stepped through the French door and felt a cool evening breeze.

He saw Lady Rimes immediately. She was strolling with Sparks along a path leading away from the house, but Jane was not with them.

Robert crossed the lawn in long, swift strides, a carefree feeling reminiscent of his youth rising inside him. He called out as he neared them, "Sparks!"

The couple stopped and both looked back. Sparks gave Robert a slanting smile and turned fully, while Lady Rimes merely glared.

"I did not expect to see you here, Robert?" Sparks stated.

Robert's feet were firmly rooted to the spot. He could not find any words to ask them about Jane without being bloody obvious. "I thought..." He stopped. *Lord in heaven*, he felt like he had at nineteen when he'd first expressed his feelings to Jane. It was idiotic. The only thing to do was just ask. It was hardly out of character for him to chase a woman. "Where is the Dowager Duchess of Sutton? I'd presumed she would be in your company, Lady Rimes." He gave her a swift, brief bow, then cast her one of his most charming smiles.

She waved a hand at him in a dismissive gesture. "You need not seek to win me over, Barrington. She shall not heed my opinion, and besides, she is not here. She is not feeling well."

Confused, Robert merely stared.

"She has the headache, my Lord," Lady Rimes clarified. "Perhaps because you have been hounding her. You take advantage then flaunt yourself with another woman. Her Grace is…" She stopped, offering him a flint-like stare which clearly judged and weighed him worthless. But then her voice dropped to a confidential tone, "She is not one of *us,* my Lord." Her slim eyebrows lifted in arch punctuation of her words. "Do not toy with her. She is no flirt, Barrington, and she does not have the resources to fend off men like you. If you have any honour left in your soul, you will leave her be."

Her head spun to look up at Sparks. "Forgive me, my Lord. I find the company not to my liking. You may seek me in the card room later." With that and a swish of lemon silk, the woman was gone.

Robert looked at Sparks. "I take it Lady Rimes does not like me overmuch."

"Not if you upset her friend," Sparks answered then held out his hand. "Good evening, Robert. Do you want to get a drink?"

Robert nodded as they shook hands, then he fell into step beside Geoff, and together, they walked back across the lawn.

"She's right though."

"What?" Robert queried, his gaze drifting across the various couples spread about the lawn enjoying the first lukewarm night of the season.

"Violet is right about the Dowager Duchess of Sutton. She is not your usual sort. I would back off if I were you."

Robert stopped, and Sparks stopped too, his eyes turning to Robert.

"Has she been speaking of me? What has she said?"

Sparks laughed.

"What?" Robert felt suddenly irritated.

"Calm down, old friend." Sparks's hand lay on Robert's shoulder. "It is just she asked the same of you, in a roundabout way, and no, she has not spoken. Your little widow is a very private person from what I have seen. I doubt she would even share her secrets with Vi. But both Violet and I know because we saw you bring her home."

Robert felt heat rise on his skin. Why should he feel remorseful? She was not a sixteen-year-old virgin with a reputation to lose any more. She was a widow with a life of her own, and, no doubt, a list of lovers in her past. She had been married to a man older than her grandfather, for God's sake.

Still, he felt the need to preserve her reputation. "Then you will also know nothing untoward occurred. If it had, she would have been home at dawn." Robert answered Sparks's knowing gaze with a look that said *"you're wrong."*

"As you say, Robert, but the warning stands. She's vulnerable. If I were you, I would leave her alone."

Robert smirked. He did not like being told what to do, and no matter how much he liked Sparks, Robert was not about to be warned off the only woman he'd ever considered his. "No." Answering in one syllable, he moved to turn away. Sparks caught his arm.

"Robert, think about it and take care." Robert yanked his arm free. *"I mean of her,"* the man said to Robert's back.

~

Jane weaved through the people promenading along Oxford Street and glanced back at Violet's footman following two paces behind

67

her. He carried a bonnet she'd bought, in a box, and the ribbons and lace she'd purchased as a gift for Violet.

Jane had come out to clear her head, having spent hours thinking about how to beat Joshua and receiving no God-given inspiration. But now her head was aching again as the afternoon crush of shoppers hindered her path.

Ahead of her, a curricle slowed in the road. It caught her eye because the movement was odd. Glancing up, she was greeted by the sight of her stepson.

How on earth had he found her?

Preparing to climb down, Joshua handed his reins to a groom clothed in yellow and brown striped livery.

Jane immediately turned and began forcing her way back against the tide of shoppers.

"Your Grace!" the footman called as she pressed on in a sudden panic, twisting and turning between the passers-by, leaving him behind.

She was in no mood to face one of Joshua's scenes in such a public place.

"Your Grace!" Violet's footman called again.

Jane glanced back and saw Joshua had not dismounted after all. His curricle was creeping along a little behind her, his horses following her at a walk while he watched her.

She would not outrun him in the crush of people. He would keep his pace beside her no matter what she did. As usual, he had the advantage.

She pressed on, weaving through the human traffic, and sifted through her options. She was not far from Violet's. As she approached the junction to Bond Street, she considered turning there, but the crowd was currently protecting her. If she did so, she would lose that protection. She did not turn.

When she reached the curb, a road-sweep boy stepped down

to brush a fresh path for her and two gentlemen who walked behind her.

The boy held out his grubby hand.

Jane reached into her reticule for a coin and heard another deep voice hail her from along the road.

"Your Grace!" A voice she recognised with an instinctive lift of her heart, even though she knew it came at the worst moment.

Oh heavens, could this get any more complicated?

Dropping a two-penny piece into the road-sweep's dirty palm, she glanced up.

Robert sat on his high perch phaeton, pulled by a magnificent pair of blacks, approaching the junction she'd crossed. He was smiling, and he lifted his hand.

She turned away, refusing to acknowledge him while Joshua was watching. She just caught Robert's expression slip into a confused grimace.

There was a bookshop a little further along; holding her breath, she headed for it.

When she glanced back, she saw Joshua's eyes focus on a large town coach which had pulled across his path to turn into Bond Street.

Ahead, Robert climbed down from his curricle, having handed his reins to his groom.

She sighed in frustration, then finally, the bookshop was there, and she darted inside.

The bell above the door rang.

"May I help you, Ma'am?" A mouse-like shop assistant was immediately at her side. Jane dismissed him with a flick of her hand.

"I have merely come to browse."

Her heart was still pounding in a steady thump, the pace of a grandfather clock. She could see Robert's curricle through the shop window. It stood vacant.

Hiding her agitation, she took an aisle between the narrow shelves and hurried to its end, then slipped about the corner and stood with her back against the end of the row. Her breathing was ragged and unsteady.

The shop bell rang again.

Glancing along the back row of books, Jane saw a middle-aged gentleman studying the shelves at the end of the next aisle. She busied herself reading the spines of the books on the shelf facing her.

Heavy, confident strides echoed along the aisle beside her.

Jane held her breath, unsure whether to try to run or simply stay and face whichever one of her antagonists it was.

"Jane."

Robert.

Her breath slipped out on a deep sigh, and, despite herself, she had a sudden feeling of relief. His familiar face was a comfort, even if he was glaring at her.

"I was on my way to call upon you. I do not see why there is any need to avoid me? I am surely not such a monster. I believe the other night was—"

She shot him a meaningful look and turned her gaze to the gentleman further along the aisle.

Robert looked contrite when she faced him again. "Perhaps we could look for a tea shop?"

"No, thank you, my Lord. I am busy." Her initial relief had waned. She had nothing to say to him, after all, and he was the last person she would wish to know of her problems with Joshua.

She moved to pass him, but he gripped her elbow, though not painfully, just with a pressure she felt sought to deliver some message he could not speak in public.

"I was bringing your winnings," he said in an over-earnest voice, his eyebrows lifting, "and—"

"Look, my Lord, I gave you no money, they are not really my winnings. Keep it. Please. I am shopping." Whatever it was he wished to say, she did not wish to hear it. She had enough concerns without Robert making her life more complicated.

His brow furrowed, and his eyes studied her with greater intensity. "Ja—"

She glared at him and moved her eyes to remind him of the gentleman playing audience.

He recommenced, "*Your Grace*, I thought only to offer to take you for a drive. If you are busy today, what if I called tomorrow?"

Jane lost patience. She was in no mood for his dogged denial. She'd slept poorly the night before, and she was far too tired to play Robert's cat and mouse games. She neither had the time nor the inclination for it. She was still feeling shaky from her flight from Joshua. She just wished Robert would accept that no meant no. "Or, my Lord, you could simply not call." Jane knew her reaction was waspish, but she was exhausted. He knew nothing of her now.

His eyes narrowed. "Not call?" His voice said he thought her completely mad.

Jane backed away a single step, her arm pulling against his grip. Why must he make things even harder? Her gloved hand lay on his chest, on his morning coat, over his heart, holding him back as he would have stepped forward. "Please, my Lord, just leave me alone. I have enough to cope with at the moment."

His expression clearing, he answered curtly, "If that is what you wish." Then his fingers let go her arm and lifted to the brim of his hat, and he bowed. "Your Grace, excuse my interruption." He turned on his heel and began walking away. But at that moment, the shop bell rang again.

Jane looked along the aisle and saw Violet's footman, and beyond him, through the glass door, Joshua's curricle stood before the shop.

Damn the man.

She looked back at what was currently the lesser of two evils, her gaze narrowing on her former swain's back. "Lord Barrington! Wait! If you would?"

He halted and turned back, lifting his gloved hands in an expression of disbelief.

"Either you wish me to stay or you wish me to go? Which is it, Your Grace?"

Fully able to swallow her pride for the sake of security, Jane rushed forward and gripped his arm. "It is stay. Please, my Lord, would you take me home? My head is aching. I do not feel up to walking now. If you would take me up in your phaeton, I would be extremely grateful."

"Lord, Jane, you do blow hot and cold," he whispered in a growl.

She said nothing, but, gripping the crook of his arm, let him lead her along the aisle.

"Jack," she said to the footman as they reached the door, "Lord Barrington is going to escort me. I will no longer be walking."

"Your Grace." The man bowed, but she caught his look of confusion as he rose.

"Your Grace?" She turned her attention back to Robert, at the question in his voice. "Is something wrong?" His words were solicitous and quietly spoken, his deep burr just for her ears as he drew open the door for her. "Are you truly unwell? You're shaking."

She looked up and met his gaze about the rim of her bonnet and offered him a restrained smile. "I will be fine, my Lord, if you would *just* escort me home."

Chapter Six

Robert eyed Jane with uncertainty, taking her hand then helping her up into the high seat of his curricle. He could feel her fingers trembling. She was nervous and agitated, and he would swear there was something more to this he did not understand. One minute she'd been brushing him off, the next asking for his assistance. "*She's vulnerable.*" Sparks's words echoed in Robert's head.

Did Lady Rimes know something no one else did?

He walked about the curricle then climbed up to sit beside her.

She was balanced on the edge of her seat, her back rigid and her fingers clasped over her reticule on her lap. Her profile was half-hidden behind the rim of her bonnet as she faced forward. All he could see was her pursed lips.

His groom passed up the reins then returned to stand on the plate at the rear.

Jane's teeth clasped her lower lip as she kept looking ahead.

Robert faced the street and saw a vehicle disappearing about a corner further along. He flicked the reins, got his animals underway, and saw her fingers lift to her brow in the periphery of his vision.

Her head turned to look at the shops on the other side of the street, leaving him with a view of the back of her bonnet.

He felt frustrated, and if he were truthful with himself, a little riled. He waited for a gap in the flow of traffic then turned the team, taking them off Oxford Street, away from the bustle and hum, on to Bond Street.

Once he'd negotiated the turn, he glanced at her again. She was still silent and apparently intending to ignore him for the whole journey.

"*Is* something wrong, Jane?"

He did not remember this quiet, stubborn woman at all.

She did not answer.

The silence was filled by the sound of the horses as their iron-shod hooves struck the cobble, their whinnies and heavy breath, the creak of leather and jangle of the metallic tack, the rattling approach of other carriages passing, and the occasional shout from street vendors.

"Jane?" he pressed again at length, drawing the carriage to a halt, waiting to turn into a side street which would lead them back to Grosvenor Square.

He sensed her look towards him as he negotiated the turn.

"Nothing is wrong. I didn't sleep well, that is all."

Why would he swear she had picked that moment to respond simply because she knew he would be distracted? There was something more. He was certain of it. More to the point, he did not think it was anything to do with him, otherwise, why would she have suddenly requested his escort?

Glancing across at her, he saw she was facing forward again.

"You know, Jane, if there *is* anything wrong, you only need tell me and I would help."

She looked at him then, meeting his gaze and appearing uncomfortable, and yet desperate, as though she wished to believe him but did not.

Reluctantly, he broke the silent communication, turning his eyes back to the street.

The next moment he had chance to look across, she was facing forward again, her thoughts, he would swear, somewhere beyond him and the street.

He made no further effort to break the silence, concentrating on the short drive to Lady Rimes's address.

As the phaeton traced about the iron railings enclosing Grosvenor Square's central garden, Jane finally piped up, "I suppose I should at least offer you some refreshment for your kindness, my Lord."

Robert glanced at her before pulling up. "Not if it is purely out of obligation."

Once the groom had taken the reins, Robert climbed down and came about the phaeton to help her descend. When her fingers gripped his, they were no longer shaking. It was only more evidence that he had not disconcerted her, but something else had.

It was a strange feeling that transferred from the senses in his hand to his gut as he helped her down – compassion, longing, need. Or just pure hunger? He had no idea. It was nothing he'd felt before.

Once she was on the ground, her fingers gently tugged for freedom.

He did not let go, waiting for her to lift her face so he could see beneath her bonnet.

She did not.

Quite deliberately, he would guess.

After a moment, he let her go.

Without a word, she hurried up the steps, deserting him, but then she stopped as the door opened, and looked back as though she'd just remembered he was there. "You are welcome to come in if you like?"

A mocking smile broke his lips. There was absolutely no predicting the woman. Well, he was willing to take whatever crumbs she threw him today. "For a moment only. If you are certain?"

She gave him a sharp nod and went inside.

Robert told his groom to wait with the horses then jogged up the steps and lifted his hat from his head.

"Your Grace. Sir." The butler bowed to them both then held out a hand for Robert's hat as Jane untied the ribbons of her bonnet.

She handed it to the butler then undid the buttons of her spencer.

In a gallant mood, Robert took the garment from her shoulders, his fingers accidentally brushing the skin above the neckline of her gown.

She shivered as she'd done the other night.

It sent a sharp knife-thrust of desire into his groin.

Ignoring it, he handed the garment to the butler.

All this black was trapping the vibrant Jane he'd known beneath it, sucking the colour out of her. She was a mere shadow of the real Jane. If he could peel it all away, as he'd done the other night, would she be free of what bothered her?

"Selford, Lord Barrington and I would like tea," she ordered of the butler. "We'll take it in the drawing room. Is Lady Rimes at home?"

"Her ladyship is, Your Grace. Lady Rimes retired to her chamber an hour ago."

"Thank you, Selford. Do not disturb her on our account then," Jane acknowledged before moving on. "My Lord." The call was for Robert to follow.

Watching her in a place she felt at home was different again, but Robert felt like a bloody lapdog trailing after her. Still, he could enjoy the view, the slimness of her bare arms beneath the short, puffed sleeves of her day dress and the snug fit of her black muslin bodice. The way the material hugged the curve of her breasts and waist. Her black hair was simply dressed in a neat coiffeur, pinned back from her face, apart from a few wispy curls which had escaped to brush her brow.

She led him upstairs and along the hall to a pink room, heavily perfumed by a vase of roses in full bloom, then pointed to a chair. "Do sit down, my Lord. Is tea suitable? Or would you prefer something stronger? I could ring if you'd prefer brandy."

He took a step towards her. "Nothing, Jane, except to know what I've done to upset you. Why were you hiding from me today? You have no right to hold a grudge, you know. I admit, I may have pressed you a little fast the other night, but..." He left the sentence there, prompting for her explanation.

Her expression slipped from diplomatic Duchess to the new wary, *vulnerable* Jane, and her fingers clasped together before her waist. She glanced towards the window when she spoke. "You have not upset me." When her gaze returned, the Duchess was back. It hit him with the strength of steel. "It is just that..." She stopped, swallowing back her words, then began again and threw her words at him instead. "For heaven's sake, Robert, it is hardly five weeks since Sutton died."

His eyes scanned her face wondering what the hell was going on, and his hand touched her arm.

She moved back.

"But you are in London, regardless, Jane, and attending entertainments." She could hardly claim to be really mourning Sutton, no matter her blacks. She was flouting convention. How did she expect him to take that explanation? Her behaviour hardly said she had been devoted to the man.

She turned away and walked across the room. "I am visiting a friend, nothing more. I did not come here for the season or the entertainments."

He caught a glimpse of her figure through the loose folds of her gown as she moved, the fabric brushing her hips and thighs. When she turned back his eyes lifted first to her bust, then to her face.

"So you do mourn him then?" he pressed, not moving, letting her run if that was what she wished. Taming her would be like training a mare to the saddle, a step forward and then withdraw. Giving her time to grow accustomed to each stage.

She sought refuge behind a sofa across the room, her fingers gripping its back. "In a fashion. But it is none of your business."

"No?" He did step forward now.

"No, Robert." She held her ground.

"Then explain exactly why you came home with me the other night, and why you then changed your mind?"

She sighed as if irritated by his question.

He continued walking forward.

She did not move, although her eyes followed him with a steady look.

"I did not change my mind. I had not intended to..." She stopped, blushed and glanced upwards, as though the ceiling, or God, could give her the words. Clearly, something had as she refocused her gaze on him, the hardened Duchess again, daring him to challenge her and argue. "All I wished to do was talk. I did not mean to hurt you then or now, but I do not want to commence a flirtation with you. The other night was a mistake."

"So you told me yesterday." His voice was a mocking growl. He was annoyed despite himself. "But I think you are unhappy, and I do not believe you are grieving. So why *are* you miserable?"

She blushed harder and leaned to pick up a copy of *La Belle Assemblée* from a low table, before dropping into a seat on the sofa. He knew she was trying to appear casual. She did not succeed.

"I am happy."

She was not, her intonation was thoroughly unconvincing and her movement taut.

Occupying a chair opposite her, he answered, "*Liar*," letting a lilting smile catch his lips to ruffle her feathers.

A blush painted her ivory cheeks, and her gaze popped up again, the purest emerald cloaked by long, dark lashes. "I am in no mood for your games, my Lord."

"Robert," he snapped, leaning forward in the chair, resting one elbow on his knee. "Do not try to hide behind formality, no matter your feelings. And I am not the one playing games. I took you to my house because you asked to go, and then you changed your mind and I brought you home. I offered you your winnings. You refused to accept them. You asked me to leave you alone at the bookshop, and I obeyed, but *you* called me back. It is not I playing games, is it, Jane?"

She was silent as she held his gaze, then she coloured up again and concluded. "I am in a difficult position, Robert. Please, do not make it harder?"

"*She's vulnerable.*" Robert stood with a sudden need to understand her predicament and crossed the room to occupy the seat beside her on the sofa. Then he gripped one of her hands. "Confide in me, Jane. Something is wrong. I am convinced of it today. A problem shared is a problem halved, as I recall. What harm is there in telling me? What is going on?"

Her eyes met his, saline making them gleam in the bright sunlight streaming through the window, defining the emerald green like the jewel itself.

He was not, in general, a man of much depth. He did not seek to know people well, and he certainly did not wish to take on other people's problems. But this was not just any other person. This was Jane. As he waited, earnestly willing her to speak, a sharp pain settled in his gut, the age-old need and longing he felt for this woman. He was like a starving man in her presence. Bloody desperate was what he was.

79

Her fingers pulled from his grip.

Even holding her hand made him lust after her; his groin was heavy. He thought she was tempted to tell for a moment, but then her eyes clouded and her gaze dropped.

Jane felt the intensity in Robert's deep brown eyes silently urge her to speak, and daylight caught the lighter shades, turning them gold as she watched him. She couldn't speak though; it was not fair to drag him into this, she'd hurt him enough once.

Her eyes dropped back to the magazine. "Nothing is wrong, my Lord."

His knee touched hers, and she felt his muscle stiffen. Then he rose sharply and paced across the room. "*Liar,*" he said again when he stopped and turned back. His tone was sharp and condescending.

He was angry with her, and she could hardly blame him. She'd told him to leave her alone then called him back and imposed upon him to convey her to Violet's.

And, of course, he had no idea she'd only done it to avoid Joshua. She'd told herself she'd invited Robert inside out of common courtesy, but she knew she had invited him in because, despite the fact this man was not her tender-hearted Robert, she still felt safer with him. She simply did not want to let him go yet. She just needed time to feel confident again.

He was watching her.

She looked up, her gaze skimming over his sculpted, tailored, slim, athletic figure. He was so infuriatingly handsome, despite oozing anger and arrogance. The magnetic pull exuding from him dragged her awareness towards him as his brown eyes challenged her, seeking every detail of her thoughts.

"*If,*" he began, his pronunciation expressing bluntly that he still thought her words a lie, "you think to dangle me, Jane, you are playing with fire, not a fish."

He stepped closer, and sensing that he intended to lean over her, Jane thrust the magazine aside and stood, too.

It brought her up face-to-face with him, and he towered over her, merely a foot away. Her eyes fixed on his mocking smile, and a lead weight dropped from her stomach to the aching point between her legs.

She said nothing, and his fingers came up and lifted her chin, bringing her gaze to his.

"You are such a liar, Jane."

His tone was no longer angry, but it held a cynical humour, and the pupils in his eyes had widened, large, onyx circles darkening his gaze with long, dark lashes defining it.

A warm ache settled somewhere in her chest then spiralled to her womb like a rolling penny when his lips lowered to hers, catching at them gently, a soft caress.

She echoed it without thought. Her eyes closed as he continued to kiss her, and she opened her mouth when his tongue touched her lips. Her very bones melting, her arms reached about his neck, and her body pressed against him, and then he stopped and pulled away.

Her eyelids lifted. She faced a knowing smile and felt the chill of his desertion.

"As I thought, a lie, Your Grace, all of it. You *do* want me. Like it or not, Jane. Admit it or not. You want me. You are found out, my dear." His eyes narrowed as he continued. "But why not admit it? I cannot make you out. And there I presume is the dilemma which has you so distracted and upset. Whatever it is that prevents you admitting it, I mean."

His hand rose suddenly and tapped her under the chin, before dropping again. "Such a tease, Jane. You don't know me very well, do you? These games do nothing but inspire me to persist."

A knock struck the door she'd left ajar. "Tea, Ma'am." The maid's voice reached into the room.

"Come in." Jane felt a blush rise again, realising the maid must have heard at least part of their conversation.

Jane turned her back on Robert to hide her embarrassment, then crossed the room and looked out the window.

She waited there, listening as the maid laid out the tea tray.

"Thank you," Jane said, when she heard the maid withdraw, looking down towards the square and the park below.

Joshua was there, sitting in his curricle.

He'd positioned it in the far corner of the square and sat with one arm stretched along the back of the double seat while he smoked a thin cigar, looking up at the house. A gloating smirk lodged on his face as he spotted her.

She stepped back and turned away only to find her path blocked by her other pursuer, the Earl of Barrington.

Her fingers lifted and rested on the front of his coat, steadying herself and holding him back as she met his gaze. A flint seemed to spark between them then and caught to a flame. She could see it in his eyes and feel it in her blood.

She did want him physically. She always had. Robert Marlow was a heart-wrenchingly beautiful man. But the problem was, he knew it, and he knew exactly what he did to her, too. She had to stand firm, despite her memories and the feelings which still burned inside her from the old days. He was not her haven against the world. Right now, he was nothing but a wolf in sheep's clothing, as dangerous as Joshua in his way. But, God forgive her, he made her want to be devoured, no matter how much she knew it could only bring her pain, and clearly he wanted to devour her, because, regardless of the anger still bristling in his eyes, and his right to be aggrieved, his head bent and his hands slid about her waist.

The embrace was fierce and impassioned. She was breathless

in moments, and her heart thumped hard as her fingers clung in his hair, hanging on against the flood.

His hands slid down over the contours of her body, moulded to the shape of her buttocks, then pressed her to him. A lustful groan slipped from his mouth into hers as she felt his arousal.

"Huh-hum."

Robert let her go instantly, and Jane felt her face turn crimson as she looked across the room and met Violet's reproachful gaze.

She stood in the doorway, her hand still gripping the door handle.

Of course, they had not shut the door.

Jane glanced guiltily at Robert, only to see him expressing no remorse at all.

Instead, he wore a wolfish grin, looking full of scornful satis-faction as his fingers lifted and swept back the lock of hair she'd dislodged.

Ignoring their reaction, Violet walked into the room and crossed to the tea tray. "Shall I pour?" Her tone bore as much humour as annoyance.

Feeling ashamed, Jane accepted with a nod.

"Selford said you had a visitor. I presumed you would need some company." There was censure in Violet's voice.

Jane smiled an apology and moved to collect her tea. Then she returned to the sofa and sat.

"My Lord?" Her friend sent Robert a quelling gaze.

Jane assumed he would instantly withdraw with some excuse to leave, but Robert was not so easily daunted.

He nodded and walked forward to collect his cup then sat beside Jane.

It seemed a deliberate move. She was very aware of his muscular thigh pressing against hers. She felt a blush again.

"To what end do we owe the honour of your visit, Barrington?"

Violet said, taking the chair opposite.

"His Lordship kindly gave me a lift home," Jane interceded before Robert could respond.

Despite the charming smile on her face, Violet glared at Robert. "Your kindness was well rewarded, I saw."

Jane coughed, choking on the tea. She set it down. When she looked up, it was to see Robert smirking again. He looked like he was almost laughing.

"Actually, I was on my way to call upon the Dowager Duchess. It was merely the hand of fortune that brought us together sooner." He drained his cup and set it down before reaching into the breast pocket of his morning coat. He withdrew several folded notes and held them out towards her.

She stared at them. "Your winnings, Your Grace," he prompted.

"My Lord, I—"

His expression darkened at her denial, and he interrupted. "If you do not want it then give it to a charitable institution. I said I would lay the bet for you, and I did." He tossed the money on to her lap and rose.

Jane picked it up and put it on the table by her cup, then rose, too. She felt as though there was a tumultuous moat of misunderstanding and maybes separating them. Their impulsive embrace of moments ago was like a lost memory already.

"Your Grace." He bowed. "If you will excuse me, I should be off in any case." He turned to Violet, stepped forward and, bowing, held out his hand, indicating for her to set her hand in his. She did not. Jane watched Robert rise and smile in a dismissive gesture that told Violet he did not give a damn. "My Lady," he intoned scathingly, before turning away then striding from the room with an assured step.

Oh. Jane looked at Violet, unsure what to do, but then, without any real thought, she set off in pursuit.

"My Lord!" she called, halting his pace as he reached the top of the stairs. "Wait, I'll see you out."

A knowing smile curved his lips.

The infuriating man was driving her quite mad.

When she reached him, she gripped his arm and led him on to the stairs, speaking in a whisper, "Robert, I do not want you to think—"

"To think what, Jane? That you do not find me attractive? That you are indeed playing games?" He leaned closer to her ear. "Or that you want me still? Or that you wish now that you'd not been so hasty in your retreat the other night?"

Her fingers fell from his arm, and as he took the next step, she did not, setting a distance between them. "What I wish for, my Lord, is that you would leave me alone."

He scowled, and his fingers curled into a fist. His voice was bitter when he spoke. "That is hardly the response I expect after what your friend observed."

She supposed she deserved that.

He climbed a step.

She took another upward, backward, only to stumble.

He caught her arm, his grip firm and secure, stopping her fall, and he shook his head at her. "You need not be afraid of me, Jane, no matter what Lady Rimes has said to you. Surely you know that?"

Her gaze met his, and she answered truthfully, "I trust you, Robert, but perhaps I do not trust myself, and there is nowhere for this to go from here."

His head bent to whisper again, and his hair fell forward in that familiar way. "Why? Is there someone else? I thought I had shown you the night before last where this could go. Is pleasure not enough for you? That was just a taste, Jane. It could be good between us, if you let it be."

Robert watched Jane's skin pale at his words and her eyes searched his. She looked shocked. Had he just hit a mark? Was there someone else?

He let go of her arm and faced those sharp green eyes as they darkened to jade. Her beauty was enough to knock a man off balance. *My dear Jane.* He wanted her still. Desperately. No matter what she wanted, he could not just walk away. He would not, and he would not bow to any competitor either. He could not think of her with anyone else. She was his.

"I don't know what to do," she whispered. "I hardly know how to live or breathe any more." Her voice was breathless and weighted with an emotion he didn't understand.

She sighed. "It is not you, Robert."

What on earth did she mean by that? That she did have another man?

"It hardly matters what I want. My life has never been about choice. You have yours. Just leave me alone. That is what would be for the best."

The woman spoke in blasted riddles, hot and cold as the bloody English weather. Leave her alone indeed, when her body begged in her every move and look for him to stay. "And if I choose not to, Jane, what then?"

Her palms lifted in an expression of lack of control. "I don't want your friendship, Robert. It won't help."

"It is not your friend I want to be, in any case."

Her eyebrows arched at him in apparent annoyance and disbelief. "No? Then perhaps that is exactly why you are so bad for me."

He'd made her angry now.

Love and hate, the two emotions were closely linked. No one knew it more than he. He had learned it from Jane.

They both engendered passion.

"Sweetheart." He smiled, applying a wolfish gleam in his eyes which always drew women to him. They liked the promise of something dangerous. "*That*, I would never deny. I shall be very bad for you, indeed, and I promise you shall love every bloody minute of it."

Her expression crestfallen, she climbed a step backward again, gripping the banister. "I wonder now if I ever really knew you."

Those words pierced him in the chest with an inexplicable pain. His weakness made him angry. He bit back just as sharply, his knife honed by years of knowing that this woman had cast him off for riches and status without a second thought. "Well, *I know* I never really knew you. At least on this occasion, I face you with my eyes open, Jane. Throw me out, if you will, but believe me, your body shows your words up for the pathetic lie they are. No matter how many times you tell me nay, I shall not just walk away."

Jane's breath stuck somewhere in her chest as she watched Robert bend his head in a scathing bow. "Your Grace." Then he lifted her hand and kissed her knuckles.

His lips were warm, and his thumb brushed across her palm.

"My dear Jane." His breath whispered across the back of her hand as his eyes looked at her face.

When he rose up, he smiled wickedly and added in a challenging tone, "Until we meet again." Then he let go her hand, turned away, and jogged down the stairs, whistling a tune to himself as he reached the bottom step.

The man was so self-assured, so content in his skin, and he wished her to follow his every beck and call.

It would be easy to do so.

She watched him accept his hat and gloves from the footman, but he did not look back before he left.

There was a dreadful pattern forming here, a pattern she should be wary of.

She was using Robert to escape Joshua, and in more ways than one. When faced with the worst of two evils, she was seeking solace in Robert. It was his familiarity and the memories she had of him when they'd been young which promised a false sense of security. He'd been her refuge years ago. But he was no refuge now. Those cursed memories were deceiving her.

He'd made her feel happy then. He made her angry and afraid now. He was not the same man. And he was not safe.

The Robert Marlow her heart clung to did not exist. The Earl of Barrington was a renowned seducer, a man who took and walked away – a man who was as much like sanctuary as the pit in a dog fight.

She thought again of his wolf-like, predatory stare. God help her, her innocence left her like a lamb to the slaughter. The man would consume her whole if she let him, and she had no defence with which to fight. He already had her in his claws.

Chapter Seven

"Lord Sparks and Lady Rimes!" the all black-clad butler yelled to the open ballroom.

Clasping the cord of her fan over-tightly, Jane's eyes passed across Violet's and Lord Sparks's shoulders as they progressed to the receiving line. The sparkling, colourful, extravagant view of those milling throughout the long hall a few steps below was overwhelming. It was a portrait gallery serving as a ballroom. Tonight, the picture was the gathered mass of London's elite.

"Geoffrey," their hostess exclaimed, kissing Lord Sparks's cheek. "I am so pleased you came." Violet had told Jane earlier their hostess was Lord Sparks's elder sister.

"Lady Rimes."

Violet lowered into a shallow curtsy. She'd declared herself more than a little nervous of the Marchioness of Kent's welcome. She had spent a lot of time in Geoffrey's company recently, and rumours had begun to spread.

"It is pleasant to see you," the Marchioness said with diplomacy.

Jane smiled, realising the woman was a skilled politician. If she disapproved of her brother's *friendship* with the notorious widow, there was not a hint of it in her voice.

"My Lady," Violet responded as Geoffrey gripped his sister's hands.

"Sophia, you know I always appreciate seeing you. Where is Frank?"

"With Wellington, already."

Jane's heart thumped as she waited patiently, wondering if Joshua was here.

"I will find you later, Geoffrey. We must have a proper talk," the Marchioness closed, and Lord Sparks moved on with Violet clinging to his arm, the image of a London rake.

Jane's gaze reached past them to the bottom of the steps to another such rake.

The Earl of Barrington stood there, his athletic frame ready to advance, his eyes fixed upon her in a statement of possession.

"The Dowager Duchess of Sutton!" The Marchioness's butler called to the room. Jane sensed a sudden shift in atmosphere, and several eyes looked towards her. Then they looked away and heads bent as people began to whisper.

Jane faced the Marchioness, ignoring them. "My Lady."

"Your Grace," the other woman stated formally, taking one of Jane's hands. They both curtsied.

"Thank you for extending me an invitation."

"I am most sorry to hear of your loss. My condolences."

At that, Jane found herself with no words.

"Of course, my husband knew the late Duke of Sutton," the Marchioness continued. "They quite often met at Westminster. He was sorry to hear of your husband's passing."

Jane wondered if she was offering censure, as the other women in the room were. Jane had heard enough whispers to know society disapproved of her socialising while in full mourning. *"Who does that little upstart think she is?" "It is disrespectful to the old Duke." "She was nobody before she wed the Duke." "A money-grabbing, little chit."*

Jane lifted her chin, but made no comment.

The Marchioness leaned closer and dropped her voice to a conspiratorial tone. "Pay no heed to others. I know I do not give a fig for their opinion, and you have the advantage of being a Duchess and a widow. You may do as you please. I am sure you are in need of a little light-hearted company if all my husband has said of Sutton is true. Enjoy yourself, my dear, and feel free to call upon me if you are in need of another friend."

Jane smiled, grateful for the kindness, and said, "Thank you." But she knew she would not call. Her necessarily private nature of previous years was now instinctive. It would be unthinkable to offer any sign implying the Marchioness's judgement was correct, and she certainly did not wish to speak of it. Having taken her leave, Jane descended into the long, narrow hall, where she immediately faced her next obstacle, the Earl of Barrington.

"Your Grace." He stepped forward, instantly enveloping Jane in his overpowering presence, and his fingers touched her elbow as though claiming her for the evening.

"Jane?" Violet intervened, her voice full of questioning concern over Robert's sudden occupation. Her eyebrows lifted too, visibly asking if Jane wished for help.

Even Lord Sparks threw Robert a look of rebuke.

Gently shaking her head, Jane warned them both not to make a scene.

"What do you say to a hand of cards?" Lord Sparks interceded, looking at Violet.

"An excellent idea," Robert responded, despite the fact the invitation had not been offered to him. "We could make up a four for whist. How do you fancy that?" he asked Jane as Lord Sparks sent him another warning look. Violet spun away, deserting them all.

Lord Sparks threw Robert an even blacker look before following.

Robert's fingers increased their pressure on Jane's elbow, and he began leading her into the crush, his head bending to hers a little as they walked. "Well, it appears the card game is off. What about a dance instead?"

Jane looked sideward at him, her back stiffening as his gentle touch became a caress, his fingers slightly stroking her elbow. "I cannot dance, as you well know, my Lord."

"Forgive me. I had forgotten." His response dripped with disdain. "Of course, you're grieving."

She was tempted to pull away and leave him standing. Across the room she saw Violet disappearing into the card room and Lord Sparks following.

"He is hooked, you know."

The comment made Jane stop and turn to Robert.

A smile slashed his face, one of those smiles which had turned her stomach to water when she was young. Now that it was delivered with an artful rakish prowess of sheer deviltry, it transformed her entire body to aspic, scattering her wits. She echoed his words, "Hooked?" her train of thought not following his at all.

"Sparks," he answered, the smile fixed firmly on his face. "With your friend. She has him by the—"

"Robert." She stopped him before he could utter the vulgarity.

"Well, I am only saying what others think. The man's panting after her all day long. Sadly, once she's had her fun, she'll throw him off."

"Robert," she chastised again. The grip on her elbow firmed, and he led her on, weaving a path through the parties in conversation about the walls, while undaunted, he continued their conversation with a jovial vein of dismissal.

"Why, Jane, did you not know what she is like? I have long thought it why she so dislikes me, because, in me, she sees herself reflected, and so chooses not to face the ugly truth. We are both restless souls, my dear." The humour-filled comment was thrown away, and yet Jane could not help but sense something far more intense beneath it.

She stopped again, looking up, and met his unfathomable deep brown gaze.

He ignored her observation, reached to the tray of a passing footman and grasped a glass of champagne for her. She accepted it, and he reached for another. "*So*, no dancing, no cards." He smiled at her in a dark flirtatious fashion. "What option does that leave us then?"

Ignoring his innuendo, she looked at the dancers.

Robert followed her gaze, as she looked at those dancing. He felt more out of his depth than he'd done for years. Yet, when he turned back to her, he saw longing in her eyes. She may not be allowing herself to dance, but she desperately wanted to.

Lord, she was so beautiful. When he'd seen her standing alone and uncertain at the entrance, behind her far more confident friend, he'd felt an age-old ache in the region of his chest.

Her dress was black satin with a deep V neckline, revealing a delicate but ravishing show of cleavage. And the V was mirrored in the back between her shoulder blades. As she moved, the gown reflected light, a soft shimmer flowing over the outline of her limbs. The fabric ran across the plane of her stomach and the contours of her hips and thighs like water, and, far from giving the appearance of a woman in grief, the black stood her apart from all others, like a desultory beacon. It drew every eye in the room, setting her beauty up on a pedestal no one else could reach. Even Lady Rimes did not compare. Yet something told him the gown was not Jane's choice, but her friend's.

His gaze skimmed over the back of Jane's head. The waterfall of dark jet curls coiled about white rosebuds and descended artfully to her nape.

He was beginning to like Lady Rimes considerably, despite her objection to him. How could he not like a woman who put such effort into setting Jane up so well? Jane's appearance put every woman who condemned her behaviour in to shadow.

"Where did you meet Violet?" His gaze continued absorbing every detail as she turned back to face him.

Her dark sculpted eyebrows arched. "My Lord?"

She'd been busy picturing herself among the dancers, he realised. "Your friend, Lady Rimes, where did the two of you meet?" he said above the orchestra's crescendo at the close of the minuet.

She hesitated, clearly trying to read his expression and understand the motive for his question. Then finally, she gave a slight shrug and answered, "In Bath." She sipped her champagne, and he knew she'd given him a useless answer deliberately.

He smiled at her and let his gaze chastise her refusal to engage.

She looked away to watch the couples exchanging partners. The musicians began a country dance. Robert touched the soft skin visible at her back between her shoulder blades, and his gloved fingers slipped ever so slightly beneath the fabric of her gown. He longed to caress her without boundaries.

He bent to her ear, and his lips brushed the upper curve. "As we can neither dance nor play cards, what do you say to a walk in the garden?"

Her face turned, her eyes darting up to meet his again. There was uncertainty there, yet, equally, he saw his own need reflected, the same hunger which had brought her to him in Violet's drawing room this afternoon, the same impulsive attraction which had drawn her to his bedchamber that first night. It was addictive.

Desire darted to his groin as she turned.

The pressure of his fingertips allowed him to guide her from the room via the open French doors and out on to the terrace. It ran the length of the Marquess of Kent's town villa.

A few other couples promenaded in the lukewarm night air,

illuminated by a string of lanterns.

He did not stop there, but guided her on towards the steps which dropped to the vista of the lawn.

It was lit only by the bright silvery full moon. In the distance stretched the ink-black Thames, glittering in the moonlight.

At the foot of the steps, Robert turned Jane to the left and followed a narrow gravel path. He heard a fountain somewhere behind the tall yew hedge which lined the central lawn, and followed the sound.

She did not speak, but he could hear her shortened, nervous breaths.

The path disappeared behind the hedge. He followed it, guiding her into the first garden room.

Robert had stayed here with Sparks as a boy, on holiday from Eton. Sparks's older sister had been more like his mother in Sparks's latter years at Eton, and they'd played numerous games throughout the formal garden rooms.

Robert drew Jane on through a Tudor love knot woven in box hedging.

The next room was divided into quarters and heavy with the thick scent of many roses in their first flourish of blooms. He did not stop but carried on, passing through. Each room was dressed in pitch-black shadows cast by the moonlight.

Stepping through another arch in the hedging, they reached the square room he'd been looking for. The fountain stood in the centre, water spilling from a conch shell in the palm of a mermaid. It sent shards of sliver moonlight spinning about the high yew hedges which boxed them in.

Jane sighed. It was an unearthly scene. Like something from a gothic novel. She walked forward, away from him, her fingers gripping her gown to lift the hem, then she stepped up and stood before the fountain.

A broad stone rim edged it about two feet above the step she stood on. She put her glass down on it and let the fabric of her dress fall, then began working loose her gloves.

Even that tiny, artless gesture had his groin stirring. It was the imagined images of her disrobing which inspired it rather than the actual act of her removing her gloves.

She laid her gloves down beside her half-full glass then leaned over, one hand on the rim of the fountain, the other reaching towards the flowing water. It ran through her fingers before her hand dropped to the dark pool. It was dotted with lily pads. She stirred the water.

Robert's gaze lifted to the heavens. He saw a shooting star streak across the sky.

"It's cool. Touch it." Her voice beckoned his gaze back.

He swallowed the thick lump of desire lodged in his throat and looked.

She had rested her hip on the stone, half sitting, while leaning sideways and trailing her fingertips through the water, watching the ripples spread across the pool.

Black night and pale light, dark dress and ivory skin, this shadowed, unearthly world seemed to belong to her. She picked up her champagne and sipped it, her eyes still fixed on the movement of the water.

He struggled to regain his sanity, stepped closer, and recommenced their conversation where she'd left off. "*So,* you met Lady Rimes in Bath. Where?"

Her nearest shoulder lifted in a little shrug. "Hector was there taking the waters."

"Hector?"

Her eyes lifted and met his, black as onyx in the silver light. "Sutton." With her expression etched in light and dark, he could not judge her thoughts, but her voice seemed to dare him to react.

He sat beside her and tugged off his white evening gloves, then shifted, lifting his leg on to the stone so he could face her. He draped his gloves across his thigh.

She took a sip of champagne. So did he, as he dipped his fingertips in the water just once.

"I cannot imagine Lady Rimes finding the company of a man in his dotage interesting," he responded, meeting her gaze again. "Or will you seek to convince me the man was still capable of a brisk country dance as an octogenarian."

"I wish you would not be so condescending and sarcastic. I met Violet in the pump room. Of course, we did not attend the assembly rooms. Hector was far beyond that sort of entertainment. He hated the crush of such affairs as this in any case. I believe Violet took pity on me. She began calling in the afternoons when Hector was resting. Our friendship grew. What more is there to say?"

Another little shrug and a sip of champagne.

He took another sip himself.

"What more, indeed?" He put the glass down beside him and leaned forward, reaching out his hand, then clasped her nape and pulled her mouth towards his.

"Robert, I—"

"No more words." He took the glass from her hand and set it aside, then kissed her, his lips barely grazing the soft texture of hers. He could feel her willingness in the softening of the muscles in her neck as she gave herself over to his ministrations, volunteering her mouth for his exploration as her lips slowly parted and their kiss deepened.

This woman was a drug. She got into his veins. God help him. He was lost to her. His other hand settled about her ribs just below the high waist of her gown, and his thumb stroked the first curve of her breast.

"I shouldn't," she whispered, standing to escape him, but he caught her hand, stopping her retreat.

Still sitting on the stone rim, Robert opened his thighs, drawing her to stand between his legs, and looked up, holding her uncertain gaze.

"You definitely should," he answered, one hand still holding hers while the other lifted, and he brushed the backs of his fingers over the full curve of her breast, his eyes falling to watch it.

She didn't move away but let him touch.

His hand turned, and his fingers slipped her gown from her right shoulder. Her skin was softer, silkier than the high-priced material. His fingertips followed her collar bone.

She sighed, and he looked up, meeting her gaze. She was watching him.

His fingers dipped beneath the fabric and cupped her breast.

She did not stop him.

The constant splash of running water rang in the air. He kneaded her gently as she stood still.

She was like a statue cast in marble and dressed in shadows, except she was warm. Her breathing quickened and pressed her breast more firmly into his palm.

She wore no chemise tonight, no stays.

Desire roared inside him like a ravenous monster, waiting for its moment to be freed from its cage.

He watched her gaze turn visionless, focusing on feeling rather than him. Then he lifted her breast free from the satin fabric, let her hand go, and clasped her buttock, too, as he kissed her nipple.

An odd, startled sound escaped her throat, and her outstretched fingers slipped into his hair.

He took her taut nipple into his mouth. It was delicate, exquisite, and cupping it on his tongue, he sucked her with a gentle tug.

The woman was a wonder, such innocent, unadulterated giving. Her body arched, pressing closer, and her head tipped back, lifting her breasts a little. Her breathing had fractured.

"*Robert.*"

He liked his name on her tongue, especially when it was spoken with such primal longing. He rose, suddenly desperate for more, a slight groan escaping his throat. His hands settled at her waist, holding her steady as he kissed her again, heatedly taking all she'd give.

"I want to be inside you," he whispered into her mouth, pulling away a little.

Her eyes had been closed, but they suddenly opened and literally shone with desire.

"I need you so badly," he urged again; her body was so compliant, it felt like butter to his touch.

"Yes, Jane?" he asked as he hastened her backward, stumbling the few steps it took to press her to the hedge. He kissed her again, and her mouth clung to his, kissing him back with just as ardent hunger. It was answer enough for him. His fingers began working up the fabric of her gown, bunching it in a clawing grip, until his hand finally breached its hem. Then his fingers were touching hallowed ground. She wore no underwear at all. He worshipped her, *there*.

A soft whimper left her throat. It was an exquisite sound that expressed gratitude and disbelief as his fingers worked the elemental pattern of entry and withdrawal, and he kissed her, deeply.

Her head tipped back against the hedge as she lost the power to kiss him back, and she whimpered again, a slight, impassioned sound.

He knew she had forgotten where they were, forgotten they were in a public place. He pressed her on, wishing her to reach conclusion, and he knew it was coming when she bit her lip and gripped his shoulders. He set her adrift and felt her tumble, felt her fluid warmth as she cried out.

He reached to undo his flap.

Sod his desire for slow exploration with Jane. He wanted her, and now, she'd be his. She was ready, and he'd not risk waiting. A desperate hunger and thirst dried his mouth as he fumbled with the buttons and kissed her neck. Then he was free and his hands cupped her buttocks to lift her from the ground. "Put your legs about me," his desperation declared in a dry, throaty growl against her ear.

It was as though he'd thrown her into the water, she changed so dramatically. Her fingers clawed and bit into his scalp, and she thrust him away.

"No!"

He stepped back, his hands gripping her waist again to steady himself. "Jane?" There was a hollow note of pleading in his voice he really did not like. He could not believe she'd done this to him twice.

"What the hell?" His temper rose like a floodtide, overflowing.

Her hands were at her sides, gripping at the thin branches of the hedge behind her. She looked startled, *vulnerable*, and absolutely terrified. Yet a moment ago, she'd been soft clay in his hands, her little sighs of pleasure echoing into the night.

He turned away and secured his breeches, leaving her to straighten her clothing, too. Then he stalked back to the pond, leaned over the water, cupped his hands and doused his face. It struck his skin, harshly cold, before dripping away. He used a handkerchief to dry his face, then slicked back his hair with shaking fingers.

Hell.

Her gentle touch settled on his back.

"I'm sorry, Robert. I... I am... I cannot. Not here."

He turned to look at her, filled with desperation more than

disappointment. "Where then, Jane? And when?"

Her gaze met his, loaded with apology and regret.

The answer was clear; probably never – nowhere. This was a bloody game of chance, like the tricksters that worked the streets, drawing you in with one win, only to find that after that the damn queen of hearts was nowhere to be seen.

"Never mind," he whispered roughly. "I'll take you back."

"I don't want to go back," she countered, her fingers gently capturing his before he had chance to turn away. Her eyes shone in the moonlight. "Can we not just talk for a moment? I need you to understand, it is not because it is you. I am just not ready for this. I don't want a fleeting affair or a single liaison. Not with you. Not with anyone, Robert." Her gaze was intense, as though what she was trying to say was something completely different.

She utterly confounded him.

She must have realised he was in no state to comprehend her silent message, and she sighed with what sounded like exhaustion. "I'm sorry. I understand if you're angry with me, but actually, I have changed my mind. I think I would like your friendship. Yet, I cannot offer you anything more, Robert." She let go of his hand, and her eyes looked at the pond. "I don't think I could cope with your desertion at the moment, if you did not..." Her whisper drifted away somewhere in the direction of the pond.

Did not what? Stay with her? The implication hit him in the gut. She'd bloody well deserted him. But regardless, he slipped his fingers beneath her chin and turned her face up to him. It was in shadow; the moonlight lay on her hair.

The tumbling fountain played on beside them, and over it, he heard the first few, clear notes of a waltz stretch from the ballroom beyond the hedges.

He could be angry. He could be nonchalant or vindictive. But this was Jane, and, God help him, even if these small tokens of affection and friendship were all he got in return, he wanted to be in the game, no matter what the stakes. If all she did was throw him a bloody scrap beneath the table, he'd still come to heel.

He pressed a soft kiss on her lips, telling her with the touch of his mouth, if not with words, if this was indeed all she could give, he would take it, just as it was, just this.

"Shall we begin again?" he whispered over her lips, then stepped back and took her hand before bowing over it. "Would you care for this waltz, Your Grace?"

The silver moonlight caught her lips as she gave him a warm smile. "I would be honoured to accept." This was his fictional Jane.

He needed no further encouragement and lifted her hand, clasping it more firmly and forming the frame for the dance. His other hand settled at her back, his thumb on bare flesh and his fingers over the silky satin.

Her hand settled on his shoulder.

He began to move, leading her into the steps and feeling her muscles play along her spine. They danced about the fountain, his eyes holding hers.

After a moment, she whispered, "We never danced a waltz before, did we?" crossing the divide of years to the treacherous territory of the past.

He'd been thinking the same thing, and somehow, the memory of things they'd done, the kisses they'd shared, the conversations they'd held, the things which had made her feel a part of him, half of him, did not make him hurt at all any more.

"No," he answered simply, very unsure of this marsh-ridden ground. But she'd longed to dance in the hall, he'd seen that, and this was a peace offering.

"You are very good," she whispered.

"If you say so."

Silence.

He knew his stilted responses had scared her back into herself again. The woman was as skittish as a virgin. What did she expect him to say? *I have danced with thousands of women over the years. I am not the nineteen-year-old green youth you deserted. Of course I can dance well. I have danced in courts across the continent.* Instead, he changed the subject, perhaps not quite as ready as he had convinced himself he was to leave off being vindictive. "So, did you love Sutton then? Do you mourn him?"

She pulled back a little, he presumed to see his face better, but did not stop following the steps he led. He could see her deliberating on how he'd intended the question, trying to judge if he was being callous, cruel, or belligerent, or if he was genuinely interested, which it appeared from her expression, she very much doubted.

He smiled, gently, to fox her assessment, the tight smile which always had the ladies equally bewildered and enthralled, then wondered if, perhaps, she was, instead, working out how to answer, as she sent him a pathetic half smile back, full of self-consciousness.

She looked over his shoulder. "I would rather not talk of Sutton."

She clearly did not dare answer. He supposed because she did not wish to upset him and open old wounds. Well, unfortunately, his wounds, he was fast discovering, were far from closed. But at this moment, he was inclined to let it drop. The pleasure of having the woman in his arms, her lithe, warm, softly pliant body so close to his, was too valuable.

Each movement generated a new caressing contact between them. Heaviness settled in his groin, and his voice dropped an octave or two as his throat dried with his thirst for her. "What do you wish to talk of then?"

As he posed the question, he deftly spun her backward, distracting his senses.

Her eyes met his once more. "Tell me about your estate, and Edward. How are things at home?"

"Home?" he asked her, his voice low and mocking. She had not lived there for years, and Sutton had sold off her father's estate, neighbouring Robert's, when her father had died. Edward had bought the seventy-acre plot on Robert's behalf and leased her father's manor out years ago.

"You know what I mean." She shook her head at him a little, clearly annoyed. "I grew up there, on your land as much as my father's. I cannot help but still think of your estates as part of me. Just tell me how things are. Is Davis, the butler, still there, for instance?"

Was this telling, that she still thought of his home as hers? As a child, she'd spent more time in his parents' home than in her own. His mother once had a miniature painted of the girl, alongside his own and Edward's. Jane had always been the daughter she'd longed for. Perhaps that was where he'd got it all wrong years ago, while he had fallen for her, she'd fallen for his home and family?

Anyway, he chose to answer. It appeared he was in an obliging mood. He'd do anything to keep her in his arms. "Yes, Davis is still there and as judgemental and bossy as ever."

Suddenly, she narrowed the gap between them and rested her head on his shoulder. It was a sweet balm for his injured pride as her hair caressed his neck and her warm, supple body pressed against his chest. His hand cradled her against him, and he felt her thighs trace the steps against, and in between, his. Desire turned his blood as thick as treacle as a fierce lust sliced into his groin. His need for this woman was pain and pleasure.

"Edward is married, as I am sure you've heard." His breath stirred the ornate decoration of her hair as he sought to restrain his physical response to her.

Her slight nod slid on his shoulder.

"He has a stepson, a fine lad, who has just started at Eton. John has a sensible head on his shoulders, which is a good thing as he will be a Duke one day. Then there are the babies, little Mary-Rose who is two, almost three, and their newest offspring, a boy, little Robbie, a rascal. Lord. He has a set of lungs on him. I told them they cursed the poor lad naming him after me."

Her head lifted from his shoulder. "But Edward is obviously still proud of his older brother if he chose to name his son after you."

Robert smiled. His thoughts of Edward's family probably showed in his eyes. "I doubt it was Edward's doing. It was more likely Ellen's idea. My sister-in-law is determined to out me to the world as a fraud."

"A fraud?" Jane's brow furrowed.

His smile broadened, he was not at all inclined to explain. Ellen was the only person in the world who saw through him. Even his brother could not.

"Nothing for you to fret over," he answered as the strains of the waltz drew to a close and he stopped.

For an instant, she did not move. Her breath was slow as if she did not really wish the dance to end. As if she savoured the moment. But then she pulled away.

He let her go and felt as though something was wrenched from inside him.

"We ought to go back." She turned to collect her gloves. "Violet will be wondering where we have gone to."

"I doubt very much she has missed *me*." He bent to collect his own gloves from the ground, then straightened and added as he put them on, "You know, if it is Lady Rimes who has set you against me—"

"I am old enough to think for myself, Robert."

Yes, of course, he knew that. He'd learned that when she was sixteen.

Robert offered his arm and felt a jolt of excruciating awareness when she laid her fingers on it. He began walking her back, but when they reached the exit of the last garden room, he stopped and turned to face her.

"I am willing to be your friend, Jane. Can we be friends?" Of course, friendship like that of Sparks and Lady Rimes was most appealing. Her offer had not excluded flirtation, and he, of all people, knew how to tempt a woman until she broke. "Would you allow me to take you for a drive tomorrow? Say at three, before it becomes too busy."

"I should prefer to ride." She gave him a shallow, almost hopeful smile. "I have not ridden in an age. Violet does not care for it. She had a nasty fall when she was a child."

"A ride then," he agreed, his eyes scanning her face again, wondering if there was something he was missing. But he could not really tell when her face was in darkness. "At three?"

"Yes." Her voice was breathless.

He felt conspiratorial, remembering the budding romance they'd kept secret from their families years ago. It slammed him right back into the present. He'd realised the reason she wished for secrecy after she'd thrown him off, because it had meant nothing to her, she'd been angling for Sutton and dallying with him. *What am I to her now?*

A friend. He heard the answer repeated in his head, spoken from her lips. He was not satisfied with it. He wanted more. He would have more.

Lord, if she was playing with him this time and angling for someone else, he'd kill her. He let her climb the steps ahead of him, then followed and led her back into the ballroom. His eyes scanned the gathering as they entered to see if anyone particularly noted their return, thinking of her reputation. For all his bold words, this was Jane. He would beg for every crumb this beautiful, incomparable woman tossed him. Already, he would be hard-pushed to ever simply walk away.

His gaze hit the current Duke of Sutton's. The man was staring at Robert with a look of speculation.

Well, Sutton could go hang. He was married with two mistresses. He could hardly judge. The man had not even donned his blacks because he'd not been on speaking terms with his father. He did not have the moral high ground.

Robert mentally dismissed Sutton as no threat. If Jane was true to form, if she was after another man, she was after money, and she had all of Sutton's. Everyone knew about the old Duke's grand gesture in leaving his fortune to his pretty, young wife – gratitude for services rendered. God, it was no different to whoring, really, this *ton-ish* fashion of marrying someone four times your age. His gaze turned away from Sutton without acknowledgement, and he followed Jane, slipping a possessive hand beneath her elbow again.

Robert's touch sent a shiver of sensation across her skin, a reaction to the knowledge of his strong, agile body. Yet she felt anxious too, concerned over what the attention of such a man meant. Despite her protestations to only accept his friendship, her heart still raced at his close proximity, and her skin felt hot. She was susceptible to him. Every fibre in her body craved his. She was aware of each step he took beside her, of his hip glancing hers occasionally.

Their kiss, his caress, their dance, had awakened turmoil inside her again. She was breathless still. She longed to learn the full conclusion of intimacy with him. But common sense held her back. She didn't dare give in to him. What if he rejected her afterwards?

They entered the card room, and Jane spotted Violet. She was winning handsomely at *vingt-et-un*, or so it seemed from the pile of notes at her elbow. Violet caught Jane's eye and gave her a questioning smile. Jane knew the unspoken words were, *has Barrington behaved, or has he upset you?*

Jane smiled in reply, to show she was not upset.

Robert had said Violet was like him and playing games with Lord Sparks. Yet Lord Sparks seemed happy with *their* arrangement, brief affair or not. Jane inwardly sighed; she was not like them.

In Bath, Violet's vibrancy had drawn Jane, and when she'd come to London, even though she'd been escaping Joshua, she'd looked forward to experiencing a life beyond her reach through Violet. Yet instead Jane had cast a cloud across it, in her blacks. She was keeping Violet from her usual enjoyment of life. She did not dance with Geoff, because Jane would not dance.

Suddenly, Jane felt isolation engulf her. Even here, with the one woman she had been able to call a friend, and the one man she had ever felt close to, she still felt alone. Neither of them really knew her, and that was her fault. She felt too ashamed to share her secrets with Violet, and besides, she did not wish to cast an even greater shadow on their friendship.

Yet nor could she share her fears with Robert, he was not the man she'd known.

But if he proved himself trustworthy?

Despite his reputation, she had a sense of hope when she was with him.

But if she sought to trust the one man Violet disliked, Jane risked offending her only friend.

She was too tired of this charade to continue pretending... Surely God's judgement upon her would be worse for lying than taking off her blacks. Their sentiment was false. She *was lying*. Robert was right.

She was a fraud.

If I could just persuade Violet to give Robert a chance, then perhaps...

Forcing a smile, she turned from Violet to Robert and proposed they indulge in the game of whist Robert had suggested earlier.

Violet agreed, but insisted on pairing men against women,

stating she wished to thrash Lord Barrington, but would dislike thrashing Jane.

Robert concurred with a hard smile.

Jane knew he enjoyed provoking her friend's animosity. There was a wicked streak which ran deep in the new Robert. Yet it only proved again how little Robert cared what others thought.

Jane took her seat, wishing she did not care. Her whole life was the whim of others.

When she looked at Robert, he gave her his charmer's smile and winked. She knew he did it only to irritate Violet.

Jane looked at her cards, ignoring Robert's and Violet's hostility. Why did she care what others thought?

I am going to do it, she decided suddenly, relief sweeping in. She would stop hiding behind her blacks.

If the *ton* cut her, so what, let them. As soon as she had decided how to resolve this thing with Joshua, she would leave town anyway. She need not care what people said.

An hour later, having successfully trounced the men and ending several pounds the richer for it, Jane left them to refresh, in company with Violet.

"Where did you and Lord Barrington disappear to?" Violet whispered as they climbed the stairs to the second floor.

Jane felt colour rising on her skin. "We walked in the garden."

"And?" Her friend persisted.

"We talked."

Violet's eyebrows lifted. "My dear, a man like Barrington does not just talk."

"No." Jane's blush rose by degrees. "But he has agreed we shall just be friends."

"Friends?" Violet gripped Jane's arm and leaned close so her voice would not carry. "Are you sure that's wise, Jane? I mean, with Barrington?"

"I know you disapprove, but we were close as children, and he..." Jane stopped and breathed in, her mind racing through how to describe her feelings for Robert. He made her feel young, safe, wanted, she liked him, regardless of the risks. "He makes me feel better, Violet. I like his company."

Violet was speechless for a moment, and her gaze held Jane's. She was Jane's only friend. If Violet truly disagreed with any association with Robert, it could cause a rift between them.

Violet sighed then answered. "It is your life, Jane. I shall say no more, but if you need to talk, I am always here for you."

Jane gripped Violet's hand and squeezed it. "Thank you. I could not wish for a better friend. I am grateful, Violet, and... Violet, I have decided to give up my blacks."

Chapter Eight

When Robert arrived, Jane was watching the street from the drawing room, and she rushed downstairs, reaching the hall just as he stepped across the threshold. She felt good today, still much in his charity after his excellent company of the night before. Even Violet had conceded their game of whist had been fun.

"You look well, Jane." His smiling eyes made a quick sweep of her attire. Her riding habit was a very dark green with black frogging. She'd not bothered renewing it with her mourning attire. She'd never had a reason to wear it, and it was already dark. She wore the matching mock-up of a gentleman's hat at a slight angle, its thin gauze veil covering her face. She smiled.

She knew she looked well in her habit. She also knew how scandalous her behaviour would be viewed over the coming days. She and Violet had spent the entire morning shopping for a new wardrobe.

"Thank you, my Lord." Jane bobbed a slight curtsy, hearing the bright note in her voice.

His smile tilted sideways, as if he speculated on the reason for her change in mood.

She lifted her shoulders, shrugging in answer to the challenge in his eyes.

She felt a little like Violet today, light, confident. The power of the decision she'd made had filled her with a boldness which had never been in her nature.

A look of roguery glinted in his eyes, and his lips lifted in a wolfish grin.

Jane tapped her riding whip against her skirts, ignoring his rakish behaviour, and walked past him to the door, stealing a sideways glance at him as she did so.

Lord, he looked good today, too. His hessians and tight buff unmentionables extenuated every muscular curve in his thighs and calves. His redingote was cut to the line of his broad shoulders and tapered to his narrow waist, outlining the slender hips his unmentionables hugged. The man was too handsome for a woman's health.

"You're ready?" he prompted, following her.

"Ready apart from my horse; Violet's groom is bringing her about."

"Lady Rimes did not decide to join us?" There was a teasing note in his voice.

"You need not mock, my Lord. Lady Rimes is, in fact, in excellent humour with you today, having trounced you so thoroughly at whist. You may even have an invitation to take tea after our ride if you continue to be upon your best behaviour."

He laughed, and she smiled in the image of his favourite mocking look. Narrowing his eyes, he shook his head at her in silent reproof.

"Your Grace, if you will allow." He held out his arm, and she took it as she heard the mare being led out. They stepped out into bright sunshine.

The sky was clear, not a single cloud could be seen, and the world felt like a brighter place. They descended the few steps to the pavement, then Jane let go his arm, walked to her chestnut mare, and patted its neck.

It looked a sprightly thing from its impatient steps. It was really a carriage horse, but had taken a saddle before.

"Here." Combining his fingers, Robert formed a step for her. The gesture made Jane's heart ache. He'd done it a thousand times when they were young. The sole of her boot pressed into his grip, and he lifted her weight, boosting her into the saddle. The groom handed Jane the reins as she shared a conspiratorial smile with Robert. He had remembered, too. She knew it from his look.

He left her and set a foot in his stirrup then hoisted himself up into his saddle with ease.

Reaching for his reins, he ordered his groom to follow at a distance.

She was far beyond needing a chaperone, and yet, it was comforting to know he thought of her reputation.

"Shall we progress?" He smiled, waving her forward.

She nodded, tapped her heel, and touched the whip against the animal's flank, holding the reins tight to ensure the feisty mare knew who was in charge. Robert lifted into a trot beside Jane, rising in his saddle.

Hyde Park was not far, but the streets at this hour were busy, and she found her attention totally absorbed by the traffic and keeping her mare in check. It meant they shared no conversation, yet she doubted Robert would have heard her anyway over the ringing sounds of hooves and carriage wheels on the cobble.

When they reached Hyde Park, she passed through the gates with relief.

Instantly, Robert stirred his black stallion into a canter.

Jane followed.

He rode on, setting a distance between them and the general crowd.

It was earlier than the fashionable hour, and yet, there were still a number of carriages and riders on the ring.

Excitement stirred in Jane's blood, and the mare felt it, before Jane had even kicked her heel the animal launched into a gallop. Jane leaned low over its neck and gave the mare her head, thundering across the open grass towards the Serpentine. Robert galloped beside her, the thuds of their racing hoofbeats pounding on the ground. They'd ridden like this many times before. She thought of the day things had changed between them.

Robert had come home to visit his parents for Christmas. It was his first year at Oxford. Edward, his younger brother who'd been at Eton, had stayed with a friend. She had ridden to Farnborough as soon as she'd heard Robert was back, and nagged him to go out riding with her. The three of them had always loved riding at full tilt through the fallow fields.

As soon as she'd seen Robert that day, she'd sensed a difference in him. He'd grown up. Truthfully, she had been a little in awe of the handsome, cultured youth who was becoming a man. Yet he'd not denied her. He'd agreed and acted as though nothing had changed. But it had. She'd known it. He'd looked at her differently. His gaze had swept over the fit of her long riding habit, and she'd realised then that during the last weeks he'd been at university, she'd grown, too.

Together they had ridden out, and she'd kicked into their normal gallop, laughing as she'd pulled ahead, teasing him across her shoulder. She'd not paced her mare for an approaching wall, and the animal had jumped awkwardly and landed heavily, unseating her. She could remember the impact even now, as her back hit the frost-hardened, cold, unrelenting ground. It had forced all the air from her lungs, not knocking her unconscious, but shaking her significantly. The next thing she'd known, Robert's stallion had flown over the wall beside her, almost over her, and he'd leapt from the animal, his expression sheer terror.

She'd always wondered since, if they'd not had that shock, would what happened next have come to pass?

He'd dropped to his knees and leaned over her, one hand on the cold ground as his other had followed the lines of her limbs, skimming swiftly across each bone and joint checking for injuries. Then his hand had fallen on to her hip.

Her breathing had been quick and she'd seen his eyes suddenly change. They'd darkened, and his look had become fixed. She'd seen longing, relief, and uncertainty. Then his fingers had slipped to her breast over the cloth of her habit, and his mouth had descended to hers, urgent and needy. It had been the kiss of youth. It had borne none of the skill his kisses did now, and yet, it had stolen her very soul. She'd given everything she was to him that day. From then on, their rides had become a means to an end, the opportunity to seek time alone.

Each time he'd returned during the holidays, they'd sought each other out, developing dozens of ruses and excuses to meet and lose poor Edward, keeping their lovers' trysts a secret from everyone else, because she'd been afraid of their parents' reaction.

It was heaven, until the day he'd come, full of expectation and hope, to ask for her agreement to speak to her father and request her hand in marriage. Her world had already been shattered by then. She'd been promised to Sutton. She'd told Robert it was too late. Her father had already agreed to her marriage to the Duke.

Robert had not even stayed to speak of it. He'd not offered to help her seek a way out. He'd just walked away without a word and not looked back as he'd mounted his horse, kicked his heels, and ridden off.

Through the intervening years, she'd told herself he'd been too young. It was foolish to expect him to know how to help. How could he have risked offending his father? He might have lost his inheritance. After all, her father had no title, and Robert was to be an earl. Yet, in her heart, she'd always felt it was because he'd not loved her enough to take those risks and steal her away.

But these thoughts were making her morbid again. She refused to be morbid today.

Robert raced in front, the stallion's longer stride giving the animal a head's advantage.

Jane's attention was diverted by an open landau crossing their path a distance away. She slowed her mare and straightened up when she saw its occupant, the tenth Duke of Sutton's wife, Emily, with her eldest daughters, who were near Jane's age. The woman had spoken barely two words to Jane in over half a dozen years.

Jane's mare now standing, Jane watched the woman stick her nose in the air and turn her head away.

Emily endlessly spurred Joshua, not that he needed spurring, but Jane knew Emily's bitter accusations only made Joshua worse.

Jane had heard her taunting her husband, accusing him of letting Jane usurp his position.

Emily had said Jane had spoken against Joshua to his father, deliberately trying to steal Joshua's inheritance.

Jane had never done so, and even if she had, the old tyrant would never have listened to *her*.

She turned her horse, cutting the woman, too, and her gaze struck Robert's.

He looked from her to the landau then back, an unspoken query in his eyes.

She ignored it. She would not let thoughts of either of the Sutton men spoil this newfound rush of freedom.

"Walk on," she said to the mare, clicking her tongue in command as her heel urged the animal forward. Robert's larger beast slipped into stride beside her.

"Sutton's wife?" he said.

She nodded.

"I take it she is not your admirer?"

Jane smiled. "No," she said then shrugged. "The woman is a bitch."

A deep laugh left his throat.

Jane felt the woman's stare burn into her back and fought the urge to look.

"Good grief, you've changed," Robert teased. "I never thought to hear you curse. The saints shall be turning in their graves. Jane Coates, a sinner. Who would have known it of such a prim and proper, perfect little girl?"

His words chased out a brief laugh. It was true. The Jane of her youth had been a sheltered child. She'd seen the world through the eyes of innocence.

She smiled at him gratefully. She knew he'd deliberately sought to dismiss her thoughts of Emily. He must have seen that it hurt her. She tried to pretend it did not, but it did. "Whereas you, my Lord, are an out-and-out sinner. You were then, and you are now."

He kicked his stallion into a canter again and called back. "Oh, but I'm a happy man now I know I shall have such fine company in hell."

She kicked her mare, too, to keep up. "That is wicked, indeed, my Lord, to will me to an eternity of hell's fire."

When she drew alongside him, he sent her a look which turned her stomach in a sharp flip-flop.

"Of course, once you are in for a penny, why not throw in for a pound? As you are already a lost cause, I could educate you in all the pleasures of sin. I would be a willing teacher, if you agree to be an apt pupil."

"Robert!" she chastised, then laughed, knowing she was tempted despite herself. "Friends!" she chastened, forcing her expression into one of rebuff. She could not hold it and smiled again.

"I wonder, Jane, are we to be friends that kiss? A friendship in the style of Lady Rimes and Lord Sparks's I think I may endure."

"Robert, stop it." Her voice was more serious, censuring his words. She really did not need this.

Glancing in her direction, he clearly realised he'd gone too far. "As you say," he answered lightly.

For several strides, they rode in silence.

"Have I upset you?" Robert prodded.

"No." She refused to be upset. She wished to enjoy today, enjoy their ride, and enjoy his company.

"No?"

She glanced at him. His voice had gained that tell-tale lilt of charm.

"You are a master in your art, Robert." She smiled again, and he smiled in answer.

"And what art would that be?" he queried with satire.

"The art of lechery, my Lord."

"You wound me." One gloved hand left his reins and pressed to his chest over his heart. "I am mortified, my dear. Have you not heard of my prowess in other fields? My knowledge of Roman and Greek artefacts is renowned. I lived upon the trade abroad."

"Trade, my Lord?" She laughed. "Your father must have been disgusted."

He threw her a look which said it all. His father and he had fallen out. She'd heard that and forgotten it. He pulled the stallion back to a trot. She followed suit. "I'm sorry. I did not mean to offend you."

"You did not." He didn't look in her direction. "Actually, he never spoke to me again after he told me to go abroad."

That struck her dumb. She stopped her horse, and, after a couple of paces, he stopped, too. "Robert?" How awful.

He'd been close to his father as a boy. Her parents had never cared for her. She knew how much it must have hurt him. Yet a man like Robert would not seek her sympathy.

118

His expression said it was nothing, but of course, it was. He slid his feet from the stirrups and swung down, dropping to the ground. Then he lifted his hand to her. "Shall we walk the horses for a bit and give them chance to get a second wind before we ride back?"

She gripped his hand and nodded as a sharp spasm of longing stirred low in her tummy. She ignored it, unhooking her knee, then slid to the ground. For a moment, they stood a foot apart, looking at each other, his brown-black gaze penetrating hers.

She stepped back. He let her hand fall. Then they turned together and began walking towards the long stretch of water which crossed the park, leading the horses behind them, each gripping the animals' reins in one hand as they walked.

"Why did you go?"

He threw her a wry smile. "Life was dull. I like pleasure. My father thought the grand tour would sober me up. Unfortunately, no one had told him what it was really like abroad. The wine and the women there are worth a dozen here. He disapproved of my pastimes. But then, of course, there was always Edward – the white to my black. My brother was ever the knighted hero as far as my father was concerned. But believe me, I am not bothered by it. I had my fun, made merry while it lasted, and as the estates were entailed, he could not fully cut me off. For a while, I thought I would leave it all to Edward, let him get on with it and stay abroad."

"Yet you came back?"

"I would have gotten to that," he answered, a deep laugh resonating in his chest, but it sounded hollow. "Am I boring you?"

"Don't be silly, Robert, you were being serious."

"I am never serious, Jane. My friends shall tell you. Ask Sparks. I came back because, in the end, I was bored of it there, too. I fancied something different. Have you never heard how shallow I am?"

Her gloved fingers touched his arm. He did not stop walking.

119

She dropped her hand and kept his pace as the horses trailed behind them. "I do not think you shallow. Complicated, yes. I have heard your reputation. Who has not? You've made a point of compounding it since you came back to London. Yet..." She stopped, even though he walked on. "I don't think I believe it."

"You don't believe me?" He stopped, too, looked back, and shrugged. "Pray, tell me, what on earth is there to not believe?" He was mocking her, she realised, but he was mocking himself, too. There was a bitter look in his eyes.

"You are different, Robert, but I don't think you are what you portray yourself to be." He just stared at her, revealing nothing. She felt as though he deliberately sought to confuse her, to confuse everyone. He wanted to shut people out and shield the truth. But what was the truth? "Is it because you were hurt by your father?"

His eyes suddenly focused sharply on hers, but then he shook his head and turned away.

She followed, but his strides were quicker and longer; she could not keep up. One hand lifting the hem of her habit, the other still clinging to her mare's reins, she yelled after him, "Robert!"

"That is the end of that subject," he barked, neither turning nor slowing. "I do not wish to speak of it."

"Robert, wait!"

"Wait!" she called again as he continued striding ahead of her. "Oh, for goodness' sake." She stopped, giving up her useless pursuit. "If you do not stop, I shall just go back."

That caught his attention. He halted and turned, waiting for her to catch up, his eyes following her, his jaw clenched.

"So, what of you?" he said as she approached. "Have you made merry with Sutton's fortune? I assume, with a husband half in the grave when you were wed, you have had ample opportunity for sport."

"There is no need to be mean just because I touched a raw

nerve," she answered, then pursed her lips.

He gave her his charmer's smile. "I did not intend to be mean." He laughed, acting as though he had not been annoyed a moment ago. She knew he had been.

"Then explain to me in what context you asked your question."

"In the context, my dear, that while I have been earning a rakehell's reputation, you have been tucked quietly away in your country house, silent as a mouse. Yet, you must have lived quite well. Sutton was hardly poor. You have had money to spend and entertainments to host as a duchess."

Jane was still unsure of his intent. Was he trying to hurt her in return? She chose to respond anyway, not wishing to close down another topic, although she was as uncomfortable with this subject as he'd appeared to be with the last. "Hector liked to live quietly. He was not a man for grandeur. Hence, I did not indulge in overspending, or fancy, or even socialising."

"*Hector.*" Robert's tone was one of distaste as he held her gaze, his dark eyes visibly trying to look into her thoughts, and then, again, he simply turned away and walked on, but at least this time he did not rush. His horse whinnied. "And did you and *Hector* get along well?"

"Well enough," she answered cagily, still unable to assess if he was mocking her or not. Well enough, if you considered being used, ignored, or disparaged *getting along*.

"He did buy you things, then, treated you lavishly, I suppose. I mean, that was what you wished for, was it not? That was why you married him, for the pomp and finery."

Her gaze rested on his broad shoulders as he walked a pace ahead. The air between them seemed charged with something she really did not understand. It was more than conversation. She'd cared for none of the pomp and finery and it certainly had not been worth its price, and the greatest cost had been losing Robert.

121

When she did not answer, he pressed again, changing tack. "I mean to say, you benefited well from it."

Oh, let him think what he wished. She really did not care any more, Hector was gone. She had a chance for freedom, and she was damn well going to chase it. "My parents did, I'm sure," she answered cryptically.

They walked on in silence, Robert looking at the shore of the Serpentine as they drew closer, while she studied him, a chasm standing between them.

When they reached the gravel path surrounding the lake, letting go of his horse's reins, he bent down and picked up a single flat pebble, then he spun the stone and skimmed it across the lake. Her eyes followed it as it skipped on the water nine times before plopping beneath the surface, each bounce spreading a ring of ripples out across the surface. It brought back their childhood so vividly, the three of them together at the lake on his parents' land. Whenever she'd succeeded in skimming stones, the brothers were never looking, and they'd refused to believe her.

He turned back and viewed her with a sceptical expression, but smiled. "Well, as it seems we cannot find a safe subject for conversation, perhaps we ought to return to my original idea and be lovers. We would have no reason to converse then. We could just kiss. We seem to manage that well enough."

"Robert," she admonished, glancing left and right to check no one was close enough to hear.

Robert looked at his groom who'd hung back and beckoned him forward, then asked the man to hold their horses. Afterwards, he took Jane's hand, wrapped it about his forearm, and began walking along the gravel path, his fingers covering hers as he bent to her ear. "We used to be able to talk well enough. If I remember correctly, you had a habit of never shutting up, well, not unless I found another use for your lips."

"Robert, don't." Her voice complained, yet her body responded, and her fingers clung to his arm. She liked him like this, teasing as the old Robert would. It was as though the sunny youth she remembered occasionally reached through his dark clouds.

"Do you remember that night?" he asked in a low, husky tone.

Oh yes, she remembered *that night*. He'd taken her out on the lake in a punt. His parents had held a garden party, and her parents had been asked to stay. She and Robert had planned a late night rendezvous on the lake. They'd met at midnight. Then, as quietly as possible, they'd freed one of the shallow, long boats, and Robert had pushed them out into the middle of the lake to a place where they could not be seen. They'd lain together in the hull on a bed of cushions, the clear night sky above them, so many sparkling stars piercing the darkness their only audience.

They'd kissed for a long while, entirely wrapped up in each other, and yet, he'd never pushed her for more. Then they'd talked of the future, of the life they would have, of how their children may look; their future marriage a mutual unspoken agreement. It all sounded foolish now. She'd been so blind then.

But that night had been in her dreams ever since, and in her dreams, he'd undressed her and loved her. They were only dreams. Yet for years, she'd regretted letting that opportunity go.

The next day, Robert had returned to Oxford, and her parents had begun to arrange her match with Sutton. When Robert had come home at Christmas, he'd arrived with a ring in his open palm, and he'd said "*I want you to marry me now. Let's not wait. May I speak to your father?*" But her father had already signed the agreement with Sutton. He would simply have told Robert to go away.

Lost in thought, she'd not realised he'd continued speaking, until he stopped, turned her to him, and gripped her chin. "Jane? I'm sorry. I should not have spoken of Sutton. I did not mean to upset you."

Her eyes met his, and she was mesmerised by the sincerity she saw there. They caught the daylight and turned to honey, his long, dark lashes framing them, his dark eyebrows outlining them. She felt out of her depth and overwhelmed by need for him.

She stepped back, out of reach. "I was not thinking of Hector. I was thinking of you," she whispered, astonished the words had slipped from her lips. She blushed and turned away, lifting her hem from the ground, and started back towards the horses. "We should go. If I am too long, Violet will worry." When she glanced back, hearing him follow, she caught his puzzled expression, but he did not speak. When she reached the mare, Robert's groom bent and locked his fingers together to make a step, so she was already in the saddle by the time Robert returned. He swung up on to his, and they rode back across the park in a gentler canter, silent.

~

"Where will you be tonight?" Robert asked as he gripped Jane's fingers in parting before Violet's door.

"You do not wish to come in for tea?"

"I think I can go without your friend's satiric observations for one afternoon." Their gazes locked, and he felt as though she wished to say something, but did not dare. The woman captivated him. He studied the light which caught the vivid green of her eyes and memorised the image for future recall. He'd been doing it all afternoon, preserving moments. The way she rode. The way she walked. The feel of her fingers on his arm. Her face in various silhouettes. The details of each expression that he saw.

Why?

He could not say. Except he was aware of a deep fear she would move on and he would lose her a second time. This time, he wished to make sure he could remember every detail of her when she'd gone.

He said nothing else. He'd upset her thrice today and that would hardly bring her about. In the future, he'd have to find some safe topic they could both converse on without prodding painful memories.

She sighed, the breath slipping through her parted lips. "Violet proposed Vauxhall."

"Is Sparks escorting you?"

"As far as I am aware."

"Then would you permit me to accompany him? I'm certain he would agree." Damn it, he sounded as desperate as he'd been at nineteen. But then, he probably was. Still, it earned him a very pretty smile. He realised then how little he'd seen her smile in recent days, when as a young woman she'd smiled constantly. If she would let him get close enough, he vowed he would make her smile all the time again. Just for him.

"You would dare to suffer Violet's reproach then?"

He let her fingers go and set his hand over his heart. "For you, anything."

She blushed, smiling even more. "I'll tell Violet."

"And I shall find Sparks and tell him he has company."

"I am sure I vex them in any case, tagging along when they would rather be alone." Her smile slipped. He'd sensed a deep sadness in her ever since that first night. Now he was starting to believe it *was* grief. Perhaps she'd really cared for Sutton, and if she had, maybe his adolescent impression of her, before she'd thrown him off, had not been awry – and yet, she had taken the route of a fortune-hunter.

"Your company could never vex anyone, Jane." *It is the lack of it that sets a man into the mire of despair.* He bowed valiantly. "Until tonight then, fair maiden."

That had the smile back on her lips.

"Until tonight."

Chapter Nine

"Your Grace, my Lady sent word to say their Lordships are waiting in the hall." Violet's maid bobbed a curtsy, her fingers resting on the handle of the open door.

"I will be down in a moment." Jane looked into the long cheval mirror again, and her hands skimmed across her gown, smoothing out creases which did not exist.

She felt nervous, even though when she had returned from seeing Robert she'd felt elated. She hadn't been able to stop smiling all afternoon. Violet had said dryly, "He wasn't a bore then," when she'd seen Jane's smile.

He had been anything but. When Robert played charmer he had Jane completely in his palm. It was dangerous befriending a notorious seducer.

Violet had even said she might grow to like Robert, if he could make Jane smile as he had.

Now Jane felt uncertain again, though. Afraid to go forward, and yet not wishing to go back.

"You look exquisite, Your Grace," Meg, Jane's own maid, commented.

Jane's jet-black curls were secured behind a thin silver tiara decorated with pearls, and she wore a matching three-stringed necklace which drew the eye to the flesh above her low neckline.

The dress was an emerald green silk and the high waist tucked beneath her breasts. She looked well. She knew she did, and yet, she'd never worn anything which drew attention so vividly before. Her courage was faltering.

Still, there was nothing to do but go. She'd made her choice. It was too late to change it now. Filling her lungs with a deep, slow breath, she told herself she was going to have fun. She was with friends. What on earth was there to fear, for heaven's sake?

Jane turned so Meg could set the black shawl she held across Jane's shoulders. It fell and looped across her elbows, hanging beneath her bottom at her back, framing the dress rather than spoiling its lines.

~

"Ah, and here she is," Lady Rimes stated. Robert looked up and found the air trapped in his lungs. *God*, Jane was stunning. His gaze swept across every curve and contour. She was perfection.

"You have given up your mourning," he said as she came down. She gave him a closed-lip smile and nodded.

Sparks bowed.

Robert remembered his manners and offered her a slight bow too, but he could not take his eyes off her.

"Lord Barrington." She held out her hand when she reached the hall. Her slender fingers were coated in emerald silk too.

He took them willingly, entirely enslaved, lifted them to his lips, kissed her knuckles, and savoured the intimacy, his thumb stroking across her palm.

Her smile broadened. It increased her beauty by degrees, a beauty he'd thought beyond improvement.

Her fingers tugged, reminding him to let go.

"We are ready then?" Sparks chimed. "Shall we head off? Vi?"

127

Still suffering from distraction over the woman whose fingers closed about his elbow, Robert was vaguely aware of Lady Rimes crossing to Sparks's side.

Jane leaned closer. "Is everything well, Robert? You are not angry?" That shifted him from his reverie.

"Angry?" he answered quietly. "Why on earth would I be angry? You look superb."

"I was afraid you would disapprove."

They stepped out into the air of a warm summer evening, and above them, the orange rays of sunset gilded wispy clouds across the sky.

He looked at her again and saw bronze highlight her dark hair, but her smile had gone, and her lower lip was caught between her teeth. Her eyes were on their friends a few steps ahead. It was touching to know she cared what he thought.

"Whether you wear blacks or not is none of my concern, nor anyone else's, Jane."

With both hands wrapped about his elbow and emotion in her voice, she said, "Thank you, Robert. I admit, I am nervous about other people's response. It is far too early to be appropriate, but I refuse to live a lie any more." She smiled again, her bright gaze meeting his.

Emotion caught in his chest like a stitch. "*I refuse to live a lie anymore.*" What did that mean? Had he been wrong about her affection for the former Duke? An even bigger question stirred his heart at the thought her decision may be due to their renewed *friendship*.

Robert looked at Sparks handing Lady Rimes into his carriage. He'd brought an open-topped barouche as the night was fine.

Jane's fingers left Robert's arm and instead took Sparks's hand. He helped her climb up, and Robert saw a dainty flash of ankle and her emerald slippers.

When Sparks nodded, Robert climbed in and sat beside Jane.

Likewise, Geoff occupied the seat by Lady Rimes. He immediately took her hand and hid the gesture beneath her skirt.

"Jane has been in high spirits all afternoon since she returned from your ride, Lord Barrington." Lady Rimes opened the conversation with a sincerity that surprised Robert. He turned to view her expression. It seemed genuine. It set him off balance. Good Lord, what had he done to gain the approval of Violet Rimes? The woman had turned her back on him for years.

Jane's fingers covered his hand, which rested palm down on his thigh.

Of course, she had been petitioning on his behalf.

He looked at her. "It is, indeed, a pleasure to see you smiling, Jane. So, what is it you are in fits over? Do not tell me the waterfall? It's tawdry. You'll be disappointed, I'm afraid."

"Do not listen to him," Geoff cut across his words. "Most of the women love it, if only on the first occasion, but once seen, both spectacle and enthusiasm become a little tainted, I admit."

"Or the entertainments?" Robert quipped, slipping into the general banter he and Geoff often shared. "Now there is a spectacle, if you are into the bizarre." He laughed. Geoff did, too.

"Well, I have never been there," Jane inserted, her voice challenging, yet amused and introspective. "And I admit to a curious interest in the bizarre. It may be to my taste. And I cannot wait to see the waterfall and the fireworks. I've read of Vauxhall. I've longed to go, and I shall not have it ruined by your jaded opinions just because you've both been so many times you are bored of it."

Geoff laughed. "Have no fear, Your Grace, I'll ensure I appear enthused by every moment."

Jane looked at Robert, and their gazes clashed in what felt like a deep connection. "I'll have no need to pretend. With you as my companion, I shall be in wonder all over again."

Her cheeks coloured, and she looked away, but not before he'd seen her smile lift.

Surely this was more than friendship, no matter what she'd said.

"And I say pah to the both of you." Lady Rimes leaned forward and tapped Jane's knee with her closed fan. "Ignore them, my dear. I love it always, just as much as on my first occasion. It is such a vibrant place, so full of life—"

"And dark pathways," Robert interjected, throwing Lady Rimes a wicked smile.

"*Robert,*" Jane chastised.

Oh dear, he'd blown the image of a paragon Jane had tried painting.

But Lady Rimes was made of sterner stuff. She shot him an answering smile, lifted Geoff's clasped hand from beneath her skirt, and set it on her thigh. "The walks, decorated in lantern light, are indeed very romantic, my Lord. Perhaps that is what you lack. To appreciate the beauty of Vauxhall, Lord Barrington, you need romance. You see, my dear friend Jane is a romantic at heart. Can you not tell? Hence, she is drawn to it, as am I."

So, Jane had not succeeded in overriding her friend's low opinion of him, just in making her play nice and offer only polite insults and mute warnings instead of open hostility.

Very well, he'd bite. "Of course, Lady Rimes, you would only be in a position to comment upon the level of my quixotic aspirations if you knew me at all, which, of course, you do not. In that case, you may withhold your judgement until you do." He met the blue-eyed blonde's gaze. For a moment, she stared at him, and he knew she was trying to establish what he was thinking. She gave up and looked away.

No doubt she wished to know his intentions towards Jane. Well, perhaps she should be more concerned about whether her friend would hurt him. After all, he was still walking about with his bloody heart on his sleeve, like an utter idiot, while the woman for whom he'd spent years pining just wished to be his *friend*.

Jane's fingers still covered his, and he turned his hand and held them possessively.

"So, what is on our list of things to see and do then, Jane? As it is your first time, you must have the prerogative and direct us all," Violet continued, brushing aside his hostility.

Jane looked at him, her eyes wide.

It reminded him of how she'd looked at him years ago. He'd thought her in thrall of him then. She'd looked at him as though he was master of the world and had the power to order everything as he wished.

"I would like to walk about the paths both before the sun sets and after, and I want to see the tightrope walker," she hesitated, longing shining in her eyes. "And dance. Most of all, I wish to dance."

He was in awe of her, and a spasm wrenched his heart. He swallowed against the lump in his throat and countered, "You can dance any evening."

"I know, but it has been so long." Her eyes looked suddenly uncertain, as though she feared he'd deny her. Of course, he would not. Whatever she wished, he'd do. She'd cast off her blacks, but she had a new shadow — him.

"Then you'll dance," he whispered, squeezing her fingers gently. When her gaze left his, he turned to find Lady Rimes and Geoff watching him with speculation. He shrugged in a defiant gesture and looked past them at the street. "It is a beautiful night for it anyway." His voice refused their conjecture, deliberately impersonal.

"It is indeed." Lady Rimes took up the theme.

"A night for revelry." Geoff sent a smile to Jane.

Jane sighed. "Yes, I am so tired of being wrapped in propriety. I am quite of a mind to break some rules."

Glancing at her, Robert saw her eyes sparkle. His blood heated. If she was in a mood for naughtiness, he knew just how to feed her hunger. Violet had said Jane was a romantic at heart. Well, a walk along the softly lit avenues would get the woman in the mood for him to steal a kiss or two. "And I shall be exceedingly happy to break them with you." He sent her the smile which had brought numerous women across the world to his bed.

"You have no need to be obtuse, Barrington," Lady Rimes threw at him, chastening his attempt to seduce her friend.

"I am not being in the least obtuse, my Lady, merely acting supplicant at Jane's altar." The back of Jane's hand stroked his thigh. He knew she did it to ask him not to argue, but it did nothing to cool his ardour.

"You are too smooth by half, my Lord," Violet swept back.

"Now, now, you two, play nicely," Geoff challenged good-humouredly.

Robert laughed then quipped, "I will if she will."

"On my part, Lord Barrington, I am still *withholding judgement*." The woman cast him a mocking smile.

"If we are to attempt neutral ground, Lady Rimes, perhaps you should call me Robert."

In answer she leaned forward, holding out her hand. "Very well, let us shake hands, *Robert*."

"Lady Rimes." He set his voice to charm, took her offered fingers, leaned forward, and kissed them.

"I suppose I must let you call me Violet," she said as he let them go.

"Violet," he said.

Jane slid closer, implying she marked her territory no matter her claims to only want friendship, and her thigh pressed against the length of his as she gripped his arm. "Robert, tell me what was your favourite thing, when you first went?"

~

Glancing up at the canopy of green leaves, Jane's gaze absorbed the perfect contrast of the orange sky above them. Vauxhall was as beautiful as she'd imagined, a Garden of Eden. She gripped Robert's elbow and looked along the broad central avenue. Violet and Geoff were walking together ahead, and at the end of the promenade, she saw the terracing from which guests could view the entertainments. They passed another pathway stretching away from the main thoroughfare, and Jane saw a mock-ruined Roman temple in the distance. She tugged on Robert's arm.

"May we walk that way? It is still an hour before we are due for supper. Violet! Geoff!" The couple, now a few paces ahead of them, stopped and looked back.

"Jane has a desire to explore some more!" Robert explained.

"Would you mind?" Jane added as she and Robert walked on and narrowed the distance between them.

Violet smiled. "Of course, we do not, Jane, but I have seen it all before. You and Robert go. We will secure the supper box."

"If you truly do not mind?"

Violet tapped Jane's arm with her closed fan. "Do not be silly. Why should we mind?"

Jane smiled in gratitude, and they agreed to meet in half an hour.

"Do we not sound like the perfect set?" Robert mocked as Violet and Geoff walked on.

Jane gave him a challenging look. "You can be a prig sometimes, my Lord."

"And you should not worry about what she thinks." Robert turned towards the side path.

She gripped his arm, looking forward. "She is my friend, and she's taken me in as her guest. I think it only polite I do nothing to offend her. I am very aware she is unable to live life as she

133

normally would with me in tow."

"No, but if Violet invited you to stay, she can hardly complain."

Jane looked up at him. "She did not ask me, Robert. Well, in an open invitation in Bath, perhaps. But I am afraid to admit, I did not even write. I just descended upon her. Do you think that is awful of me?"

His brown gaze bored into hers, and she smiled, wondering if she was a gullible fool to feel so happy in his company. "It seems, Jane, I cannot think you awful, no matter what you do. Come along. Let's investigate this ruin." He smiled, too, and a melting, quaking sensation settled in her stomach.

Her heart raced.

"It's beautiful, do you not think so?" she commented as they reached the high columns and half-built walls. She let go of his arm, peeled off her gloves, and gripped them in one hand while the other lifted to trail her bare fingers over the rigid granite columns. It felt cool and smooth.

"From my jaded perspective, Jane, it is a waste of time and effort. Who would build something to make it look as though it has fallen down?"

"How can you say that?" She turned back to him, her fingers remaining on the stone, and faced that beguiling smile. Her insides became aspic. He looked very handsome in the orange hues of the setting sun. She turned back to the ruins and began weaving in and out of the columns which formed an arched colonnade, her fingers skimming over the stones. "Violet is right. You have not one romantic bone in your body. *This* is romantic."

He laughed, still standing a few paces from the ruin. "*This* is a pile of old stones. Do not tell me Sutton built you one of these things. Follies are named as such for good reason. "

She stopped and leaned her back against the stone, her hands against the cold granite. "Hector would have agreed with you, and he certainly never did anything just to please me."

Her words seemed to surprise him, and his expression turned from humorous disinterest to one of question.

She never spoke of her marriage to anyone. She didn't know why she'd said it. She pushed away from the column and started walking through the row of arches again. She'd always been too embarrassed to let anyone know what had happened. She'd thought people would think less of her "However, *I* admire follies. I think they are even more beautiful because beauty is their only intent. If I ever had an estate of my own, I would build a folly. I expect this is stunning when lit up after dark." Her voice sounded whimsical.

"Jane." Robert caught her elbow, making her jump, then turned her to him, hiding them behind one of the broad columns so they would not be visible from the distant avenue. Her gaze met his. His brown eyes were intensely dark, his pupils distended. She couldn't breathe. "I don't understand you. Do you mourn Sutton or not? You send so many alternate signals. What am I to think? I cannot judge."

She looked from his eyes to his lips. She wanted him, just as much as he obviously wanted her. *Friends?* She could not be just friends with this man any more than they had been just friends years ago.

"Jane." His voice was husky and full of restrained emotion as his head bent. Then his lips touched hers. Her arms reached about his neck, and she kissed him back, her gloves dropping to the ground. His hair was soft and thick, and he cupped her bottom through her gown. Her body arched against him, and she felt the evidence of his arousal.

"Oh God, Jane, don't," he spoke into her mouth then stole one more brief kiss before pulling away.

"Don't what?" she whispered, resting her temple against his cheek and fighting to catch her breath and her sanity.

"Arch your body to mine like that. You drive me mad with want. If you still expect me to play your friend, I cannot do it, Jane."

She looked up. He had such beautiful eyes. "You make me feel happy," she answered, knowing her answer did not provide the response he sought. Her hands clasped his upper arms and pushed him back a little, setting a distance between them. Why was she so drawn to him? "But *this* is truly folly."

"Folly?" he repeated, his eyes baring a depth she assumed was unreleased desire.

"We should get back." She stepped aside, moving into the view of those promenading along the main avenue. For a moment he just stood there, watching her, half in shadow. "Robert?"

"Jane." His voice was back to a mocking note. "All hot and cold again, are we not?" He bent to collect her gloves from the ground. When he left the colonnade, he passed them to her.

She took them, but could not meet his gaze. "I'm sorry, I—"

"Never mind it." His voice was abrupt, as though he did not wish to hear her words. "So, tell me." His tone changed completely. "Did Sutton treat you well?"

Jane deemed to answer solely because she wished to set their embrace aside, as it seemed he did, and slipping her gloves back on, very aware he watched her intently, she said, "If you really wish to know, which I am sure you do not, Hector paid me very little attention. My husband's passions were for gloating and encouragement of envy. I was his showpiece."

Jane gripped Robert's arm once more, and together, they turned to stroll back towards the promenade. "He brought you to London, but did not bring you here then?"

She'd no idea where this was going, but with her heart still racing and her blood as thick as honey in her veins, she was in no state to think her way out of the conversation. "No. I mean, no, he never brought me to London, let alone to a place he would have considered purely licentious like Vauxhall. This is the first time I have visited the capital."

"But surely he attended Parliament?" Robert's voice was high-pitched with astonishment.

"I believe so, but I think he avoided entertainment other than his club."

"Then if he liked to gloat, why on earth would he not bring his wife?"

After a few moments' silence, she looked up at his perplexed expression. She had never understood why her husband had kept her virtually imprisoned. "I hardly know." Her voice sounded a little choked. She did not wish Robert, of all people, to see her insecurity. She forced her lips into a smile and shrugged.

"I could make a guess," he quipped in return, smiling too.

"Do tell." She waited, pretending not to care. She did. She desperately wished to understand Hector's cruelty, if you could call isolation cruelty. It had felt like it to a seventeen-year-old girl.

"A diamond like you, Jane, it's obvious. He didn't want to let you out in front of London's bucks. He probably feared you'd stray."

She'd stopped walking without even realising it.

He turned to face her, his brown eyes full of concern. "Is something wrong?"

"No." She closed her eyes and shook her head, wondering if Robert had guessed right to some degree.

Hector had liked control, and he'd allowed his friends to taunt her, but that was under his watchful supervision. If she'd met someone else beyond his power, maybe he thought she could have slipped his leash.

She swallowed back against the lump lodged in her throat and set a smile back on her lips. "I should think it was more because he liked to come across as holier than thou. I would have spoiled his town image. In the House of Lords, he liked to be envied for

137

his politics and power, not his wife. Come along." With that, she walked on, dismissing the subject, and turned her eyes back to the avenue ahead.

"If you have not been to London before, have you already visited the sights with Violet?"

She laughed. "Violet? You are joking. You do not know her well, I note. Violet would consider such outings an absolute bore."

"Then you would not refuse if I offered to escort you."

She smiled at him. "I would not refuse, Robert. I would appreciate it very much. Thank you."

Robert felt something hard grip in his chest. This woman could melt him. Yet she blew so hot and cold. He had no idea where he stood with her from moment to moment. And at this moment, she was tepid. Lukewarm, that was his ladylove.

But, *by the saints*, a moment ago, she'd been heated lava in his arms. She hid it well, but the woman was not impartial to him. Still, for some reason, she refused to yield to it. Unfortunately, he was no martyr. He wanted this, had wanted it for years. She felt right on his arm. He was warm and human again with her. This was beyond sex. This was about Jane. A light flared in his heart – that familiar torch he'd always carried for her. He could never face parting from her again, and if that was so, there was only one conclusion to this.

His heart pounding a tattoo against his ribs, he felt his breath catch in his lungs and forced it out. "*Jane.*"

He longed to make her stop, face him, and urge her to accept his words and answer, yes, but he held back. He dare not pin his heart so firmly on his sleeve for her to ridicule and wound. He'd done that once before. Instead, he was prudent and phrased his proposition casually. "For me, *this*, *us rather*, I do not see it as something temporary. If you were, I mean, in the future, once

138

you are ready, if you felt that it was right..." He hesitated, having reached the crux of the matter, and knew he was making a hash of it, but all he could do was lay his cards on the table. "What I mean to say is, I would not be against the option of revisiting my previous proposal."

He felt the gentle tug of her fingers on his arm as she stopped walking. He stopped, too.

"Did you just propose to me?"

Astonishment or outrage? He was not sure. Just in case, either way, he put up his guard. The same armour he'd been using for years. The very same defences he'd learned at her hands years ago. Lord, he was a glutton for punishment.

His mask of indifference was set firmly in place as he faced her.

Her fingers slipped from his arm.

He felt her rip his heart right out.

"Robert, what on earth are you thinking?"

Was that not just the point? He was smitten and *not* thinking. That was the issue in a nutshell. He was quite obviously *not thinking*. Or at least, nothing of any sense if he was fool enough to make such an offer to a woman who clearly did not have the measure of his worth. Who, in fact, thought him worthless – *else why did she take Sutton over me?*

There it was again, that damn question.

The question that had disturbed his sleep for years, to the point he'd had to bury it behind sex. *Why not me? Why Sutton?*

He'd answered himself a thousand times, too. Money. Power. Status.

Yet those answers never satisfied him, and certainly never stopped his subconscious asking and analysing the question a million times more.

God help him. He'd not even dared let any other woman close enough to risk them finding out his faults, for faults there must

139

be, otherwise, *why?* But then, of course, none of them had ever measured up to Jane either. But, who the hell *was* Jane?

He could surely not love a woman who would toss his love aside like soiled linen? Twice.

Could he?

It was a bloody, sorry state for a man whose reputation declared him a heartless rake.

Aloud, he said, "It was no more than a suggestion, sweetheart. Take it or leave it. If you have an interest, you need only ask."

She burst into laughter which echoed along the pathway.

It seemed he damned well could love a woman who saw no value in his affections. All he was worthy for was kisses. Those she liked. He knew that, if nothing else. At least his damned reputation remained intact then.

"Sorry, Robert," she whispered when her laughter died.

He paid little mind to the insincere apology. Whether she was sorry or not, she still did not want him, and that was the rub, and God, but it hurt.

"I just did not expect it. You need not be gallant for my sake. I've survived one marriage. I do not intend to launch into another. So you may come off your guard."

Speechless, Robert turned and walked on. Her gentle, slender fingers gripped his elbow. He felt them about his heart as she chattered on in her sweet, sing-song voice, merrily extolling all the novelties of the pleasure garden.

The setting sun sent the last shafts of pink and gold across the sky. In the distance, it was turning to a royal blue, a perfect romantic sunset, and on the third finger of her left hand, clutching his arm, her gold band caught the light, beneath the ostentatious emerald engagement ring.

He was a bloody fool. But when he turned to hear her words, he saw the golden light catch her beauty, gilding her cheekbones, her magnificent green eyes, and her full red lips. She stopped speaking. His feeling must be in his eyes. He'd never understood why she'd cast him off, but nor had he ever stopped loving her. *Jane.* He suddenly could not quite believe that, after all these years, she was here.

He may be a damned fool, but he could not walk away from her.

He covered her fingers with his own. "Come along then. Let us do some more exploring."

~

Hours later, leaning one elbow on the table within their private supper box, tucking her fist beneath her chin, Jane took the opportunity of Violet's and Geoff's absence to steal a sideways glance in Robert's direction.

The male tightrope walker, suspended over the heads of a hushed crowd, drew a sudden sigh of fear from his audience. Jane was not at all afraid. He was as comfortable on the rope as any other man was on the floor, and yet, his talent was indeed awe-inspiring. She looked back when the crowd let out a chorused gasp. The nimble fellow landed a somersault. His audience applauded.

Jane applauded, too, then transferred her gaze back to an even more enthralling sight, Robert in repose. He made no response.

He was everything she wished for this evening, attentive and considerate – wonderful – everything was wonderful. He'd paid for their expensive yet sparse supper and they'd danced half a dozen times, because none of the rules of society counted here. There were no matrons or patrons to judge them.

Even the hawkers and harlots who'd flooded the gardens after midnight and flaunted their wares, moral and immoral, did not tarnish Jane's pleasure, and on the signal of the bell, Robert had taken her to see the cascade of water. It glittered in the lamplight.

Then afterwards, he'd led her through the lit and unlit pathways, seeking temples and fountains. As they'd walked, they'd heard other couples in the darkness – whispers, laughter, and squeals carried on the balmy night air. This really was a pleasure garden. It stimulated every human sense. It willed you to abandon restraint and revel in vice. She was not immune.

The memory of their brief kiss had haunted her thoughts, and she ached between her thighs for him. Perhaps she'd had too much champagne, or was it the wonder of dancing with him that had seduced her? They'd laughed as they'd skipped through the zealous steps of a country dance to the sharp, jolly ring of a brass band, and her hands had clung to him when they waltzed. Or it could have been the way his fingers had protectively gripped her waist or her hand as they'd walked along the dark paths? But whatever was making her wish for another kiss and more, he'd made no attempt to repeat it, and she felt as though, despite his attentiveness, since they'd kissed, he'd somehow withdrawn from her.

She turned towards him, to watch him better, and tried to unravel the puzzle that was Robert. She knew he wasn't concentrating on the tightrope walker. His thoughts were somewhere else. He'd not shown any tendencies of his youth tonight. He'd been witty, pleasant, entertaining, but never truly sincere, not since they'd kissed. The old Robert was in retreat behind the solid, insurmountable wall of charm he'd built for his defence.

She smiled, absorbed in his sober expression and his familiar profile. The way his hair, in a Brutus cut, swept a curl or two across his collar and hung over his brow. Had he meant his proposal, or was it a joke? He'd said he wasn't known for his seriousness. Did that mean for his lack of sincerity, too? She'd taken it for a joke. She didn't dare risk thinking of it as anything else. How could she accept him, even if it was real? Pain lodged in her chest at the possibility of being forced to reject Robert again.

"You're staring, Jane. I believe one's eyes are supposed to be upon the entertainment." He spoke without turning, and yet a rakish smile twitched at the side of his lips. The wolf. Barrington, the soulless rakehell. That was the Robert of tonight.

"I'm caught out," she whispered.

"Indeed, you are." His head turned and his gaze met hers. She still stared, smiling and studying the contours of his face.

"Your Grace?"

The smile instantly fell from her lips, and her heart thumped harder. She turned immediately, standing up as she moved. Robert stood, too.

What on earth was Joshua doing here? What had he seen? Of course, he knew none of her history with Robert, but even so, anyone, anything, anywhere near Joshua was in danger.

"You will, of course, dance with me."

Jane felt herself blanch and lowered her head as she dropped a restricted curtsy, deliberately but surreptitiously insulting him.

What could she do? She'd rushed into giving up her mourning, engrossed in thoughts of dancing with Robert and desperate to be free of the cage Hector had built about her during his life, only to forget entirely the cage he'd forged for her on his death. She'd played directly into Joshua's hands. He could approach her now whenever he liked. She could not say no without making a scene, and she refused to have her humiliation known, especially by Robert. Robert moved to her side in a possessive, protective gesture.

"Of course," she answered, her voice wooden.

She did not look at Robert, but moved forward. What would he think of this? Everyone knew Joshua disapproved of her.

Joshua offered her his hand. She took it, a tattoo drumming in her chest as his fingers gripped hers.

They walked from the shallow steps of the supper box to the dance floor, and she felt Robert's gaze on her back. Somehow, she knew he was still standing.

The music suddenly changed tempo to a waltz. "I asked for it," Joshua whispered against her ear. A shiver ran the length of her spine.

Robert watched, unmoving. He'd seen Sutton's wife cut her in the park. He thought he'd rationalised it. The son of the deceased Duke had disapproved of such an obscene age gap between his father and his stepmama. Sutton had made no secret of that in the years Robert had been back in England, and certainly, he must dislike Jane inheriting the old man's money. *But this?*

Robert's eyes followed them across the dance floor.

She was stiff, uncomfortable, no longer the carefree, laughing girl of an hour ago.

Sutton's wife cut her. Sutton did not. Sutton danced with her on the first opportunity that arose. There was only one conclusion a man could draw from evidence such as that. *Hell.* Robert did not want to accept it, but it made sense. It would explain why she kept refusing him. "*I cannot.*"

It was Robert's turn to stare at her. He leaned a hand on the rail of the supper box. He could not see Geoff and Violet among the dancers. They'd probably slipped off to seek private entertainment. What hour was it now? One, perhaps two. Pulling out his pocket watch, he clicked it open. It was one-fifteen. His gaze returned to the dancers. He could no longer see Sutton and Jane. They'd disappeared.

His breath quickened, and his heart picked up its pace. He felt strangely suspended as he descended the steps. He looked left and right then chose the promenade path leading towards the river. The area of pathways there were the darkest and particularly known for offering privacy.

By the time he reached it, he was moving at almost a run, his stride hard and sharp, crunching on the gravel, his heartbeat the only noise he could hear.

He found them in minutes, in a darkened stone alcove hidden in the hedge. It was Sutton's voice which carried, although Robert hadn't caught the words. Jane was pressed back against the stone. Sutton leaned to her ear. His hands gripped her shoulder and her arm. Robert couldn't move. He actually felt the moment his heart splintered. He was suddenly intensely cold. She was doing this to him again. The woman he'd known and loved *was* a bloody fake. His imagined Jane was not capable of this. This was her husband's son! No wonder Sutton's wife had cut her. Robert's Jane did not exist. The fiction he'd mourned was gone. This was the truth.

Thank God. I am free of her now.

She saw him and he viewed both the scene and himself from afar.

When her eyes fixed on his face, he saw horror in her expression then watched her fight free of Sutton's grip.

Suddenly released from his transfixion, grimacing in disgust, he turned away, leaving it all behind.

She was upon him in a moment, her fingers clutching his arm. He shrugged her off, neither slowing nor reducing his strides to allow her to keep up. He had no wish to hear her explanations. He did not want excuses.

"No! No! You will not do this to me again! Robert! You do not understand! Please! It is not as you think!"

The anger, the hurt of years roiling inside him like a beast over which he had no control, he suddenly stopped and spun back to face her.

She looked shocked and afraid and stepped back beyond his reach as his glare threw his revulsion at her. Tears stained her cheeks, and her chest heaved.

When he did not speak she stepped forward and touched his cheek.

Pulling back, he growled, "No, Jane. This is it, the end. How many times do you think you can make a man look a fool and expect him to dance attendance on you? No. Not anymore. I will not do it. I will leave you to your *friend*." Thrusting the words like a knife, he tilted his head towards Sutton, who watched from a few feet away, looking pleased and gloating. "Tell Geoff I will find my own way home."

With that, Robert turned and, swallowing back the anger and bitter taste in his throat, he walked away.

Chapter Ten

Her arms wrapping about her waist, Jane shivered, despite the warm evening air, and tears tracked down her cheeks. A single sob wrenched from her throat as she tried to breathe and watched Robert walk from her life a second time. If he'd ever really loved her, surely he would know she would never do what he'd thought he'd seen.

"That man is no loss to you." Joshua's voice came from behind her, deep and gloating. Her fingers forming claws, she swung about and launched her anger at him. He'd done this deliberately, for pure malice.

She understood her dead husband's pleasure now. Oh yes. It came to her in a blinding light.

Joshua simply caught and held her wrists, laughing in her face and leaving her rage impotent.

"Now, now, my little cat. Such claws Her Grace hides until she is roused." He hauled her against him and twisted her arms behind her back. "You'd better find yourself a good solicitor, my dear. You will receive a letter from my own in the morning. Shame. No more pretty dresses, Jane. He tells me my father's will is nonsense and shall never stand. I will drag you through the courts, if I must, and then, my dear, you will depend on me. You'll surrender to me in every way in the end, Jane. Do you understand? But for

147

the moment, you're lucky. Before I sate my desire for your body, I want to see you beg me to take you." He let her go. She stumbled backward. He walked away, laughing, leaving her in near darkness, alone.

A deep, tremulous breath pulled into her lungs. She wiped her tears away with her shawl and began walking, stiffening her spine, ignoring her shaking hands. She had to get back, to go on.

Joshua had manipulated Robert because he'd seen Robert as her potential ally, and, in a single move, Joshua had closed that door to her. Just like his father, he wanted to control her. She saw everything now. Her former husband was controlling them both from beyond the grave, like puppets. He'd not given her security and freedom on his death. He'd set a new key in her cage. Hector had known how Joshua would react. *Like this*. What had just happened was what Hector had willed.

She knew Joshua was right. The will would not stand, not once it was tested before a court.

It was all clear – Hector's cruel plan. He had taken as much pleasure in taunting his son as in breaking her youthful spirit and resilience. That was Hector's way, to destroy everything he envied, and make everyone envy him. His rift with Joshua had begun before their marriage. Hector had always intended writing this will. He'd married her to infuriate Joshua. She'd been a pawn for Hector to play against his son. He'd manipulated Joshua and broken her, but ultimately, he'd always intended Joshua would win. He'd left her nothing, done nothing for her, right up until the end. She would never have the chance to be happy.

It was no wonder Joshua had grown into a monster like his father.

Her fingers still shaking, she gripped her shawl, pulled it up over her shoulders, and walked blindly in the direction of the music. The sound of raucous voices echoed behind her. She looked back and walked into someone screaming as hands clasped her arms.

"Jane?"

"*Geoff.*" Both relief and distress rang in her voice, and a sob escaped her throat. But then, instantly, sanity returned. She didn't even really know him. She forced herself to be calm. "Thank goodness," she whispered in a steadier voice, pulling away. "I was lost."

"What happened, Jane?" Violet said at her side, her fingers resting on Jane's shoulder. "We passed Barrington leaving, with a face like thunder. He didn't even pause to speak. We were looking for you."

"We argued. I'm sorry. I've ruined your evening."

"Do not be ridiculous, Jane. Did Barrington upset you?" Violet's voice was deep with concern.

Jane fixed a false smile, applying all the skill she'd learned from the house of Sutton, and responded dismissively. "It was a foolish disagreement. It wasn't his fault."

"I will speak to him—" Geoff began, but she touched his arm.

"No. Please, don't. It really was not his fault. It was mine, and that is an end to it. I do not wish to discuss it further. May we go now, please?"

Violet pressed Jane's shoulder then said she was tired anyway.

~

Jane sat alone at the breakfast table with the headache and red-rimmed eyes, which Meg had failed to cure with a solution of witch hazel.

Violet had already eaten.

Selford approached, bearing a silver tray. A sealed letter lay on it.

Jane's fingers shook when she picked it up. She slid her cup of coffee away. Her nervous stomach had not been able to face food. She broke the seal and felt it crack loose.

149

As Selford backed away, her eyes scanned the neat, sharp script.

It was the writ Joshua had threatened last night. A notice advising the will was in dispute.

The only solicitor she knew was Hector's. He was the one who'd written the will. She could hardly go to him. It seemed the moment had come for her to brave sharing her humiliation. She had no choice.

Last night, when she hadn't been able to sleep, she'd come down to borrow a book from Violet's small library, and as she'd passed the drawing room, she'd heard Violet and Geoff talking in hushed voices.

Violet had spoken of her concern for Jane. Violet knew something was wrong, and she thought Robert's desertion a part of it. She'd told Geoff she wished Jane would tell her what was wrong.

Well now, Jane would. "Where is Lady Rimes, Selford?"

"I believe my Lady is in the garden, Your Grace."

Jane rose before a footman could move forward to withdraw her chair. It was about time she dared to trust someone again.

~

The good weather had held for another three weeks. The heat in the city was scorching at midday, but now it was late afternoon, and the *ton* was out *en masse* to promenade, to see and be seen along Rotten Row in Hyde Park. This was the showground for unmarried ladies, young bucks, and the leaders of fashion. Jane, however, had accompanied Violet simply to stretch her legs and seek a change of scenery. They would have come long before the fashionable hour if it had not been so intolerably hot.

With her parasol resting on her shoulder, as Violet's was on hers, Jane promenaded across the lawns with her friend towards the Serpentine, and behind them paced two of Violet's burly footmen, their rearguard, as Violet called them.

Since Vauxhall, Jane's social life had narrowed.

She'd told Violet all about Hector's cruelty, and Joshua's manipulation, and Violet had been her usual, supportive self. She had helped Jane find a solicitor and plan out what to do. The only help that Jane had refused was an offer to have Geoff speak to Robert and explain. But Jane had not wished either Geoff or Robert involved. Geoff was too much of a stranger and if Robert could misjudge her so badly, why should she care to tell him the truth? And besides, Robert might get some silly notion in his head about duelling if she did.

So instead Violet and Jane had mapped out a defensive strategy themselves, including Violet's new "*rearguard*". Moreover, Jane had ceased attending balls, or any event where the Duke of Sutton and dancing might merge, and Violet's solicitor had obtained a copy of Hector's will and begun scanning it, looking for potential flaws. But Jane had not returned to her blacks, nor ceased any other social activity. They shopped frequently, as Violet insisted Jane should spend Sutton's money while she could, and they attended musicals, at-homes, card parties, and supper nights, and overall, apart from the Robert-sized aching hole in Jane's chest, life was comparably quite good.

She had not seen Robert since Vauxhall. And she'd resisted the urge to ask Geoff how Robert was.

"What will you do this evening while I am out with Geoff? I do so hate leaving you alone," Violet said as they walked away from the hubbub of Rotten Row.

"Read probably. I am not at all bothered to be left behind, and I am sure Geoff must be weary of my presence."

"Nonsense. Geoff likes you as well as I do. He enjoys your company."

Jane gave her friend a smile, knowing Violet spoke the truth, yet also that Violet's relationship with Lord Sparks was evolving into something far more intense than a simple affair. Violet had been single for years, and, apparently, she'd never paid quite so much attention to one man. Violet's feelings seemed to be reciprocated, too, because Lord Sparks was spending less and less time beyond her friend's immediate sphere.

Violet pointed ahead of them. "Look, is that not Barrington?"

Jane looked forward, and her heart jolted. She stopped. Violet did, too. He was just a few yards away, pacing along the gravel path about the lake where they'd stood some weeks before. A warm longing surged into Jane's blood, and the hole in her chest filled at the sight of his tall, excellent figure and the proud bearing in his posture.

His hands were clutched behind his back as he walked beside a lanky youth, who was a little taller than Robert's shoulder. He was listening to the youth's animated conversation. The boy had the look of a colt, with long legs and arms, as boys did in adolescence when they suddenly sprouted inches in a matter of months. She could remember Robert looking like that.

As Jane watched, another child ran up and wrapped her arms about Robert's leg, a young girl barely as tall as his thigh, with rich ebony curls tumbling about her face. Giggling, she refused to let go. Then her hands suddenly reached up. Robert bent and picked her up. One of her arms embraced his neck, and she planted a swift kiss on his cheek. Robert tussled her hair. The boy laughed.

Something new and unknown struck in Jane's chest. Something vicious, cruel, and needy – jealousy and longing. This was just how she'd dreamed things may be so many years ago, for her, with him. Children. A family.

"Do you wish to go?" Violet whispered.

As she spoke, Jane looked to where the girl had come from and saw a man made in Robert's mould.

Edward, Robert's brother. The adopted brother of her childhood.

A woman walked with him, her fingers threaded through his, their bodies so in tune their affection was a visible force. His wife was beautiful in an uncommon fashion, slender, dark-haired and blue-eyed. She was the most attractive woman Jane had ever seen. The girl and the youth were both clearly hers.

Just as Jane was about to turn and accept Violet's suggestion of retreat, Edward's gaze spun in Jane's direction, and his eyes widened in surprise. "Good Gracious!" she heard him declare. "If it is not our Jane!"

There was no running now. Jane took a sharp breath and held it, seeking to slow the thump of her racing heart, and continued on down the slight slope. Edward and his wife, their hands still clasped, strode towards her. He grinned broadly.

"Well, well, Jane Coates," he called as they approached. "I did not know you were in town."

She made no comment, closing her lips on the hurt that wished to declare Robert knew. That he'd chosen not to tell Edward spoke volumes.

She offered her hand. "Jane Grey now, I'm afraid."

Edward let his wife's hand fall, but ignored Jane's, and, gripping her upper arms, pressed a kiss on her cheek. When he let her go, there was a glint in his eyes, stirring memories of their childhood, and he answered, "Nonsense. You shall always be Jane Coates to me, my surrogate sister."

She smiled, too, and, looking over his shoulder, saw Robert had turned his back to her. He was skimming stones with the boy. All pleasure at seeing Robert faded. Was he cutting her? Before Edward?

"May I introduce you to my wife?" Edward said. "Jane, my wife, Ellen. Darling, I believe Jane's full title is now the Dowager Duchess of Sutton."

153

The woman's eyes widened a little as if the statement meant something more than just an introduction, yet she bent her head and curtsied.

"There is no need for formality," Jane declared, blushing. "As Edward said, we are as good as family. Just Jane is fine, Ellen." She offered her hand again, and the woman took it. "It's a pleasure to meet you."

Beside Jane, Violet made a little coughing sound.

"Oh, but I am forgetting my manners, you so surprised me, Edward. Lady Rimes, this is Lord Edward Marlow and his wife." Of course, this time Edward's greeting was more formal as was his wife's.

"You will walk with us a while, Jane?" Edward invited. "This weather is so hot, we have brought Mary-Rose out to find a breeze. She is so restless in the heat at home." Jane glanced over his shoulder to see the girl balanced on Robert's arm, cheering as her brother skipped a stone half a dozen times.

"Yes, of course," Jane answered then added loudly, "I am surprised Robert did not mention I was in town."

"You've seen him?" Edward glanced over his shoulder at Robert. "He never mentioned it." Edward shrugged when he looked back. "But then who am I to be kept informed of his social life? Merely his brother."

That surprised Jane. It was unlike Edward to criticise Robert. They'd been as thick as thieves as children.

Edward offered his arm to his wife, and Jane and Violet fell into step next to them. They walked along the path leading away from Robert. "Jane was our neighbour as children, Ellen. She spent more time at our hearth than her own. Jane was the daughter my mother craved. You will have seen her miniature at Robert's country residence. It is amongst the family, just as she was. Such a little bruiser, always trying to prove she could keep up and match

154

our boyish antics."

"That is not quite how I remember it," Jane laughed. "As I recall, you were always trying to lose me, and you called me a nuisance."

"Well, you were." A bark of laughter left his throat. "But it is good to see you." He looked at his wife and added, "Jane was married quite young. I've not seen her since."

"Oh." Ellen smiled in her direction. "Then you should come to dinner. We have no plans this evening. I'm sure Robert shall not mind as you are virtually family."

"No, I—" Jane began.

But Violet spoke over her attempted refusal. "You are doing nothing else, Jane. How pleasant to have the opportunity to catch up." The look Violet threw Jane urged her to take the opportunity to patch things up with Robert.

"Robert!" Ellen called back across her shoulder, heedless, if she sensed it, of his reluctance to participate in the happy image of reunion. "Robert!" she persisted.

He glanced over and gave Ellen a quelling glower.

She turned and smiled at Jane. "Wait a moment. I will just secure his agreement." She then walked back with determined strides.

"If he's in a mood, she'll snap him out of it," Edward stated. "She has more patience than I do with him, and the two of them seem to understand each other in a way he and I cannot."

"But you were always close." Jane was surprised by this turn, and her eyes followed the scene behind Edward.

Another pang of sorrow and longing pierced Jane's heart as Ellen took the girl from Robert. He shrugged. Then his lips parted in a broad, sudden smile. He said something. Ellen laughed. She struck his shoulder with the back of her hand and shook her head. Robert then walked away. Ellen turned back.

Jane met Ellen's gaze as she approached, smiling. Ellen looked as though she had a deep affection for Robert.

Her son was at her side, as tall as she, and the little girl was still balanced on her hip.

"Robert has remembered something urgent to do. He cannot join us for dinner, but he's quite happy for me to invite who I like. So, you will, of course, come. You have to tell me all about Edward in his childhood and arm me with more ammunition to taunt these brothers with when they are churlish."

Jane smiled. How could she not like a woman who was so open-hearted? "I would love to. Thank you. I'll look forward to it."

But Edward frowned and glanced back at Robert as he walked away. "He has remembered something urgent?" Edward looked at his wife when he turned back. "What? Is he in a mood?"

Edward's young daughter held out her hands to her papa. "Uncle Robert promised me an ice."

Edward's frown deepened as he took his daughter from Ellen. "And then he disappeared? What is up with him, Ellen?"

Jane felt the heat of a blush as Ellen's son also complained. "And he'd promised to play backgammon with me..."

"John," Ellen admonished. "Your uncle is a busy man when he is in town. He will give you a game tomorrow, I am sure."

"Uncle Robert does not make promises he cannot keep, but he's broken two." The boy's words sounded arrogant, but his voice said he thought something amiss.

Edward looked at Jane. "I cannot understand him—"

Feeling the heat of a blush, Jane interrupted. "I think it is my fault. We have fallen out."

While the boy eyed her as though she had three heads, Edward's eyebrows lifted.

Jane felt her blush burn.

"It does not surprise me," Edward said, obviously seeking to ease her discomfort. Then, ending that conversation, he smiled. "And I am being extremely rude, I have not yet introduced my son and daughter."

"John, this is the Dowager Duchess of Sutton. Jane, Lord John Harding, the Marquess of Sayle. He is the heir to Ellen's father, the Duke of Pembroke."

Jane remembered Robert mentioning John was to be a Duke. She'd not really registered it then.

"Your Grace," the boy acknowledged, bowing with perfect manners.

"And this is Lady Rimes, Jane's friend." Edward said, glowing with pride. He obviously loved his stepson.

"My Lord," she and Violet acknowledged.

Jane smiled. This family bore no comparison to the Sutton's. John seemed charming.

"And this," Edward stated, his hand running over the little girl's ebony curls, as she was balanced on his arm, "is my imp of a daughter, Mary-Rose."

A sharp pain pierced Jane's breast. She'd given up all hope of children when she'd realised any child born to her would be sentenced to Hector's imprisonment, too. Now, confronted by this familial scene, that scar tore open.

"I want my ice, Papa," the child said, looking only at her father.

"You are rude, mite," John said, holding his hands out to his sister. Again the girl changed her host, now clinging to her brother's neck. "You have not even said hello to Papa's friends, and you are asking us to leave them. Are you going to be polite and say hello to these ladies? You must call this lady, Your Grace, and her friend, Lady Rimes."

The girl made a frustrated face, but then wriggled to be let down before slipping from her brother's grip and performing a perfect curtsy. "Your Grace, Lady Rimes, good day. My name is Mary-Rose." Instantly it was done, and her bright smile turned back to her papa. "Now may I have an ice?"

Edward shook his head, but Jane could see the smile he struggled to hide. "Not yet, you must wait a while. I wish to speak with my friend Jane. I shall take you to Gunter's in a little while if you are good, and patient."

Edward had taunted Jane more than Robert when they'd been children. Robert had been the one who looked out for her, while Edward had always found her presence irritating. He seemed mellowed now.

"Come," Ellen stated, picking up her daughter.

"You are very pretty, Mary-Rose. I am sure your papa is very proud of you," Jane said.

"And in debt for one ice," Ellen added with a laugh.

"She is a poppet," Violet said, her eyes sparkling.

"She is a *monster*," Edward answered in an overzealous voice that had the little girl laughing.

"A monster who devours ices," John enthused, bending to form an impression of a monster, which made the little girl squeal with delight.

They all began walking, and after a few paces, as Violet moved to speak to Ellen and pet the little girl, Edward caught hold of Jane's elbow gently and held her back.

With the others walking a few paces ahead, Edward asked bluntly, "What did Robert do?"

Jane glanced sideward at Edward, smiling, but feeling guilty. "Nothing. The blame is mine. He misunderstood something, and he would not let me explain."

Edward sighed. "My children idolise him..."

"And that is a bad thing?"

Edward threw her a lopsided, awkward, smile. "I am happy that they like Robert. It constantly amazes me just how close Robert is to them, but he is hardly the material of a hero. The children dote on him, and he on them, too, but Robert is no saint and someday

158

the pedestal they have put their uncle on will topple. The man he's become is not the boy we grew up with, Jane, as you have possibly discovered if the two of you have fallen out. What caused it?"

Jane sought for a believable half-truth. The whole truth was too humiliating to tell. "Robert saw something which caused him to make an incorrect judgement."

Edward's eyebrows lifted. "Your fault or his, answer me truthfully? Has he upset you? Because I know more than anyone how good he is at that. He returned from the continent acting as though it was I who was in the wrong."

She shook her head and met his gaze. "Mine." She changed the subject. "But why have you two fallen out? You were always in each other's pockets before."

Edward grimaced. "We were until he went abroad without any explanation. He sent no word when mother died, and when our father died, he sent me a cursory note, giving me permission to manage in his stead. I was eighteen and tied down by his responsibilities, or perhaps more accurately, his irresponsibilities'. Then, all of a sudden, a couple of years ago, he returned, expecting the world to revolve about him again. I made it plain I would not be at his beck and call. Since then, we've got along reasonably well, but our relationship is not what it was. As you can tell by the fact he did not mention to me you were in town."

Was there something behind the change in Robert? Jane looked ahead and watched Violet walking beside Ellen and leaning to brush back the little girl's curls. Jane glanced at Edward again. "Why did he go abroad?"

"I still have no idea. He dropped out of Oxford early and went carousing in town. I remember father in a rage, waving about the I-owe-yous Robert had sent home for payment."

Jane had not known Robert had dropped out of university. An odd feeling of coincidence settled in her stomach.

159

"Ellen is closer to him than I am. If you are seeking someone to talk sense into him, then it's her. The two of them have an understanding that escapes me. Fortunately, I know exactly how Ellen feels about me, otherwise, taking into account my brother's reputation, I would have cause to be a very jealous man."

"Ellen is wonderful. You're lucky, Edward, and your family is lovely."

He laughed and said, "I know."

This was a man very confident of what he had, and very happy.

She wondered, then, if the problem between him and Robert could be envy. She *envied* Edward.

Their conversation shifted, turning to the past. Smiling, Edward reminded her of when her skirt had caught on his hook when she'd insisted on fishing with them. She had lost her balance, struggling to free it, and fallen in the lake. Robert had pulled her out. She'd been covered in weeds and crying.

"You were a cruel boy," Ellen uttered.

Jane looked up, holding back her laughter as she realised Ellen, Violet and John had stopped to listen. "In fairness, I think I was a pain."

"In fairness, you were a downright nuisance. Robert was always rescuing you from one thing or another, like when you climbed up that tree after us then were too afraid to climb down."

Jane laughed again. Oh yes, she remembered. Robert had always come to her rescue. He'd rarely grumbled about it, but often chastised her for her stupidity.

"Papa!" Mary-Rose held her hands towards her father. "May I have my ice now? I'm hot."

Edward smiled at Jane, as he accepted his daughter once more. "We shall reminisce some more tonight. But for now, if you will excuse us, ladies, I have a promise to keep. We shall see you this evening, Jane."

"Yes, this evening at seven, if that is not too early," Ellen completed.

"I will look forward to it. Till then," Jane answered.

Edward and his family walked away.

"I'm sorry I did not believe just how thick you really were with Barrington when you said you'd been close," Violet whispered when they'd gone.

Jane shot her friend a dismissive look. "What does it matter? He's still angry with me."

"But not disinterested if he must run."

"You forget, Violet, I do not want him interested. It is better if he does run. Less complicated, certainly."

~

Jenkins held the door as Robert entered his townhouse, listening out for voices. He'd returned after midnight, hoping Jane would be gone. There was no sound of conversation.

Robert stripped off his gloves and took off his hat, then passed both to Jenkins.

"Robert, I did not think you would be so late."

Ellen.

Robert's fingers rubbed the tense muscle at the back of his neck. "Sorry. Did I miss your guest?"

"I should think so. It is nearly one, Jane left hours ago." Ellen arched an eyebrow.

It was the look she gave him when she knew he was fabricating. At times, it was intensely irritating how easily the woman could read him.

"I have asked Jane to come to our dinner party on Friday."

"It was supposed to be a family meal..."

"Well it seemed to me, from what Edward has said, that Jane

161

is virtually that. But she said you may disapprove."

Robert narrowed his gaze. If he argued, Ellen would know there was something more to it. If he let Jane come, he need not speak to her.

"She can come," he answered, then changed the subject. "I am going to have a nightcap. Is Edward still up? " He began crossing the hall to escape her.

"I'll have hot chocolate, Jenkins, please," she called back to the butler, following. "Edward's retired. I waited up for you."

The woman was too tenacious when she got hold of something. Ignoring her intense gaze on his back, Robert disappeared into the male sanctuary of his study, but Edward's beautiful, determined wife invaded it.

Sighing, Robert turned about and folded his arms over his chest as he leaned his bottom against the desk. "Go on, then, Ellen. Pray, have out with it. Tell my why you stayed up. What are you stewing on?"

"I am not stewing," she declared, crossing to the decanters and upturning a glass. "Which would you like?"

"Brandy," he said with little patience. He was tired. He'd been tired for days. He'd hardly slept since he'd seen Jane with Sutton.

Ellen brought him the full glass, as if the liquid contained in it could fix all ills. "Edward told me Jane married the Duke of Sutton not long before you left for the continent." Her voice was all social gossip, and yet her gaze swept his face for any sign of reaction.

Women. Who on earth would want one for a wife?

"Yes." Was his only answer, in a *so what, Ellen*, voice, as he took the glass from her hand.

"I was merely wondering if there was any connection."

"If there was, I would not wish to tell you about it," he answered, sipping the fiery liquid and watching her calculate her next move.

"Why have you fallen out with her?" Again, she watched

carefully, undoubtedly looking for some slip in his expression or demeanour.

"That, my dear, is for Jane to tell you, not I."

"She said it was her fault, a misunderstanding."

Robert's eyebrows lifted. If you could call being caught *indelicado* with your stepson a misunderstanding. "Perhaps."

"So, you agree it was a mistake? I'll send her an invitation tomorrow."

He grunted acceptance, but felt manipulated.

Ellen's hot chocolate arrived.

"I'll take it upstairs," she advised the maid before looking back at him. "Goodnight, Robert. Jane is very beautiful, isn't she?"

At that, he gave her a twisted, mocking smile, silently telling her to stop fishing, then bid her goodnight.

His sister-in-law had clearly taken three pieces of a puzzle and made a jigsaw. Well, she would find herself disappointed if she expected anything of it. Jane was not for him and never would be. He just wished his bloody heart would recognise it and stop hankering after what he could never have. Even now, the loss of her was like a lead weight in his chest. But he could not forget the sight of her in Sutton's arms. It hurt, even more than it had hurt at nineteen to be told the woman you loved had chosen in your stead a man old enough to be her grandfather.

Chapter Eleven

Jane was incredibly nervous when she arrived at Robert's town-house nearly a week later. Fortunately, Geoff and Violet were with her as the family party had been extended to include friends, a fact which Jane could not help but think had changed due to her inclusion.

She hadn't known what to say when Ellen had invited her. The idea of making Robert feel uncomfortable in his own home had appalled her, but Ellen had been persuasive, and Jane had accepted, providing Ellen confirmed Robert's agreement.

Geoff and Violet were not the only friends Robert had asked either. There was quite a group of their acquaintances, enough for Robert to avoid any need for welcome as they entered. Ellen immediately filled the vacuum and introduced them to her distinguished relations, the Marquess of Wiltshire and his wife – Ellen's eldest sister and her husband, the Earl of Preston and his Countess – Ellen's middle sister and her husband, and the Duke and Duchess of Bradford – Ellen's youngest sister and her husband. Heavens, for a small family affair, a quarter of the House of Lords were in attendance, and the conversation buzzed vibrantly.

But later, when Jane sat silently on a sofa in the drawing room after dinner, watching the various activities and conversations, she was left with the familiar feeling of loneliness despite the crowd. She stole a look at Robert's tall, immaculate figure. He was speaking with friends including Geoff, and, therefore, Violet, in the far corner, a move Jane would swear was deliberate. Over dinner, she'd been placed three seats from him, and yet, he'd successfully managed the conversation to ignore her.

He was hurt, and she had a feeling there would be no truce this time.

But even so, as she watched his back and noted the way his hair curled at his collar, the contour of his calves and thighs, his narrow hips and his broad shoulders, she knew she still loved him – longed for him.

The current pianoforte music ceased, and Jane was drawn back from her contemplation as a hand settled on her shoulder, a warm, male hand, Edward's. "You're quiet, Jane. Is everything well?"

"Yes," she answered, forcing a smile. "I was just listening to Ellen. She has a wonderful voice and plays with such skill."

A proud smile lodged on his face. "Quite. The first time I heard Ellen and John both sing, I admit, it took my breath away."

Next, the four sisters sang together, a truly remarkable sound, as good as any professional performance. Once the song was over and the applause received, Ellen relinquished her seat at the pianoforte and came to stand beside her husband.

"Why don't we play whist?" she said to Jane before calling across the room, "Robert, you will play?"

Jane blushed and longed for a hole to fall into.

"Sorry, I have just agreed to play billiards. Someone else will step up," Robert answered bluntly, trouncing Ellen's manoeuvre.

It was an obvious put-down, and Jane felt as though she would expire from humiliation as Ellen tried to persuade him. Jane rose, excusing herself and claiming she wished for some air. Then she slipped through an open French door, on to the balcony beyond. It was folly coming here. She should have known she was not welcome, and yet, some stupid, girlish hope had stirred in her chest when she'd received the invitation with a note confirming Robert's agreement. It was obvious now, he had not agreed, merely complied.

The warm night air was barely any different to the close air indoors, thick with the scents of floral perfumes from the garden below, but the night was bright and starry. It reminded her of the night she'd lain in a punt with Robert, looking up at them.

She felt tears in her eyes.

Perhaps she ought to go back to Bath?

Perhaps she ought to just accept her fate and let Joshua have everything. She was still young, after all. She could become a governess or lady's companion. Lord, how the *ton* would laugh at that, the Dowager Duchess destitute and forced into service. But what did she care? Nothing for such shallow people who knew her not at all.

"Jane."

She jumped at the sudden intrusion into her solitude. Ellen stood behind her.

"I see how you look at him and how he looks at you," Ellen said quietly. "When Edward and I met, Robert did his utmost to push us apart, not because he did not care for Edward, but because he does. He has a tendency, when he is afraid someone may forgive him for something for which he cannot forgive himself, to push that person away."

Jane knew Ellen was speaking on Robert's behalf, apologising for him, undoubtedly without his knowledge.

Jane looked at the garden and set her palms on the stone balustrade. "That is not the case with me. The fault really is mine."

"But you have feelings for him? And he for you?" Ellen's words were spoken as a question, but her voice said she already knew the answer. "Was there something between you before your marriage?"

"Yes."

Ellen's fingers touched Jane's shoulder. "Then why not now?"

With a self-deprecating smile, Jane faced Ellen. "A better question would be, how? Who we were, then and now, are very different people. It was a long time ago, Ellen. The past is gone." Jane felt a sudden affection for this woman. She'd become a friend.

"Need it be, if you both wish it to be different?" Ellen's eyes were silver and jet in the darkness, her features white and black. It would be so easy if all things in life were black and white in clarity, but the truth was, things were many shades of grey. There were ifs and buts, not just yes and no.

"It's too late," was all Jane could answer.

"In my experience, it is never *too late*, Jane. I know my brother-in-law's reputation, but I have seen his immeasurable ability to love the children. You have seen the way he is with them. I think you are alike; both longing for more than life has dealt you. Why not try to find it together?"

Jane sighed, her heart hammering at the thought, yet she shook her head. "You do not understand, Ellen. It is too complicated."

Ellen squeezed Jane's shoulder for a moment then let go. "*Life* is complicated, Jane, but we must live it. Surely, it is best to do so with the person you choose beside you."

Tears filled Jane's eyes as she shook her head again. That was what she wished for, but it could never be. Ellen passed Jane a small handkerchief, then, after embracing her briefly, disappeared.

~

From the billiard room, Robert watched Jane prepare to leave. She'd worn amber silk tonight, a colour which engaged with her green eyes. Having Jane here was like having a living, breathing work of the masters in his home. Despite himself, he'd found his gaze wandering in her direction all night, just as it had now. With his shoulder resting against the door frame, he watched her in the hall, his cue gripped in his hand.

"Robert! Your shot!" someone called behind him, and as they did so, Jane turned in time to catch him staring. He could see a question in her eyes. A question which welcomed his attention and offered more.

No, not any more. I have had my fill of being kicked in the gut by you. I'll not let you knock me down again.

He narrowed his gaze in disgust and turned back to his game.

It was a good two hours later, after all their guests had left, that Ellen approached Robert to say goodnight, and when she leaned to bestow a sisterly kiss on his cheek, she whispered, "I knew the old Duke of Sutton. He was a manipulative man. If I were to make a guess, I would think Jane's marriage was forced and certainly sour. I would feel sorry for her, if I were you."

At her words, a cold shiver ran across Robert's skin, and a sick feeling rose in his stomach.

Ellen did not stay to talk, instead she pulled away with a little smile that said quite bluntly, *go to her*, before turning to take Edward's arm and retire.

It left Robert in a state of flux, all sorts of unwelcome thoughts racing through his head. Thoughts that told him perhaps *he* was the villain. Thoughts Robert did not want to face with a clear head.

"Forced?" It implied the day he'd ridden away, when she'd told him of her engagement to Sutton, he had *deserted Jane*. Had she needed him then? When he'd left her there. *Had he left her to endure something that had not been her choice? Had she loved him then, truly, and been made to marry another man? A man old enough to be her grandfather.*

To drown out the voice of conscience, he retired to the study and befriended a decanter of brandy.

His feet on his desk and his ankles crossed, Robert leaned back in his chair and put the doubts Ellen had generated to rights.

Jane had turned him down. She'd thrown his proposal back in his face. For God's sake, he'd seen her in the arms of her stepson – *that* could not be explained away.

Bloody interfering woman.

Ellen had spoken to stir his guilt, he knew it. But if it was true, he had guilt to be stirred.

But he'd have seen it in Jane's eyes that day, surely, or heard something since.

He kept drinking.

Wouldn't he? Perhaps her affair with the son was a sign of her unhappiness and not her debauchery.

Hell!

He filled his glass again and remembered his seething anger that day. Anger that was enough to make him blind and deaf to details he did not seek to see.

Hell!

He took another swig of brandy and let it numb his mind, unwilling to look at the past with any logic, as he cursed Ellen. Ignorance was bliss. He did not want to know.

Did he?

Hell!

~

Come morning, Robert awoke where he'd sat the night before, the shattered decanter on the floor amidst the last of the brandy. His head thumped, but his thoughts were clear. He needed to know the truth. He had to understand what had happened, if only to silence his conscience. He needed to see Jane at least once more.

It was far too early for polite calls when he left, clean-shaven

169

and clothed, to look at least half-decent in comparison to his previous half-dead appearance.

He walked to help clear his hangover, his mind continually racing.

Was Ellen right, had Jane been forced into marrying Sutton? Had he ridden away that day and left her to endure a life sentence?

By the time he approached Grosvenor Square, it was just after eleven.

As he walked along the street, his cane rapped on the pavement, matching his long, quick, restless strides.

A few yards from Lady Rimes's property, a man yelled down from the driving seat of a dray.

Robert's progress was suddenly arrested. He was stunned as his eyes took in the scene. Jane was on the far side of the street, and the driver of the dray shouted in her direction. She looked horrified. Robert followed her gaze and saw Sutton.

He'd jumped down from his curricle, abandoning it in the middle of the road. As his tiger, the groom, ran to grab the horses' harnesses, Sutton approached Jane. His body taut with anger, he moved almost at a run, bearing down on her. When he reached her, he yelled something in her face.

She did not flinch. She seemed to stand more erect, and her chin tilted.

Sutton's hand lifted in an instant, and in the next, he dealt her a sharp blow.

She fell back, knocked to the ground by the force, even though her maid tried to catch her.

Robert was in motion before he knew it, and ahead of him, the street exploded in reaction.

Jane's maid screamed abuse, and a couple of vendors and a bulky workman who'd been seated on the back of the dray surrounded Sutton.

He raised the whip, dangling from his hand, in threat against them all.

When Jane said something from her position on the ground, too quiet for Robert to hear, Robert thought Sutton would use the whip on her.

"Sutton!" Robert's yell reached over the general hubbub.

Some of the gathering crowd expanding about Jane looked his way.

"Don't you dare!" Robert ordered as Sutton's gaze struck Robert's. The rage in it turned Robert's innards to ice.

What was this man capable of?

Sutton began backing away, growling one last threat at Jane, which Robert could not make out. Then the Duke turned and yelled at those about him, cursing until they parted and let him through.

By the time Robert reached the scene, his cane was gripped so tightly in his hand it was cutting into his palm. He realised then that, instinctively, the frippery had unconsciously become a potential club. He used it indiscriminately, but not viciously, to push through the crowd in order to reach Jane.

The onlookers had not guessed the abused woman was a dowager duchess and the man who'd attacked her, her stepson, a Duke. If they had, the tale would fly through the gossipmongers. It would be on the tongues of the *ton* by dinner and in the news columns tomorrow.

Robert let his cane fall to the pavement and heard it hit the stone with a dull, wooden rap as he dropped to one knee, uncaring of the dirt. His fingers touched the red mark on Jane's cheek.

"Good God, Jane, let me help you."

She looked at him with apparent relief, her eyes bright and sharp, as though he was a branch to grasp in the aftermath of Sutton's storm. Then Robert saw her realise what he'd seen and her gaze dropped as her skin darkened in a deep blush.

He rose and turned to the crowd, intolerant of their ogling. "The show is over! Go about your business!"

At once, there was a change of tempo in her audience. Voices grumbled, gossiped, and surmised, but they started to disperse.

He turned back and helped Jane stand.

Too many emotions roiled inside him to fathom them all, but among them were sympathy, outrage, protection, and *love. God, there was still love.*

Once she was up, he gripped both her hand and her elbow.

"Are you up to walking?" he asked quietly, receiving a nod as her maid behind her continued a tirade against the Duke of Sutton, even though the man himself was long gone.

"Meg!" Jane silenced the woman, although not quite, her ranting only became unintelligible.

At least Jane knew the risk of revealing her identity.

"Here, take my cane and go ahead. Have someone fetch a doctor," Robert directed the maid, to get rid of her. "I'll take your mistress home."

The maid went.

Despite claiming to be well enough to walk, when they moved, Jane's grip suddenly clawed on his arm, all her weight on him.

"Do you feel faint?"

"The street *is* spinning, I'm afraid." Her voice was full of embarrassment and agitation.

"Cling on then. We will have you back at Violet's in a moment." With that, he shifted his grip from her elbow and took a firm hold at her narrow waist, encouraging her to lean her weight more fully on to him as they walked slowly across the street and along the path to her friend's front door.

It was open, Meg having reached the house before them, and inside, Violet's butler barked orders, calling for a cold compress, tea, smelling salts, and anything Her Grace may possibly need.

Robert led Jane to the drawing room and bid her sit. She did so, head bowed, her fingers trembling as she tried to untie her bonnet. She merely pulled the ribbons into a knot. Then her beautiful eyes looked up to him, begging silently for help.

He dropped to one knee and moved her hands away. They were cold and shaking. He focused on the stubborn knot and had the damn thing free in moments. When he drew the ribbons loose and removed her bonnet, she spoke for the first time.

"You were always rescuing me."

Her gaze met his in apology, but he saw the memory there, and embarrassment. It wrenched the tender wound she'd opened in his heart. The wound she'd taken a knife to the other day with Sutton, a man who apparently was prone to hitting her.

Could Robert be placed any lower in her pecking order, the old and infirm, and now the abusive, all above a man who would offer her everything and expect nothing in return?

Robert leaned back on his heel and smiled. *What else could I do?* Angry at her he may be, but he was not the type to turn his back on a damsel in distress, and after all, this was Jane. *So much for not playing her fool again.*

"And it would seem things do not change. You were always getting yourself into trouble. Has Violet got any liquor in here?"

"In the bureau. Over there." She pointed vaguely, but it was enough of a direction for him to spot the walnut cabinet.

He rose and crossed the room. Inside the cabinet, he found a decanter of sherry and glasses. It would calm her nerves. He poured a small measure and took it to Jane. Her eyes followed his movement, staring at him as though he had two heads.

"Drink, it will stop you shaking."

He knew she'd never liked strong liquor, and her nose wrinkled, but she drank it anyway. It made her choke, and she pressed the back of her hand to her lips.

He took the glass away and set it aside on a chest, giving her a moment to recover before turning back.

When he did, he stood, looking down on her.

She seemed ridiculously small.

He waited for an explanation.

She looked up and met his gaze. No explanation came.

He folded his arms across his chest. At least she had the decency to blush, but still, she did not attempt to explain.

A knock struck the semi-open door and Jane called, "Enter."

A maid bearing crushed ice wrapped in a linen towel came in. Jane took it. "Thank you, Penny. Tell Mr. Selford not to send for the doctor. I am fine now—"

"Ignore her, Penny. Her Grace has had a blow to her head. She is giddy and shaky. She should see a doctor whether she wills it or not. I will stay until he arrives to make sure she does."

As the maid left, Jane threw him a look, implying he was being overbearing.

He hardly cared. He'd just watched her struck by the man she'd thrown him over for. He was in no mood to be obliging or conciliatory.

He pulled a spindly satinwood chair up and sat facing her, leaning forward and resting his elbows on his knees, a gesture his friends would recognise meant business. It stated he was not about to be fobbed off.

Jane clearly did not know the look as she leaned back away from him, one hand pressing the ice pack to her cheek, the other laying in her lap. Her eyes looked up at the ceiling.

"Are you not going to tell me why he hit you?" he challenged.

She sighed and lowered her gaze again. "No."

A wash of mixed emotion racing through his blood, he straightened. He was angry, yes, but disappointed and helpless, too.

His hand lifted in exasperation. "Very well, as you wish, but I was calling on you in any case. I wanted to discuss something."

"Discuss what?" She eyed him warily, long lashes flickering, the ice pack still pressed to her cheek, her voice hesitant.

"I wish you to tell me something, honestly, Jane. Something has come to my attention that makes me think – wonder..." He stopped, watching the uncertain expression on her face. A sigh escaping his lips, he leaned forward, once more resting his elbows back on his knees.

He could not force her to answer. She would or she would not. All he could do was ask. Half of him did not wish to know anyway. The answer may well be unpalatable. "Were you forced to marry Sutton?"

It was as if she'd received a second physical blow. The hand gripping the ice pack fell, and there was horror in her eyes, and suddenly, she seemed unable to catch her breath. She opened her mouth, but only a strangled sound left her throat.

It was true. Hell. It was true. She'd no need to say it, the answer was written in every tortured expression of her body.

"God, Jane, I'm sorry." Robert's arms came about Jane in a moment, and he was on the sofa beside her.

Her head pressing to his shoulder, she cried.

He'd broken a dam she'd thought unbreakable.

His fingers brushed her hair from her temple, and his breath caressed the crown of her head as he whispered comforting words.

He said the things she'd wished to hear for years, but had thought impossible long ago. That he was sorry. That if he'd only known, understood – he would not have left her. That she should have told him. That he would have helped her somehow.

Once her tears had finally run dry, when she pulled away, wiping at her eyes and nose, he handed her his handkerchief and gave her an understanding smile.

If he'd picked any other moment to ask her, she could have found some way to avoid the answer, but after that awful scene with Joshua, her reservoir of strength was empty.

Joshua had received a letter from her solicitor this morning. He had found some clause under which to contest Joshua's claim. It would appear Joshua didn't like it, and, in answer, he'd resorted to violence. But she was not going to drag Robert into it.

She blew her nose in a very unattractive fashion and realised she was half sitting on him, one hand clutching at his shoulder. She moved off him and stood. The cloth full of ice lay on the floor.

He did not rise but watched her.

She gave him a half smile. "I'm sorry, Robert, I did not mean to involve you in this."

"In what?" he responded with a far too perceptive gaze.

"In the middle of Joshua and I. I'm sorry." She couldn't tell him more. He would do something stupid if she did, like call Joshua out. She did not wish Robert hurt.

He did not question her, but returned to his last topic. "Tell me what happened that day. Tell me why you turned me down?"

Jane dropped into the chair he'd vacated, facing him as he sat on the sofa. She felt too exhausted to have this conversation and shook her head.

In answer, he threw her a rakish smile. His weapon of feminine destruction. "Just humour me. Tell me how it was as you saw it. I want to know the truth, Jane."

She sighed. "I cannot see why. It was a long time ago, too long ago to make any difference, Robert."

"Say it anyway." Strong emotion suddenly burned in his eyes. The rake left and Robert shone through.

"Oh, very well." She did not have the energy to continue arguing. Her fingers clasped in her lap and her eyes fell to them. "Within days of you leaving after that last summer, my father was speaking of a beneficial marriage. Not for me, of course, for him, but then, I was only ever incidental in my family's scheme of things. He talked of gaining influence and standing. I thought he was speaking of you, that he'd guessed, but I was presented to the Duke of Sutton a few weeks later. I'd seen him once previously when he'd called on your father."

"Why did you not write and tell me?"

Robert was looking at her intently when she lifted her gaze. Undoubtedly, he did not like what he'd heard.

She would not sweeten the story to make it palatable for him. He'd asked.

"That is not hard to work out, Robert. You were nineteen. Whenever you came back from Oxford, you were full of adventures and spoke constantly of opportunities. If I had written to you, I know you would have felt honour-bound to marry me. I was younger than you. I did not have enough confidence. I could not force you to surrender the future you spoke of. You may have held it against me for the rest of our lives."

"I offered you marriage. I would not have surrendered my future, but let you share it."

"I knew that afterwards, but not then. Do you not see how different it was when it was a choice you'd made? Anyway, it is of no consequence now." They could not go back. Waving her hand, she dismissed the argument and carried on. "I did not write to you. Nor did I know how far things had progressed. The marriage contract was apparently signed a week before you came home. Two days before, the Duke of Sutton had visited my father. I thought he was there on business. When I was called to the office, I was still blissfully unaware of the truth. In that half-hour interview, my life changed completely.

"Father introduced me to a man four times my age, who I

hardly knew, as my future husband. Hector had obtained a special licence, and we were to be married in four days. I was not even to be given time to adjust to the idea. You know the rest. Do you want some tea?" She moved to rise, but Robert caught her wrist and held her still.

"Why do you think I know the rest? As I recall, I sent word for you to meet me, and you came, but when I showed you the ring I'd bought, and asked to speak to your father, you just said I could not because you were already engaged. You said none of this then, Jane."

She pulled her arm free, losing her temper. "And as I recall, you did not stay to hear it. That was the moment you disappeared, without seeking any explanation and without a single thought for me. Forgive me, but I do not recall saying I wanted the marriage, nor that I had agreed to it, nor that *I would say no to you*. Of course, you could not speak to my father. He'd already signed the agreement with Sutton! When I received your note, I foolishly hoped you would not let it happen, that you would take me away. I did not have the courage to write, but I'd prayed you'd come home and help me."

She jabbed a finger at his shoulder, remembering her desolation, anger, and despair.

"And what did *you* do, Robert? You rode away, without even looking back, and left me to my fate. So, do not sit there and condemn me as the villain of the piece. You played your part, and I do not believe I ever heard of your suffering as a result. All I have heard of the Earl of Barrington is what a merry time he's had of it, how many women he's bedded, his racehorses, and his life abroad. You are in no place to judge me. So there, you have your story. You have wheedled it out of me, and what good has it done you?"

His mouth half open, Robert neither moved nor spoke. Her

outburst had stripped his rakish façade bare.

Instantly, she regretted it, but she did not have any chance to ease the insult to his ego as Violet burst into the drawing room.

"Good grief, Jane, Selford has just told me what happened." Violet stripped off her gloves and bonnet. "The doctor has just arrived. Selford is taking his hat. I thought we'd agreed you would not go out without Graham and Frederick."

Jane rose and turned, her receding anger leaving her feeling thoroughly deflated. "I didn't think he'd be about at this hour. It was foolish of me. Fortunately, Robert rescued me."

She looked back to see he'd stood, but he remained silent and looked as though he hadn't heard her.

"Of course, we must thank you, Barrington," Violet chimed. "Thank heavens you were there."

He bowed to Violet. But Jane had an odd sense of the years tumbling backward. She could feel his disengagement as she had done that day. She knew he was leaving. He'd already done so mentally. He mumbled some acknowledgement of their joint thanks, barely looking at Jane. Then he left.

Her feet turned to stone. She couldn't follow him. She couldn't move, trapped by uncertainty as she watched him go with a dreadful feeling he'd gone for good.

She felt dazed as the doctor entered, and Violet immediately began fussing over the bruise on Jane's cheek.

~

When Robert got home, it was after dark. He'd spent hours walking the streets and parks, struggling to make sense of everything, but it simply would not fall into place. The story she'd told was entirely different to the one he'd spent his life stewing over in anger and resentment. He had slept with dozens of women, measuring them

179

all by Jane and finding them all wanting. But God, he was honest with himself at last. He had not been seeking another Jane all these years. It had been vengeance. He'd blamed all women for what one had not even done.

God, how would he ever face himself in a mirror again? He was an evil, bloody bastard. An arrogant, self-obsessed idiot.

If I'd stayed to hear her out, then?

If I had listened to my heart, not my head?

He'd always known the image of Jane he'd created – the woman who'd thrust his love away – was at odds with the girl he'd fallen for.

If I had believed my instinct?

Instead, he'd deserted her at the point she'd needed him most.

Well, he would not do it again. He'd made his mind up on that in his hours of tormented melancholy. No matter what drove her to seek comfort from her stepson, whether she loved the man or not, Robert had seen how Sutton treated her, and he could not just stand by and let it happen again. He had to get her away from that man and give her time to come to her senses, and there was only one way he could think to do it. He had to get her out of town.

Ignoring Jenkins' offer to take his hat and gloves, and with a cursory grunt of recognition at Edward and Ellen's greetings called from the drawing room, Robert went straight to the study. There he withdrew paper from a drawer, dipped a quill into the ink pot, and began writing the letter he'd been mentally drafting for the last hour.

Chapter Twelve

"A letter for you," Violet stated, entering the drawing room with a smile which implied her interest in its contents.

"Not Joshua?" Jane exclaimed as Violet let the envelope fall into Jane's lap.

"Not as far as I can tell. Go on, open it. I am itching to know who it is from. You never have letters."

"Because my social life is miniscule. You are getting excited over nothing. It will be something mundane, perhaps about the lease on my property in Bath." Violet laughed and Jane smiled.

Since Joshua's assault yesterday, Jane had felt sullen and been prone to silence and tears, more due to the conversation which had followed than to the injury.

She'd tried to keep her thoughts on other things today.

She put aside the embroidery she'd been using to occupy her mind and picked up the sealed paper.

She knew immediately who it was from. Violet knew, too, the minx. The seal was the Barrington coat of arms, Robert's. Her fingers shaking and her heart beating harder, she broke it.

Why had he written? Why not come in person?

The familiar writing made her heart ache as she began to read.

Dear Jane,

Sentiment or formality? She could not tell; it was the same address he'd always used.

I have done little but think of what happened and the things you said. I wish to make amends to you, if you will allow it. Come home with me, Jane, on Saturday next, for as long as you like. If you are worried over appearances, I shall, of course, ask Edward and Ellen to accompany us. I am sure they shall, and I will invite anyone you wish me to ask. Ellen may play hostess. I hope you accept, not for my own benefit, you understand, but for yours. If Sutton is your choice, so be it, but I will not turn my back a second time and let you do this without thought. Come away with me. Take some time at Farnborough to think things through. After all, it was as good as your home, too, once. When you are certain of your choice, then you may do as you wish. But just give yourself some time away from Sutton, to think. The man hit you, Jane.

Forgive me, it is none of my business, I know. I am not offering myself as an alternative, you understand, but just as a friend, as you wished, a place to think things through, and a person to talk them through with, that is all.

Well, that is it my offer exactly. Take it or leave it. If you accept, write back to me and I will set everything up, just as you request, and send word to let you know when my carriage shall collect you. I will go on ahead to check all is in order and meet you there.

Yours forever, in friendship, for as long as you need me to come to your rescue.

Robert

Her hand, which held the letter, fell to her lap, and Jane stared at it.

"Well?" Violet prompted.

Jane lifted it and read it once more. No, she had not imagined the intimacy and sincerity in it.

"Do tell, Jane," Violet urged.

"He has asked me to attend a family party at his country house. The invitation is extended to you and Geoffrey, if you wish."

"It says more than that. Your face speaks another story."

Jane gave her friend a *mind-your-own-business* smile, but deemed to throw a little more seed to her pecking. Violet had been her greatest support, after all. "He is apologising for our falling out, that is all."

"In pretty verse?" Violet prodded. "Barrington does not strike me as the poet type. No, I would say he is more a man who would deploy heartfelt sincerity to win the ladies, and you are blushing, so I am right. He is gushing, and you have fallen for it. He gets you to his country home and takes you to his bed, woman wooed and won, and that will be an end to it, and you shall never hear of him again."

"And thank you for cheering me up with that remarkably cutting assessment. I happen to believe his gushing, and I think I shall accept his offer and go. But if you intend to do nothing but disparage him, I ought to leave you here. Perhaps I am tempted by his bed and do not wish you putting me off at the last hurdle."

Violet sat beside Jane and laid a hand on her knee. "If you fancy his bed, I am certain it would not be unpleasant, so go to it with my blessing, as long as you are well aware of the possible outcome. And indeed, I should not come, as I fear I shall be too tempted to disparage him. If you are set on this course, Jane, go. All I wish for is your happiness. I will be overjoyed if you prove me wrong."

~

The countryside whipped past the open carriage window as the warm summer breeze flooded in, and Jane felt her stomach flip for the fifth time that morning. She'd been very bold in defence of her decision to Violet, but in practice, the thought of going back to Farnborough, to Robert, had set her on edge.

She'd deliberately decided without thinking. She'd chosen with her heart not her head. The moment she'd read the letter, she'd longed to be here, with him. There could be nothing between them now. Too much had happened in the years in between, but she could escape Joshua, and she could be at home again, and feel safe, as she had not done for years.

The passing landscape became familiar. The journey had taken four days. Robert had planned it, every change of horses, every inn, so that none of the concern was hers. She leaned closer to the open window, and her fingers gripped the sill. The breeze swept back her hair from her face beneath her bonnet as they crossed a narrow, humpback bridge over a shallow river that was depleted by the drought. Ahead, she saw the postilion rider on the lead mare as the carriage turned a corner. Her sense of excitement and nervousness grew.

Oh, but it felt good to see familiar scenery, even if the grass was less green from the lack of rain; it was still home. The hills, the dales, the moors, the rivers, *home*, all of it, a part of her that she'd lost for so long.

She'd mourned this place more than the loss of her parents.

Pollen-laden, fresh summer air filled her lungs. She could smell the grass, the clover, and the heather.

The team of horses pulled the carriage about the final bend and in through the gates of Farnborough, on to the long avenue of horse chestnut trees. She could see the sprawling mansion in the distance. It had developed through generations from medieval times onward. Its familiarity hit her hard in the chest, and her heart figuratively lifted to her mouth.

Home. It did feel like hers, even though it was Robert's, and it *was* her sanctuary now. She'd be safe here, for the first time in years.

Her heart thumped as the carriage slowed, pulling before the front of the house.

She'd never thought she'd be here again.

The sound of churning gravel beneath the carriage wheels and horses hooves filled the air as the carriage drew to a halt. She could see the front entrance into the courtyard. The sounds outside the carriage became voices as grooms and footman surrounded it.

A footman put down the step. Then she saw Robert beyond him, emerging from beneath the arch of the portcullis.

She took the footman's hand to descend, watching Robert stride across the gravel drive. Her stomach turned a summersault inside her, and her heart clenched tightly. She longed to run to him and throw herself into his arms as she used to do.

"Jane." He was there, taking her fingers from the footman's and leaning close to speak confidentially as her foot touched the gravel. "I am so glad you agreed to come. I hope you do not mind the informal welcome, but I thought you would prefer it. You were always a no-fuss girl, as I remember. But if I was wrong, feel free to chastise me. You may be a part of the family or spend time alone as you wish. There is no pressure. This is *your home,* for as long as you wish it to be. I expect nothing of you, nor will Edward."

"What have you told him?" she asked as Robert let go her hand.

"Nothing," he said with a smile. "You are family. I told him I'd seen you, and you needed a bolt-hole. He cares for you too much to pry, just as I do, Jane. And that's an end to it. You are not here for explanations. I offered you a place and space to think. You'll have it. I promise I shall hold my tongue. Your life is neither mine nor Edward's business. But if you want us, we are here. If you do not, it is your choice. Eat in your room, read in the library, whatever you wish."

"A horse," she said as he stepped back a pace to lead her in.

At her words, his eyebrows lifted. "A horse?"

"Yes," she expounded, her voice breathless, the words seeming distant to her tongue. "I would like to ride, not read. I think better, feel better, when I ride. I would like to be able to ride, if I may?"

"Then later, you shall pick a mount, or three. Try the whole damn stable, Jane. My staff know to answer to you just as though you were me. They will do anything you ask."

The man before her was not one of the foremost rakehells of the *ton*. He was all the youth she'd fallen for. An urge to hug him rushed over her again, and to kiss him. But it was hardly the thing to do when the vein of his introduction was kindness and friendship. It would be silly to stir up those impotent feelings between them, no matter what she felt for him, or he for her. There could be no outcome from it. Instead, gripping his elbow, she said, "Thank you."

"You are welcome." He smiled. "Come along then. Let's get you settled." Freeing his arm from her grip, he clasped her hand and drew her forward under the raised portcullis and into the cobbled courtyard where the central fountain sent the sound of running water bouncing back off the surrounding walls of the house. They passed through the stone portico and into the old keep. There, he released her, and her eyes scanned the familiar room, the square twist and rise of the stairs. The house still felt huge to her, even as an adult.

"Well then, what do you wish to do? I'll leave it up to you. Are you tired? Do you want to stop for refreshment, or would you rather I have Mrs. Barclay show you up to your room and give you chance to freshen up? I've no need to show you about, of course. I'm certain you remember it all. You're in the yellow room with a view of the garden."

Jane realised he was nervous, too. He seemed to be trying overly hard to do and say the right thing. She smiled broadly, a smile of gratitude straight from her heart. "Heavens, is Mrs. Barclay still here?"

He smiled. "Yes, and Davis, as I told you. They are itching to meet you, but I did not want to overpower you with well-wishers the minute you arrived." His eyes moved to the bruise still visible on her cheekbone, and his hand lifted. His fingers brushed across it, as if he'd wanted to touch it since he'd first seen her and could no longer resist. "It is getting better. Does it still hurt?"

"Only if I touch it." She laughed. Instantly, his fingers fell, but his touch had been too gentle to hurt.

"What is it to be then, tea or a warm bath?"

"Good Lord, nothing warm!" Jane laughed again, fanning her face with one hand while the other tugged the ribbons of her bonnet loose. "What would be nice is some lemonade. Do you think you could rustle some up?"

"Not personally, but I'm sure Mrs. Barclay will manage it."

Jane grinned. "If I hurry upstairs and freshen up, could we drink it outside? Having been shut up in that stuffy carriage for days, I could do with some fresh air. I would love to see the gardens and take a stroll."

His gaze ran over her face then settled on her eyes. "Lemonade in the garden, it is then, Your Grace." He bowed slightly, giving her his rakish grin.

She lifted off her bonnet and shook her head to loosen the sweat-dampened curls from her brow, batting his arm with the straw confection. "Tease!" Then, instantly, she sobered as an intruding thought unsettled her. She did not want to be alone. "You will sit with me though?"

"If you wish." His smile had fallen, perhaps because he'd heard her concern.

"I do. If you are not busy?"

His smile lifted a notch again, closed-lipped and not rakish at all, just Robert's. "I'm not busy. You have my undivided attention, if you wish it. Shall I meet you on the terrace?"

"Yes. Thank you. I'll be as quick as I can."

"Do you want a maid to take you?"

"No, I remember it. Meg should be upstairs by now. I'm sure one of your footmen will have led her up."

"Very well then, I'll see you in a moment." He gave her another slight bow then watched her take a step backward before she turned. She hastened upstairs, glancing back a few times to see him still standing below, following her progress with his eyes. He smiled each time she glanced down. She smiled back, feeling light-hearted in a way she'd forgotten she could ever be.

Silly woman, she told herself as she reached the landing. It was beyond stupid. It was definitely imprudent to feel so overjoyed at his attention. But she did, and she virtually skipped along the landing, she felt so happy.

Reaching the yellow room, she found Meg bent over an open portmanteau. Jane tossed her bonnet on the bed and began peeling off her lace gloves then threw them there, too. "Heavens, Meg, find me a fan and my parasol. It is so hot. I am going to sit in the garden, but I refuse to put a bonnet back on."

Barely minutes later, having washed quickly and dismissed Meg so the maid could also seek refreshment, Jane rushed on to the terrace with a bounce still in her step. Robert was there. He was leaning on the balustrade which ran the length of the house at the back, looking out on to the parterre gardens. The air was full of summer scents, honeysuckle, jasmine, roses, and lavender, and the blue sky and sunshine were the perfect backdrop to the riot of colours in the formal gardens below. Summer sounds echoed about the grounds, too, a wood pigeon cooing, a little flock of sparrows chasing and calling through the box hedge, the water fountain running in the distance, and laughter. A child's laughter, and the cracked laughter of a youth not quite a boy, but not yet a man. "John and Mary-Rose?" she said as she started to cross the terrace to him.

He turned, and in that first instant, there was a depth to the dark brown of his eyes that was almost sad. But then he smiled, the rakehell's smile, meant to charm.

She was charmed, utterly. Something clenched low in her stomach, a tight, sudden spasm which disappeared just as fast as it came.

"Do you wish to see them? They've decamped to the shade of a plane tree on the other side of the haw-haw. Mrs. Barclay has indeed risen to the occasion and prepared lemonade. It will be served there or here, wherever you wish."

"There, I think. I would love to see the children." Jane unfurled her parasol and rested the shaft on her shoulder.

"Well then, there we shall go," Robert stated, offering her his arm. "Ellen has little Robbie up, too. He was too restless to sleep in this heat."

Jane flicked open her fan and began wafting it. "I do not know how you can stand to wear a coat."

"I admit, it is a bit warm."

"Then take it off."

"You are barely here an hour, Jane, and are already undressing me!" he stated with a satirical laugh.

"I am giving you permission not to stand on ceremony. You said my visit was to be informal. If I am family, treat me as such." Her words were reproachful, but she touched her voice with humour to match his.

"Very well." He raised his arm higher. "Help me with the damn thing then. The day is like a boiling pot."

She snapped shut her fan, let it hang from her wrist, balanced her open parasol on her shoulder, then helped him take off his coat.

When they walked on, it lay over one arm, while her bare fingers gripped his other, embracing firm muscle beneath the thin cotton of his shirt. They did not hurry, but discussed her journey, Geoff and Violet's growing romance, his staff, and the changes he'd made at Farnborough, while their footsteps crunched on the gravel paths.

It was at least half an hour later when they reached the sunken wall which formed the haw-haw. Robert took her hand to help her down the slope to the gate which led through the steeply sided ditch into the fallow grassland. Usually, livestock were grazing there, but there were none today, and Jane looked to the sound of laughter and saw the edge of a rug behind a tree.

She let go his grip, very aware of the intimacy of holding his warm hand. Its heat seemed to reach inside her, and memories of his touch on the first night they'd met in town came to mind. She could picture him without clothes easily in this heat, in this field, doing intimate things. An exhilarating tremor ran through her innards. She glanced at Robert, certain she was blushing, but he was looking towards the tree.

"Your Grace! Uncle Robert!" It was John who saw them first. The boy looked pleased to see her, or perhaps he was just pleased to see his uncle.

She wondered then if they had been deliberately dismissed to a place beyond the formal garden so the house would be quiet on her arrival. She'd seen no one but Robert before this.

The boy ran towards them, stripped to his shirt, too, his sleeves rolled up and a ball gripped in his hand.

"Papa and I are playing piggy-in-the-middle with Mary. Will you play, Uncle?"

She sensed Robert smile without even needing to look. "Poor little minnow, how does she stand a chance?"

"The whole game is thrown. You know it is. She always wins. Will you play?"

"Not at the minute, John. Give Jane a chance to get settled. And where are your manners? You have not even said a proper welcome."

Instantly, the poor boy looked mortified, as if hurt by Robert's chastisement. Blushing and holding the ball to his chest, John bent into a deep bow. "Your Grace, my apologies. Of course, we are glad of your company."

He spoke with the perfect pitch of a future duke. She smiled and waved his words away. "Just Jane, please. Both your father and uncle think of me as a sister."

"Aunt Jane then," John replied, rising up, his voice slipping easily back to that of a rambunctious boy.

"John," Robert challenged as if to deter.

But Jane gripped Robert's arm. "Aunt Jane is perfect. I'm happy with it. There is no need for formality, is there?" Robert's eyes met hers, and they were warm with affection and rimmed by dark lashes. It was a look he'd have given her when he was only a little older than John.

She smiled at John. "Come on then, John, lead me to the lemonade." With that, she let down her parasol then clutched at her skirt, lifting her hem a little so she could keep up with John as they progressed through the uneven grass.

Robert followed, watching Jane listen to John's eager chatter. It felt so good to have her here. She looked different already. She'd lost half a dozen years. She was no longer the Duchess, just Jane. *His Jane.*

Not *his* Jane. He couldn't say that. He'd promised her space and a place to think. He was determined to let her have it. If afterwards, she chose to continue her affair with Sutton, at least Robert would

191

know he'd tried to help her. At least he would not have to live with guilt over the son. He'd been enduring it for days over the father. The thought pierced Robert's chest even now.

It was his fault, all of it. Now he had to make amends.

Jane knelt on the edge of the rug, greeting Ellen, and bent to little Robbie while Ellen introduced her youngest child and John poured Jane's lemonade.

The baby was lying on his back, watching the leaves rustling on the warm breeze above him, his legs and arms in constant movement as he squealed with ridiculous pleasure at the sight. Jane touched the child's bare toes, and her expression slipped to melting appreciation.

"He is beautiful," she said in a whisper.

"Isn't he?" Edward shouted from a distance away. Robert looked to see Edward walking towards her. He was in his shirtsleeves, too, tossing the ball John had thrown him from one hand to the other. He was bragging indecently, but it amused Robert to see his brother's pride. Edward's smile admitted how atrocious his vanity sounded anyway.

"Edward is biased, ignore him," Ellen interjected.

"Edward is a proud father," Jane answered, her eyes not lifting from the little boy as she took his tiny hand and his fingers clutched her thumb. "You *are* gorgeous," she said at his babyish giggle.

"Your lemonade, Aunt." She took it from John's hand and smiled a thank you.

"Did you want some, Uncle?"

"Yes. Please," Robert answered as Mary-Rose's possessive grip captured his leg. He picked the little scamp up and swung her high. She squealed.

"Uncle Robert, horsey."

"Not at this particular moment, sweetheart." He sat her at his waist.

Her arms circled his neck. "I like to play horsey!"

"But I do not like to have grass stains on my knees before Aunt Jane," he whispered to her ear. "Play ball with your papa, and we shall have a game of tag later. Will that do?"

She gave him a determined nod and stretched her legs in the familiar gesture which said, *let me down*.

Watching Mary-Rose run to Edward, Robert caught Jane watching him. She smiled, but there was a glint in her emerald eyes which suggested she was close to tears. She looked away and sipped her lemonade.

Did she want children? She'd had none with the old Duke. She could not have them as his son's mistress. Had she birthed children and been forced to give them up?

Robert moved to kneel beside her on the rug and accepted a glass from John.

"This is cool and very welcome," Jane said in comment of the lemonade, looking at Robert again, with eyes that no longer bore tears.

"Yes," he answered, but as he said it, he tried to tell her in a look that he understood. She smiled and looked away. Heavens, she'd been here little more than an hour, and he felt as though he was fast unravelling at the seams.

"You'll not play?" Edward called as John returned to their game. Robert turned and found his brother's gaze observing far too much.

He'd told Ellen and Edward little more than the servants. If Jane wished to tell them anything more, it was up to her. Ellen had not challenged him. He assumed she'd guessed there was more to it, but her sensitivity meant she surmised it was best not to delve. Edward, however, lacked his wife's diplomacy. He'd asked numerous times. *Why had they fallen out? How had they made up?* But he'd not registered that Robert and Jane had once shared feelings far deeper than brother and sister. Until now.

Robert watched the knowledge dawn on Edward's face. Even if Jane's current affections were for Sutton, there was still that something between them, and the summer air had felt thicker and heavier since her arrival. He had a feeling it was the same for her, and, evidently, the attraction was not invisible to others.

Edward's smile lifted awkwardly, and he answered himself. "I take it not then."

Robert drank his lemonade. What Edward thought was his concern. It was what Jane thought that mattered.

And so Robert told his brother later when they were left alone to drink their port.

"You are a sly bastard," Edward answered in response. "So, when did this little affair of yours begin? You have kept it all cloak and dagger."

"I have not kept it anything. Nothing is happening. It is no affair, and for God's sake, do not let Jane know you believe it is. You will have her running a mile to get away from me. "

Edward's face puckered. "Then why is she here, Robert? What *is* going on?"

Leaning back in the chair, looking at Edward, Robert wondered whether to speak or not. He'd never shared the story.

Edward waited.

Robert lifted his glass of port to his lips and looked at Davis, silently sending the servants out.

"Nothing," he said once they'd gone, before leaning forward and resting one arm on the table. "It is as I told you. She had an accident. She needs some time and somewhere to get over it. I owe her the opportunity. But if you must know, my relationship with Jane was not fraternal while I was at Oxford."

"What!" Edward's mouth dropped open, and his eyes widened.

"See, you do not know all you think you do. We had feelings for each other then. We used to meet in secret."

"Bloody hell! And I thought you more distant then because you had outgrown our company."

Robert smiled. He'd *let* Edward draw false conclusions. "I offered for her, but she was already promised to Sutton." Robert looked up at the ceiling, angry with himself again for his ill-judged behaviour. He took a breath to fight back the agony of guilt and looked back at his brother. "Anyway, the short of it is, she told me she was already engaged. I charged off in a rage, thinking it was her doing and she'd played me for a fool. She'd been forced into it though..." Robert's voice cracked, lost in the pool of emotions roiling inside him.

Edward's expression was disbelief, then concern. There had been a measure of understanding this afternoon, but now, Robert saw it was all slotting into place in his brother's head. "*She* is why you dropped out of Oxford and left for the continent."

Robert nodded. He did not like to admit it. He'd never told anyone. Yet now it was out it seemed better just to tell the whole. "Father sent me abroad. He loathed my behaviour in London. I did not wish to tell him how much I hurt inside. I did not wish to mar the high opinion he had of Jane. I did his bidding. I still thought her the villain then."

"Good God," was all Edward said.

"See, little brother, for all these years, you've hated me for deserting father. It was father who banished me."

"But why not return when he died?" This had been Edward's bone of contention for years. Robert knew it. Edward had taken on the responsibility of their father's estate at barely eighteen. He'd never forgiven Robert for not coming back to take it over himself.

"Because, by that point, I could not stand to even be in the same country as her."

Edward shook his head in astonishment. "Then why not tell me when you came home."

"Because it was none of your business. I am only telling you now because you have guessed half of it, and I do not want you to run off with the wrong idea in your head." Fixing a hard stare on his brother, Robert said, "She told me she was forced to accept Sutton when I was in London before we left. That is why I have asked her here. Sutton treated her badly. I'm giving her time and a place to recover. She told me if I'd asked, she would have run away with me before she'd married him. I did not ask. I turned my back, let her down and blamed *her*. I owe her this. It is nothing more. Do not make it so, or you'll make her uncomfortable. Heavens, even Ellen has backed off, because she's realised the girl has suffered enough."

"Ellen knows?"

"Ellen's guessed, I think."

Edward drank from his glass of port then said, "Jane and you. God, you are a dark horse. How? I never noticed. We must have all been blind?"

Robert smiled and shrugged.

"And now? What do you feel for her, now?"

Robert did not answer.

"You love her," Edward answered for him. "What does she feel for you?"

Robert shrugged again. "Who knows? I think she feels something, but she has made it clear, on several occasions in London, she does not want me." He did not say there was someone else, although, suddenly, he longed to share it. He longed to share at least a little of his pain with someone. He'd carried her loss for so many years.

"Is that why you fell out? She said it was her fault."

The memory of that moment at Vauxhall was suddenly vivid in Robert's mind. "Yes," he breathed then added, "but I did not know the truth then."

Edward drained his glass, set it down, then rose and walked about the table to lay a hand on Robert's shoulder. It was the most conciliatory gesture they'd shared since Robert's return from abroad. For the last couple of years, Edward had tolerated Robert, but not liked him. "You can charm her. Make the girl fall back in love with you. After all, is that not your greatest skill?"

Robert laughed and set his hand over Edward's briefly. "Sadly, it does not seem to work on Jane. Believe me, I've tried."

Edward laughed and tapped Robert's shoulder. "Well, now you have Ellen on your side. Jane had better watch out. She has no idea the power my wife can wield."

Robert rose. "It is only thanks to Ellen she's here at all. Your wife had to hint to me that there was more to Jane's marriage before it occurred to me to ask."

"At least now I know your affections lie elsewhere. I need not worry about you and Ellen," Edward concluded in a dry tone.

"You had no need to worry anyway, Ellen adores you." Robert felt wounded. "She just saw the truth in me years ago, hence why when she spotted Jane, she worked it all out. It is hardly my fault if you are blind while your wife is not. At least a broken heart is something you've never had to bear."

The look he received told Robert that Edward finally understood. Both Robert and Ellen had been cut off once, wounded, and they'd recognised it in each other.

"You'll win her back," Edward answered. "Smile," he charged. "You'd better turn on the charm."

They entered the drawing room a few moments later, in more accord than they'd been in since childhood, smiling exuberantly and causing both women to look at them a little oddly.

"What have you done to him?" Ellen leaned to Robert to whisper a little later over her hand of cards as they played whist.

"Told the truth," Robert whispered back.

"Well, it is about time," Ellen answered a little louder. Robert watched her throw Edward a cajoling smile, and Edward's eyebrows lifted, blatantly inquiring what they were talking about.

"For what?" he challenged verbally when he received no response.

"For you and Robert to kiss and make up, that is what, Edward Marlow."

"I can think of nothing worse," Edward answered, but then he lifted his glass and looked at Robert. "But I shall drink to him, though. A toast, ladies, if you will, to happy endings!"

"To happy endings!" the women echoed. Robert reached for his glass and knocked the rim against Jane's, his eyes fixed on hers. She was the only one of the four of them who hadn't a clue what they were toasting. Poor woman, he'd promised her space, but she was about to become the obstacle of a major family onslaught.

She laughed, none the less, and clenched Edward's hand, then let it go.

Chapter Thirteen

Jane could not remember when she'd felt this happy. First thing in the morning, while the day was cooler, she and Robert would ride out across the estate, just as they had done in their youth, racing across fields and ditches, Robert's hounds in chase.

His hounds were a new addition to the fold, three of them, pale gray deerhounds. Long-legged and sleek in shape, they could run like the wind, but once they'd had their play, they were as docile a creature as could be found. When they lounged in the drawing room, washed down after their run, Mary-Rose would sit and coddle them. Even on four legs, the dogs were taller than her, but the child loved them, and they seemed to love her, too.

Jane ate luncheon *en famille*, a homey affair with the children, and afterwards, there was always some game or merriment, cricket, chess, cards, catch, chase, or hide-and-seek. This often had Jane in fits of giggles with Mary-Rose. Jane adored the little girl. They spent hours making daisy chains in the meadow or playing with dolls and sharing imaginary teas.

The evening meal always included John, and Jane understood this was when Edward and Ellen gave their eldest son their full attention. John was at the gateway to adulthood. At times, he reverted back to childish ways, while at others, he thought Mary-Rose's antics beneath him. But he was good-hearted and Jane enjoyed conversing with him.

But most of all, Jane loved little Robbie. The infant was a jolly, restless, little soul, who did not like being cosseted, yet what he did like was to be carried. They shared many walks about the garden, looking at the flowers, the fountains, and the fish pond. The little boy stole such a place in her heart, she was overawed with a broody longing for her own child, a longing that would never be fulfilled. The need became a physical pain. At times, it was so overwhelming, Jane was certain Ellen must know, but she never spoke of it. Nor did Jane.

She would not have children. All she could do was make the most of others', and six days into Jane's stay, Ellen answered Jane's unvoiced longing. She asked Jane to be Robbie's godmother. The baptism was planned for two weeks hence, and so, Jane's time became absorbed in helping Ellen plan the celebration.

It was their current activity.

"I thought perhaps tomorrow morning we could have breakfast served on the ridge when we ride out. Do you fancy it?" Robert was leaning about the door frame of the drawing room, speaking to her in passing as she and Ellen sat at the little desk, with invitations spread about them.

Jane nodded. "It sounds a lovely idea, yes."

"Then I shall have Mrs. Barclay organise it." He smiled and lifted his hand in farewell as he left.

"You two are getting along famously," Ellen commented, a searching note to her voice.

"We always did." Jane's eyes lifted to the miniatures on the wall, Robert's mother and father, him and Edward, and her, the surrogate little daughter of the family. When she'd been sixteen, she'd thought Robert her destiny. *And now?* Now, she dare not even think of it for fear this island of happiness she'd discovered would disappear. She did not want to do anything which would shatter the illusion she was living in.

"The bruise on your face has healed. Robert never did say what happened..." It was a tentative question.

Jane smiled. That particular secret was too raw to share. "I feel much better. Thank you."

Ellen studied her for a moment then smiled with a look of apology before turning her attention back to the list, clearly accepting Jane did not wish to discuss the matter. "Here, you write these. I will start on the menus."

When Jane took the list, she had a strange sense she saw the future. But it was not an image, it was a feeling – a feeling of despair, as though she mourned this blissful utopia, and if she mourned it, it was gone.

~

The next morning, breathless and exhilarated after their gallop, Jane watched Robert swing down from his saddle. He left his stallion to graze and strode towards her.

She unhooked her leg from the side-saddle, and once she'd done so, he was there.

His hands gripped her waist and lifted her down.

Her awareness of his touch was stronger than ever today, but she resisted the urge to pull him close and kiss him, and instead took a step away.

He smiled, hands falling to his sides, making no comment on her censure.

She turned and walked towards the rug the servants had spread out beneath a beech tree when they had brought the hamper up from the house.

The rug and the hamper had just been left on the ground, together, in a pre-arranged spot, for Robert and Jane to find. The servants had all disappeared again now.

Jane could see down into the valley and across it to the moor.

Robert walked beside her, then knelt on the rug and flipped open the lid of the hamper. "What do we have?"

Hands on hips, Jane watched him, smiling. The annoying sense of impending doom had not left her since yesterday, but she refused to acknowledge it.

He looked up, all boyish charm. "I do declare, Mrs. Barclay has done us proud again. We have a feast, Jane. Fresh rolls, butter, honey, ham, plum cake, cheese in three varieties, and a bit of the cold rabbit pie from yesterday, and to top it off, strawberries and champagne. How decadent shall we be?"

"Very." She swept the skirt of her habit beneath her as she knelt, too, and peered into the basket of delights.

"What would you like?" he asked.

"I should serve."

"Nonsense, you're the guest."

The guest? Perhaps that was why she sensed something going awry. She'd been so busy playing happy families, she'd forgotten she was only a guest. This was neither her home, nor her family. "Very well, I'll have plum cake and cheese."

He smiled and tossed a cushion at her. "Make yourself comfortable. Do you want champagne, Your Grace?"

She laughed, but relaxed, leaning sideways on one hand. "Of course, but if you are playing the gallant, before you serve me, you must kiss my hand." She presented it to him as she said it, teasing.

A wolfish grin formed on his face, and he gripped her wrist while his other hand tugged off her glove. Then he pressed a warm kiss on the back of her bare hand. "Your servant, Your Grace," he whispered over it afterwards.

A blush burned her cheeks, and her heart raced, which meant he knew how he affected her, for his thumb was pressed to the point of her pulse in her wrist. He paid no heed to it, or so it appeared, and let her go, then turned back to the basket.

After they'd eaten, feeling a little like a stuffed goose, Jane lay back on the rug and rested her head on the cushion. Robert had tidied up and put the hamper aside for the servants to collect later, when they returned. He lay beside her with his head on his palm as he propped himself up on a crooked arm and his other hand began playing with a stray curl of her hair which lay on the rug.

"This weather cannot go on forever," she said, her awareness of his closeness growing and her breath becoming scarce. She could feel his body heat along her side.

"No," he answered, his voice distant.

"Is the drought affecting the crops?"

"Probably."

She turned her head and looked up at him. He smiled, his eyes focusing heavily on her. She remembered that first night in London and the predatory, brooding hunger she'd seen in his eyes then. This intensity was very different. It appeared to be true affection, love even, but it burned with longing. The lock of hair he toyed with tugged her scalp as he played, and she felt a now familiar tingling warmth race across her skin and settle between her legs.

"Robert." His name meant so many things she could not say, and perhaps it was the deep-seated fear of losing him soon, or the level of attention he'd shown her, or just that her resistance had finally failed, but it was she who reached for him. Her fingers lifted, gripped the back of his neck, and drew him down.

He came willingly. She felt no hesitation.

As his mouth touched hers, her lips parted, welcoming him. Greedy, she was the first to slide her tongue into his mouth.

He answered in equal measure, his tongue dancing with hers.

Her body arched, longing for more, her breasts pressing against his chest and her pelvis touching his hip while her fingers braced his scalp through his hair.

His leg shifted and urged her to part hers. His knee settled in between them over her riding habit. His upper thigh pressed into the pulsing place between her legs.

She pushed back against him, kissing him, feeling the weight of his body as he kissed her harder.

His hand slid upwards from her waist and closed over her breast.

A whimper of pleasure and need escaped her mouth. It was caught in his.

Robert's fingers began working loose the buttons at the front of her habit, popping them free with one hand without ceasing the kiss.

She was so hungry for him, so in need of him, so aware of every lean muscle in the body which lay half over hers, and again, it was so different to the night she had first met him. This was no longer the need of the past and sexual tension. This was about now, and him. She had come to know him and love him all over again, more than she had done years ago. Her tender-hearted, very dear, Robert.

With a low growl, his warm fingers slipped inside her gown, beneath the cloth, and found flesh, closing over her breast again. The intimate touch sent a shaft of sharp pain to the place where his thigh pressed hard between her legs.

His kiss left her lips and began covering her face, her neck, as she felt the evidence of his arousal, hidden in his breeches, press against her hip.

He began rocking against her and kissed the skin he'd bared at her chest, then her breast.

With beautiful, delicious pain burning inside her, she shut her eyes and just felt as he rocked his hips, and she followed his lead.

Air touched her breast when his mouth opened and his tongue circled and flicked, while his firm grip squeezed her soft flesh and his thigh pressed hard against her.

This thing he could control was wonderful.

His warm mouth sucked her breast again and he shifted a little so the top of his thigh sat more snugly between her legs, as she rocked against him, maintaining the rhythm he'd set, though now he'd stilled.

She sighed, pressing her head back into the cushion on the rug, her fingers on his shoulders while his gripped and released her breast in tune to the movement of her hips.

She loved him and she could feel *it* building, the feeling he'd taught her in London. The wave flowed into her, the crest of it rising higher.

It broke and she cried out as it flooded her, sending her senses reeling then numbing them, leaving her weak and exhausted as it washed over her and ebbed away. Her breath left her lungs on a sigh.

His forehead rested against her collarbone, his hair tickling her skin. His body was no longer taut. His leg lay loosely between her thighs, and his hand was on the ground beside her.

"I'm sorry." She barely knew why she apologised, but it was just the way he lay over her. "Did I do something wrong?"

He laughed and his head came up. "Hardly." Then he took a deep breath and released it on a heavy sigh.

She felt the heat of it on the swell of her breast through her open gown.

He moved his leg away and returned to the position he'd begun in, propping up his head on one hand, while the fingers of his other hand trailed about her cheek and brushed aside her hair.

She re-secured her buttons without rising.

His finger touched the corner of her mouth.

She smiled, her gaze meeting his, and touched his cheek.

"God, you're beautiful," he whispered.

"So are you."

"So, what do we do now?"

"I don't know."

"You started it, Jane. Do you have any idea how much I want you? It's been hell trying to keep my hands off you. But if that is what you want, I will."

She shook her head and shrugged her shoulders against the ground. "I have no idea what I want."

He sighed, still watching, but then he rolled away suddenly. "I suppose we ought to get back anyway. Come along." He stood and held out his hand to help her up.

Beside the horses, he folded his hands to make a step.

She set her foot in it, and, like so, he lifted her into the saddle.

"Are we going straight home?" she asked.

He smiled up at her, his wolfish rakehell smile.

"One kiss, my Lord, and you are back to being predatory."

He laughed as he set his foot in his stirrup and pulled himself up with an agile grace that had her admiring every inch of his muscular physique. But once he'd mounted, he said, "Actually, I was smiling because I like hearing you call Farnborough home."

Home. But it was not, was it? It had always felt like home. It was the only place which had ever felt like home. But the truth was, she had no home. None but this borrowed one. No real place where she could feel safe and happy.

Jane turned her horse and lifted into a trot.

He moved to ride beside her. "Did I say something to upset you?"

"No. What shall we do?" She sensed him look at her.

"Do you really wish me to answer that? Beyond taking you to bed, I can think of nothing to suggest at the moment."

"While your brain is still in your breeches, you mean?" she mocked, as he had mocked her, kicking into a canter.

"Now, now, Jane, such foul protestations are not becoming. I did not hear you complain a moment ago while you took your pleasure from me." His tone was churlish and sarcastic, the humour hollow, as though he was actually offended.

She stopped the mare's stride and swung the animal about in a sharp turn to face his approach. "Are we arguing?"

His stallion stopped then danced sideways. "Are we? I hardly know any more."

"Nor I," she replied, her gaze searching his face, although she didn't know what she looked for.

"Then we are not. Come on, a gallop, a race. That will knock the tension out of both us and the horses."

She nodded, then turned her horse, and kicked her heel. Her mare took off.

The fields and trees were yellow and brown, not green.

Surely the drought had to break soon.

~

The rest of the day was odd. Whatever she did, she was aware of Robert, and he seemed just as aware of her. Even when he and John were indulging in a game of backgammon and Jane was sitting on the drawing room floor, playing with Mary-Rose and the dogs, Jane's gaze kept catching and locking with Robert's.

In answer to the uncomfortable physical awareness she now felt in his company, she started avoiding him, and, over the next few days, she ceased spending time alone with him.

In response, Robert watched her even more, with a soulful look in his eyes, which she could see asked her to explain what on earth was going on. But he did not voice it, and she knew he was letting her withdraw.

After a couple of days, he gave up asking her to ride or walk with him and spent more time on business and less with the family.

When Ellen asked him why he was suddenly so busy, in front

of Jane, he made some excuse about having left the business to others for too long, and it being time he took up the reins.

Edward broke into the conversation then and began speaking about the crops and herds and harvests.

When Mary-Rose's baptism grew closer, and Ellen's family descended on Farnborough, Jane knew then her prediction had been right. Her little pretend family started drifting apart.

She liked Ellen's sisters and their husbands, but with so many young children here, Mary-Rose and Robbie mostly stayed in the nursery, and John had his real aunts and uncles to entertain him.

Then friends arrived from a neighbouring estate, and cousins of both families. Jane only knew Robert's cousin Rupert, who'd married a year ago. He'd introduced his wife, Meredith, but even Rupert was like a stranger to Jane. She'd only met him twice when he'd stayed at Farnborough as a child.

Feeling out of place, Jane spent more time alone, retreating to her room to read, as she'd done today. She was sitting quietly on the window seat, bathed in summer sunlight.

A warm breeze swept in through her open window, catching at her hair. Her feet rested on the cushion before her, and a book lay open on her lap as she looked out the window. She hadn't been able to concentrate on reading.

A single, sharp tap struck the bedchamber door. It made Jane jump, but turning and gripping the book to stop it slipping to the floor, she bid whoever to enter, expecting to see a footman.

It was Robert. He held a letter in his fingers, and he looked at her from the open door, but did not come in.

"This arrived for you." He held out his hand.

Jane rose, leaving the book on the window seat, and went to collect it.

"You need not have brought it yourself," she said as she took it.

"Why, because you don't trust yourself near me? I would have thought I'd proven myself capable of restraint by now, even if you have not." His words were cutting and his expression sullen. He didn't move from his spot beyond her chamber door. But then he changed character completely, shrugging it off and sighing as he looked past her to the open window and the curtain caught on the warm draught. "Never mind. I did not come up here to argue. I just wished to know you are well. You have been hiding, I think." His gaze came back to her. "What is wrong, Jane?"

She shook her head. "Nothing."

"Just saving yourself for Sutton," he whispered in a low breath, as though he had not intended her to hear it, or perhaps had not even intended to voice it, but could not quite help himself. It stung.

Her mouth opened to say something in response, although, heaven knew what, but he lifted his hand and shook his head.

"That was mean of me. I'm sorry. Ignore me. I'm just in a truculent mood, bored of my own company probably. Anyway, what I came to say is, we are having a game of cricket in the meadow after luncheon. Will you come down?"

She nodded, but she couldn't keep letting him believe there had been something between her and Joshua. It hadn't seemed to matter, but now... "It is not what you think, Robert."

"What?"

"What you thought you saw at Vauxhall. There is nothing between Joshua and I like that... He wants his fortune, that is all."

"Yet he—"

"Do not ask me to speak of it, please." She heard the bitter pitch in her voice that said she could not. She felt too ashamed. She did not have the courage to admit how terrible her life had been, and the last thing she wished for was to drag him into her current nightmare.

She should not have come here. She should have left things as they were.

209

Mentally dismissing him, her eyes fell to the letter, and she began opening it.

She heard him release what sounded like an irritated sigh but when she looked up, he was already several strides away, walking back along the hall.

She could hardly blame him for being frustrated and angry with her. She'd been a fool to kiss him. It was that which had made everything go so wrong.

She shut the door and opened the sheet of paper.

It was from Violet. She had been invited to the Marlows' exclusive baptism party but she wasn't coming. She apologised, but said she'd been unwell, yet Jane was not to worry, nor to return to London, unless she wished to.

Jane folded the letter, opened a drawer, and slid it in amongst her clothes. There would be no rescue party then. She must continue on alone. She returned to the window seat and looked down on to the gardens. Several women, including Ellen, were walking along one of the paths below.

Jane sighed. What was wrong with her? Why was she not able to be happy? What had she done in her childhood to set fate so against her? Still, whatever curse had set her on this path, she knew she could not hide from it any longer. She had to go back and face Joshua. She did not sit back down to read her book, but instead sat before the travelling desk in her room and wrote to Violet's solicitor.

An hour later, she walked through the garden in search of the party playing cricket. They were not hard to find. The sound of the hard ball striking against willow resonated about the garden, while the lower constant sound of the women's gossip and the occasional masculine cry of success or failure carried on the warm air.

When she reached the opening on to the meadow, Ellen immediately called and beckoned Jane over. Jane was not allowed to sit beneath a tree with the children though. She was kept in the heart of the conversation and asked question after question on her childhood years with Edward and Robert.

Jane wondered if Robert had said something to encourage his guests to include her. She hoped not. It would be embarrassing if they felt sorry for her.

When the men took a break to swap the teams between bat and field, they came over and stood in the shade drinking lemonade. They were all in their shirts, today, and overly hot. Jane's gaze picked Robert out and found him watching her as he approached. Jane turned back to speak to one of Ellen's sisters and her husband.

"Don't ignore me." Jane jumped a little as the sharp retort was whispered to her ear. He was behind her and obviously still sulking.

She faced him, with only a foot separating them. His gaze said everything his mouth had not spoken and his hand suddenly gripped her upper arm. He drew her a few steps away from the others.

Robert wanted her. She clearly wanted him. Why would she not just give in to it, especially if what she'd said earlier was true, and there had been no affair with Sutton? But there was something going on.

He'd assumed that letter had come from Sutton. It had taken a great deal of willpower not to break the blank seal. What had it said?

She'd looked uncomfortable when she'd refused to give Robert the details of her fight with Sutton.

She *should* be uncomfortable. But her vulnerability made Robert believe her.

Yet why, then, would she not let things progress between *them*? She just kept holding him back. She was so bottled up, even here at Farnborough, with him. Even though she'd relaxed and seemed happy until he had let things go too far up on the hill.

211

Since then, she had been pushing him away.

Her pretty mouth narrowed. The same pretty mouth which had sighed with ecstasy against his, but days ago. What did she think, that he was a corpse, completely unfeeling, without heart or soul, so he could take her torture without reaction? He'd been coping fairly well, he thought, until she'd pulled him to her, taken what she wanted, then again left him unfulfilled and panting for what she would not let him have. Well, now, he was out of sorts and tired of being toyed with.

He knew the signs her body spoke. She wanted him, no matter that she backed away. And that attraction would not simply go away because she willed it to. But she did not have to give in to it.

So where did that leave him? Frustrated and panting after her, still, like a bloody dog. She could torture him for the rest of his life if she wished.

"You're brooding," she said.

"Yes, am I not entitled to occasionally? You have done enough of it yourself this week."

"You're angry at me, I know," she sighed, the air seeming to go out of her all of a sudden. "Perhaps I should just go back to Violet's tomorrow?"

Desperation flooded him. He hadn't considered that possibility. His grip unconsciously firmed on her arm. She shook it loose. "You cannot go," he answered, "not before Sunday. What of the baptism? Ellen would be disappointed."

Her fingers tucked a stray curl behind her ear.

His gaze followed her movement, and desire cut him open like a knife. He was in pain for her, every muscle, every sinew, every bone in his body belonged to this woman. And if he could never have her, what then? For now, though, all he could think of was tomorrow. She had to stay.

"Ellen has her sisters. One of them, I am sure, would be

honoured."

"No. She did not ask them. She asked you. Does it mean nothing to you?"

She looked over his shoulder to where the children played, avoiding his gaze.

God. She could not even look at him now. He already knew from her actions she could no longer bear to be in a room with him.

"Yes, but I am not really family, am I? I think Ellen is just being kind. It would be best if I was not Robbie's godmother. It will only make things awkward in the future."

"Jane, what the hell is wrong with you? You blow hot and cold with me, and now with Ellen. Do not let her down. I mean it. It meant a lot to her to ask you. She does nothing lightly. Do not upset her." He narrowed his eyes, waiting for Jane's response, feeling hard and cold inside again.

"I do not mean to upset her. I did not think it mattered." She seemed smaller, her voice shrinking, and she still looked past him.

"It matters," he answered impatiently.

"Then I'll stay." Her chin lifted in a little show of defiance as her eyes came back to his. "But do not bully me."

He cocked an eyebrow at her. *Me, bullying her? Bloody hell.* "I do not recall hitting you, Jane. I am not Sutton. I am not bullying you. It is you who are playing the damn tormentor. I swear, you enjoy torturing me."

"Robert!"

They both turned as Edward called from a distance away, beckoning Robert to come and take the bat.

Without another word, Robert walked away then snatched the bat from Edward's hands.

When he took his place before the wicket, he still felt stiff with anger.

Forth, a friend of his, bowled, and Robert swung all his

213

frustration into the strike. He hit the ball hard, and it went flying with a sharp crack.

"Six!" someone shouted, meaning he'd no need to run.

He heard groans ring from the fielding team who had to fetch it in the heat. Then he leisurely swapped ends with Edward, passing his brother midfield.

When he glanced at Jane, he caught her watching, but, immediately, she looked away, pretending to be absorbed in the women's conversation.

She did not smile at him any more.

He was certain the fear which had haunted him over the last few days had come to pass. His Jane, whom he'd sheltered and entertained in his home for the past weeks, had gone again. His chance to win her was over. She would leave him the day after tomorrow, and he would have to let her go.

He hadn't a clue what he'd do then. Stay here, he supposed.

On Robert's next bat, the hard ball whizzed past him and crashed into the wickets, sending the rods and pins askew. The opposing team mocked him good-humouredly while Edward accused Robert of deliberately not lifting his bat so he could get out.

Robert handed the bat to his cousin, Rupert, and strolled away from the game.

He'd bury himself in the damned country. That's what he'd do. If running to the continent had not worked, he hardly thought any distance would make him forget, but at least he would not have to look at her. He would not have to see the grace with which she moved. Nor the frown which formed a line between her brows when she thought, as it did when she played chess with John. Nor the lost-in-love look which always came over her when she picked little Robbie up. Nor would he have to hear her girlish laugh erupt, as it did when she played her games with Mary-Rose.

A constriction gripped about his heart, a pain that hardly let him breath.

How the hell could he let her go? But he had to. He'd promised her he would.

Chapter Fourteen

If he'd been brooding in the morning, by the evening, Robert was in despair.

All togged up in their finery, the women decided they wished to dance. So Ellen played the pianoforte, and Edward sat beside his wife, turning the music. All the other men expressed a preference to dance with their wives. It left Robert to offer to partner Jane.

He thought about retreating from it, but then he remembered how much she liked to dance and couldn't bring himself to leave her out, though he was surprised when she accepted. His eyes had barely left her all evening, and she'd not looked at him once.

Lovesick fool that he was, his heart lurched merely at the pressure of her hand in his. It was then Ellen struck up a waltz. Robert glanced at his sister-in-law. Of course, she and Edward must have seen it all turning sour. They weren't blind. But what could they do? No more than him. Jane was slipping through Robert's fingers, and there was nothing to be done.

"You are quiet tonight?" she said.

His eyes turned to her face.

"You're still angry?"

He forced a smile. "Not at you, not really." *Just bleeding to bloody death for the love of a woman who does not want me.* It was himself he was angry at, for idiotically creating false and flawed

216

expectations in his head, *and his heart.*

He supposed, when Jane returned to London and told her friend, Violet would think it justice.

Jane was studying him, following the steps he led. She felt so good in his arms.

He should have had Ellen play before, one evening when they were alone, but then it would have been foolish, just the two of them dancing. Yet even now, he could feel the magic working between them. It always did when they were close. Her body moved nearer and he leaned to smell her hair, his cheek brushing against her ebony curls.

Her head then rested on his shoulder, and they were dancing as they'd done weeks ago in a dark London garden.

No one noticed. No one cared. The married couples forming the rest of the party all danced closer than was standard.

He felt her sigh, and her hand slid from his shoulder to his neck. "Do you want to walk in the garden?" he whispered into her hair.

She nodded against his chest, then pulled back. He was unwilling to risk her coming to her senses and swiftly gripped her upper arm, then paced across the room with her in tow and out through the open French doors. He did not stop on the terrace, but drew her on through the garden, his grip shifting from her arm to hold her hand. He walked quickly, knowing she was taking two paces to his one.

She did not try to pull free. Instead, her hand gripped his just as tightly as his held hers.

It was as if they'd found something to cling to amidst this madness which possessed them. Or that was how he felt, and he hoped she felt the same.

When they reached the circular rose garden his mother had planted, an arbour hidden far away from the house, he stopped, tugged her back into his arms, and held her, physically willing her to stay.

His chin rested on her crown as she melted against him, and her arms wrapped about his waist.

A physical need gripped inside him. He was a man after all. He needed sex. But he wanted *her* more, and he would not risk losing her company tonight just because he'd overstepped her boundaries. This could be the last night he had it.

"Why?" she asked against his chest.

He smiled, knowing exactly what she meant without asking. "Who knows?" he whispered, stirring her hair. "There is magnetism between us. I can neither explain nor understand it either, Jane. We are just drawn to each other whether we will it or not."

She lifted her head away from his chest and met his gaze. "Kiss me," she beckoned in a siren call, her eyes bright with bodily lust.

This was madness. He ought to keep a cool head. She would regret it minutes later. "No, Jane, not this time, sweetheart. I've learned my lesson. You do not really want to. Tomorrow, it will be me you paint as the one in the wrong. No. Go back to London on Monday, Jane, and let us leave things as they are."

She did not move, did not pull away, just looked at him, her eyes implying he was a fool.

He was.

He laughed, a choking, cracked sound. "What? Don't tell me you're surprised I am able to say no?"

She smiled.

It broke his damned heart.

"I am thinking I shall not accept no for an answer actually. Take me out on the lake, Robert."

"The lake?" His voice was virtually a whisper. What was she saying? They had both admitted in London they remembered that night. It was the night he'd made up his mind to marry her. There would be no repetition of that.

"Yes, please?" Her hands still gripping his waist, her smile turned cajoling.

What is this?

She let him go, slipping from his grip. "Come then," she whispered before running off along the path heading towards the ornamental lake.

What the hell is she up to? His heart pounded. Perhaps he would wake up in a moment and this would be a dream. He followed regardless. If it was a dream, he was going to relish it, confound his instinct for self-preservation. He let his good intentions sail away like dandelion seeds blown on the wind. If she'd be gone after tomorrow, he'd take what she offered tonight and hang on to the memory for the rest of his life. It would help him endure the parched years to follow, without Jane.

She stopped at the edge of the arbour and held out her hand.

He took it again, clutching it tightly.

In minutes, they were at the edge of the lake. The wide expanse of water stretched out before them.

His grandfather had added the ornamental lake. It was only shallow, hence, they'd always used punts on it. Plus, the flat-bottomed boats were more conducive to comfort.

Jane climbed in as he held her steady.

His servants had clearly guessed the boats may be used during the house party because they were laden with freshly aired cushions.

He did not speak as he untied it and climbed in.

Nor did she.

Everything about it took him back to the night years before when they'd crept away from the house after dark.

Water swilled about the hull as he dipped the pole in and pushed them out. It lapped gently against the wood as the shallow boat slid across the lake, sitting low in the calm water. An owl called from somewhere in the trees at the edge. Another answered it.

Jane sat on the cushions, her arms wrapped about her knees, holding them to her chest, and her stocking-clad toes peeked from beneath the hem of her gown.

They'd both left their shoes in the boathouse.

"Stop now," she whispered when they were in the middle. "Sit with me."

His pulse thundered through his veins, his blood as thick and heavy as molten lead, and a weight of need hung in his groin. He sunk the pole into the mud on the bed of the lake and tied the punt to it.

She moved the cushions while he did so, spreading them along the hull so they could lie across them.

When he joined her, she wrapped her arms about his neck and pressed her face into his shoulder.

Barely able to breath, he asked, "Jane, what is happening here?"

She lifted her face, but he couldn't see it in the shadow of the silver moonlight which etched all else about them clearly. She was in black again, colourless and wreathed in mystery, as she'd been the first night in London. "I don't know," she whispered. "I just know I do not want to leave you."

A pain pierced his chest. "You don't?"

"No, but I don't know what to do. This is the only place which has ever felt like home to me, and yet, it is not my home."

Sighing, he closed his eyes. The holding back was unbearable, and yet, going forth, only to have her stop him again, was worse. "So, it is my house you want, not me?"

"It isn't the house. It is you. It was you in London only, and I felt it then too... I..." She paused, catching her breath. "It would not feel like home if you were not here."

"I was not the one who said you should leave." He was very aware she could see his face while he could not see hers.

"I know, but I cannot stay forever, can I?"

"Why not?"

She did not respond. Instead, her slender, elegant fingers slid up his neck and delved into his hair.

"Stop talking and just kiss me. Please?"

He gave in. He couldn't not. His mouth touched hers and felt her lips part. Then his tongue slid into her warm mouth. She tasted of red wine.

Her body arched to his, just as it had done up on the hill.

She was so needy when he got her going, but he could not bear for it to stop again. If she let him take more from her tonight, she would have to let him take it all.

He offered her nothing beyond his lips, ignoring the insistent pressure of her hip against his.

"Robert," she said, just as she'd done the other day, begging him for more, for some form of release from the desire raging between them.

Heaven knows, he was not a selfish lover, but he wanted *something* from this. His hand reached to the skirt of her flimsy muslin gown, and his fingers began working it up.

In anticipation, her fingers gripped his shoulders, but he sensed there was a fear in her grip, too.

Pray God, she did not force him away tonight. He was hard for her again, and his desire felt like a bloody battering ram, waiting to be unleashed.

When he touched the bare skin above her stocking, her body jolted, and as he slid his fingers across her inner thigh, he felt her breath catch against his mouth. Then her hand lifted from his shoulder for a minute, and he thought she would stop him, but instead, she began trying to release the buttons of his coat.

When she could not, a frustrated sound came from her throat.

He moved, shifting back on to his knees.

He could see her then, and watched silver moonlight play across her face as he stripped off both his evening coat and his waistcoat and left them in the rear of the hull.

She smiled, giving him that feminine come-hither look.

It sent a dagger of aching awareness to his very tip.

She sat up a little and half-heartedly tugged the end of his cravat, her hair already falling from its pins.

He took off his neckcloth and left it in the hull.

When he leaned forward again, her fingers began pulling his shirt from his waistband. Then they touched skin beneath it.

There was just something so uncertain and hesitant in her touch. It felt different to being touched by any other woman he'd known.

He pulled his shirt off and threw it aside, too.

Immediately, her fingers ran across the contours of his chest.

He was unwilling to be the only one in a state of undress though, and so, gripping her arms and interrupting her indulgence, he drew her up and reached for the buttons at her back.

Once they were free, he slid her dress from her shoulders and helped her free it from her arms. It was too awkward in the boat to take it right off. But he helped her work off her chemise, too, until she was bare to her waist.

She was shaking. It was not from cold; the air was hot.

When they lay down on the cushions again, the soft flesh of her breasts pressed against his chest, and she groaned into his mouth.

He drew the sound into his lungs. He wanted to be a part of her. *Oh God*, he wanted to be in her, but not yet, not until he was certain she would not say no.

His hand reached between their bodies.

She was aroused, hot and damp.

His index and middle finger slipped into the heat, and his thumb pressed and caressed. He would drive her so mad with want she would be incapable of saying no.

"Jane?" he whispered to her ear.

"Yes." Her voice was breathless.

"Do you want this? Are you sure? You will not make me stop this time."

"Oh God!" Her hips pressed to his palm, and her fingers cradled his scalp.

"Do you want this?" he asked again, needing to be sure.

"Yes! Yes! I want this!"

"*But do you want me?*" he pushed, determined to be certain.

"Robert, I want you! Yes! Just!" Her hands suddenly gripped his shoulders, her fingernails cutting into his flesh. "Please!" she cried out hard. He felt the wave of ecstasy hit her as her pelvis bucked against his hand.

"I want to be inside you now. Yes?" He spoke cautiously, still fearing the answer might be no as his fingers left their moist haven and moved to undo the flap of his breeches.

"*Yes.*" She nodded, but as the silver light caught her eyes, he saw a sudden element of fear.

What did she think? That he would hurt her? Had someone else hurt her?

Once he was free, he did not rush, remembering that night in the garden. Lifting her hand from his shoulder, he pressed a kiss into her palm. She was beautiful. He wanted her to be sure. He lowered her hand.

Her breath caught as he closed her hand about him.

Her touch was tentative and uncertain.

He supposed because it was him, because they'd waited years for this. If it happened? He was still not convinced it would. He dared not hope.

"I'll not hurt you, Jane, sweetheart. I promise," he whispered as she grew more confident with his tuition.

Her legs had fallen slack.

He let her hand go and touched her, trailing his fingers over

223

her thighs and lifting her skirt up over her bare stomach.

Her leg lifted and lay over his hip, her body clearly craving to be closer, while her hand worked harder.

He gripped her luscious, pert bottom.

He longed to be within her. But not yet. He was not sure enough to try it yet. Just a moment more.

God, he felt like a green youth, afraid to take the final step, and he disliked this unsure man.

His hand suddenly moved to stop the movement of hers. "Now?" he whispered to her lips.

She stilled instantly, and it felt as though every one of her muscles solidified.

He lifted a little, met her gaze, and held it as he moved over her, covering her.

She had not said no, but she was silent, and her breathing was short and sharp, and her body lay still, but not relaxed.

It felt like worship to him. This would always be the most precious moment of his life.

"It should have always been like this," she whispered as her palms pressed against his cheeks.

He lifted his hips.

She closed her eyes and bit her lower lip.

He held his breath, watching her face, then plunged quickly. Her warmth overwhelmed him, flooding through his body as time slowed a dozen times, and then he felt a sudden sharp pressure and her body jolt. It burst instantly and let him through.

He was motionless suddenly, but seated deep inside her.

Extreme cold washed over him as understanding dawned.

The uncertainty in her touch, which he'd sensed on that first night, and again now, had not been *like* a virgin's. She had *been* a virgin.

She had been a virgin! The animal roar rose inside him.

She was his.

Claimed by him.

Owned by him.

His.

The breath, which had been stuck in his lungs, expelled suddenly on a single word. "*Jane?*"

"Carry on. Please, don't stop." Her hands gripped in his hair and pulled his mouth to hers, and she whispered again before she kissed him, "Robert, *please don't stop.*"

He moved slowly, and he could feel her taut, slender body beneath him, stiff with uncertainty. Or perhaps pain.

He kissed her. Hard. In gratitude. In awe. A kiss which sought to distract and possess. Slowly, he felt her legs slacken again, and her core relax, adjusting to his deep intrusion.

Her hands left his hair and pressed over his shoulders, fingers spread wide.

He kept his pace steady and whispered into her mouth how much he loved her, how beautiful she was, how no other woman had ever been able to compare to her. When he increased his pace, he felt her arch against him. Her palms travelled down his back and her fingers gripped his hips.

He made his movement more controlled, quick and sharp.

She was panting in moments, her fingernails sinking into his hips. Then sweat suddenly coated her skin.

She'd break again soon.

He waited for her to fall. But she seemed to hold back, hovering on the edge of it, as though afraid to cross the bridge.

"Let it happen, Jane," he whispered as he had done in London. "It shall be so much better if you do."

Almost as if his words were the final caress, he felt her tumble, her pelvis pressing hard against his, and burning warmth surrounded him.

He loved her. Loved her to distraction. She was the only woman who'd ever been in his heart, and he'd learned much from others, but now, he was going to give it all to her. He could give her pleasure she had never known existed. Once he was done with her, she would not be able to bear leaving him.

She was shaking and silently weeping, clinging to him as he progressed, seeking to enthral her with the constant charm of his invasion. He wanted her cast adrift and he was never going to let her return. He could feel her body dissolving in shivering spasm, as he made a sudden sharp thrust. But then... He growled into the night, sounding like a wolf as he fought the release he didn't wish to come yet, before stilling and admitting defeat as he let it overtake him and held her tight against him.

In answer she wrapped her legs about his hips and her arms about his shoulders and clung to him, hugging him with her whole body as he felt her tears run across her cheek.

She was his. This should have happened years ago. It was how things were meant to be.

His body lost tension, and his forehead rested on her shoulder.

She was as damp with sweat as he was.

She let her grip loosen, and her hands slid down to lie on his back.

He moved, lifting up, looking down at her, and withdrawing from inside her. "Why did you not tell me?"

She smiled and brushed back a lock of hair from his brow; the gentle gesture gripped as a spasm in his chest. "Hector left me all his money. Joshua wants it back. With that knowledge, he could claim the marriage was never real, and he would win."

"You think I would have told anyone?"

"You were not in good humour with me when we first met, Robert. After that, I was just too afraid of what would happen next."

"What do you want to happen next?"

226

"I don't know. I do not care. Just take me to your bed."

Robert laughed, and let his fingers run across her cheek, brushing away the tracks of the tears she'd shed as they'd made love. "You're *fast*, aren't you?"

"Fast!" She bucked, trying to push him further off her, reminding him, as she had once done before, of a temperamental colt.

He should have opened his mind like his eyes when he'd thought it. Perhaps he'd have seen what her skittish temperament meant then. *God*, she'd shied away every time he'd become too intimate, and it had never been playing games, just maidenly uncertainty.

She'd been reserved, and he'd been overzealous and scared her off.

He stroked her hair and kissed her cheek. "I'm only teasing, Jane. You are hardly that, sweetheart." He kissed her brow, then nipped at her neck. Her head tilted back and her body arched.

"Not here, darling, not again," he whispered to her skin.

He leaned to press a last kiss on her bare breast before pulling up to kneel at the end of the shallow hull. "You're right. Let us withdraw to a bed," he said, looking down at her. His breeches were slack about his hips leaving him virtually nude.

Her gaze swept over him, and she bit her lip as she sat upright, too, naked to her waist, her wrinkled gown only covering her middle and leaving her long, slender legs glowing pale in the moonlight.

The peaks of her small firm breasts invited him back. She looked shameless and wanton, with her hair loose and hanging to her shoulders – she was anything but – *she looked gorgeous*.

But his observation must have made her self-conscious, because she began covering herself, lifting her bodice, then sliding down her skirt. She was such a *vulnerable* woman. He wasn't used to that. He would treasure her all his life though. The knowledge of her virginity left him totally undone, and an instinct to protect

227

her burned strongly within. She'd only ever be his.

His heart pounded and his head spun as he secured his breeches and slipped on his shirt and waistcoat. He left that hanging open.

She would only ever be his. Lord, he wanted to shout it. Regardless of all his years of self-flagellation, angst and pain over this woman, *she was still his.*

He untied the boat in silence then began pushing it back to shore. Water lapped at the hull, while above, small bats swooped and circled in the night air.

At the boathouse, he held Jane's hand to help her out, then he secured her loose buttons.

He threw his coat over his shoulder and wrapped his cravat about his neck, not bothering to dress properly.

If anyone saw them walking silently back to the house, hand in hand, he knew it would be blatantly obvious what they'd been up to. He didn't care.

They met no one.

To avoid his guests, he led her in through a servant's entrance and up the back stairs.

Halfway up, he caught her sharply to his chest, stole a passionate kiss, and left Jane breathless and laughing. He silenced her by pressing his hand over her mouth, fearful of his guests hearing, but her beautiful eyes laughed on.

He was smiling broadly when they carried on. He felt as though he was nineteen again and none of the intervening years had existed. Jane was his world.

On the first floor landing, he opened his bedchamber door tentatively.

Archer was busy tidying clothes in a drawer, and his head spun to Robert.

Robert raised his eyebrows, *get out.*

Archer's eyes widened as he nodded, before closing the drawer and disappearing.

As the dressing room door shut across the room, Robert pulled Jane in. A single candle burned on the chest near the bed. It was nothing like the sophisticated scene he'd led her to in London. The room was the same as when he came to bed alone. With any other woman, the honesty of it would have made him feel stripped. Not with Jane.

"Robert." Her arms came about his neck and her untutored kiss pressed over his mouth. His hands slid down her back and gripped the flesh of her buttocks.

Before Jane knew it, they were moving across the room, Robert half lifting her. Then her gown was loose once more, and he was slipping it, along with her chemise, from her shoulders. She was naked in moments and felt the abrasive sensation of his clothes against her skin, and in answer she slid off his waistcoat and tugged his shirt over his head.

When he let her go to allow it, his eyes skimmed across every inch of her body, hunger dark in his gaze.

She couldn't believe this was happening at last, that she had let it happen, and yet it was always meant to be. It should have happened so many years ago. That was why she had cried in the boat. She felt so full of emotion – of love.

He was wonderful, beautiful, and yet she was under no illusion; she knew who he was, half her Robert, tender and kind, half the Earl of Barrington, rakehell and seducer, determined to devour her.

"I want you so much, Jane," he whispered.

She touched the hair across his chest which narrowed to a dart reaching into his breeches, and her hand slid down to touch him there as she remembered how their lovemaking had felt in the boat. She was no longer afraid. It had hurt in the beginning, but then it had become a blissful agony. She opened the buttons of

229

his flap and heard his breath catch as she pushed his breeches and underwear from his slim, muscular hips. They slid to the floor, and her thumbs settled on his hip bone for a moment while her fingers gripped his hips, feeling the lines of bone and muscle.

His body was so lean and muscular and beautiful. Like nature had crafted it with a chisel.

When she took hold of him, he was busy freeing his clothes and stockings from his feet, but a heavy sigh left his lungs. She did not look up, but explored slowly.

His muscles jolted when she used her thumb to caress him.

She had power over him, she realised; just as he could control her, she could master his instincts and control him. It was a liberating and exhilarating thought. Her thumb moved and his muscle shuddered.

She looked up, smiled wickedly, and tightened her grip about him.

His shining, wide eyes, held her gaze.

She let go, too unsure of what to do yet. Instead, her hands travelled over his midriff and chest again.

He took control.

In moments, she was flat on the bed. He'd half thrown her there, having gripped her buttocks and toppled her back. She was breathless already, but she wished to play an equal part in this. She did not wish to be charmed by the rake and done to. She wished to be with Robert, loved not worshipped, the two of them equal.

She pressed him to his back and straddled his thighs. Naked skin caressed naked skin, Robert's naked skin.

"I want to be inside you immediately, Jane. Will you forgive my haste?" he whispered up at her, with no argument over his prostrate position.

"I want you there," she answered. She ached for him, despite the soreness from the first time.

Strong hands clasped her hips, then he impaled her.

This was the two of them, as it always should have been, equal and the same. Loved and cherished in balanced measure.

A wolf-like growl came from his throat.

She watched his body moving beneath her and learned the pattern he created, then moved for herself and felt his grip loosen.

When she looked up, his eyes glinted with intense unreadable feelings.

"I cannot believe you're really mine," he said in a hoarse voice.

Her fingers brushed his hair back from his brow. "I have always been yours, Robert, just not like this."

"Jane," he whispered, emotion seemingly overwhelming him.

It made him even dearer to her, if that was possible, and as his hips lifted and his hands rocked her pelvis, she felt her body bow with pleasure. Then the warmth of his mouth was at her breast.

The sensations tingling through her seemed to connect and tangle up as her fingers clawed on the mattress. She fought to keep her head and his rhythm, refusing to be passive and desperate not to be left behind but to travel this crest together.

Her skin felt hot.

He was too good, too knowing. It was so hard to keep up with him. He changed patterns continuously, enthralling her, and his hands travelled everywhere. The more he worked, the less she could think.

She sat upright a little more to draw away from him, but the movement brought her breast back to his mouth, and he nipped it swiftly with his lips.

A sigh of pleasure escaped her, sensation swirling about inside her. She was burning hot and ready to burst into flame.

When she looked at his face, he gave her a sudden wicked rakehell smile, and his thumb slid down between them, found the sensitive spot he favoured, and pressed. He'd won her over.

She broke, her muscle trembling as *it* raged through her, and, at the same time, she felt his motion change to determined, strong, deliberate strokes, racing towards the final hurdle. She hung on, breathless and boneless, unable to compete. He was too good. *Too knowing.*

"Oh, Robert," she whispered, "don't stop." Looking down, she watched the firm ridges and hollows of muscle tighten across his stomach each time he moved.

"Robert," she said again more loudly, her voice wobbly.

"Robert!" She broke once more and could no longer hold herself up. Her arms bent at the elbows and she collapsed. Then one of his hands gripped her scalp, pressing her head to his shoulder while the other splayed over her back, holding her secure and safe.

A sound of passionate pain left his throat when he broke, too, and pressed deep then stilled.

"Robert," she whispered one last time.

With a deep growl, he moved, rolling over and tipping her back on to the soft bed.

His body covered hers, and she held him close as he'd held her, while her lips brushed his cheek and his brow.

He nipped at her neck, using his teeth.

Her heart thundered.

"Are you well?" His breath caressed her shoulder. Then he lifted a little. His brown eyes were matte now. One of his fingers traced the contours of her face then slipped over her shoulder and breast.

She nodded, suddenly tired and overwhelmed by a flood of emotion as her senses returned to earth.

He rolled off her then pulled the sheet up over them. He kissed her hair as her head pillowed on his shoulder.

"Sweetheart," he whispered, "you cannot imagine how much I love you. It is beyond any explanation."

"If it is how much I love you, I can," she answered, her eyelids

232

already falling.

When she woke, the candle had burned down to a short wax-encrusted stub, and Robert was kissing her shoulder as his fingers slid across her stomach.

He said nothing, but just held her gaze as he pressed her back on the bed, parted her legs and began loving her again.

This was Lord Barrington, the London rakehell, administering his art. She knew it, but it was wonderful. She did not fight it. She was too tired and too blissfully relaxed.

His intense gaze held hers, burning into her, and like his eyes, the emotion in his touch was raw with need.

This claiming was an unadorned expression of lust, but it was bestowed in *love*. She could see and feel the depth of it.

Afterwards, he held her tight as she lay on his chest, and she fell asleep again as he stroked her hair.

The next time she woke, she was lying on her stomach, and his fingers were running over her back in tender exploration. She stretched luxuriously, extending her body, intensely relaxed, and opened her eyes. The room was light.

She should not be in his bed.

His lips touched her shoulder, and she sensed him smile as his fingers traced the curve of her spine down to her bottom.

"Robert!" she laughed, lifting to her elbows as his fingers slipped lower. "We need to get up."

"Who says? It is time to get up when *I* say so, sweetheart. I'm not letting you go until I've had my fill. You've made me wait long enough for this, Jane." He moved, grasping a pillow, before urging her to lift her stomach. Then he slid the pillow beneath her.

"What *are* you doing?"

"Showing you another way to make love," he stated bluntly as he knelt behind her. His fingers explored again, as though her body fascinated him, and she sensed him watching what he did.

Then his fingers gripped and parted her thighs.

Her legs became braced open by the pressure of his when he came down over her and into her all at once. She was held wide for him and utterly in his thrall.

The wretch, he knew what he was doing, forcing her to let him have all the control.

"Does this feel good?" he asked against her ear after a moment, his weight pressing her into the bed.

"Yes, it feels good," she answered as she felt the magic swirl through her.

"How good?" he urged in a vocal caress.

"Very good," she answered as she became a little breathless. "*Robert.*"

His fingers were still playing as he moved.

"Do you love me, darling?" he urged in her ear again, holding her body and mind hostage. She longed for a ransom to escape the earth; he could quicken the feeling in her so easily.

"I love you very much, Robert! I do. Very much!" she cried out as a wave washed high, but he changed his pattern so it broke in ripples and not a rush, teasing her. The rogue.

"Robert!"

Oh, he was mean when he wished to be. He was playing with her.

His undulation possessed every element of her thoughts. The London rake, the Earl of Barrington, was busy binding a spell about her.

"Do you like it this way?" he whispered again. "Is it truly good?"

"*Yes.*" It felt good. He felt good, and wicked, and the sensation was all-consuming as he pressed her legs painfully wider.

A whimper escaped her lips. She had not intended it to. But the sound was pleading.

"Yes, sweetheart?" he echoed.

It was not wicked. It was cruel.

234

Her breath came to the pattern of his movement as her finger-nails sank into the pillow.

"Yes, darling?" His low voice filled the air.

"Yes, Robert," she answered, half screaming as she longed to break or escape. She wanted to say stop. She wanted to grip his hips and stop him, but the feelings inside her were beautiful and terrible all at once, and the beautiful element longed for it to continue, to get faster and harder, but he did not change his torturous pace. Her body bowed to better receive him.

"Do you want it a little more vigorous?" he asked in a low voice. She could hear him almost laughing. "Say it, Jane, if you do."

She gripped the pillow harder and clenched her teeth, feeling every muscle in her body tense in battle against the distracting, glorious discomfort of his possession, but she only endured a little longer. "Robert, please!"

The change was instantaneous. She wished she could see him. She could imagine his face now, set with concentration, his eyes dark and intense, watching his work as he determinedly drove her towards heaven.

She realised she was shouting out with every stroke. She hadn't even known.

"Ah!"

"Yes."

When she crossed the gate, he did not stop, and she lay there, semi-conscious and delirious, and let him have his way.

His weight lifted off her suddenly, and his hands pulled her up.

He concluded their lovemaking kneeling on his haunches with her kneeling astride his lap, impaled and only half-aware of what he did as he bit her shoulder and adored her in his own way. His end came on a harsh cry, as though he'd fought it and hadn't wished to give in even then. Afterwards, his fingers swept her hair forward over her shoulder while his other hand splayed on her stomach and held her steady.

235

She leaned her head back on his left shoulder as he kissed her right. "You are mad, Robert Marlow," she said to the air.

"I am starved," he answered. "I have waited years for this, for you, Jane. You will forgive me, surely, for being a glutton now. I've slept with no women since you came to my room in London. What I am, Jane, is famished."

She slipped from his grip and turned to the edge of the bed, looking back. "Well, I am going. You cannot keep me here all day."

He moved to grab her, but she slid off the bed and snatched up her clothes.

"I can," he growled, following her.

Her hand lifted to hold him back. "We have to go to the church, Robert."

"Church?" He sat back on the bed. "Hell. I'd forgotten."

"I had not." Picking up his shirt and breeches, she tossed them at him. "Besides, I do not want Meg spreading rumours below-stairs if I'm absent."

Robert laughed. "Just because we did not see the servants last night, my love, does not mean they did not see us. They have a way of merging into nothingness so they are never seen. They were there. They know our secret already."

"*Robert*." The idea horrified her. He stood, naked and gloriously beautiful, his hand held out to her. She stepped back. "I am going."

"I would put some clothes on first though, darling." He laughed again as his eyes perused her naked body with a lustful gleam.

"You are wicked, Robert Marlow," she threw at him as she put aside her dress and began slipping on her chemise. "I am surprised you even dare set foot on holy ground." She carried on dressing, but when her dress dropped into place, Jane remembered leaving her stockings in the boat among the cushions.

Jane's fingers shook as she turned to face him. "I left my stockings outside."

Bless her. She was precious, *and his*. He wished to stand on a hill and yell it to the sunrise. *Jane is mine! She's only ever been mine!*

He smiled. "They are in the pocket of my coat." He moved to fetch them. His heart felt so damned tender as it thumped steadily in his chest. He felt like a virgin himself. This was new to him, too. Making love to a woman he *loved*.

She smiled back at him when he gave them to her, and once she'd put them on, he secured the buttons at her back. Then he embraced her firmly. "I promise I'll let you go," he whispered, but he just needed to hold her one more time before he did.

She hugged him, too, and they stood there for a moment before he kissed the crown of her head then pulled away. She took a deep breath.

"You're crying?" he said, his hand at her waist. "Why?"

She smiled, though her eyes still glittered. He wiped the tears from her cheeks with his thumbs, but more overflowed. Had he been too rough or too insistent? Should he have let her rest?

"I'm just happy," she said on a sob.

"Happy?" he echoed, laughing roughly. He kissed her brow. "People don't cry when they're happy, sweetheart."

"They do." She pressed a kiss over the stubble on his jaw. He held her tight again and let her cry, and felt like crying, too, though he was not a man who did. It was relief and joy and disbelief he felt – *and love – a hundred tons of love.*

His hands slid down her arms and gripped hers. "Come along then, sweetheart, you need to go."

He began walking backward, leading her towards the door as he held her gaze. Her emerald eyes were shining, but they were no longer welling with tears.

"I would like to make you lose control," she said as they reached the door. "You never quite let go, do you? I'd like to do to you what you do to me."

Jane. No other woman had ever compared. They'd all taken, not given. Not that he'd cared. He'd had his pleasure, but God, he knew that to be a shallow feeling now.

"Believe me, Jane, you are quite capable of knocking me senseless." Red spots bloomed on her cheeks. Was she still unsure of him? "I've adored you since we were children, Jane, I've never stopped. You need only turn your gaze away and I am lost. You will stay here, won't you? With me?"

"I should get back to my room. Meg will—"

"She will know anyway, Jane. I'm sorry, but your dress is creased beyond repair. You'll not hide it from your maid. If you wish, though, I'll tell my valet, to tamp the gossip down. He'll silence any talk. Shall I ask him to order a bath drawn for you, too?"

She blushed. "What hour is it?"

"Seven," he answered, having already looked. "Only the servants will know, and anyone who says a word against you, Jane, will have a scolding from Mrs. Barclay."

Jane sighed. Perhaps he should not have mentioned the housekeeper knowing, too. He was used to disposing of lovers. He was not used to wishing they could stay, but watching them go.

He kissed her one last time. "I love you, Jane," he whispered as he pulled back and let go of her hands.

Her fingers swept his fringe off his brow and her eyes held his, deep wells of green. "I love you, too, Robert."

He wished they could forget the christening. He felt like he was losing her again. "Run along and pamper yourself," he whispered. "I will see you in a couple of hours."

She nodded, then opened the door and left. His heart thumped with a strange feeling of doubt. It disturbed his previous jubilation. But it was a foolish fear. She'd marry him now. Why would she not? She'd hung on to her virginity all these years, and now she'd chosen him to give it to. He'd not spoken of marriage, but it must surely be in her head.

Chapter Fifteen

A good six hours later, Robert stood by the font of the small village church, in the presence of his buried ancestors. Jane stood beside Ellen, holding Robbie, who was wriggling as always. Ellen's youngest sister and her husband, the Duke and Duchess of Bradford, stood with them, next to Edward. Together, they repeated the priest's words to renounce evil and reject sin, expressing beliefs on behalf of the child.

Robert's eyes turned habitually to Jane, as they'd been doing all morning. He smiled at the blush painting her cheeks, knowing she was remembering her last sin. The one he'd no intention of repenting and every intention of repeating. She was right. He should not be standing in a church.

She, however, was the perfect image of innocence today, which she had been until last night. She could not meet his gaze without turning crimson, and when he tried to speak to her or include her in a conversation, she stuttered some comment then excused herself, colouring up.

A wondrous thought struck as he watched her holding Robbie. His child could be busy forming itself inside her. He'd never released inside a woman before. He'd done so four times last night. Something clenched firmly about his heart, like a fist, gripping it. He would propose again later. He'd been considering how and where.

His heart thumped steadily again.

He remembered her accusation that he always stayed in control. She was right about that, too. Sex for him had never been just escape. It had been seeking. Now that he'd found what he sought, he didn't know if he was capable of ever fully letting go. His instinct never to trust was too ingrained. *But perhaps with Jane.* Memories slipped in of last night, and the awe of it lay heavy.

Robbie's bright eyes held hers for a moment, and his chubby little fingers gripped her short sleeve.

Robert would never tire of looking at her. His heart was full. He'd love to see their child in her arms. He hoped.

The vicar took the child from Jane, held Robbie over the font, and poured the water over his head. Robbie scowled and wailed. When Robert looked up, Ellen's gaze was not fixed on her son though. It was on him.

He smiled, silently telling her to mind her own business.

She'd questioned him this morning, before Jane had come down, about where they'd disappeared to the night before. Ellen had told him everyone had noticed. The implication was he'd been imprudent and risked Jane's reputation. He'd lifted his eyebrows and told Ellen, "You may think you rule my life, but you do not, and I might hold you in my affections, but I am not to be chastened by my brother's wife."

To which she'd answered ... "I have been chastising you for years and you have never routed me before."

His sharp answer as he'd walked away was... "Perhaps you are no longer so high in the order of my life."

Not for the world would he disconcert Jane further by letting her know his guests suspected. Nor would he acknowledge their speculation. This was private and personal. He would not even discuss it with Ellen. He wished only to shut out the world and return to his youth, when his orbit had been Jane.

Edward took Robbie from the vicar, and Ellen looked at her squalling son. Robert turned his gaze back to Jane to find her watching him. Her eyes darted away. A day ago, this event, the baptism, had been something precious he'd looked forward to. Now he longed for it to be over so he could spend some time alone with her.

He walked back to the house a few paces behind her, while John, at his side, asked for Robert's opinion on a horse he could take back to Eton. Edward had agreed to John keeping one in stables there. At least their discussion on breeds and what to look for distracted Robert's Jane-focused brain.

"Sayle!" Robert stopped and looked back at the same time as his nephew. It was the Duke of Pembroke, John's grandfather, who'd called. He was the only one who used John's courtesy title.

Robert sensed his nephew stiffen and knew John was afraid he'd done something wrong. Pembroke had spent many deluded years believing he could control his grandson because the boy was his heir.

"Sayle!" Pembroke called again as John waited for his grandfather to catch up.

Robert waited, too, unwilling to leave the boy to the mercy of a tyrant.

"Grandfather," John stated before bowing deeply as the Duke approached.

"Your Grace." Robert joined his nephew's welcome, but only bent slightly.

"How fare you, boy? I have hardly seen you for months. You must come and spend some time with us soon."

"I am well, Your Grace. I said to Mama I shall spend the last week before I return to Eton with you, if that is suitable for you, sir?"

"It shall not suffice. One must not be miserly with one's duties,

242

Sayle."

Robert had never heard the Duke say a good word to his heir. There was no encouragement, no recognition of any achievement – *no affection*.

"You will return with me today, Sayle. The Duke of Sutton's widow is not fit company for a boy your age."

Robert felt the words wind him like a punch in his stomach. What the hell did Pembroke know of Jane? Robert had not heard a single rumour of her in town and even if he had, he was in a position now to deny them all, and he would not let Pembroke insult his future wife.

"Your Grace, with respect, the Dowager Duchess of Sutton is a close family friend."

Pembroke's measured gaze settled on Robert, clearly questioning his morals.

"Go on ahead, John," Robert directed his nephew.

John met Robert's gaze with a look of doubt, then glanced at his grandfather for consent.

Pembroke nodded, and once the lad was ahead, Robert said, hands clasped firmly behind his back, "I think, sir, you should cease listening to rumour."

"And I think, Barrington, you should leave your paramours in London and keep them well away from Sayle." The Duke's bitter words burned with disdain, and Robert felt his anger flare.

"Her Grace is not that, sir, yet I hope she will soon agree to be my wife, and I shall not hear unfounded, ridiculous rumours repeated in my presence, nor in my house."

"Who said I speak rumour? I have seen her behaviour with my own eyes, Barrington. She has loose morals, and I shall not have her near Sayle. If you marry that woman, he shall not visit here again."

The urge was to ask Pembroke what he thought he'd seen, but

Robert *knew* she'd been untouched until last night.

"You may order as you wish, Your Grace, yet John shall come. Edward is your grandson's guardian. You can neither dictate to Sayle, nor to me. Regardless of what you believe you have seen, I can assure you, you are wrong. The Dowager Duchess of Sutton is of excellent character, and if you, sir, dare to defile it, I shall have you thrown off my estate, and you will not be welcome here again."

Robert lifted his hand as he saw Pembroke about to protest. "I would not, Your Grace, unless you intend to spoil this day for your daughter. I shall have you removed if you dare say one more word."

Visibly infuriated, Pembroke shouted forward to his wife then quickened his step. No doubt, he would leave after luncheon. Robert pitied the Duchess, the only person left under Pembroke's influence.

"What was that about?" Edward said, catching up.

"How you put up with such a father-in-law, I shall never know," Robert answered.

"I do just that, put up with him, but you know Ellen wishes to see her mother and will not have John cut off from her father. John is to inherit, after all."

"In my opinion, it would be a blessing if John *were* cut off from Pembroke. He had the audacity to insult Jane. Some nonsense about her moral stature."

Edward's hand gripped Robert's shoulder. "If he is using last night as an example—"

Robert shrugged it off. "He is not, and mind your tongue."

"Then perhaps you should be a little more discreet. You disappeared from a small gathering with her, Robert. Do you think us all blind?"

Robert sighed. It was true, of course. "Were comments made?" Jane would be mortified.

"Our guests are friends and family. They are too polite for that, but they wondered over your whereabouts, and I am sure they are capable of drawing the same conclusion as Ellen and I. Still, at least, I assume you have won Jane over?"

Robert smiled. He could not hide his joy.

"I knew it. You did, you devil. You had better make an honest woman of her or I shall call you out. She is as good as a sister to me."

"I will ask her when everyone's gone. That celebration is too personal."

"She is not leaving then? She said she was returning to London."

Robert smiled at his brother, convinced. "She'll not leave."

When Robert quietly opened the door of Jane's bedchamber later, it was almost one in the morning. The house had taken hours to settle, but the comments made by Ellen and Edward had made Robert more discreet. He'd not spoken to Jane all day, unwilling to draw any further speculation, and aware Pembroke was watching her. That had seemed to unsettle Jane enough. She'd spent most of the day silent, hiding amidst a crowd.

Robert shut the door carefully and whispered her name. The room was flooded with moonlight. She did not respond. She was in bed, and all he heard were her steady, slow breaths. She lay on her stomach, sleeping, naked in the heavy, humid air of the hot summer night.

He felt as though his heart stilled.

The single sheet covering her had slipped to the hollow of her back, and her dark hair splayed over the white cotton of the bed.

An owl hooted outside. Perhaps one of those they'd heard last night. She'd left the sash window a little down, but there was no draught. The night air was too dense with heat.

Robert let his silk dressing gown slide to the floor, lifted the sheet, lay beside her, and drew her close. She didn't stir. He kissed her hair, his arms about her as he moulded his body to hers and breathed in her familiar scent. Then he drifted into sleep, content to just lie beside her.

~

Jane woke to the sound of lashing rain. She'd left the sash window down for air, but it had been so warm and heavy, there had been no draught. Now, though, a stiff breeze kicked the curtains, making them fly out like flags as she heard rain hammering hard against the windowpanes and pound on the dry ground outside. The drought had broken. She could smell the vegetation soaking it up. A deep rumble of thunder echoed outside.

She moved to sit up, but a weight lay across her stomach. An arm? She looked back. *Robert's.* He lay behind her, with one arm about her and the other beneath the pillow. The cotton sheet fell slack across his hip. Jane sat upright and his arm slid down.

A flash of lightning illuminated the room. It was followed by a sharp growl of thunder which shook the house and made the window rattle in its mount. Robert sighed in his sleep and rolled to his back, his free arm lifting and lying above his head.

Another flash of lightning spiked a light over his features. Jane turned to face him and lay back down. She swept the lock of hair from his brow then her fingers followed his jaw. Robert. She'd thought he would seek her out at some point in the day for a private conversation. In the morning, he'd kept looking at her, but by the afternoon, he'd held back as though he did not wish to draw attention to her.

The Duke of Pembroke, Ellen's father, had stared all day, too.

He had attended one of Hector's house parties a few years ago. Hector had made much of it because Pembroke had a higher standing in the House of Lords. Hector had gloated and thought it a real coup to have such a man join his gaming soirées.

But Pembroke had not been happy when he'd discovered the perversity and viciousness Hector favoured for his games. Dog fighting was one of Hector's preferred entertainments, as well as baiting.

She could still remember the Duke of Pembroke's look of disdain for both the company and the entertainment.

He chose to leave when Hector began his favourite game: flaunting his pretty young wife and baiting his peers.

He'd liked to make her appear available, when, in truth, he'd never let it go that far.

Jane had rejoiced in the Duke's desertion at the time, pleased Hector had lost in something.

She dare not contemplate what Pembroke thought of her now. His attention had been unnerving, although her mind had been occupied by other thoughts, *of Robert*.

Casting the Duke of Pembroke from her mind, her fingers slipped beneath the sheet and explored the contours of Robert's naked body.

Lightning flashed outside, and, this time, the crack of thunder rang instantaneously, as though the house itself had been hit. It was an angry storm, but its violence, the sound and smell of rain and the sweep of cold air through the open window, was stimulating. She felt alive.

She kissed Robert's shoulder and felt the sinewy lines and furrows of his torso.

All day, she'd walked about in another world, half in the thrall of the sensual knowledge he'd taught her; her stomach and the place between her thighs whispering an ache which constantly told her she was no longer a virgin and she may, even now, be with child. A child? The thought made her heart ache.

The rain gained in intensity.

Jane felt the part of him which had invaded her last night,

lying limp in repose. It stirred, changing in density, disproving his claims. He did not need to be in control. He could become aroused even while asleep.

Another flash of light illuminated the chamber, and the thunder came on the back of it.

Cool air caressed Jane's skin as a sharp breeze swept through the window.

Growing bolder, Jane slid down the bed.

He'd used his mouth on her in London. It seemed only natural a woman could do the same for a man.

A groan left his throat, and his hip jerked.

She glanced at his face, but he'd not woken. She moved to kneel astride one of his legs and returned to her task to see how far he could go without control.

A deeper groan erupted from his throat, and the lightning flashed, followed a moment later by a clap of thunder.

His fingers slipped into her hair and he pressed into her mouth as his hips lifted and he swore in a foreign language before he said, "*Jane*," in a voice which sounded pained.

She did not stop. She could tell he liked it, as she'd liked what he'd done to her.

A sound left his throat almost like a whimper.

He threw the sheet off her back as another flash of light filled the room, vividly illuminating her love play. His groan became a growl, his fingers clinging in her hair, and he pressed her down as his hips pressed up.

"Sweetheart," he said breathlessly.

The lightning brightened the room for another instant, and the thunder was now a few minutes behind it, but the rain seemed to strike the window like pins pattering against it.

The accompaniment of nature's symphony gave her an inhuman feeling as she played master to him and felt the power of it.

Robert's hips kicked, and he clasped her scalp.

She liked having this effect on him, and, as she learned the things he liked best, his fingers began clasping then releasing in her hair while his hips pressed up and fell back.

She understood what he'd meant about being in control now. She was observant and aware so he could simply enjoy. But she ached with arousal, too – from the pleasure of pleasing him.

Another flash of lightning struck overhead and shook the windowpanes. In the same moment, his fingers clawed and a ragged cry left his throat as he pressed into her mouth.

It was over.

Suddenly, his hands gripped her shoulders, drew her up then tumbled her back onto the bed. His kiss was urgent. It burned with gratitude.

When he ceased, he left her panting and lay beside her, his head resting in his palm, his weight on one crooked arm.

Lightning struck again, highlighting his face and his gentle smile.

"Jane," he whispered as his free hand cradled her cheek, "what on earth were you about? Duchesses do not do such things, darling."

"Did you not like it?" Had she done something wrong?

He leaned and kissed her lips in a brief caress then said against them, "I liked it. *Immensely.*"

She smiled. He kissed her cheek, then her chin, and her neck. "Why didn't you wake me?" she said to the air.

He pulled away. "I tried, sweetheart."

"I didn't know you'd come."

"I'm surprised you would doubt it." His gaze fell, and his fingers traced a path over her breast and circled her nipple.

A sharp, delicious spasm caught in her stomach and her body arched. The lightning flashed again. His eyes returned to hers, and she saw his predatory hunger there, the wolf howling to the moonlight.

"You never spoke to me all day," she whispered.

"Because, my dear, each time I tried, you blushed. I did not think you would wish it to be obvious." His fingers slipped lower and circled her navel.

"I couldn't stop thinking of you."

"And I you."

Another flash of lightning lit up his handsome face. She fought to preserve it in memory as her fingers gripped the back of his head and pulled him down while his fingers slipped between her thighs. "Know that I love you," she said to his lips, her heart bursting.

He pressed one long kiss on her mouth then moved lower and kissed her breast.

She sighed and arched, stretching, cat-like, her arms reaching above her head, and saw the letter from Violet's solicitor, which Meg had brought up earlier, discarded on the bedside table. Jane did not wish to think of the future, not now, not for one more night. In the morning she would, but she wanted just one more night with Robert. She gave herself up to his adoration.

~

Daylight shone through the window when Jane woke, as though the storm had never happened. Robert was gone. The only evidence left of his presence was the dent in the pillow where his head had lain, and the subtle smell of sex in the sheets. Jane smelled the pillow, breathing in his scent. He used rosemary in his hair wash.

Through the window, she heard the hounds barking in the courtyard on the other side of the house.

She realised, suddenly, it must be Robert. He must be there, about to ride out with the hounds.

Jane smiled and stretched, then remembered her letter. She

rolled over, picked it up, and slipped her fingernail beneath the wax seal. There were two letters, one from the solicitor and a second smaller sealed piece of paper which bore Joshua's brash scrawl.

Her heart beating harder, Jane sat up and read the solicitor's precise script first. The query he'd identified had been addressed. There was nothing more he could do. It looked, he said, very much as though the will would be overturned and the proceeds awarded to Joshua, in which case, Jane must return everything. Her fingers shook as she picked up Joshua's letter. It would place her in his debt. It was what Hector had intended all along, to tie her to his son.

Her thumb broke open Joshua's letter, and her eyes skimmed across his words. Threats, all of it. What he would do if she did not comply. How he intended to break her. But worse still, how he intended breaking anyone she hid behind. Violet and Robert were named, with reference to their financial affairs and the possibility of accidents which may befall them. The letter slipped from Jane's fingers and fell to the floor. Her hand covered her mouth as it trembled.

Outside, the hounds barked and whined for Robert's attention.

She had to go to him, be with him. It might be the last opportunity they had to be alone.

She rose in a rush, found her habit, then fought to dress alone. Calling Meg would just delay, and Robert would be gone. At least the buttons were at the front.

Moments later, Jane raced downstairs, her hair in a loose chignon secured roughly with several pins and her hat left behind. She leapt from the bottom step, her fingers gripping the newel post, and swung about it, rushing towards the door to the front courtyard. She was breathless when she reached it, her chest heaving, but the cobbles were still damp, so she had to slow her pace. Her quarry was there, checking the girth strap of his saddle. Early morning sunshine shone above them, silhouetting the ancient keep at the heart of the house against a blue sky.

"Robert! Can I come?" she called as her feet struck the cobbles in a steady rhythm, her legs slashing at her skirt.

The hounds strolled over to greet her with their measured strides, yet their tails whipped from side to side, expressing pleasure and a hope to be stroked.

Robert straightened as he looked back and smiled, his appreciation blatantly written in his eyes. He was so handsome. She smiled, too. She couldn't not. She loved him so much.

But then she noticed the groom watching, and realised how imprudent they were being. If the servants hadn't been certain before, she had just given them another sign there was something between the Earl and her.

"Hello, sweetheart," he said in a low drawl as she approached, his gaze skimming over her habit with a look of hunger.

"Good morning. May I come with you? Do you mind?" Her eyes darted to the groom, to tell Robert to cease using endearments.

He merely cast her a wicked smiled and said, "Heavens, darling, why would I mind? I love your company."

She widened her eyes in another warning.

Robert turned away. "James, run about to the stables and have them saddle up a mare for Her Grace."

As the groom obeyed with a quick tilt of his cap, Robert looked back at her and said loudly, "Did you sleep well, Your Grace?"

Oh, the rogue.

"More than well," she answered, feeling a blush.

"I did not." His eyes glinted impishly. "I was disturbed."

Her mouth opened, though heaven knew what she should say to that. She shut it again, in no state to fence with him in his rakehell mood.

"The thunderstorm," he enthused, "was extremely disturbing,

but in a very invigorating way, I suppose."

"Oh, the thunderstorm."

He bent to whisper as the groom reached the edge of the court-yard just beyond the raised portcullis and headed in the direction of the stables. "Yes, darling, *the thunderstorm*."

"I wish you would not tease," she answered as he pulled away and patted his stallion with one hand while his other held the animal's reins. The hounds wandered anxiously in circles, waiting for their chance to run.

"Do you now?" he said, not looking back. "Well, I would make a good guess you are out of luck. Sorry, love, but this is me, faults, foibles, and all."

Oh, she loved him, faults, foibles, and all, regardless. It was an unbearable pain today. How could she leave? But she had to. Joshua had threatened him, too.

"Well, *you*," she whispered a little breathlessly. "I would like to ride out to the abbey ruins. May we?"

"*The ruins?*" She had his attention again and met his questioning gaze. She refused to answer that look, not yet, not for as long as possible.

Of course, he must know it was a sentimental trip. The ruins bordered his property and what had once been her father's. It was one of the places they used to meet. She longed to preserve new memories there. If she must leave him, at least let her have one more memory to hold on to. "You do not mind?"

"It's a long ride for a morning's outing. I cannot take the hounds if we go so far."

"I know, but I have not been there for so long. I just – I want to see it again. May we?"

His gloved fingers lifted her chin then touched her cheek, communicating something he didn't speak. They dropped as his groom shouted and horseshoes rung on the cobble.

Robert looked over his shoulder. "James, you'll have to give the hounds a run. We're going too far out."

"Aye, my Lord," the first groom answered with a tug of his forelock as another led a mare into the courtyard.

The second man held the collars of the hounds as they yelped and complained, while Robert bent to check the girth strap, tugging it to be sure it was tight. Then he straightened and slapped the animal's flank before turning back to Jane. "Come on then. Let's get you up."

He made a step for her, as he'd always done, then turned to his own mount, and lifted easily into the saddle.

"Come on," he said, tapping his heels, to walk the horse on. The hounds began barking in chorus behind them. Both grooms held the dogs between them as they strained to be free; they did not appreciate being left behind.

"I think I am unpopular," Jane said to Robert's back.

Robert tossed her a smile over his shoulder. "They'll have their run. Just not with me. But we can give the horses a good stretch in any case. Let's blow away the cobwebs."

"I'd like that. You'll have to lead though. I've never ridden from Farnborough to the ruins."

He rose into a trot and glanced sideways as she drew level. "Whereas I could ride it in my sleep."

She nodded sharply as pain struck her breast. She was going to hurt him soon. This would be their last ride together, and that was why she wished to go to the ruins. It seemed to her to be the right place to say goodbye.

Robert kicked into a steady canter, the gravel crunching beneath the stallion's stride.

Jane followed.

Once past the formal gardens, he pulled the rein to the right, turning off the drive and into an open meadow where the deer herd grazed. Then he caught her out and spun his stallion instead of riding on.

She halted her mare.

"Now that we are out of sight," he said, leaning towards her, bracing her nape and lifting off his saddle – then he kissed her, open-mouthed.

She was breathless when he pulled away, and her body was wobbling aspic again.

He gave her a rakish smile then turned his horse.

She had to leave him. She had to.

For the first time since she'd asked him to take her on to the lake, she regretted her decision. Yesterday, she'd lived on a cloud. Today, she'd toppled back to earth. She knew she had to do this.

"Is something wrong?" he called back when she hadn't followed. His smile had fallen, and his dark eyes clearly sought to fathom her expression, sensing some change in her.

She shook her head. "No." She couldn't say it yet. It was suddenly very important to her that they reached the ruins. There, where they had first fallen in love, she would feel better and be strong enough to speak. She forced a smile.

"Hurry then," he called, leading on to a path running into the woods.

She kicked into a canter, passed him, and urged the mare into a gallop. Wind caught at her skirt and her hair, freeing wisps from the pins, and Robert's stallion thundered past as he gave the animal its head, riding low in the saddle.

They raced on through the grass avenue leading through the woods then out into open grassland. The animals' hooves pounded on the moist ground with dense thuds. Their pace was reckless on the slippery grass, but neither she nor Robert had ever cared for reserve when it came to riding.

She felt so many things, exhilarated, in love, happy, and

desperately sad, all at once, as they reached the gate at the edge of the parkland. She felt like leaping from the saddle and clinging to Robert as he leaned to release the gate and held it for her to walk her mare through. She did not wish to leave, but what else could she do? Once he'd come through, he re-secured it behind them.

The track they'd joined led them past some of the farm cottages, which meant they must ride at a more sedate trot. Robert acknowledged his tenants, lifting his hand.

"Lord Barrington! M'lord," one man called, beckoning Robert as he leaned on a garden wall. Jane had to stop, too, and keep her mare steady. She could hardly ride on while Robert spoke to the man. They discussed the harvest and the impact of both the drought and last night's storm, which had knocked down the ripe wheat.

It was a testimony to show her she was making the right choice. They were no longer young. Robert had responsibilities. People relied on him. She could not entangle Robert in the Suttons' games.

Robert called to her then introduced his tenant.

She blushed when he gave her name.

He'd spoken as though she was his future. There could be no fairy-tale ending. Happily-ever-after had never been her fate. That hope had died years before when Robert had ridden away and left her alone.

"Your Grace?" Robert called her thoughts back to the conversation. "Samuels was saying he remembers your parents fondly. He was offering condolences."

Her attention focused back on Robert, and her heart ached and burned with bitterness and anger.

When she faced the farmer, she saw speculation in his eyes. She was out riding alone with Robert, after all, and staying with him.

"Forgive me, Mr. Samuels. My thoughts were elsewhere for a moment. Thank you for your concern." Her voice was stiff. *But it was a long time ago and I have no fondness left for them.*

"I used to work on a farm for y'ur father, Y'ur Grace. 'E was a good man, was 'is Lordship. 'Tis a shame 'e had no son."

Jane's heart thumped as the man waited for her answer, his hand on the wall.

Behind him, Jane saw a cockerel in pursuit of a hen, strutting across the small yard. Its neck craned as it crowed.

She opened her mouth to speak, but nothing came out.

Her father had locked her prison cell. "*A shame he had no son.*" Had she been a boy, she would have inherited. Certainly, she could not have been forced into marriage.

Oh, she was in a melodramatic mood today, but she didn't care. What befell her father and his property was her father's fault. And she could not regret that she'd not borne a son. What she'd done with Robert had been beautiful. It would have been foul with Hector. Thank God he'd held that opportunity from her.

And as for her father, she had seen neither of her parents after she'd married. She'd always wondered if they'd regretted what they'd done. She hoped they'd been tormented by it.

Jane shook her head and felt her expression turn cold as she stammered out, "Th... thank you. I... It is a... A shame. Forgive me. My Lord, we should be going." The last was said to Robert as she yanked her mare's rein and turned. The animal whinnied in reproof of the sharp tug on the bit in its mouth. Jane kicked into a trot without waiting for Robert's answer.

"Your Grace," she heard the man say behind her before Robert took his leave.

"Whoa! What is it?" He called forward, over the clip-clop of horseshoes as they left the labourers' cottages behind. "Wait!"

She did not slow.

"Jane! Wait! Walk a while, will you?" he said, grasping her reins as he reached her, and forcing her mare to slow. "Pray, tell me. What happened back there, for Samuels and I are in the dark?"

257

He spoke with the mocking pitch he'd used in London.

"I hardly care." She glared at him, casting on him all the bitter, impotent anger which belonged to her father and the Dukes of Sutton.

"Sweetheart," he urged quietly, his fingers gripping her hand instead of her reins. "What is it? What's wrong?"

"Nothing."

"Nothing?" He laughed. "Then you are not the girl I remember. Becoming a duchess made you arrogant, Jane. I've never seen you address anyone so bluntly in my life."

She tried to tug her hand free, but he refused to let go, and she refused to answer.

"Tell me?" he asked, cajoling.

"Tell you what, that I have no love for a man who would barter his daughter for a title, and certainly no sympathy for him losing his lands? He sold me to Hector."

Robert let her reins go and sat back as if her words had struck him like a physical blow.

"I don't know what I'm doing here," Jane concluded, meeting his gaze. "I should not have come. I'm sorry, Robert, it was a mistake."

"Whoa," he said, gripping her reins again. "I am nothing to do with your father, or Sutton?"

Angry and tired of fighting, of surviving, Jane just looked at him. *You walked away. You turned your back on me.* The words were left unspoken. "I was going to tell you at the abbey—"

His eyes narrowed. "Then tell me there." His voice was a harsh whisper suddenly, then he let her reins go and jerked his stallion away. In a moment, he was galloping ahead of her.

She followed.

He took an irresponsible jump over the wall at the bend in the road.

She jumped it, mere feet behind him. Then his stallion kicked turf up before her through fields full of livestock, scattering sheep.

When they reached the stream, his stallion surged ahead and jumped to the opposite bank.

Her mare slowed and walked tentatively through the water.

Robert disappeared from view.

Jane pressed on and saw the abbey ruins rising towards the sky beyond the hedge. When she reached them, she found his stallion grazing, and Robert nowhere in sight. She dismounted, dropping to the ground.

"You are going back then?" He stood behind her. "With no thought to discuss the decision with me."

Jane turned around and left the mare to graze.

He was leaning in a doorway of the ruin, his shoulder to the stone, his arms folded over his chest.

She had to face this conversation. It was her fault it was harder. She had given in to need the other night, not him. She owed him the opportunity to have his say now. "I told you two days ago I thought I should."

"Yes, well, a lot has happened since then." He stood straight.

She turned and walked on, following the outer wall which towered above them. Some of it was coarse stone, but in some places the ornately carved frontage survived. The hem of her skirt began to darken in the damp grass.

"Had I known the decision was already final, it would not have," he said, beside her now, matching her pace.

She glanced sideways, only to be stilled as his hand gripped her elbow.

"Have I done something wrong?"

She pulled her arm loose, facing him and stepping back. "No, it is not you."

"Not me?" His eyes were narrow and challenging. "Why go back then?"

259

Jane breathed deeply. "Robert, I have to sort things out with Joshua. I cannot keep hiding here."

Robert didn't move. He just watched her. "Do you wish me to come with you? Can I help you?"

"No." He could not come. He would end up hurt, by Joshua, or in fighting Joshua. She had to let him go.

She walked on again.

She didn't hear him follow, but refused to look back and let him see the tears which burned in her eyes. When she reached the gap where another side door had once stood, she walked through and crossed the raised floor which had been the chancel. Walking to the end of the ruin, she looked out onto the long dale. The hill beyond was the border of what had been her father's lands.

Her arms folded across her chest and her fingers gripped her elbows. Sad and happy feelings tangled up inside her.

She finally knew everything there was to know of Robert, and she was leaving him.

"I don't understand," Robert growled behind her, clearly wounded. "Why did you give me your virginity if you intended to leave?"

She turned and her arms fell to her sides. "Why not?"

She could see the pain in his eyes as he came nearer.

Her anger was washed away suddenly, by the memories of this place, of him when they'd been young. She'd been happy then.

His fingers braced her waist. "There are a hundred reasons why not. You've kept hold of it for a long time, Jane." One hand cupped her chin. "I thought you'd chosen me. I thought it a permanent thing. I was about to offer you marriage *again*. But you still do not want me, do you? What do you wish me to do, beg you to stay?" His voice, his eyes, and his touch, all unnerved her.

"Robert, I don't mean to hurt you. But this is the right thing to do."

"*The right thing? To break me?*" He looked upward and the hand cradling her jaw fell.

She gripped his upper arms. "I'm sorry, Robert. I do not regret it. I love you, but I cannot stay."

His head dropped, and his gaze snared hers again. "Not can't, Jane. Won't. Marry me, and Sutton can go to hell. Let him have his father's fortune. I am hardly going to let you starve. I will support you. Cease being greedy, Jane."

"*Cannot*, not will not, Robert," she answered on a whisper, refusing to debate it. She would not tell him it was for his own good. No man wished to think a woman protected him.

He didn't protest. Instead, his hand slipped to the small of her back and jerked her against him. The action was fierce. Then his lips were on hers, and the fire flared between them. Memories of yesteryear were cast aside by the heated, sensual images of the last two nights.

The base of the ruined wall pressed into her thighs as he leaned her against it and began raising her skirt.

"You're mine," he said as the heavy fabric slid up her thighs. He gripped her bare flesh and lifted her on to the wall, parting her legs about his hips.

She should say no. She should. But she could not. She was desperate to know him one last time.

"I want to be in you."

She nodded. She couldn't speak. This was a foolish thing to do.

His flap was undone in a moment, and her skirt was bunched to her waist between them. Her bottom pressed uncomfortably on the rough stone as he kissed her violently again and filled her with an unbearable passion. She gripped his shoulders and held on against the vicious determination and pain with which he loved her. It was all so quick, raw and desperate. There was no art in it. It was base instinct. She had wanted to make him lose control.

261

She had achieved it. But not through loving him. She didn't like it. She felt him purging himself of her. But she would bear the coldness of his last embrace if it eased him and let him exorcise his soul and wipe her from his memory.

He gripped behind her knees and she held his hips as he moved. Oh, she would still break, even to this savagery. Oh. Her body jerked with each stroke, the stone cutting into her bottom.

His eyes were fixed on hers. She clung to his neck and his shoulder when she splintered into breathless abandon. He gritted his teeth, and she panted and moaned at the impact of his crude thrusts.

Then he said, "Jane, darling, don't go," as he neared the end.

"Robert," she said, her fingers running through his hair as his brow fell to her shoulder once he was spent. She heard him breathing steadily. His body remained still. "I have to," she whispered.

A dreadful recognition dropped inside her, falling like lead. Sex was not just his paintbrush, it was his sword. It was how he'd coped with her loss before. It was how he defended himself against hurt.

His head lifted. "And if you are with child?"

"I will worry about that when it happens," she whispered in answer. "But I promise I will tell you."

There was an odd look in his eyes. They had hardened, shutting her out as they'd done that first night in London, but they also glimmered with fluid.

"And if you are not?" he answered, his voice cracking as he drew away from her and secured his clothing. "Will I hear from you then? Is this an affair, or just a brief liaison, Jane?"

She sighed, and her fingers touched his clean-shaven cheek. "I don't know what this was. It was just the two us. Do you not see? Just because we should have always been us."

"You love me. You have said so." There was pain in his voice.

"You say we should have always been together. You say my house, when I am here, is the only place you have ever considered home. And yet, you will not stay. Forgive me for my ignorance, Jane, *but no*, I do not see at all. Why are you going?"

"Robert—"

"Robert, leave me alone? Robert, stay with me? Or Robert, make love to me?" His words were cutting. "Please, do not tell me this was your friend's idea to teach me a lesson?"

"Do not be ridiculous!" The flat of her palm struck his chest. He stepped back. She slipped painfully off the wall.

"Whether it was or not, you can congratulate yourself. You have succeeded, Jane. I give up." His hands lifted in a gesture of helplessness as he held her gaze, and then suddenly, his eyes disengaged, and he turned and began walking away. "Fight your bloody fight with Sutton then!" he yelled to the air.

She followed, her heart thumping, trying to catch up with him as he passed back through the gap in the wall.

"If the money is so important to you!" he shouted, when he reached his stallion without looking back. "Have it and not me!"

"It is not the money!" she shouted in return as he set his foot in the stirrup and swung up into the saddle.

He turned the stallion to face her as she reached her mare. His gaze was hard, the man behind it invisible. "Forgive me, Jane, if I do not find the time to say goodbye." With those cold, cutting words, he turned the stallion and rode away, pushing into a gallop, leaving her standing just as he'd done years ago.

Chapter Sixteen

Her heart was empty, but her mind was engaged in packing, and she refused to contemplate what she was leaving behind or what would happen now.

"Be careful with that," she called to Meg as her maid folded one of her evening gowns.

"You're leaving then?"

Jane looked up. Edward stood at the open door of her bedchamber. His words were inquiring, but his pitch accused. Her heart thundered. "I have to."

"Robert has gone to Forth's."

She blushed, and a lump caught in her throat, but she refused to cry. She nodded and looked back at her maid. "That will do for now, Meg. Please fetch me some tea."

When Jane looked back once Meg had left, Edward had taken a couple of steps into the room. He watched her intently. "I was wrong."

"About what?" she queried, her hands clasping at her waist.

"Robert is not callous."

"I know, Edward," she answered, turning away to pick up a pair of gloves from the bed, unwilling to face this conversation.

"He is in love with you."

Jane dropped the gloves into a trunk and looked back. "I know,

264

Edward, but I cannot stay."

"Why, because you do not trust him? If it was what I said in London, Jane, he has explained it all to me now. Father sent Robert abroad after he dropped out of Oxford, because he was on a course of self-destruction. He stayed abroad because of your marriage." Edward came closer and touched her arm. "He could not bear to even be in the same country because he loved you, and you were married to another man."

Jane made a face. "And we both know he was a monk for all those years." She turned away and collected her silver hairbrush, comb, and mirror, then put them in her portmanteau. She'd worked all that out days ago and had begun to understand the myriad of emotions Robert Marlow hid behind his rakehell shield, but her choice could not change.

"You were married, Jane. Did you expect him to wait?"

"I expected nothing," she answered, turning back to face Edward. "I'm sorry, but I cannot be the person he wants me to be, Edward. I have to go. I have no choice. I wish I could stay, but I can't."

"It is as Robert said then. You turned him down?"

"It is." She nodded, feeling the lump rise in her throat again.

"Is there nothing I may say to change your mind?"

"Nothing."

For a moment, he stood there, watching her with a perplexity that said he was still looking for a different answer. "You don't think you will regret this?"

Regret it? I shall spend the rest of my life mourning that it cannot be so, but as much as I am hurting Robert, Joshua can hurt him more. "Regret it or not, Edward, I have to go," she whispered earnestly.

He shook his head. "Come and say goodbye to Ellen and I before you leave. John and Mary-Rose will want to say their farewells, too." He came closer again and touched her arm once more.

She nodded, unable to speak for fear she'd cry.

He kissed her cheek. "You are still my surrogate sister, Jane," he said in a low voice as he pulled away. "If you ever need me..."

He turned and strode away then, but Jane called, "Edward." He looked back. "You will keep an eye on him, won't you?"

"I will, Jane. If nothing else, you've fixed things between the two of us which have been broken for years." He gave her a tender smile and left.

Jane sat on the edge of the bed and covered her face with her hands, giving in to her silent despair and tears.

~

Robert walked through the hall at Farnborough, his forearm wiping his brow, before rolling his shirtsleeves down. He'd come from the stables. His muscles cried out, complaining against the physically strenuous work of harvesting. He'd thrown himself into manual labour to distract his thoughts from Jane and joined his people in the fields each day. There was something very cathartic in taking a scythe to the wheat.

In just his shirt and breeches, sweaty and dusty, he was nothing of the London rake now. His fingers pulled the clinging, sweat-damp cotton from his chest. Archer's nose would lift in disgust when Robert reached his rooms, but at least there would be a bath waiting.

And then what? The hours of darkness were the worst, lonely hours of frustrated dreams and dark thoughts. He didn't like his own company. He'd concealed it for years by sharing the beds of women he could seduce and leave without a second thought. But after he'd physically known the woman he'd longed for and loved all his life, he had no appetite for casual encounters any more. His old life had soured.

He began climbing the stairs. She'd been gone for two weeks, and the lance of pain lodged through his chest was no less than when he'd left her at the ruins. He refused to let his mind dwell on whether or not there may be a child.

His fingers ran along the smooth polished wood of the banister. *Jane.* God help him, he had no idea how to go on from here.

"My Lord!" Davis called as Robert reached the landing.

He looked back. "Davis?" The butler was climbing the stairs, a letter in his hand.

"Forgive me, my Lord. This arrived for you. I did not like to send it out to the fields."

Robert took the letter. He must have walked past it in the hall. Davis bowed and excused himself.

Gripping it between finger and thumb and tapping it against the palm of his other hand, Robert strode on.

Archer was in Robert's chamber and instantly assessed Robert with a critical scowl as Robert threw the letter on the bed and stripped off his shirt.

"I am sorry, my Lord. I hope you do not mind but I must say it. You are letting yourself go, sir."

"Archer." Robert shot the man a quelling look. "You know damn well I do mind, so keep quiet. I cannot see anyone here who cares. Is my bath prepared?"

"Yes, my Lord—" His valet snapped, about to say more, but Robert lifted a hand.

"Leave me then. I've no patience for your chiding. I'm too bloody tired."

"My Lord," the man conceded with a bow, still sounding irritated. "As you wish."

Perhaps Robert *was* falling to pieces, but what did anything matter any more?

He sighed and continued undressing, then caught his reflection in the mirror. He'd not shaven in days, and his hair was sweaty and clung to his head. He did look awful. Yet the man in the mirror only matched the raw, wounded animal inside him. He felt numb and he cared for nothing, least of all, his appearance.

Stripped to just his breeches, Robert picked up the letter. It was from Sparks. Geoff was not normally on corresponding terms with Robert when he was out of town. Robert's thumb broke the seal, and his eyes skimmed over the words, not really reading. He saw Jane's name and started at the beginning again.

Geoff wrote as though Jane was at Farnborough. He said to warn her about Sutton. A spasm clutched at Robert's heart. She'd said she was going to London, so why would Geoff think she was here? Surely Jane should be with Violet? But if Jane was, then Geoff would know.

Robert sat on the edge of the bed. His eyes scanned the letter again. Something wasn't right. Something was, in fact, dreadfully wrong. Cold, dense fear gripped his stomach.

He threw the letter aside and rose, unable to cope with it. She'd left. She'd chosen to go. She wasn't his responsibility, and that was her choice.

Every muscle in his body aching, Robert finished stripping then walked to the decanter. His stomach growled with hunger, but he ignored it, tipping brandy into a glass. He took it with him to the brass tub, stepped into the water, and sank down, submerging his body up to his chest and resting his elbows on the tub's edge. He sipped the brandy then rested the glass on the tub's rim, clasped in his hand. He laid his head back and shut his eyes. The warmth of the water seeped into his bones.

Jane. He thought of her beautiful face, her almond-shaped, dark-rimmed, emerald eyes and felt the image calm him, relax him.

"My Lord?"

Robert's body lurched, swilling water over the edge of the tub on to the floor as his eyes opened. His mind was stunned, and his breath stuck in his throat as his heart pounded. In his dream, he'd been on that street, watching Sutton strike her, and it had been so real, he'd almost felt the blow himself. His vision returned to his dressing room and looked at the glass still gripped in his hand.

"Forgive me, my Lord. You shouted. I..." Archer ceased speaking, but kept walking towards Robert. He had the oddest look on his face.

"I don't need you. Get out!" Robert said impatiently.

"My Lord." The man's eyes said it all. He thought Robert was losing his mind.

"Just give me that letter on the bed, Archer, and go."

"Sir, I think you should eat."

"Archer, I do not need a nursemaid. Just send up some bread and cheese. I'm in no mood for dinner."

"My Lord."

Archer's concern was irritating. Robert did not need a bloody keeper, yet he knew he ought to appreciate it. Archer was under no obligation to show concern. He picked up the letter, brought it to Robert, and passed it into Robert's outstretched hand. Then, with a sharp nod and a pathetically insulting bow, Archer turned and left.

Taking another sip of brandy, Robert read the letter again. Geoff said Sutton's behaviour had become erratic. He'd been bragging about his ability to control his father's widow in White's. Geoff urged Robert to keep Jane in the country. He also said Sutton had overturned the will, and Jane must hand everything back. Geoff feared Sutton would not be satisfied with just the money.

There was no date on the letter. Robert turned it over. A date was scrawled in the corner over the address. It was dated less than a week ago. Could Jane have taken that long to return to Town? Perhaps she'd taken a detour. Robert let the letter fall to the floor

269

and sipped the brandy. He saw a vivid picture of Sutton striking her. Angry, he downed the brandy, set the glass on the floor, and ducked his head beneath the water.

He couldn't ignore it, no matter how much he wished to. Concern for the woman lodged inside him. He would never forgive himself if anything happened to her and he did not go. "*You were always rescuing me.*" He had always felt a need to protect her, even before he'd fallen in love. Now it was simply instinct.

At least Archer would be happy when Robert shaved.

~

Seven days later, Robert stood before a bay window in White's and looked down on the street, his hands clasped behind his back. White's had always been a retreat, a place where he could recoup from the concerns of life. Perhaps it was the masculine scents of tobacco, leather, and brandy which eased him. They reminded Robert of his father's office. Yet today, the quiet male conversation and heavy scents did nothing to restore Robert's natural air of calm.

He'd been waiting half an hour for Geoff.

Sutton wasn't in London.

Neither was Jane.

Apparently, Sutton had taken his wife and children into the country. It was not unusual for the time of year. The season was over. Most of the aristocracy had fled the city's stale air.

"Barrington."

Robert turned. It was Ellen's father, Pembroke. He was not a man Robert expected to see in London at this time of year. Nor would he have expected Pembroke to acknowledge *him*.

"Your Grace." Robert bowed, but not deeply.

"You seem distracted, Barrington," the Duke said, studying Robert with his arrogant, silver-eyed gaze.

Robert took a breath, but gave no answer. He had nothing to say to Pembroke.

If only Robert knew where Jane was, he would feel better. He felt jumpy and unable to relax until he did. He'd hardly slept since she'd left Farnborough, yet he did not feel tired.

Pembroke continued "I have had my man research your future wife."

Robert's eyes widened at the audacity, but in an odd way he wished to laugh. There was not a hope-in-hell's chance Jane would ever be his wife. Pembroke had wasted his time and money. But then, the pain of Jane's loss swept in again, and Robert felt bitter. "I do not want to hear it," he growled, scowling and moving past Pembroke. The man caught Robert's arm.

"Hear me out, Barrington. You will not dislike it. I did it to protect my heir. I do not want the boy corrupted."

Robert glowered and yanked his arm free. He knew the price Pembroke placed on protecting his heir. Previously, Pembroke's daughter had borne the greatest cost. Yet perhaps Pembroke knew where Jane was.

An ache in his chest, Robert chose to relent, but it felt like betrayal to publicly interfere in Jane's affairs. "Well?" he pressed impatiently.

Pembroke did not speak, so Robert pushed again. "Tell me, Your Grace, if you must, but pray, do so promptly. I am due to meet a friend."

"I misunderstood what I saw when the late Duke of Sutton was alive, Barrington. I owe her an apology."

The man could have punched Robert in the face and he would not have been more shocked. Pembroke did not apologise lightly.

"Will you take a drink with me? I ordered port."

Stunned, Robert nodded. They occupied two leather wing-chairs in the bay window.

"If you were wrong, then what can you have to tell me, Your Grace?" Robert posed, leaning forward, a hand resting on one knee. Pembroke leaned back, relaxed, and arched one eyebrow.

The attendant arrived, and Robert waited, anxious and irritable, as the port was poured.

Once the attendant had gone, Robert urged sharply, "Tell me what you know, Your Grace?"

Pembroke laughed. It was a deep resonant sound. "*Patience* is a virtue, Barrington."

Impatient, Robert answered, "It is not a virtue I have time for." But despite his words Robert sat back, his hands gripping the chair's arms, rigidly holding himself in check.

"Very well. I discovered the Dowager Duchess was not a willing party in Sutton's amusements."

"Amusements?" Robert scowled.

"The late Duke encouraged his guests to be, how shall I say, less than respectful to his wife. Apparently, Sutton took pleasure in tormenting her in other ways, too. He forbade her many things, riding, walking, and dancing, for instance. She had no freedom, I believe. My man also discovered that Sutton forced her father into debt to secure the match. I always thought the late Duke of Sutton odd, but now I wonder if he was mad. He kept her like a bird in a cage."

Robert rubbed his jaw, silent. He remembered the conversation he and Jane had had at Vauxhall. It was the only time she'd spoken of Sutton, "*and he certainly never did anything just to please me,*" she'd said.

"I will warn you, Barrington, my man thinks her inheritance is disputable. He believes the will a ploy to taunt the son. It is likely to be overturned if contested. It appears the late Duke of Sutton intends to keep his bird caged even from within his grave."

Robert's mind reeled. What if the son was as mad as the father?

What if Jane was with Sutton? "It has already been contested. He won. Do you know anything of the current Duke?"

Pembroke's expression turned sour. "He has a reputation for erratic behaviour and violence. He seems a man in the image of his father, inhuman."

Pembroke was hardly one to judge. He, too, had been inhuman for a time towards Ellen, although never violent, just cruel.

Robert drank his port with an urge to go, but go where?

"Robert!"

Geoff. Robert stood as Geoff crossed the room and lifted his hand.

"Excuse me, Pembroke," Robert said, looking back. Then he gave the man a stiff bow before adding, "Thank you for the information."

"You have not heard it all yet," Pembroke interjected. "My man heard the current Duke intends to obtain your fiancée as his mistress. I do not believe he intends to give her a choice. I thought you should know it. I am sure Sutton will not hesitate in disposing of any obstacles, Barrington."

Robert's eyes narrowed as suddenly the sum equalled four. But he had no intention of sharing his thoughts with Pembroke, yet he was grateful the man had spoken. Bowing again, more deeply, Robert said, "Thank you," once more. Then he turned away.

He had to find her.

"Remember, Barrington," Pembroke said behind him, "if there is any trouble, I do not wish my grandson caught up in it."

Robert glanced back. "I would not wish it either, Your Grace."

He crossed the room to meet Geoff. "Shall we find a coffeehouse? There are too many ears in here."

Geoff nodded.

Half an hour later, leaning over a coffee as black as treacle and with arms crossed on the tabletop, Robert looked at his friend. The

273

air in the little shop was thick with the aroma of roasted coffee, and tobacco smoke helped screen them from the other occupants. "Did Violet write to Jane's address in Bath?"

"Yes. The letter was returned saying Jane's tenancy had terminated. The house has been closed up. Her butler answered and asked after her. Apparently, he thought it odd. Violet said he'd followed Jane from the late Duke's household. There is no word on Sutton?"

"He's gone to Berkshire." Why would Jane leave herself no property to return to? It was odd. Unless she'd gone into hiding somewhere.

"Safely out of the way then."

Robert's fingers rubbed his jaw. "Pembroke just shared some tales I'd sooner not have heard. What does Violet know of Jane's marriage?"

"Very little, I think," Geoff set his coffee cup on its saucer, his eyes on Robert. "The old man was seriously ill at the point Vi met Jane. I believe they only spoke when he was incapacitated, and Vi would not betray Jane's trust to me, but she did mention Jane was very different in Bath. Vi said Jane was wary of censure from the old man. She is hardly outgoing, though. If Jane was more reserved, she must have been virtually silent."

"Oppressed," Robert stated.

"That was my assessment, yes."

"When did Violet's solicitor last hear from Jane? He can give me no leads?"

"None. The last communication was the letter he sent to your place."

An attendant passed with a pot of coffee, and Robert lifted his hand, beckoning for him to refill Geoff's cup. Robert hadn't known Jane had received a letter from the solicitor. She'd not said. Had that been the letter he'd given her?

Geoff waited until the waiter moved on then said, "Apparently, French enclosed a letter from Sutton, too. It had been delivered via Sutton's solicitor. I believe French wrote to inform Jane they'd lost."

"What was in the letter from Sutton?"

"Who knows? French did not open it. It was addressed to Jane."

Silent, Robert felt his heart thudding, and his gaze fell to his untouched coffee. Pembroke's words tumbled through his head, "*He forbade her many things…he kept her like a bird in a cage*". Robert remembered the night he'd seen Jane watching other people dance, when she'd still worn her blacks, longing to dance herself. "*A horse*," she'd asked at Farnborough, as though she'd claimed the crown jewels, and in town, she'd confided, "*I have not ridden in an age*." He could picture the bright light in her eyes every time they'd ridden. He thought of their last night, "*know that I love you*", of that last day at the ruins. Why had she let him make love to her when she was leaving? All these things just did not knit together.

An ominous thought struck him. What if Sutton's letter had summoned her back to her cage? But she'd escaped. Why would she go back? If Sutton had threatened her, why had she not spoken of it? Robert had offered to protect her!

"*I am sure Sutton will not hesitate in disposing of obstacles.*" Robert suddenly understood everything. Pembroke had implied Robert was an obstacle. That scene at Vauxhall came to mind – Sutton pressing Jane back against the stone. Had Robert been disposed of then?

"*I love you – but I cannot stay – cannot, not will not.*" Jane's words. *Good God!*

What if Sutton's threat was aimed at *him*? Would she have gone *for him*?

Was she protecting *him*?

The more Robert thought it, the more he believed it. Sutton was threatening her with what he could do to *him*.

The clever bloody bastard.

Sutton knew her far better than Robert ever did.

He'd spent years thinking her selfish when Jane's only fault was selflessness.

Her little outburst before his tenant had been Jane straining against the bit. She had not wanted to go.

If Robert had pressed, if he'd made her explain instead of losing his temper, he could have given her the power to break her bonds. But in the image of his behaviour years before, he'd ridden away.

No wonder she did not trust him.

Geoff nudged him. "What is it?"

Robert leaned back, feeling suddenly helpless. "Sutton has her; I'm certain of it. He threatened her, I think, with what he would do to me. I believe that was the content of his letter. Pembroke thinks the man's mad. He's also heard Sutton intends to force himself on Jane. Having seen him hit her, I would not be surprised if it is true. She's in danger."

"You are fond of her?" Geoff's gaze said he knew the answer.

"I have always been. I loved her when we were young, before she married. I failed her then. I'll not fail again. No other woman ever stood a chance. They've always been in her shadow."

Geoff's gaze filled with compassion. "My sister was right. I think you've even convinced Violet. I dare say Jane will believe you, too, when you find her."

A low growl of self-disgust slipped from Robert's throat. "I'm not certain. She proved the level of her faith in me by leaving Farnborough. She has no belief in me. If she did, Sutton's threats would have been worthless."

"Or perhaps she cares too much about you to take the risk."

Robert said nothing. It was only salt poured into the wound.

"At least, if you think she is with Sutton, you have your lead. He's gone to his estates, so follow him. Jane will either be there

276

or not. Either way, you need only sit it out in a nearby inn and wait until he leads you to her."

Robert nodded. He'd thought the same. He stood. "Thank you, Geoff," he acknowledged as his friend stood, too. They shook hands, and Robert gripped Geoff's tightly. "You will forgive me for my haste."

"Of course. You will keep Violet informed? She is beside herself with worry. Jane did not deserve the life she's had."

"No, and I intend to spend the rest of my life making up for it. Good day, Geoff. Tell Violet I shall write when I have news."

"May luck go with you, Robert."

~

Silent, sitting in the dark, occupying a threadbare armchair, Jane clutched her knees, tucked inside her skirt, and listened intently, waiting, wondering – terrified.

She didn't know the hour, but she could hear the clock ticking in the hall outside. It was a steady, unrelenting rhythm which matched her heartbeat.

Joshua was late. It must be well past midnight. Did it mean he wouldn't come tonight? She didn't imagine for one moment he'd given up his game.

Her eyelids were heavy and kept falling, but she dare not sleep. Forcing her eyes to stay open, she looked towards the dark shadows near the door. She'd pushed a chest before it.

Fear prickled in her nerves.

Hector had tormented her for years, but he'd never physically hurt her. Joshua had. He was sadistic, not simply cruel. She had good reason to fear him.

Robert slipped into her mind. He did so constantly. When she was most afraid, she sought refuge in halcyon memories of the summer. He was secure. That was a constant balm.

Then she heard it, the first heavy footfall in the hall. The ring of hardened leather heels on wood.

Silent, she gripped her knees harder to her chest, and her bare toes curled over the chair's rim. She was too afraid to even breathe.

Strike. Strike. The rhythmic steps grew nearer.

She was no fool. If Joshua wished to open it, he would. He was strong enough to push the chest aside. The barrier would simply buy her time to contemplate her fate.

Strike, strike.

There would be no point in crying out. No one would come. No one would help her here.

Her heart pounded.

She was in a third-floor room. There was no escape.

"Jane." His deep baritone stretched along the hall, heavy with threat, and she saw light break a crack above the door.

Strike, strike.

He was two steps away.

Strike, strike.

Her heart thumped harder as his footsteps stopped outside the door.

"So tempting." His voice resonated through the wooden door. His tormenting words reaching into the room. "Do you lie awake thinking of me, Jane?"

She jumped half out her skin and gasped when the door handle suddenly jolted, twisting sharply. He'd won again. He'd heard her cry out. He knew she was awake, and he knew she was afraid.

Deep, callous laughter echoed about the hall outside as he rattled the handle several times with no intention of coming in. He had the key. He was just tormenting her.

She clutched her stomach. Until this morning she had held on to the chance their might be a child within it. But now her courses had come and she knew there was not.

He walked on. She felt sick as she heard him go and she ached everywhere from the bruises of his violence. She had not tried to bar her door in the day because she'd needed food to stay alive in case there *was* a child.

He had held her by the throat this morning, and she'd thought she would die as he'd cut off her air. But then he'd let her go. That was when her courses had come. Now she was unsure whether it was best to be alive or dead.

His footsteps and laughter faded with the light. She could doze now, for a little while, but she would not dare lie down.

He'd played this game three dozen times, sometimes thrice in one night, deliberately disturbing her sleep.

In London, he'd said he would wait until she begged him to take her. Now she understood. He was torturing her until she would rather suffer rape than fear.

Chapter Seventeen

Robert paced back and forth across the courtyard of the small inn. He'd been evicted from the taproom, unable to simply sit. His heart raced with a galloping beat. It had done so for days now. He wondered, and not for the first time, just how much more of this he could take before he expired.

His boot heels struck the cobbles, and he turned and forged the same path back again. He had no outdoor coat on, and the day was cloudy and cold, but it didn't permeate his distracted senses. A breeze swept the dust up in a sudden eddy. Summer had departed, and autumn was on the way.

With a shudder that twisted his shoulders, he refused to think too far ahead.

James, Robert's groom, was established in Sutton's stables. Two days ago, James had gone there, cap in hand, seeking employment. It had gotten them access to the house. They'd tried more subtle investigations, interrogating the local populace with obscure questions about visitors who stayed with the Suttons. Robert had claimed to be an associate of the old Duke and wondered how his widow fared. Robert's staff had deployed various ruses, claiming to be former employees or staff of friends of the Dowager Duchess. But no matter the tack they took to question, no one had seen anything of Jane.

Robert hoped James had gleaned some knowledge of her. At least he must have seen when Sutton came and went. Sunday was normally a day the staff had time off. Robert had been waiting hours, believing James would come back to the inn.

As he turned to pace the yard again, Robert thought, thankfully, of the quickly scribbled note he'd passed to Jenkins to deliver to his man of business before leaving London. The special marriage licence he'd acquired had arrived this morning, four days after Robert had arrived. This time, Robert was not giving Jane a choice. When he got her away from Sutton, he would insist she accept his protection.

In the street beyond the courtyard, he heard the approach of a carriage, horses, the jangle of harness, the creak and roll of wheels. Shouts flooded the inn's courtyard, and grooms ran from the stables as a large mail coach rumbled beneath the arched entrance. Stable hands rushed to unharness the horses and replace the team. Robert stepped back out of the way and watched the driver jump down. The top was heaped with luggage, and two young men sat on top of it.

Robert sighed, his patience suddenly running dry.

A drop of rain struck his brow. He looked up and saw the gray cloud was now painted black.

Another spot of rain touched his face, then another his hair. He looked down and saw rain speckling the gray cobble.

His fingers swept back a lock of hair which had fallen forward over his brow. He would feel much better if he knew he was in the right place – that Jane was definitely here with Sutton. The sound of the patter of rain striking the roof tiles began to increase, intensifying. Robert's eyes turned to the activity about him, but his thoughts were still elsewhere. The stable hands walked the winded horses. Their coats were thick with sweat. Fresh, eager-spirited horses were being secured in the traces of the mail coach.

Robert knew how they felt. Blood flowed thick and fast in his veins, pumping adrenalin that had his muscles ready for fight or flight. The issue was he could do neither, *yet*. He could do nothing but wait.

The rain fell in earnest now and struck his shoulders, his hair, and his face with force. He lifted his forearm and wiped his brow, but his sleeve was already wet.

He had no idea how to endure this waiting.

"Lord Barrington!" His gaze whipped to one of the inn's attendants. "There is a woman wishing to speak with you, my Lord!"

Robert shifted out of the way of a lad running with a bag which had been thrown from the mail coach, and saw a young woman behind the attendant. She was no one he knew, and in service by the look of her.

The heavy rainfall dripped down his face and plastered his shirt and waistcoat to his skin, but Robert paid no mind to it as he crossed the courtyard.

"Lord Barrington?" the woman questioned as he walked the last few steps. The attendant bowed and disappeared.

She cast back the hood of her cloak. "James, the groom, sent me, my Lord, with this." She withdrew a letter from beneath her cloak. "He said to say not to worry, but he promised you'd give me a penny for dropping it off."

Robert shivered, a chill running across his skin beneath the damp cloth of his shirt. "Thank you. Come in a moment, please." He took the letter and encouraged her to go before him.

Inside the inn's lobby, a chambermaid was waiting on the stone flags to pass him a linen towel.

Accepting it, Robert nodded his thanks, wiped his face and hair, then thoughtlessly passed it back, too distracted by the letter in his hand.

James couldn't write. It would not be from his groom, but it bore no address so there was no handwriting or mark to determine its origin.

"This way." Holding out a hand, he directed the young maid to the private parlour he'd hired. Embers still glowed in the hearth, warming the room. The woman waited just within the open door as he unfolded the letter and saw Jane's neat script. *She's here.* His heart pounded, but his concentration was disturbed by the movement of the maid.

She watched for his reaction.

He reached into his pocket and handed her a couple of coins.

"Thank you, my Lord. Jim said you'd be grateful. Did you want me to take anything back, sir?"

His eyes narrowed on her. "Are you on another errand? Could you come back?"

He received a brisk nod. "Yes, sir, if you want." With that, she bobbed a quick curtsy, and, in a swirl of skirt, was gone.

Robert walked to the door and called for writing materials, then turned back and reread Jane's note. There were just three lines.

Your offer is gratefully accepted. I shall be free tomorrow at the larks. Meet me at the fore.

His heart set up a thundering pace again. The message was written in code, a code they'd developed in their youth, to hide their affair from their families. What it told him was that she'd feared the note being intercepted and the consequence if it was. She asked him to meet her at six, at a crossroads. But what crossroads? He'd need to find out.

She was being kept against her will, watched and censored, if she must write the note in this brief code.

Pembroke's words rang in his head. "*He kept her like a bird in a cage.*"

A few moments later, sitting before the writing desk, Robert's fingers shook as he withdrew the cork from the bottle of ink and considered his response. A hundred words he'd left unsaid ran through his thoughts. The soft tip of the feather tapped against his chin, and his fingers gripped the nib in inactive preparation. Finally, he dipped the quill into the indigo ink and merely scratched *Agreed. R* on to the paper. Words had failed him. There was nothing he could express which would not give her away, and yet, there was so much to be said. It would have to wait. All of it.

~

The black stallion beneath Robert stepped sideways, pawing the ground impatiently, as restless with waiting as he was. Easing his grip on the reins, Robert sat back, aware his tight hold was probably transmitting his tension to the horse. He'd sent his carriage on ahead. His gaze turned from one lane to another. It was a quarter past six. Apparently, these were the only crossroads she could have meant.

A sharp breeze swept at the trees, rustling leaves. The sky above was blue. The morning sunshine bright, if not warm.

He looked along the lanes once more in each direction. Nothing. The horse puffed, whinnying and shaking out its neck.

Listening intently, Robert absorbed every sound. Several young rooks played on the breeze above, letting the air catch their wings, cawing merrily. Then he heard in the distance the thud of hooves on compact, moistened ground. More than one horse. Cautiously, he walked the stallion back to conceal himself in the trees. From there he listened to the riders approach, watching for his first glimpse. When they turned the bend, he felt his heart lurch into his throat. A woman and a man. The woman sat astride with her skirt drawn up, and her cloak flew loose behind her as she rode at pace, heedless of propriety. *It was Jane* with James.

Robert kicked his heels to the stallion's flanks and rose into a trot. Relief flooded him with an intense pain. *He had her*. He was not a man to cry, but if he were...

Heading in their direction, he watched her gallop towards him, low in the saddle.

She eased up as she drew nearer, rising and pulling her mount back into a canter. He could see her face. She was smiling a broad, excited smile. It struck him right in the heart. He smiled in answer as she slowed to a trot a few feet before him. God, she was a blessed sight. He stopped and sat back in his saddle.

She drew up her mare, and it danced about his impatient stallion, setting his beast sidestepping again.

"*Robert*," was all she said, his name breathless on her lips.

It said so much more though. The same hundred words he'd not said in his note. He could hear everything he felt in her voice.

Despite the presence of his groom, Robert found himself reaching forward to touch her face. He had to touch her just to be sure it was not a dream. His fingers stroked over her cheek reverently then slipped to her nape and pulled her to him to receive his kiss.

James coughed behind her. "Huh hum, my Lord."

Robert broke the kiss and smiled at her, then at his groom. "Yes, James?"

"My Lord, the horses may already be missed, and once they know they're gone, they will look for Her Grace."

"You're right, James." Robert looked at Jane and drank her in. Her ebony hair was swept back in a simple plate, her gown plain, yet she looked so beautiful. Her bright, shining, emerald eyes were the only jewels she needed. "Are you happy to ride on?"

She nodded. "Anything you say."

"Come on then," he responded, as though it was no more than one of the morning rides they'd shared frequently at Farnborough. "This way." He turned the stallion.

"That way?" she echoed. "It goes south."

"*Anything you say,*" indeed. He cocked one eyebrow at her failure to comply so soon. He'd thought it too submissive for Jane. She was clearly still not willing to trust him. "Exactly," he answered. "Sutton will expect us to head for London or North, so we will go the opposite way." His smile dared her to disagree.

She did not. Nodding, she kicked her heels and was off. In a moment, the three of them were at full tilt, setting as much distance as they could between Jane and her cage.

The brisk autumn breeze cooled Jane's face and her bared stocking-clad legs which gripped the mare's flanks. It caught at wisps of her hair, too, pulling it loose.

She hadn't dared risk searching out her riding habit, too afraid of being seen. If anyone had seen her in it, they'd have guessed her intent. She'd never ridden there before.

As it was, she'd been terrified, creeping through the quiet house in the wake of the maid James had communicated to her through.

Over the last weeks, in the dark hours of night, she'd longed for Robert and regretted leaving him, even though she'd known it was right to protect him. But when she'd discovered he'd sent his groom, her heart had leapt in her chest, and she'd forgotten everything but being with Robert. She'd not stopped to weigh the decision. She'd merely grasped the chance. Now, she was here, riding beside Robert, free. But she was not. She never would be. Joshua would never really let her go, he'd find some way to force her back by threat or foul play.

Robert was pale. He'd lost weight, too. He looked at her, reached across, and clasped her hand over the reins. The gesture moved her, and she felt tears glaze her eyes. His grip eased their pace to a canter. "We should get rid of these horses."

Robert let go her hand and pulled to a halt. So did she and

his groom.

"You must take the horses back to the inn, James, and ask them to run them up to the house. Make sure they don't see the direction you leave in. We'll meet you at The Fox Inn as planned."

"Jane, sweetheart." Robert's eyes were back on her, rich brown and tender. "Slide over to my saddle. I'll not have you hung for a horse thief when I've gone to so much trouble to save you."

Their animals drawn together, she dropped her reins and reached for his shoulders as his hands gripped her waist. His strength pulled her over to his saddle.

Her bottom rested on his thigh and she laid her cheek onto his shoulder.

"James." She felt the deep rumble of Robert's voice in his chest.

"Aye, my Lord," the man acknowledged, catching up her mare's reins. Then wheeling both horses about with a nod and smile to her, the groom rode off.

Robert gripped her waist and held her closer. Jane looked up. "*Robert.*" Their lips touched again, as they shared a lingering kiss, which was about love, not lust. Her heart ached when she broke it and whispered, "I missed you."

"Did he touch you?" was his answer as his brown eyes flashed anger.

She shook her head. Not as he meant. Not yet.

"You shouldn't have gone to him."

She held his gaze for a moment, but said nothing. Then she let go of him and shifted in the saddle to sit astride before him, hitching up the skirt of her plain grey walking dress to enable it. Her bottom rested against his thighs and groin.

"I didn't go to him," she said at last, her fingers gripping the pommel as she looked ahead.

"Well then, I wish you had not left me." His words were caustic. It jolted a pain in her that brought tears to her eyes. She was glad he couldn't see.

He kicked the horse into a walk, rocking his hips forward to encourage it.

"I had to leave you; I didn't want to involve you," she said to the road ahead.

His reins still in one hand, he splayed his other hand over her stomach and pulled her back against him firmly. The touch was gentle and protective. His heels kicked again and set the stallion into a trot. "And now I am involved anyway. How could you think I'd want you to give yourself up to protect me?" Jane moved to turn, but couldn't. "Yes, I worked it out in the end. It doesn't make me feel particularly proud knowing you think I can't protect myself or you from Sutton, Jane." His voice dropped to a low, cracking note. "It hits my pride. I *will* protect you." His fingers pressed against her stomach, and his breath stirred the escaped curls at her temple.

She laid both her hands over his, one on the reins, the other on her stomach, holding him as best she could. He didn't know the Suttons' perversity or their power. She did not want him to.

He sighed, and his cheek rubbed against her hair. "Don't leave me any more, sweetheart. Swear it. I can't bear to grieve for you again."

She nodded and tears tracked silently down her cheeks. She wiped them away. She should not be here, but she knew she couldn't bear to be without him either.

"Then you'll marry me?"

At that, she tried to twist back to see his face, but couldn't.

"You're not saying, no. I shan't listen. It's settled. Archer has gone ahead to find us a vicar. Within an hour, you are going to be my wife, Jane."

A strange sound left her throat when she tried to speak, half sob, half laugh, and when words came, they sounded strangled. "You're mad! We can't marry today. We need to have the bans read."

288

His lips pressed to her ear. "Not if the man you are to marry has the common sense to bring a special licence from London."

"You did not!" She struggled to look back. The pressure against her stomach held her tight. "Robert, my agreement is required."

"You are taking my name," he said determinedly against her ear. "Once you have it, you may do as you like. If you really will it, you can have a marriage in name only, but taking my name is the only way to permanently break Sutton's hold on you. You will not be legally dependent on him. You have sacrificed yourself twice, Jane. I believe it's my turn."

His words took her breath away. He was not just asking her to marry him, but offering to give up his life and the chance for an heir if she agreed to his foolishness, just for her safety. "May we stop? I want to walk."

She felt him stiffen, armouring himself against her potential refusal.

"Sutton – Jane, I'll—"

She squeezed his hand which gripped the reins, gently silencing him.

"You said yourself, he will not come this way. Just for a while, Robert. Please?"

He drew the stallion to a halt and held her steady as she slid her leg across the saddle and slipped to the ground.

She waited with her arms clutched across her middle as he swung his leg over then dropped effortlessly. For a moment, he just stood there, as she did, holding her gaze, his eyes a vivid, bright brown. She was the one to step forward and take his hands, but he was the one who pulled her close and kissed her, his fingers threading through hers.

This time, there was lust as well as love, and when he broke away, hunger burned in the wide, onyx pools at the centre of his eyes. He feared she would argue; she could see it. He looked as he had at the ruins on that last day.

"Yes, I will marry you," she whispered. "A real marriage, Robert. Not a pretend one." No matter what happened, she could not walk away again. It felt good to make the decision.

He let go of her hands and braced her cheeks. "You mean it?"

She nodded.

"Good girl," he answered with his rakish, charmer's smile. Then his lips were on hers again, and her arms circled about his neck as they kissed open-mouthed. She was breathless when he pulled away.

"Come on then. We wouldn't want to be late for our own wedding. What a to-do that would be."

Her fingers squeezed his shoulders. She so longed for him to be the hero she needed.

"Let's get you up before you change your mind." He smiled and gripped her waist. In an instant, she was up on his saddle and he was lifting to sit behind her. She didn't turn to sit astride, but put her arms about his sinuous midriff and snuggled close, her legs across his thighs.

"You are not alone any more, sweetheart," he whispered. "Do you understand? You may stop pushing me away and holding me at a distance now."

She pressed a kiss on his jaw. "Yes, my Lord."

~

An hour later, Jane stood before a humble altar, watching Robert gently slide a plain gold band on the third finger of her left hand. She had left all her old jewellery behind.

They were bathed in coloured light. Her eyes lifted and caught the hint of a smile on his lips and reverence in his brown gaze. He looked as though he was wishing the years away and imagining this was the wedding they'd spoken of in their youth, their families lining each side of the church.

She'd have worn a white dress from the pages of *La Belle Assemblée,* and the church would have been full of roses.

But the church was bare, their appearance commonplace, and their only audience, Robert's valet and groom. Yet it was a dream come true. She had Robert, at last, and that was all she'd ever really wanted.

Robert's grip on her fingers pulled her closer, and his lips brushed her cheek. She smiled and met his tender gaze. The vicar snapped the book shut he'd held open. "I now pronounce you man and wife."

She was Lady Jane Marlow. No longer a Duchess. No longer a Sutton. But Robert's wife.

In a daze, she thanked the vicar then let Robert lead her to a table to sign the register. It was done. She stepped outside into dazzling sunlight and breathed fresh air. Robert's fingers slipped about her waist.

He took her back to the inn where they awaited the arrival of the coach over a hurried breakfast.

She'd thought herself not hungry until it was laid out before her, then found herself ravenous, causing Robert to laugh over the size of her appetite.

He steered her straight to the coach and handed her up.

When she sat against the leather squabs, exhaustion washed over her as she listened to him give orders to the driver.

"You need not ride inside the carriage just to keep me company," she said as he entered after her and dropped into the seat. James closed the door.

Smiling, Robert looked askance at her, set his arm about her shoulders, and drew her close. "A charming greeting for your husband, wife. *You may ride outside,* indeed."

"I meant nothing by it." She laid her cheek on to his shoulder, feeling relief and safety. Robert, her island, was now her property. "*Husband*. It sounds insanely silly to call you that. I only meant you needn't feel obliged to keep me company. I'm too tired to ride, but if you wish to, I won't take offence."

"*I* will take offence soon if you're not careful, *wife*." He played with the word on his tongue, and she could hear the smile in his voice. "Silly? I do not think it silly to call you wife. I refuse to let you mock it. *Wife*. I like it very much, and I've waited so many years to say it, I think the novelty will last. And I shan't desert you after less than half an hour for a saddle. I'm very happy here. If you're tired, set your head on my lap and sleep. I want to appreciate my acquisition."

She laughed. He stretched out his legs and set his booted feet on the opposite cushioned seat, crossing them at the ankles. She willingly followed his suggestion and tucked her feet up on the seat with her knees bent, then used his thigh as a pillow, one hand beneath it and one on top.

Robert reached across and picked up the blankets from the far side, then slipped one beneath her head and the other he threw across her.

"Comfortable?" The carriage lurched into motion.

She nodded once, her eyelids already falling.

Robert toyed with a wisp of hair behind her ear, winding and unwinding it. She was his. Jane Marlow. God, that sounded good. Tomorrow he'd send an announcement to the papers. Let Sutton argue with that.

Jane. *His wife. Lady Barrington*. He liked it. He liked it so intensely he was concerned for his state of mind. Should any man be so bowled over by claiming the woman he wanted as his wife? Apart from Geoff, his friends would think him insane, and, of course, the women of his acquaintance would think him changed. He *was* changed. He'd be a damn recluse for Jane if it made her happy. Anything which made his wife smile would be his new obsession.

He pulled off his gloves, disturbing her sleep. Her fingers gripped his thigh, and her eyes opened with a start, the emerald glittering with urgency and fear.

He tossed his gloves to the opposite seat and stroked her temple.

"Robert?" she questioned, returning from a dream.

"Aye, the same." He saw the concern ebb from the contours of her face. She laid her head back on the blanket.

"I thought..." she mumbled as he continued to stroke her hair. "We really are married, aren't we?"

"Yes, sweetheart, we really are. *Wife.*"

She took a deep breath, then her eyes closed, and she slipped back into sleep. Her weight increased on his leg.

"Darling girl," he whispered.

The tenderness in his chest absorbed her image with an enduring ache. Even if she forgave him for his past failures, he'd never forgive himself.

When the coach rumbled over the cobbled yard of the Crown Inn in the market town of Stourbridge, Jane was still asleep, and as James opened the door, Robert lifted his finger to his lips, bidding his groom quiet.

So it was that he carried his new bride over the threshold and laid her upon their marriage bed, sound asleep.

He ordered a scant supper sent to their room, and a bottle of the inn's best champagne which remained unopened while he sent for a bottle of brandy. When it came, he drank one glass of it before making the decision to take off his coat and join her on the bed.

He lay down behind her, carefully settled his hand on her waist, and curled into the shape she'd made. She didn't wake, but stirred. After a moment, his eyes closed, too.

Chapter Eighteen

When Jane woke, Robert watched her and he saw her eyes open wider as though her mind jerked into wakefulness. He lay beside her, his head resting on his palm, as he balanced on one arm. He smiled. She smiled, too. He touched her cheek then her lips.

"We were in the carriage," she said against his fingers.

"And you, sleepyhead, slept right through. You left me to dine alone."

Jane propped herself up on her elbows. "It's morning! Did I sleep a whole day and night?"

He nodded. "You slept through our wedding night."

"You rogue." Sitting up further, she pushed his shoulder, tipping him backward onto the bed. Then she leaned over him, her palm falling on his chest. "Why on earth did you not wake me?" Her eyes flickered with light, which implied she was more grateful than angry.

"Because it would have been mean of me, when you were obviously exhausted. I'm really not the wretch you think me, Jane. I can be sensitive."

For a moment, she didn't answer, but then she said, "You've never been a wretch to me, Robert Marlow. I know you too well to believe your façade. Although I will admit, I was deceived at first when I saw you in London, but you'd worked hard casting your damned reputation. I've never thought ill of you though, even that first night you were kind to me. I've always seen *you* buried beneath the rake."

His fingers lifted and brushed her hair from her temple. "No need to sugar the medicine, sweetheart. I was angry with you that first night. I had no cause to be. You had every reason to be angry with me for leaving you to face a marriage to Sutton. I'm sorry, Jane. I should have stayed and listened. I knew you better than to believe you were willing. I've hurt you over the years, I know. I'm going to make it up to you. But you may wish to know it was not your father's fault."

Her eyes widened, and she pulled away, sat up and knelt on the bed. "How can you know that?"

Robert lay on his back with one hand behind his head. "Edward's father-in-law has an unfortunate habit of thinking he owns everyone. When I mentioned I intended to marry you, he had your history traced. One of the things he found out was the former Duke of Sutton put the thumbscrews on your father to gain your hand. He forced him into debt."

She said nothing and shut her eyes. He sat up and reached for her.

She leaned back. "I cannot think of him kindly."

"I'm sure you can't." With his arm still raised, Robert beckoned her to come to him. "I don't think I'd be able to either if I were you. He played his part. If he'd managed his affairs better... So many ifs and buts, Jane, yet no matter how I wish it, sweetheart, I cannot change the past."

She came to him, her arms circling his ribs as her face pressed into his neck.

"We're changing the future though, darling," he said gently and kissed the crown of her head.

"I hope so." The words were whispered to his shirt. Gripping her shoulder, he held her back a little and lifted her chin with his fingers.

"I know so." He dropped a swift kiss on her lips. "But for now you must be hungry. Let me order breakfast."

"What?" She leaned back laughing.

His eyebrows lifted.

"A notorious rake like you, deserting a woman in his bed? *I* am your *wife*. Perhaps it has put you off? I do profess, *my pride* is wounded."

He deliberately set a wicked smile that promised retribution, leaned forward sharply, and toppled her backward.

She squealed as his hands grasped hers.

He pinned her to the bed. "I can oblige you, if you wish, wife, but I had thought only to increase your stamina first."

Her smiling eyes met his gaze. "Pray, do tell what I need stamina for, *husband?*"

He kissed her, invading her mouth as a lance of sexual hunger ripped through him.

Her hips pressed upwards and her fingers wove between his.

The woman was a wonder. His emotions raged beyond desire. He felt so warm and human inside. He'd always felt coldly determined with others.

Her soft breasts pressed to his chest through their clothing.

He could easily raise her skirt and set himself inside her — he wanted to — but this was their first time as man and wife. He wished to make a memory they could keep, and it would not come from a hasty coupling.

Forcing himself to stop, he let her hands go and rolled on to his back, sighing as his forearm fell over his brow. He fought to quell the desire burning in his blood.

"What is it?" Her voice was small.

"Not like this," he said without lifting his arm from his eyes.

He felt her move and sit astride his hips. Then her hands rested on his chest.

"Why not like this, when I want it so? *I want you.*"

Lifting his arm, he looked at her warily. "I want you, too, but I'll not hurry it, Jane. Let us make the first time for us as husband and wife special."

She pouted then climbed off him and moved off the bed, her back to him. "I suppose you wish for lavender and roses."

"No!" He followed her, angry that she would thrust that at him at this moment. "You cannot compare that!"

"I did not..." she began as she turned back. Then she started again, "I'm sorry, you're right. I'm just hungry. Call for breakfast."

His gaze held hers. He still felt hurt. But he shrugged. He was hungry, too. "Well then, apart from me, what do you fancy?"

The smile she gave him in answer was censored. "Anything will do, cheese, ham, eggs."

"Coffee and bread, as well, and we are done then. Do you want me to send a maid up to you?" He echoed her smile, pulling on his boots.

"Hardly, I have nothing to change into." And her gown was badly creased from a night sleeping in it.

He stood. "I'll send a maid to find something else you can wear then. Besides," he said as he tossed her a lopsided roguish smile, the one he knew could melt most women's defences, "you need wear nothing for the rest of the day regardless. I intend to keep you very busy in this room." He left then, in search of a maid and breakfast, not that that was what he was starving for.

~

Jane finished her last mouthful of ham and eggs then rose. They'd breakfasted in their chamber, for privacy's sake. Jane rested one hand on her stomach. "I'm stuffed."

"I wish you were," Robert chimed, leaning back against his chair and stretching his legs.

"Sometimes, my Lord, you can be too crude."

"And sometimes, my Lady, I am not indecent enough. You cannot have it both ways."

She smiled to mollify his irritation, but turned away and went to look out the window. A carriage pulled into the courtyard below. She'd hurt Robert, she knew. She should not have mentioned the scene he'd set for Lady Baxter, but she could not help thinking about it. He'd hurt her through the years, too, through his desertion and his public pursuit of other women. That wound would not be easily forgotten.

He was the only one; she was one of hundreds.

Footsteps struck the floorboards behind her, then his palms slid about her ribs, as his lips brushed her neck with a gentle kiss. "I want you, wife."

Just the words sent a power wave of desire racing beneath her skin. She nodded and leaned her head back on to his shoulder. His fingers began working loose the buttons at the back of her high-necked gown. His lips brushed her neck gently as her gown tightened then slackened when each button was freed, and once her dress was loose to her hips, his fingers slid beneath the fabric over her stomach and upward to cup her breasts. He was too good at this for the sake of her sanity.

He slid her dress from her shoulders and it fell to the floor. A deep breath caught in her lungs. But then he stopped and was silent.

She turned, wondering why.

His eyes were on her throat and he reached out and touched the bruises.

"You said he didn't touch you." There was pain in his voice.

"He didn't, not as you meant."

Sorrowful eyes glanced up and met her gaze. He looked down again as his fingertips brushed over her arms. There were bruises there, too. She stepped back.

"The man's a bastard. I'll have to kill him." His hands fell, clenched then flexed. She stepped forward and clasped them.

"I'm free, you said it. Don't seek to stir up a hornet's nest, Robert."

His gaze met hers. "I want to call him out," he whispered in a bitter voice.

"I knew if I'd stayed at Farnborough, it would end that way. That is why I left, because I knew you would fight, and I will not see you harmed. He would kill you before you got near him. Don't take any risks, Robert, please."

His eyes focused heavily on hers for a moment, then, suddenly, he lifted his hands free and embraced her instead. "I'm sorry, Jane. I should not have let you leave. I should have forced you to stay. Can you forgive me?" His jaw pressed against her hair, and she hugged him, too, and felt his anger ebb.

"I chose to leave," she said to his shoulder. "You rescued me."

He sighed, pulled away, and tapped her beneath the chin. "I wish you would cease getting into trouble so there would be no need for rescue."

She lifted to her toes and kissed his lips. "Thank you."

He hugged her again. "Come along then. Crack to it, wife. Let us get your clothes off."

"Such charm, my Lord," she mocked.

"Sod charm. I am impatient. Besides, you have promised to obey. What need have I for charm?"

"You had better charm me, Robert, or you'll get nowhere. It is your charm I fell for." He was joking to make her forget Joshua. She loved him even more for it.

"I'll charm you with my body, Jane. You shan't need words."

The sentiment in his pitch made the muscles in her stomach spasm. "Robert," she said the moment before his kiss brushed the corner of her mouth. Then his lips touched her chin and her throat, gently pressing over her bruises as his fingers slid upward from her waist.

When she lay naked on the bed, watching him finish undressing, she saw *her Robert*, not the rake. It touched her heart.

He grinned at her, all art gone from his look as he came to her.

He'd been with others, but they didn't know him as she did. "Do you like what you see?" he asked as he lay down.

She did not reply. He did not give her chance; he kissed her.

She felt as though she had been made for him. This was so very right.

"I love you," he said as he came into her.

His loving was slow and intense, heavy with emotion which burned bright in his eyes.

"Sorcerer," she breathed as she felt a wave sweep towards her, its crest not yet broken. Her fingernails dug into the skin of his shoulders, and she cried out as the first release came already, flooding her body in a blissful tide of eclipsing sensations.

"You're the witch," he whispered to her ear when a second flood swelled throughout her. "You captured me years ago, Jane. I've been under your spell all my life."

"Robert," she breathed as another wave rose.

His hands pressed into the mattress, supporting his weight and making the movement in his hips more precise and controlled.

Her fingers fell to grip the muscle at his waist.

"You are holding me as though you think the tide will wash you away." His gaze held hers, the brown depths full of passion, but there was laughter, too.

"It may." She bit her lip and her head titled back into the pillow as her feet pressed into the mattress and her toes curled. Another shattering release sent her adrift.

She heard him laugh lightly from far away as he changed the tempo of his movement to a slight pulsing beat half inside her.

"Are you trying to drive me mad?" she cried when he suddenly withdrew.

"When I have been insane for you forever, I think it fair."

"*Ahh, Robert.*" Her fingers clawed into his hips and his movement quickened and deepened.

They tumbled together at the end and he cried out.

After a moment, he rolled away and pulled her with him, his hand running over her hair. "I love you."

"I know," she answered, "and I you, which is a good thing as we are married now. You cannot turn me out."

He laughed. "I would never want to, Jane." His fingers brushed her hair behind her ear.

For a little while they lay there in each other's arms, talking, remembering their life together years ago. Then Robert pressed her back with one long kiss, and began all over again.

As she lay back, his kiss moved lower, to her breast.

She sighed and arched.

His fingers began their skilled manipulation and his mouth captured her nipple in its warmth.

She felt so loved.

Her hands settled on Robert's hair as she watched him kiss her breast, while his fingers caressed her internal planes. She captured every feeling and held on to it, then cupped his face and pulled his mouth back to hers as, already, she felt her first crest break.

He kissed her hard on the lips for a moment then pulled back and knelt between her legs, resting back on to his heels as his hands laid on her parted thighs.

She watched him hesitate, as though he felt the awe that she felt too. They were married now, at last.

The sun shining through the window of their inn room illuminated his beautiful body.

His fingers gripped about her thighs and pulled, sliding her body down the bed to him, and then, as he knelt over her, and with her legs draped over his open thighs, he plundered her body in the pattern of hard thrust and slow withdrawal.

His determination was exquisite agony. "You are too good at this," she whispered as she felt it melt her bones.

"You can never be too good, Jane," he answered as he filled her to the brink, making her moan breathlessly and feel like weeping.

When she cried out later, his thumb pressed into her mouth to silence her. "Not so loud, darling. There are other guests here, remember?"

Biting down on his thumb, she fought hard to be silent as he took her over and over again, with delicious deliberation, tantalising her senses and driving her mad with need. Her fingers gripped his back and clawed, and the soles of her feet pressed on to his shins. Then she fell, toppling in ecstasy.

With a low growl, as though spurred, he claimed her body in more urgent strokes which had lost all of their finesse.

"There is no woman like you," he said, as she hovered in that heaven-like place, her senses reeling. "I love you, Jane," he ground out a moment before he broke, too. She pulled him down, bracing his head against her shoulder as they rode the storm of beautiful release together.

Then he rolled to his side and pulled her head to his chest.

She lay with a hand on his chest and her leg over his thighs, nestled under his arm, listening as his breaths slowed and he drifted into sleep.

She was wide awake.

She slipped from beneath his arm and crept off the bed, then collected her clothes and dressed.

It was strange to be here with him, married to him, after all that had happened. She sat at the far end of the bed with her back against the bedpost, her knees tucked up and her arms wrapped about them, and watched him sleep.

He lay there naked in all his glory, perfect and relaxed. He had no idea what he'd taken on.

She did, and had grabbed this chance to claim the fate which should have been hers without any hesitation. But she should not have done it. It was selfish to involve him. They couldn't really go back to how it was, or could have been, before she'd married Hector.

What would happen next? She couldn't guess. She'd live each day, each minute, waiting for Joshua's orchestrated disaster to descend. He would do something in revenge. Of course he would.

But she would not let it spoil her time with Robert. She was going to savour every second they had together and pray Robert would not be hurt.

~

Sutton's first assault came six days after Robert had helped Jane escape. He'd expected it to be physical, but it was not. It came in the form of a letter from Robert's man of business. When it was set down on a silver tray in the private parlour they'd been using at the inn, Robert knew what it meant.

Jane was busy buttering a piece of toast for him.

Unwilling to trust his skill in dissembling, Robert folded the letter and shoved it into the inside pocket of his morning coat, disregarding it as though it was another note from his estate manager at Farnborough. He was determined to ignore it until he could find a moment alone to read the thing so Jane would not see his reaction. He knew she was waiting for this even though she hadn't spoken of it.

Since he'd shown her the announcement he'd posted in *The Times*, she'd lapsed into a withdrawn, thoughtful state.

True, he could tease her out of it. She'd smile and laugh, but those sentiments died too quickly.

She was worried and still living with clipped wings.

He longed to see her fly again and she'd not be able to if she was involved in Sutton's puppetry any longer. This was Robert's problem now, not hers. He'd promised to protect her, and he would.

To buy time to read the letter in private, he sent Jane and a maid from the inn on a shopping spree, with money to spend on hats, as many as she wished. It was a believable excuse to lose her for an hour, because she'd left everything at Sutton's, and, so far, they'd only purchased a few gowns for her to wear while they stayed at the inn.

Once she'd gone, he retreated to their chamber. It was the one place Jane escaped her trepidation in full. When they went to bed, she was free of all the chains of her past.

He broke the seal and dropped to sit in a spindle chair near the fire as his eyes scanned his business man's brief script. After a minute, his hand dropped as he thrust to his feet and crushed the letter in his fist.

Jane had been right about Sutton's influence. This was more than Robert had anticipated. The majority of shares in a shipping business Robert had invested in had been bought out by the Duke of Sutton, and he'd instantly closed the business down. Robert's shares were now worthless. Obviously, Sutton was willing to toss away the fortune he'd forced out of Jane. If Sutton continued this tack, Robert would end up penniless in debtors' jail.

"But not yet," Robert said aloud. At least he had the common sense to keep his investments spread over several different companies. He would have to go to London though, as Murray had requested. They'd have to move his other investments before Sutton played this trick again.

Damn. Jane would know something was wrong when he told her they were going back. But she must know they could not hide away forever.

His good intentions failed within hours though. The next strike came the following morning before he'd spoken to Jane of their impending trip to London, and it came in Jane's company, when he was unprepared to present a false front. This time, it *was* a letter from his estate manager at Farnborough. Foolishly, Robert thought it unimportant and slit it open.

Someone, Malcolm wrote – Sutton, Robert thought – had bribed the bidders at the local corn market not to bid for wheat or barley from the Farnborough farms. The entire crop had been left unsold. This time, Robert could not control his anger. It did not just affect him. It affected the people who depended on him. He screwed up the letter in the palm of his hand and tossed the damn thing across the room with a growl.

Jane, who was sitting in the chair opposite across the breakfast table, pouring them tea, looked up with a start, her eyes wide and her cheeks pale.

He knew this was the moment she'd been dreading. He saw understanding written plainly on her face.

"What is it?" Her voice as she posed the question said instead, *what has he done?* There was little point in denying who was behind it. She wouldn't believe him if he did.

Angry with himself now, too, for letting her see his reaction, Robert fought for control of the sneer which twisted his lips as he sought to alleviate some of her fear. "Nothing to worry about, Jane. I'll handle it. Is my tea poured?" He reached for his cup.

Jane put the teapot down and stood in physical protest, all indignant anger, even before her verbal protest began. "*It is not nothing.* It's about Joshua. Tell me what he's done. "

Desperately wanting to deny it, Robert hesitated, but his hesitation gave him away. He'd been right about his inability to dissemble. It seemed the only thing he was right about at the moment.

"Jane, don't worry, please. I will handle it—" he started, rising and stepping towards her. She stepped back out of reach, refusing consolation.

"Just tell me what he's done, Robert?" Her arms were at her sides. Her hands curled into fists.

"I have to go back to London, that is all. Do you want to come? If you do not, I could take you to Farnborough first?"

Her eyes suddenly shone with green fire, and she gripped his arm. "You will not dismiss me. I know what he can do. You do not. You will not call him out, will you?"

He braced her slender waist. "Did I mention that? I am not even contemplating it, Jane. I'm going back to London to meet with my man of business. I need to secure my investments. He is threatening me financially, not physically. He is trying to bankrupt me. I need to return and ensure my investments are inaccessible."

He watched her fear abate a little as black lashes veiled her eyes and she took a breath.

She opened her eyes again. "Tell me what he's done?"

If she must worry, he supposed, she ought to worry over reality and not imagined fears.

"He's closed down one of the businesses I invest in and left my shares worthless. It was only a small amount. I can suffer the loss."

"But there's more?"

He felt the world-weary façade he'd worn for nearly a decade slip over him. "That letter," he said, indicating the crumpled note he'd thrown on the floor, "told me he's stopped Farnborough's grain crops from selling. No one will bid."

"Robert, no!" His hands gripped her arms before she could turn away, but she pulled free. "I should go back! They are innocent people! I'll not have them hurt because of me!"

"Do not be foolish. You cannot choose to go back anymore. You are naught to do with him now. Think how it would look – my wife going back to live in her previous son-in-law's house? He would likely throw you out just to mock you. No, Jane, I will solve it. But I do need to go to London."

"I knew this would happen," she whispered as he pulled her close and held her. Her anger appeared to ebb away.

"Sweetheart, I know you did, and I did, too. But let's not argue, it is precisely what he wants. I will compensate my tenants. I'll not let Sutton win."

She pulled free and met his gaze.

Her eyes were as sorrowful as the first time he'd seen her in London.

"And what about next year? If you have nothing left, how will you compensate them? If his father would not even allow me freedom after his death, how do you think you can stop Joshua? You cannot. He won't give in. That is why I left Farnborough. I should not have come back to you."

God, he wanted to shake her. Instead, his fingers cupped her cheek. "Would you rather I'd left you to your fate then? So you'd be the martyr and me the villain again? Forgive me, Jane, I am not playing that part any more. I can no more continue watching you suffer than you can bear watching Sutton attack me. Whatever the outcome, we face it together. Do you understand?"

Her gaze did not meet his.

"Jane, look at me? Sweetheart, do not draw back from me. *Please?*"

She shut her eyes.

This was the caged Jane. He could see it now. He'd looked straight through it in London. Behind those flashing eyes and her rigid spine was a lack of confidence and an undercurrent of constant fear, waiting for Sutton to claw her back.

"I don't care what Sutton does. I will not let him touch you. If we have to leave England to avoid him, I have properties abroad. Trust me, Jane."

Her eyelids lifted, and long, ebony eyelashes framed her emerald gaze. A cramp of sharp pain bit in his chest.

"I'm sorry," she whispered, shaking her head. "I suppose I am too used to being afraid of him and unused to being loved by you. I do trust you. I don't want to lose you though."

"You won't lose me, Jane. Rail at me, if you like. Ring a peel over my head, darling. Just stay, and you shan't lose me. I don't care about the money or even Farnborough. I do care for you."

She lifted to her toes and hugged him, her cheek against his.

Chapter Nineteen

They arrived in London three days later, just before midday, and, within an hour, Robert ascended the steps to his solicitor's office in Mayfair, with Jane on his arm. A light rain fell in an unrelenting mist, coating her new scarlet pelisse and bonnet with a sheen of dew.

The autumn weather had been in no mood to lift Robert's spirits on their journey to town. It had rained persistently the entire time, turning roads to impassable muddy tracks, slowing them down. He'd not even stopped for tea on their arrival, but sent word straight to Murray that he would call within the hour.

His fingers pressing beneath Jane's elbow, Robert steered her through the front door as Murray's clerk held it open. "My Lord, my Lady." Etched on the glass was the title of the offices: "Messrs Murray and Bishop, Solicitors".

Jane had been nervous, silent, and frequently distracted since she'd discovered Sutton's manoeuvrings, and her hard-won smiles were even rarer than before.

The clerk stepped back and opened Murray's office door for them.

When they entered, Murray greeted Robert with raised eyebrows, having glanced at Jane. Then he remembered his manners and bowed, his cheeks colouring. This was Robert's future – to watch other men's appreciation of his wife, no matter their age.

"My Lady, forgive me. I did not expect you."

No. He would not have. Robert had no wish to bring her, but she'd refused to be left behind. He'd only agreed because he did not feel comfortable leaving her alone.

Having greeted Jane, Murray then shook Robert's hand. "Lord Barrington, I am glad you were able to return. I'm afraid I have had to make some distasteful decisions, but there is little choice now; everything is here for you to sign." Murray waved his hand at two chairs before his desk. "Do sit." He then looked at the clerk. "Tea, I presume, Perkins."

"No. Thank you. Not on my behalf, Mr. Murray," Jane stated, dropping to perch on the edge of one worn leather, winged armchair. Robert seated himself in the other and relaxed, feeling determined.

Now he was here, he could cease to worry and start fighting.

He looked at the clerk. "None for me either, Perkins. Thank you."

"Something stronger then, my Lord?" Murray asked, sitting down behind the desk.

Robert shook his head. Beside him, Jane glanced about the room.

Murray was not a man of tidy habits. There were stacks of files everywhere, but Robert knew from experience, the man could lay his hand on anything he wished in seconds, despite the apparent mess.

She was nervous.

Robert realised, now, she'd been nervous all the time when they'd been in London before. Because of Sutton? Undoubtedly.

God, I was such a blind idiot at Vauxhall.

Jane's profile was hidden behind the rim of her bonnet. All he could see was the spray of artificial rosebuds on it. But she sat with a straight back, her fingers gripping her reticule in her lap.

She still had the look of a duchess.

Robert reached across and clutched her fingers. The grip on her reticule eased, and he brought their joined hands to rest on the arm of his chair. It forced her to sit back a little, too.

"My Lord," the solicitor said, drawing Robert's attention.

Murray had steepled his fingers beneath his chin, and his elbows rested on the desk. "Obviously, you appreciate the urgency of the situation, else you would not be here, Lord Barrington. But I am sorry to say, I have agreed to sell a large proportion of your shares, certainly all those in companies where you do not have the majority holding. However, as I was certain you would not wish to leave your funds un-invested, I have found some commercial property for sale. If you purchase it, you can make your return in rents, my Lord. I am happy to secure it under a business name so the Duke of Sutton shall be in no position to trace it. If he discovered it, I do not doubt he would find some way to stop it from being let. He has already begun making moves on your other investments, so there is no time to lose." With that, the man drew up a pile of papers which had been prepared for Robert to sign.

Robert nodded. "What of my properties abroad?"

"They are safe as far as I know, but the Duke of Sutton's access to information seems to be without bounds."

Robert rubbed his chin feeling a need to expend energy which had no outlet. Jane's fingers tightened about his other hand. Murray set down a quill and ink.

"You know of his involvement at Farnborough? You will send some funds there to be given to my tenants, to make up for the loss, you understand?"

Murray looked up, met Robert's gaze and nodded. "Of course, my Lord."

"How will I know if he is tracing my properties?" Robert shifted forward in his seat, letting go of Jane's hand to take the quill from

311

Murray.

When Robert signed his name, he registered the sudden shift in his life. In less than a week, it seemed he was signing away most of what he'd previously thought important, his bachelorhood, and now his business interests. But Jane came above everything.

"I have taken the liberty, my Lord, in employing men to stay in the vicinity of your properties. If anyone begins to ask questions, we shall know. That is the only way I can think to counteract him. If I voiced any concerns in my own circles, I may draw attention rather than deter it. The Duke of Sutton seems to be able to bribe or blackmail every trade."

Robert scratched the quill across the final page and set the paper aside, then let the quill drop and leaned back with a sigh, meeting Murray's gaze again.

"If we can keep things hidden for long enough, he'll grow tired of the chase, I'm sure," Murray stated.

"*No*," Jane chimed in with vehemence.

Robert looked at her as she faced him, shaking her head and shifting forward to the edge of the chair. "He won't stop. His father stole my life. Even when he died, he did not let me go. Joshua will not stop."

Robert laid one hand over hers as it gripped the arm of his chair. "No need for melodrama, darling. You'll scare Murray off. I'm sure Sutton has his limits, the same as any other man. He is a man, isn't he? He does bleed like one, doesn't he?"

Her mouth twisted at his glib wit, and her hand pulled from under his, but he caught it and hung on.

"Well, then, my Lord, I'd better ensure your investments are doubly secure," Murray interjected, nodding in Robert's direction.

"What I wish to do is attack him."

"You will not get close," Jane interrupted.

"Lady Marlow is right, my Lord. Unfortunately, the Duke has

too much power. You do not have the fortune it would take to manipulate a man like that. I did attempt some inquiries, but there are too many people in his pocket. There is no hope of attack. I'm afraid, my Lord, we cannot move against him. We can only hope to hide your investments."

Minutes later, angry and frustrated, Robert found himself stewing in the carriage. He'd expected Murray to have some ideas to establish a counterattack, not shut him down. Robert was slumped back against the squabs with arms folded over his chest and one ankle resting on the other knee while he stared out the window at the busy street, unseeing. A little cough rang from the opposite corner of the carriage.

Jane sat with a straight back, her hands clasping her reticule.

She eyed Robert warily when he looked over. *I am not the damn villain.* "So, what do you wish to do then?"

"What do you mean?" she asked quietly, her almond-shaped eyes widening.

"If Sutton is so unstoppable, then what do you wish to do? Run?"

Jane watched Robert, and heard the same edge his voice had held at the abbey ruins. Her mouth opened to answer, but before she could speak, he continued. His words were as brooding and sulky as his body language. "I thought you said you did not want him to win, yet, at the moment, you seem devoid of any desire to fight. Therefore, I presume you'd rather retreat. If so, we'll go abroad and leave him chasing his tail."

Sighing, she crumpled back against the seat, and her eyes turned to the passing carriages and drays. "He'll follow us there anyway. He will be in London in a day or two, as soon as he knows we are here. He won't let us run, Robert. He'll follow."

"Every man has an Achilles' heel, Jane. Mine was always you. Sutton must bloody well have *one*. There must be something, some weakness we haven't seen."

Her eyes spun back to him. He looked less angry now, but still determined to disbelieve her. "You don't know the Suttons, Robert. I do. If your skill is sex, theirs is destroying people. They are masters at it."

"So, all I am good for is taking you to bed? You certainly know how to put a man in his place, Jane. It's nice to know you have such confidence in me."

She sighed again. She was angry and frustrated, too. Why did he not understand? She should never have come back to him. This is what she'd known would happen. "Don't be silly. You know that is not what I meant."

"*Silly?* You annihilated my character before my man of business with your lack of faith. I am not incapable, Jane. And Sutton is just a man. Not the damned devil. There will be a way to beat him. I just need to find it. But it would help, Jane, if you had some belief in me and stopped criticising me."

Her ire rose, and her fingers gripped the edge of the carriage seat as she leaned forward and let her temper fly its leash. It had never done before. "I am not criticising you! I am telling you the truth! Is it not better you know it rather than set yourself up to fail and lose everything? Why would I lie to you? I don't want you to get hurt!" She turned away again, her fingers still gripping the seat as she looked out the window.

The stubborn, belligerent man, he simply refused to listen. She was worn out with worrying and fighting. What was the point when they could not succeed? "I should not have come to you. I should have stayed with him."

Within a second, Robert moved. His fingers gripped her elbow, and she was hauled unceremoniously across the carriage on to his lap. He braced her chin with one hand while his other arm was about her shoulders, and his dark, thunderous gaze bored into her.

314

"If I hear that from you one more time, I will not be responsible for what I do. Do you understand?"

"So now you threaten me?" she whispered.

"Yes! You deserve for me to thrash you. But I'll think of another form of recompense." His voice had dropped an octave and turned seductive, and she was instantly physically aware of him, of the muscular thighs beneath hers, and the firm chest her fingers pressed against. His brown eyes glittered at her with anger and desire.

She'd never dared shout at anyone. It felt good to have shouted at him. She wasn't afraid of him. She felt better for it.

"Bloody hell, Jane." His tone had gentled, and there was a soft glow in his eyes suddenly. "*Just trust me*. I will find some way to win, but it will be much easier if you are on my side, not working against me. No more talk of regrets." His eyes swept every feature of her face, as if looking for disagreement.

She so wanted to believe in him. She just knew better. But she'd made this choice, and now must simply make the best of it. If he needed her to support him, she should.

"Silly girl," he continued, all anger gone from his voice. "I know you're frightened, but I will not let him near you."

His hand left her chin and fell to her thigh. Then they kissed, her arms about his shoulders. She lost herself in it and felt him slip the ribbons of her bonnet free and toss it on to the opposite seat. Then his hands were in her hair and his tongue in her mouth and they were in a carriage, on the busy London streets, in the middle of the day.

She broke the kiss, her palm slipping to lie over the lapel of his coat, over his heart. "You are wicked, do you know that?"

"But you love it."

"I love *you*," she answered the moment before he began kissing her again.

When he broke the kiss a little later, he whispered, "And I, you, sweetheart, but just trust me, please?"

She met his gaze.

"Why did he want your money so badly? Did he not have enough?"

She shook her head. "I told you at Farnborough. It is not all about the money. He is like his father. He needs control. It's in his blood. My escape will have vexed him, and your instigating it will rankle. He will be unable to focus on anything else until he has the two of us brought to heel."

The black of Robert's eyes widened. "And how will he do that?" He was fighting against his anger, she could see, but he was listening.

"I don't know, Robert. I've never escaped him before. Even when I was in London or at Farnborough, I knew he was simply biding his time. I was still trapped. This is the first time the Suttons have had no chain on me. I don't know what he'll do."

He kissed her sharply once on the lips then shifted her off his lap, seating her beside him. Her arms remained about his neck, pulling him with her. He laughed. "We are nearly home, sweetheart. Time to look respectable."

She kissed the corner of his mouth then whispered, "I hate being respectable. I prefer being wicked, with you."

He pressed another sharp kiss on her lips then reached to unlace her arms from his neck. He laughed. "I like you wicked, but not right now."

"Take me up to bed," she answered as the coach drew to a halt outside his London townhouse, and her fingers trailed across his clean-shaven jaw.

He caught her hand and squeezed it as the carriage door opened. "There are things I should do. I ought go to my club and find out what gossip there is on Sutton."

"Don't leave me alone," she said as he moved to descend. "Do as you wish later. Stay with me now." She tried to keep her voice light, but the tone was hollow, giving away what she really wished for, to forget Joshua and think of Robert.

He sighed and glanced back, his expression concerned as the groom lowered the step and stood back. She let Robert go, and he climbed out, then waited for her on the pavement, lifting his hand to help her down. She took it, and once she was beside him, gripped his forearm instead. A sharp crack of a whip cut the air, and she looked beyond him.

Shock imprisoned the breath in her lungs, and an ice-cold chill solidified her blood. "Joshua." She said his name aloud, without even realising it.

Robert looked.

Joshua was sitting in his curricle a little further up the street, a groom holding the horses steady. Joshua had clearly flicked the whip to draw her attention.

"Ignore him," Robert said, turning back. Jane looked up at the front door as her heart thumped in her chest and her hand slipped from his arm.

She measured her pace, but she could think of nothing but getting inside. Jenkins, Robert's butler, already held the door open, which surely meant Joshua had been there long enough for him to cause the household some concern.

He'd been awaiting their return.

They had been in town for three hours, and he'd found them.

Robert was close behind her when she crossed the threshold, and the door shut immediately once they were through. Her fingers pressed to her throat, and she felt as though she could not breathe. Her hands shook. She let them fall and struggled to remove her gloves. Robert caught her hands and held them still until she looked up and met his gaze.

317

"I'll not go out," he stated bluntly. Then he turned to Jenkins. "Fetch Lady Marlow a glass of brandy." His fingers worked loose her gloves, and when they were off, he gave them to a footman as Jenkins returned with a bottle and a glass. Robert took both in one hand and gripped her elbow. "Come on, girl, you are made of sterner stuff than that. Let's go upstairs."

She gave him a shaky smile and let him lead her. He took her to his bedchamber – their bedchamber. Once there, he kicked the door shut and let her go, then uncorked the bottle with his teeth, poured some brandy into the glass, and held it out to her. When she didn't immediately take it, he said jokingly, "It's a good medicine for nerves."

She couldn't smile, though she knew that was what he wished her to do, but she took the glass. "I didn't think he would be this quick. But I was right. He came. He has nothing else to divert him as much as we shall now."

"Just drink it, Jane. Forget about him for a bit."

She sipped the burning liquid, more to appease him than because she wanted to. Its heat slid straight into her veins. She closed her eyes and felt the warmth relax her muscles.

A shout rang out in the street below the window. Jane opened her eyes and turned.

It was a distinct, deep, masculine voice, the words indefinable, yet the threat clear. Then a hullabaloo broke out beneath the window. There were numerous voices, shouting and barking orders, arguing. Jane lifted the glass and drank all the brandy as she'd seen Robert do, then coughed, choking as it burned her throat. Robert took the empty glass and set it aside. She crossed to the window and held back the swathe of curtain so she could look from behind it without making her presence obvious. A group of eight rough-looking men were addressing Joshua in loud voices, ordering him to move on.

Jane sensed Robert at her shoulder and glanced back as he also leaned over and looked down. He smiled.

"My new footmen," he stated, as though they watched nothing more than someone taking a picnic in the park. "Jenkins has a good eye. I wonder where he got them. I'd make a guess at the docks. Handy that they are not in uniform yet. Sutton cannot blame me. They'll look even more impressive when they are though. They are to be our own private army, Jane. What do you think?"

"You will just rile him further."

Robert straightened and looked at her. His brown gaze was deep with satisfaction, clearly congratulating himself on winning this round.

"Upsetting him suits me." His fingers gripped her waist as he spoke. He bowed his head, and her arms came up about his neck. They kissed. It was tender and full of thirst, and when he broke it, he whispered across her lips. "Now, where were we? Ah, yes, I remember. You were begging me to stay and make love to you. I have decided to concede, sweetheart. Come along." He took her hand and began walking backward towards the bed.

She smiled at the devilish glint in his eyes – of avarice.

~

Robert loved her with a hard, intense determination. He wished to make her forget. He hurried into the main event to that end, bringing her on top of him, so she could feel some control over her life and know she could have that with him.

They were hidden from the world within the shroud of her long, dark hair, but once she'd broken, she was too languid, and her limbs too weak to move, so he took charge and concentrated on dominating her thoughts, dropping her weight hard and thrusting up, burying himself deep within her, over and over.

319

This was bliss, this, now, when she was utterly in love with him and thought of nothing else. She was so beautiful when she was like this, completely free of burdens.

He tipped her back on to the bed so he could move more freely, one hand gripping her breast as he continued besieging her senses, deliberately driving her mad for him while he gritted his teeth, refusing to race towards his own end.

He desperately wanted her mind free of Sutton and full of *him*. He wanted her to trust him and cease thinking and speaking of Sutton.

"Jane," Robert whispered as he drew nearer the end.

She loved him, he knew that. Her body gave him its faith, her heart, too. He just had to convince her head.

When she broke one more time, he followed her into that sea of serenity, his shoulders shivering as she gripped them, and his forehead fell to rest on hers as he braced himself against the torrent of feeling that swept into every vein, muscle, and nerve.

He was damp with sweat, and his muscles trembled when he lifted his head. She smiled. He smiled, too, feeling a warm pain about his heart.

Rap, rap. Two sharp strikes hit the wood of the bedchamber door. The pair of them jumped. Robert rolled off her and on to his back, his breathing not yet steady.

"My lord?"

Jenkins.

Surely they'd got rid of Sutton.

"What is it?" Robert called.

"Lord Edward is at the door, sir. Shall I let him in?"

"Yes, I'll come down." Robert rose and reached hurriedly for his clothes as he saw Jane do the same. Her face was crimson.

Gripping his garments in one hand, Robert went to the window. There was no sign of the Duke of Sutton's phaeton, but there was a black hansom carriage pulled up before the door. Robert couldn't see Edward. He must already be in the hall. Which meant Jenkins must have responded with something like *I'll see if his lordship is at home*, which meant Edward must know Robert was here and was probably already upstairs waiting.

He looked back to see Jane hurriedly dressing and did the same.

"I'll greet him," Robert said quietly once he was fully clothed. "There's no need for you to rush; call for a maid and take as long as you like. I'll tell him you are resting or something."

"Don't say that," she hissed back at him, her eyes bright from their lovemaking and her hair all mussed.

He smiled.

She frowned. "You look a state, Robert. Pray, do not say I am lying down, because he will know who has been lying down with me."

Laughing, Robert turned away and pulled the cord to ring for the maid. Then he left.

When he stopped at a mirror in the hall, to run his fingers through his hair, and straightened his pathetic attempt at tying his cravat, Edward appeared from the drawing room. "There you are, Robert. I am offended. News of your wedding is published in the papers before I hear a word. Where was our invite? Ellen is positively peeved. I believe she has taken it as a personal affront. How could you not even tell us?"

"We told no one," Robert answered as Edward came towards him. "There was a need for haste. No insult was meant, I can assure you. I'm sorry. I know Jane would have preferred it if you could have attended, but it was not possible, otherwise, I promise, I would not have had you miss my shackling for the world. I am sure it would've amused you."

"Hardly." Edward held out his hand. Robert shook it. "My brother marrying my surrogate sister suits me fine. She is truly my sister now. You're happy, both of you?"

Robert nodded. Edward let go his hand. "Fine, Ed, things are just not straightforward, that is all."

"Problems then?" Robert fell into pace beside his brother, and they walked back towards the drawing room.

"Just a few." Robert shrugged, not wishing to drag his brother into it. "What news is there about town?"

"I don't know myself. We've just arrived for the Rochester ball."

Robert looked sideways. "You are not staying here?"

"We saw the knocker in place and progressed to the Pulteney Hotel. Ellen refused to invade during your honeymoon. But I insisted we at least call. I couldn't not congratulate you, could I? And my sensibilities are not so great." Edward smiled. Robert scowled as they entered the drawing room.

Ellen rose from a sofa.

Her mouth came open then closed. She smiled. "I told Edward we should send a note first, but he insisted on just dropping in. I'm sorry. We have arrived inconveniently." She walked across the room as she spoke then her fingers were at his neck. "You or Jane shall have to learn how to tie your cravat, brother. You have given yourselves away." She undid it then retied it, finishing just as Jane came in.

"*Jane.*" Ellen took Jane's hands. Jane blushed. But Ellen did not press the point of their indiscretion. "I was so excited when we saw the news. Edward wrote to Farnborough, but they sent a letter back to advise you were not there. I am very glad to find you both in town, so we may at least offer our felicitations. You are obviously happy."

Ellen turned to Robert and kissed his cheek.

Jane received a similar greeting from Edward.

"I'm pleased for *both of you*," Ellen whispered as she drew away from Robert.

She had always disliked his nomadic ways. But she'd been the only one who'd seen through him to realise how much he'd longed to be settled.

He smiled awkwardly then took Jane's hand, threading his fingers through hers.

Edward grinned again, his hand resting on Jane's shoulder. "Jane Coates, now a Marlow, just as it should be, I suppose."

Jane smiled, her blush diminishing, and her fingers gripped Robert's tightly.

"I suppose I should call for tea," she said. "Do you wish to stay for dinner?"

An odd sensation raced through Robert. It was a novelty to have a woman take on these domestic tasks. In the past, Ellen would have hosted herself.

Ellen's hand lifted in refusal. "You need not entertain us. I told Edward you would not want to be disturbed, but he insisted on wishing you well. We shall go directly."

Jane shook her head. "Do not be silly. Of course, you are welcome. Tea. I shall ring for it. Sit down, do." She let go of Robert's hand and looked at Edward at the last.

Ellen smiled. "Thank you, but we shall not stay for dinner. We are expected at the Rochester ball this evening."

Robert glanced at Jane as she walked to the bell pull. He had an invitation, too. A ball would be a good place to introduce them to the *ton* as a couple. Sutton could cause no trouble there.

"Perhaps we ought to go, Jane? I have an invitation. I am sure the Rochesters would understand our reason for not submitting a reply."

Her hand fell from the bell pull and she turned back. Although she smiled, he saw the wariness and hidden concern in her eyes.

He was learning to read her. She wanted to go, to dress up and dance, but she was afraid of Sutton. He could see it.

Well, they would go then. He would simply deny Sutton's hold and chase the shadow of that damned man from her mind.

"We'll go." He held his hand out to her.

She came to him, accepting it.

He pulled her into a hug and whispered to her ear, "I know you want to."

Chapter Twenty

Jane clutched Robert's arm overly tight as she stepped into the Rochesters' ballroom. She wore bronze silk, and he fashionable black, which set off the colour of her dress beautifully.

Robert's eyes had darkened by degrees when he'd seen her dressed. Then he'd fetched a gold and emerald necklace which had been his mother's.

As he'd fixed the heavy jewellery about her neck, she'd felt its weight settle into the valley between her breasts, like a caress. Even now, she could feel it there, reminding her how much he cared.

His fingers covered hers on his arm.

He bowed to Lady Rochester. Jane curtsied.

Even with the threat of Joshua's retribution hanging over her, Jane felt lightness in her heart. She was not alone any more.

Robert took Lady Rochester's hand and pressed a kiss upon the back of her fingers. She cast him an odd, tense smile then looked at Jane and blushed.

A chill ran up Jane's spine.

Jane gave Lady Rochester another shallow curtsy, feeling the woman's discomfort, then turned to Lord Rochester. Was Lady Rochester one of Robert's past conquests?

Jane's heart thumped.

Robert shook Lord Rochester's hand, but he scowled at Robert then glowered at Jane as she dropped a swift curtsy.

Once they passed, Robert's hand lay over hers on his arm again, and he whispered through the side of his mouth. "Perhaps they *are* miffed we attended without accepting."

Both her hands gripped his arm. It was not what she'd thought then, if he could jest like that, but her heart still thumped, and her gaze reached to the room. There must be women he'd lain with here. She shut out the thought, her gaze moving into the crowd, seeking Edward and Ellen.

Someone beside Jane moved quite suddenly, turning away. The movement captured Jane's attention, and she realised others were doing the same. Robert kept walking, and the action followed them like a wave.

Oh Lord, we are being cut.

"What have we done?" she whispered. More people turned. "Robert?" But as she said it she saw Joshua across the room, in the far corner, surrounded by people.

The conversation in the room had dropped to hushed tones.

"Heaven knows," Robert answered, looking about them. "But it must be something to do with Sutton."

Jane lifted her chin defiantly. She'd lived through worse than this, but not in such a situation. Lady Marshall scowled directly at Jane, tutted, then turned away.

Ignoring the urge to stop and yell, *what am I meant to have done?* Jane carried on serenely, pretending nothing was wrong.

The Ripleys stood together in a large family group. She'd spoken to two of the wives on numerous occasions when she'd been with Violet, but even they refused to meet Jane's eye.

The quadrille came to a halt and the dancers bowed or curtsied then parted. There was laughter and chatter in the room again as couples separated and found new partners. The musicians struck up the more evocative notes of a waltz. Robert turned to Jane.

He smiled, but it was the mask he'd used in town before. It was a hard, cold smile. "We'll dance then, shall we?" He gave her no chance to refuse, already capturing her waist.

Her right hand settled on his shoulder as her gaze darted all about the large room. He immediately spun her into the heart of the dancing, amongst numerous others.

Her heart was thumping, her feet following his movement with no great art.

One couple looked at her and Robert, stopped dancing, then left the floor. They were followed by a second couple and a third. The floor began to clear. Couples stopped and turned away everywhere.

"Look at me." Robert's tone was a sharp order.

She did, her gaze striking his and absorbing the reassurance he sought to offer.

"It is Sutton. He's in the corner, holding court."

Glancing across the room, Jane saw Joshua glaring at them in sharp accusation and whispering something to a man beside him.

Her eyes turned back to Robert. A closed-lip smile was fixed on his face. He spun her. "Do you want to go?"

She shook her head.

"Neither do I," he whispered, drawing her closer.

She smiled genuinely, her hands and her eyes clinging to him. It did feel wonderful to have someone to help her fight.

"It appears we have the floor to ourselves," he stated, spinning her with flourish.

"It is at times like this, I wish I came from a large family," she answered, seeking to be as light-hearted and dismissive as he was.

He gave her a genuine smile, not the guarded one. "Well, that is one wish you now have answered, Jane." His head tilted to where Edward led Ellen to the floor.

"Edward, yes, but..." she began, about to say one brother did not a large family make, yet then she saw other couples taking

327

to the floor. It was an explicit resistance. They glanced about the room, glaring at their audience. "Ellen's sisters and their husbands?"

Jane met Robert's gaze again.

"See," he whispered with pride, his tone challenging her earlier disbelief. "You are a part of my family now."

Her heart filled with a soft pain, and tears blurred her vision as Robert continued to lead her across the floor. More couples slipped from the crowd.

"Ellen's extended family," Robert whispered.

Jane saw the Marquess of Wiltshire across Robert's shoulder. He was Ellen's brother-in-law and heir to the Duke of Arundel, and his judgement clearly held great weight within the *ton,* more weight than Joshua's. His glare brought more couples to the floor. Numbers continued to swell as others started to realise, if they continued to ostracise the Earl of Barrington, they were likely to be the ones set apart, and by the time the waltz ended, there were as many couples on the floor as there had been when it began.

Jane lifted to her toes and briefly kissed Robert's cheek. She believed him for the first time. She believed they could succeed against Joshua. They could fight and win.

She took Robert's arm, and he led her to the edge of the dance floor while Joshua watched them with an intensity which promised another assault.

Jane lifted her chin and looked right back, telling him he had no hold over her any more, yet then, he began walking towards her. Jane froze, her fingers digging into Robert's arm. Robert turned.

"You will regret this, Barrington," Joshua growled. Then he was gone, leaving them both standing amidst the crowd.

Edward, Ellen, and Ellen's sisters surrounded them in a moment, and Jane allowed the women to lead her away to the refreshment hall. The men followed.

"What rumour did he start?" Jane asked Ellen.

It was Ellen's sister, Penny, who answered, "He told everyone you were having an affair with Robert during your marriage to the old Duke."

Jane turned. "But that is plainly nonsense. Robert was abroad, and half of them are having affairs anyway. Why should they even care?"

Ellen's gaze met hers. "Robert was not abroad for the last few years. There are those who believe Sutton, and as to people's judgement, you are clearly unused to the holier-than-thou aspect of the *ton*. They will turn a blind eye until scandal is shared in plain sight. Then they all act disgusted, as though they have not done the same."

"But *I* was never in town."

Ellen smiled. "Unfortunately, it only gives them more opportunity to believe Sutton, if they have seen no evidence to dispute it. Robert has stayed with us frequently. He was not always in town. They could imagine him anywhere."

Jane glanced back at Robert, who was talking with the men. She saw he had just received the same news. There was nothing they could do but ignore it. *Ton* marriages were riddled with affairs, and the gossip would die down. If this was the worst Joshua could do, then he would hardly break them. She still felt triumphant.

~

The following afternoon, still abuzz with the success of the night before, Jane ran to greet her husband. She leaned on the banister and looked down as she heard the front door bang shut.

Robert was there in the hall. She'd not expected him back for at least another hour or two. He'd gone to his club, White's, to find out what he could about Joshua's intentions.

She would have gone to see Violet, but, when Jane had asked

after her friend the night before, she'd discovered that Violet, and Geoff, had left town.

She hadn't minded Robert leaving her here though. She'd gladly spent some time with the housekeeper and got to know the staff. She felt happy today, like there was a future to plan for after their victory last night. For the first time, she truly believed she could win against the Suttons. Robert had said so, and she was learning to trust him.

When they'd made love last night, she'd felt entirely free, and she'd slept soundly in his arms. So soundly, he'd left her to take breakfast in bed when he'd gone to his club.

Her fingers trailed on the banister as she raced along the landing and downstairs.

He glanced up, but then instantly looked away, focusing on his gloves as he tugged them off.

As she reached the bottom step, Robert virtually flung his gloves at Jenkins then lifted off his hat and thrust that at his butler, too.

Something was wrong. "What is it?" she asked, pausing with her hand on the newel post.

He looked her way with a deep sigh and gave her his insincere, rakish smile. "Nothing for you to worry about." There was a lethal edge to his words.

Her hope drained, and Jane felt as though a stone had dropped to the bottom of her stomach.

Joshua had done something else.

She walked to Robert. "Tell me what he's done?"

He shrugged her fingers off as she laid them on his upper arm and turned towards his study. "Later, Jane. Jenkins, is there brandy in my study?"

"Yes, my Lord," the butler answered as Jane followed Robert's long strides.

"Robert!" she called, unable to catch up. "Robert! For heaven's sake, tell me what Joshua has done!"

Robert thrust aside the office door, and it banged back against the wooden panelling as he disappeared.

When she followed him in, he'd stopped at the secretaire with one hand on a decanter and the other on a glass. His back was to her. "Leave me alone, Jane, please. I don't trust my temper."

She stood staring at him, not knowing what to say, all the wind knocked from her sails. She'd felt so happy.

Instantly, Robert felt guilty. He silently cursed, but didn't turn back, focusing instead on pouring a drink.

He'd been swearing all the way back from White's. He'd even traitorously blamed her in his thoughts, as much as Sutton. He was not in the mood to talk to her.

When he turned around after sipping the brandy, he saw she looked crestfallen. She'd been beaming this morning after their success last night. Now she appeared vulnerable again. Her beauty struck him hard in the chest though, as it always did. But sadly, the sight did not diminish his anger.

He was in a rage.

He downed the remainder of the amber liquor in one swift draught then turned to pour more.

He drank that straight down, too, but it did nothing to ease his anger. Spinning round suddenly, he threw the glass at the stone hearth. Satisfaction rushed through him as it shattered, but Jane leapt back to avoid the splintering glass.

"Robert! Tell me what he's done!"

Mixed emotions writhed in Robert. "They have blackballed me at White's."

Her brow furrowed. "They what?"

Of course, a woman would not understand. He had a seat in the House of Lords. He needed the respect of his peers.

331

Robert turned back and snatched up another glass then stalked towards her, his voice rising with each step. "They have voted me out of my club, Jane." He flung the second glass at the marble hearth and liked the satisfying reward as it shattered and knocked a chunk off the marble.

"I'm sorry."

He'd felt her smallness last night as they'd danced that damned waltz, her fragility. He was reminded of it again when her hand touched his arm.

It is not her fault. She'd been forced into her marriage, into her connection with that bloody family. But even so, he wanted to spout poison and lay the blame on her. He felt devoid of gentlemanly etiquette today, primal.

Jane had been right. Sutton was bloody playing with them. They'd won a single battle last night, not the war, and Sutton had probably already known he had the next foray in hand.

Robert's hands curled to fists. "It's not your fault."

He turned away and sought another glass. This time, he filled it and drank, then waited while the strong liquor diffused the anger in his veins, his hand still gripping the glass as it stood on the side.

"What will you do?" She was beside him. Her fingers wrapped about his as they held the glass, her other hand resting on his shoulder and her cheek against his back.

Kill him. As the thought crystallised in his mind, the silent words formed in his head.

A duel sounded very appealing. It would end this.

Robert imagined running a blade through Sutton.

Jane must have sensed his thoughts. "No!" She moved away, letting him go again. "You are not a murderer. You are not to do anything stupid. I shall not let you do it."

"You'll not let me?" He spoke to the decanter, not turning, anger soaring in his blood again. A repugnant sneer touched his lips, and he turned around. He may love her, but it was about time he held his own reins again. He would be lord and master in his home. She'd been stringing him along all summer. She was not going to dictate to him any more.

He needed to get out. He needed to get away from her before he said something he did not mean.

"Robert, do not be foolish!" she said as he started moving. He did not stop to listen. "I know Joshua," she urged behind him, following as he left the room. "He does not fight fair. I doubt he would even risk his own life!" Her words followed him across the hall as he heard her rushing to keep up. "He would have someone else dispose of you before you even have a chance!"

"Robert!" she screamed his name again as he kept moving.

"Do not do it!" It was the last thing he heard as he went out the door without his hat, his gloves, or his greatcoat.

~

Jane knelt on the drawing room window seat, her brow against the window pane. It had been raining for an hour, a light drizzle which clouded the view and traced its path in little rivers down the pane of glass. She'd been watching the street since the door had slammed shut behind Robert three hours earlier, praying he'd gone to Edward and hoping Edward had persuaded Robert against anything rash. Traffic came and went on the street outside, others' lives continuing as normal while hers fell apart once more.

She had known how this would end. She should have been stronger. She should have stayed away from Robert. Yet she couldn't think of losing him now.

A man of Robert's build entered the square in the far corner with a long stride. Her fingers touched the windowpane.

It was him.

Jane pushed herself off the seat and ran to the hall, racing to the front door to pull it open before any of the footmen. She did not wait for him, but ran outside, down the steps into the street, and threw herself into Robert's arms as he came along the pavement.

Her satin house slippers were soaked in a puddle, but she didn't care.

"Jane, we are in the street," he chided in a deep burr. He was soaked through.

She let him go and took his hand, smiling at him. He smiled in return, closed-lipped, and let her lead him up the steps.

Inside, she began unbuttoning his morning coat.

"I am not an invalid," he whispered. "I can manage."

"I know, but you're all wet, and I am so glad you're home." She hugged him again and pressed a kiss on his cheek.

He kissed hers in return, but then his hands settled on her waist and pushed her away. "Let's go upstairs."

She nodded her agreement as he slipped off his wet morning coat. She was very willing to escape their audience – Jenkins and two footmen.

"You did not do it, did you?" she asked, following him as he walked upstairs.

He did not reply.

She looked back at Jenkins, who held Robert's wet coat. "Send for some tea. Lord Barrington will need something to warm him."

When she entered the drawing room behind him, she shut the door and leaned back against it. "You did not, did you?"

"Did not what?" he queried, facing her.

He stood beside the hearth, warming his hands. His brown eyes asked the question, too.

"Call Joshua out. Where have you been? Did Edward persuade you against it?"

He came towards her then, amusement suddenly in his eyes,

and when he reached her, he said, "No, Jane, I have neither called Sutton out, nor spoken to Edward." His fingers settled on her shoulder and began toying with a lock of her hair.

"Then where were you?"

His gaze dropped to her lips. Her hands pressed against his damp waistcoat to stop him from leaning forward. He was in an odd mood, and she was suddenly angry with him.

"Robert!"

"In Hyde Park."

"In Hyde Park? So now everyone knows we are at odds and Joshua has even more fuel for his rumours."

"I have been walking off my temper."

She wished he'd simply talked it out with her. He was her sanctuary. She wanted to be his.

"Are we at odds?" he questioned, his voice sullen and his eyes brooding.

"You walked out. All I wished you to do was speak to me. I did not cause your anger."

His gaze was heavy on hers and uncommunicative, and his fingers let go of her hair and fell from her shoulder.

One of his eyebrows arched before he turned and walked back to the hearth. He leaned one hand on the mantel and reached the other towards the fire. "A man has a right to vent his spleen, Jane. I just wish there was an end to this muddle."

She saw his shoulders shudder. He was cold. Compassion swept through her.

A knock struck the door, and a maid called, "Tea, my Lady, my Lord."

"Bring it in," Jane answered without taking her eyes off her husband. He did not turn.

She remembered that day at the ruins, when his anger had been addressed at her.

Once the maid had set down the tray, Jane dismissed her. The girl bobbed a curtsy and left, shutting the door behind her.

Looking at Robert, Jane asked, "What do we do now?"

He did not turn. "Who knows? I have no idea. It seems he has the power to do whatever he likes while I play his bloody fool."

"I'm sorry." A sharp pain raced from her heart into her breast. Joshua was attacking Robert because he'd helped her. She felt guilty.

"It is not your fault," he answered, though his voice was unconvincing. It sounded as though he was trying to convince himself, too.

She went to him and hugged him, pressing her cheek against his damp waistcoat at his back, desperately seeking to impart to him how much he meant to her.

He straightened, tension ebbing from his body as one forearm lay over hers.

They stood like that for a moment in silence before he turned and embraced her, kissing her hair and whispering, "God, Jane, remind me why this is worth it."

With tears in her eyes, she lifted her mouth to his, and his broad hand encompassed the back of her head. The kiss was searing, hard, and passionate. A coil of desire swirled through her stomach and slipped between her legs. She thought of the ruins, of how he'd lost his tight control and made love with ruthless need.

"Come to bed," she whispered. "Ease your anger through me, Robert." He'd always helped her. She could do this one thing to help him.

Both his hands settled on her buttocks and sharply pulled her pelvis to his as his brown eyes glittered with a dark heat, but his words refused her offer, even though his body was already saying yes. "No, Jane. I don't want to hurt you. I haven't got a grip on this yet."

"You won't hurt me. You wouldn't. I know you couldn't, Robert."

Her lips brushed his, urging him to accept, but he held back and did not deepen it, yet she felt his muscles shiver with restraint.

She met his gaze again.

He didn't speak.

She began undoing the buttons of his waistcoat as his heavy-lidded gaze watched.

Her fingers pressed over his rigid stomach. His shirt was wet, too, and his skin was cold. He shivered.

"You need to get these wet things off." She looked up to his eyes, and began tracing his waistcoat from his shoulders.

He sighed, but she could see he was not thinking of being wet and cold.

Turning away, he took off his waistcoat.

"Robert," she whispered, when he turned back to her, lifting her arms about his neck as his hands settled on her waist. She shivered, but it was not from the damp seeping from his shirt into her dress.

She loved this man. She always had. They had made a mess of the past, and it haunted them today, but they had each other now, despite it.

"Do you know how much I love you?" his voice rasped from his throat, a desperate hunger in his tone. "I'm sorry I've let him anger me. I know it is not your fault, Jane."

But he'd laid some blame on her. She heard it in his voice, yet, how could she be angry at him for that? She had involved him. She'd accepted his offer of marriage. She could blame him, too, if she wished. He'd left her alone all those years ago to be trapped in the Sutton's net, but she did not, not anymore, not now that she knew he'd carried his own pain all these years.

"I love you, too," she answered, her fingers against his cheek. She pressed her lips to his.

His floodgate broke, the passion in him overflowing, and she hung on as it swept her away. He was such a physical, elemental person. All his emotion pressed into activity. Sex had become his armour and shield, she had seen it as a weapon. It was not; it was his retreat. He'd escaped from her loss with others, and now, she wished him to become used to losing himself in her. She wanted so much to be his solace, to become his shield.

Her fingers ran through his silky hair, and a strange thought struck her. How would things have been between them if they'd married when he was nineteen? Not like this. He was not so strong and passionate in character then. They'd have had a marriage like his parents, staid and quiet. He'd have made love with placid adoration, not this fire. She liked his fire. She could not imagine life with him without it. She admitted to herself, she loved the new Robert more deeply than she had loved the old. Her previous love had not been so all-consuming. It was an odd feeling to think that something good had come from the separation they'd endured and the life he'd lived in between.

Breaking their kiss, he dragged a deep breath into his already heaving lungs. "Do you know how right you are for me?" His fingers caressed her thighs, working up her gown.

"Here?" She hesitated, reaching to stop his hands.

"*Here. Now,*" he answered, meeting her gaze, the residue of his anger glinting as a visible challenge in his eyes.

"There is no lock on the door."

A wicked, rakish smile caught up his lips before he lowered his head and began brushing her neck with kisses while his damp hair caressed her cheek. "I dare you."

Riotous, delicious anticipation danced through her. She was not afraid, not with him. He made her want to take the risk.

He lifted his head and gave her his predatory, wolfish smile – the rogue.

"You're wicked," she whispered as his eyes baited her, denying cowardice, but he said nothing, did nothing, just waited on her decision.

A sigh escaped her lips, and his eyes glowed with self-congratulation, the inky pupils flaring, making the dark brown about them only a narrow rim.

He did not wait for words. His mouth came down on hers, hungry and urgent, as his fingers continued to work up her dress.

"Undo my flap," he said as he lifted her and backed her up against the wall, his dark gaze burning into her.

Her fingers shook as she did, while his clutched her bare thighs. Once he was free, she gripped his shoulders, very aware of the unlocked door.

"Stop thinking. Just feel," he urged on a growl as he pressed into her and brushed a kiss on the corner of her open mouth. "I love you," he added in a deep, heavy, burr, as though the words were a creed.

"I love you, too."

"I won't live without you."

"You need not." She gripped his shoulders tighter. Had he thought he'd lost her? She must cease saying she'd go back or she wished she had not come. He needed her. She *was* his solace, just as she wished to be.

After a while, she had no choice but to let go of thought, because the storm of his desire ripped it away. This was no careful charm. It was rough enslavement. It was as it had been at the ruins, artless and ruthless. But it was different now. This time, he was not angry with her. This time, she relished every element of his primal assault and revelled in the free rein he allowed himself with her, repaying him with the surrender of her soul.

"I needed this, Jane. I need you," he said once she was breathless and panting and dazed. He lowered her legs to the floor then turned her and urged her to kneel.

On the floor? In the daylight? With an unlocked door? How much further could he push her boundaries?

She obeyed, kneeling on all fours. He filled her with a low growl. This was primitive pleasure. He was losing himself in physical expression and losing her with him.

She knew he was doing this for himself, not her. What she gained from it was only consequence. *Wicked man.*

His tempo shifted and became sharper and more forceful, coarse, quick strikes.

Her fingers and toes curled and gripped against the hardwood floor as his clasped her hair and shoulder, holding her still to meet his thrusts.

She was simply sensation, and she felt herself flood, time and again. Then his hands suddenly clamped about her hips, and, with three swift hard strokes, he reached his own conclusion.

When his breathing grew steadier, his fingers braced her stomach, and he pulled her upright to kneel on his lap as he dropped back on to his haunches. Her head rested back on to his shoulder, and her limbs shook as he pressed a kiss on her neck. "Did I hurt you?"

She shook her head.

"I'm sorry I was angry." His voice was husky.

"You have nothing to be sorry for. I understand, Robert." She slipped free of his hold and turned, wanting to see his face and look into his eyes. "Do you feel better?"

"I feel better, yes, but at what cost?"

"At no cost. You have not hurt me."

"No?" His eyes searched hers. "I was not too rough? I have not given you a dislike of me?"

Her fingers swept the damp lock of hair from his brow.

"I love *you*, Robert, *you*, faults and foibles and all. Passion and anger are a part of you; I do not expect you to be perfect. You allowed me to be angry the other day. I'll understand when you are. Just never shut me out."

He smiled, and his fingers came up to brush her cheek. "I'll try. But I've spent too many years seeking to be good enough for you. I am afraid of losing you."

She hugged him firmly. "You are good enough for me. I never stopped loving you, Robert, not in all the years we were apart."

The weight of his palm lay on her back, and her cheek pressed against his wet shirt.

"The first night I saw you in London, the reason I went home with you was to escape Joshua. He'd attacked me at the ball. That day in the bookshop, he was in the street. I called you back to avoid him. And I saw him watching the house after you'd taken me home. I turned to you all those times for comfort and escape." She pulled away, and his hand rested at her waist as she knelt, facing him. "Now that we are in this together, should we not comfort each other? You can lose control with me, Robert."

His lips pressed against her forehead and he hugged her.

"I wish I could turn back time," he spoke to the air above them. "I wish I had not left you alone in that glade."

"You were young, Robert. We both were. Too young to deal with what happened. Let us just think about now and discard that pain."

He sighed. "I wonder how I have lived without you."

Did she need any more reassurance that the others he'd slept with meant nothing? Her hand pressed against his damp chest as she pulled away again. "We are very similar, you and I. We *were* made for each other, weren't we? I have spent my life hiding my hurt and pain behind pride. You've hidden it behind debauchery. Both of us have acted as though we don't care. We do. We have both been through torment internally, while others thought us cold and dispassionate."

He gave her a fierce hug, his hand running over her hair, but

341

he did not speak.

It was true. They had endured enough silent pain. She had let hers out now, and she hoped he had, too.

She smiled and looked up. "Thank you."

"For what?"

"For enduring this hardship for me. I believe in you."

"Go change and tidy up, then I will take you for a drive in the park now that the rain has stopped, so everyone will know we are not at odds. And *thank you*, for loving me. It is not an easy task, I know." He kissed her cheek and finally let her go to secure his falls, saying, "Now run along, sweetheart, and get changed."

Chapter Twenty-one

Looking in the mirror of her vanity table, as she sat before it, Jane watched Robert secure his latest gift from his mother's jewels about her neck, a string of pearls. His hands brushed her skin, and he leaned in and pressed a kiss to her neck.

Her hand lifted and touched his hair as he pulled away. She looked up at her husband when he stood straight again, or rather, at his reflection. He met her gaze in the mirror. His fingers gripped her shoulders and caressed them gently, his thumbs rubbing her nape.

The action sent familiar shivers running down her spine, and an ache, a spasm, spiralled inside her.

"May we not go to the Yorks'?" she whispered, letting her head fall back to rest against his stomach.

His deep laugh resonated about the room, "I would *prefer* to stay at home." His fingers slid downward into her bodice.

Since Robert's outrage over his barring from White's, she'd barely spent any time apart from him. They'd driven in the park, shopped, and loved, hiding themselves away, denying the world, a silent resolution forming between them that nothing would set them apart. She'd been wrapped up in him, as he'd been in her. They'd been sheltering each other, she knew, and she'd treasured the intensity, shutting her mind to anything else, though nothing had happened for three days. It only meant the next attack was imminent.

The dull thud of the front door knocker reached their hallowed ground.

She took a breath. "That will be Edward and Ellen."

His hands lifted again and gently squeezed her shoulders. "Sadly, we must go then."

She smiled and took his hand. "Solidarity, my Lord."

"Solidarity," he answered, lifting her fingers to his lips.

Her other hand touched his cheek. "If Joshua plays any games tonight, do not rise to it, Robert. Promise me?"

He smiled, placating. "I shall try, but I will not stand back and allow the man to ride roughshod over us. I have my pride."

She took a breath and let it go on a sigh as a knock struck their bedchamber door. "My Lord, my Lady!" Jenkins called. "Lord and Lady Edward are waiting in the hall."

Jane braced herself.

"Stop worrying," Robert said in a low voice. "All will be well. I'll not let it end otherwise."

They left the room and proceeded downstairs.

"Ellen. Edward," Jane called, smiling.

Once in the hall, Jane found herself embraced by Ellen. Robert's fingers let hers go.

"Edward told me what happened the other day. He has an idea—"

"My Lord! My Lord!" Ellen was cut off by a shout coming from behind them.

"My Lord!" It grew louder as they all turned to the servants' entrance in the hall. "My Lord!"

James, Robert's groom, ran into the hall, arms wide. His face was dirt-stained, and his clothes were singed in places, wisps of smoke rising from spots on the cloth. He wiped his brow on his arm as he came to a halt and drew a breath. "My Lord," he said to Robert, "the stables are on fire."

Jane looked at her husband.

His eyes had narrowed, and the muscle in his jaw was visibly taut. "How?" The single word spoke the accusation. He moved forward. So did Edward.

"A torch was thrown over the wall, my Lord."

Without a word, Robert shared a look with Edward then his pace increased. They were gone in an instant, James with them, as they disappeared through the servants' door.

Jane gripped her dress, lifted her hem, and hurried in pursuit, hearing Ellen follow.

When they reached the courtyard, the stables were in flames, gold and orange tongues licking the jet night air. The fire was eating the stable block like a giant monster, crackling and growling. The internal beams groaned, and suddenly, a massive crack rang out as wood splintered and a quarter of the stable roof dropped away, collapsing with a loud, angry whoosh.

Flying splinters of burning wood and straw drifted about Jane, and the intense heat from the blaze seared her lungs and scorched her skin.

Her eyes spun about the courtyard as voices broke her shock.

Several chains of servants passed buckets of water between them. Horses screamed and whinnied. Men shouted, calling for more water. She could not see Robert or Edward, but it appeared all the horses were out, and yet, the carriages and tack would still be lost. The flames licked higher in the air, threatening the house.

"Ellen." Jane caught at her sister-in-law's hand and pulled Ellen with her to join a chain forming on the side by the house. At once, a bucket was passed into her hands. She passed it on again towards the corner of the stable closest to the house, where people sought to stop the fire from spreading. Jane took another bucket from Ellen's hands and looked for Robert in the chaos. The fire was a bright

345

torch against the cloudy, indigo hues of night. Another bucket was passed, and Jane handed it on, and then an empty one back.

"Another bucket!" It was Robert's voice.

Her eyes turned to him. He was by the stable, pouring water on to the burning wooden frame above a door, as grooms ran through trying to save what they could. "Another!" he yelled, frustrated at his chain's slow pace. Jane saw Edward at the head of another chain. She worked to speed up the passing of her own, calling ahead for everyone to hurry and listening to Robert's orders for the targets of their battle. Two additional chains formed under Robert's direction as servants from the houses around his own came to help, but they made little headway against the raging fire, its flames leaping like fingers reached out towards the house. Jane passed back an empty bucket to Ellen. Their eyes met and Jane said, "We will lose the house."

"Not if we can help it," Ellen responded, her fingers catching Jane's for a moment before passing the bucket on.

A flash of light suddenly filled the sky, and lightning stretched to earth like a crack, breaking through the black night. Thunder shook the air about them. High-pitched female squeals of fright joined masculine cries to continue the chain. Then, in answer to an unspoken prayer, the heavens opened. Rain fell in large, heavy drops hammering down, drenching the stables within minutes and subduing the flames.

Jane stopped and looked up, as did everyone about her, and some held their hands to the rain.

The fire smouldered, tamed from flames to wisps of smoke in moments, and the air stank of charred wood and burnt leather.

Buckets fell to the ground, and people hugged and laughed, thanking God.

Jane felt exhausted as she walked over to Robert. His face was upturned to the rain, and his arms hung loosely at his sides.

"Robert?" She gripped his hand.

His hair was plastered to his brow, and his coat was welded to his powerful frame. Everything about him spoke of authority and silent strength.

He lowered his head and looked at a passing stable lad.

"Is there a saddle?"

The boy stopped and turned. "Aye, my Lord."

"Then saddle me a horse."

The boy did not move.

"Now!" Robert yelled.

The lad tugged at his forelock then darted off.

"Where are you going?" Edward asked.

Jane turned.

Ellen was holding Edward's hand. Her damp dress clung to her figure.

"This ends now," Robert answered stiffly, his fingers slipping from Jane's.

Jane saw the boy throw a saddle over the back of a chestnut mare. Robert walked away.

She followed. "Robert. No."

He glanced back. "*No, Jane?*" The words were flung at her, but he did not stop moving. "Do you still not believe in me? I am going to settle this."

"Not when you're angry." She tried to grip his arm, but he pulled it free.

"Trust me." He no longer looked at her, but at the horse. She could see his mind racing towards a fight with Joshua. He may as well already be riding there. He was obviously picturing the violence he planned in his head.

"Robert, I trust you. I do not trust him! Don't go!"

"Then maybe I shall not fight fair. Or would you rather I wait until he's killed us both." His loose arm swung to incorporate the smouldering charred remains of the stables as he walked. She hurried after him. "*If this had spread to the house?*" The conclusion of that question, of how much they could have lost, he left hanging as he halted and turned to face her. "It stops now, Jane, one way or another."

She moved in front of him. "No."

"I can't not." He pressed her aside and walked on.

Jane looked at Edward, who'd followed. "Stop him! Stop him, please! He will not listen!"

Edward did not acknowledge her, but moved past her as Robert mounted.

"Robert, don't go!" Jane cried, spinning about and facing him again, rain dripping down her face.

He sat back into the saddle, ignoring her imploring words, and the look he gave her was an apologetic denial as he struck his heels to the horse's flanks, hard.

But Edward grasped the animal's reins and held it steady. "Wait! I have an idea. Just give me a moment. You know you'll never stand against Sutton alone. He won't let you anywhere near him."

"So now my own brother thinks me too weak."

"I don't think you weak. I have a secret weapon."

Impatiently, Robert's horse twisted its head against the grip of the bit.

"What weapon?"

"Pembroke..."

Robert had reached the end of his tether. All he wanted to do was face Sutton and put an end to this. His palms itched to do it.

"Pembroke's influence outweighs Sutton's by miles. Imagine if we get Pembroke on your side!" Edward still gripped the reins.

"Let me deal with this!" Robert's anger was intense. He wished this done.

"Don't be a fool. You cannot take him down alone! You know you cannot!"

Impatient, Robert inwardly cursed. He knew Edward was right, and yet, every element of Robert's being wanted to go after the man who had abused Jane and was now attacking *him*.

"Robert!" Edward yelled.

Looking at the hubbub in the courtyard, Robert saw Jane. She watched him with wide, dark, terrified eyes. She was soaked, as he was, as they all were, but the bedraggled state of her hair and dress brought him back to sanity. How would she cope if Sutton retaliated with a fatal strike? This had all begun because he'd ridden away and left her. He couldn't do the same again. She needed him.

Hell! In one movement, he swung down from the saddle.

"Tell me your idea," he growled at his brother.

Jane lost all reserve, flew at him, and hugged him hard, sobbing.

She had scaled his rakehell walls long ago, and now, he knew he had broken her defences, too. Less than a month ago, she would not have shown any feeling.

A half hour later, all still in a state of dishabille, they clustered in the drawing room, he and Edward in their damp shirts, the women with shawls wrapped about them as the fire, having been stoked, burned brightly. Both women clasped a hot chocolate in shaking fingers, while Robert and Edward gripped glasses of brandy.

"Why do you think Pembroke would let himself be dragged into this? I cannot imagine him agreeing to it," Robert challenged.

"Because he is interested in anything which involves John. You know, as well as I do, Sutton's strikes could get broader. Let us help. Let me get help. After all, you helped Ellen and me once. Let us return the favour."

"And what the hell can Pembroke do?"

Jane set down her chocolate, and her fingers wrapped about his arm. He could feel her willing him to listen, even though she never said a word, as she pressed closer to his shoulder.

"He can do to Sutton what Sutton did to you. He has the influence you do not. He can draw people to your side and threaten Sutton financially and socially. With Wiltshire's influence, too, and the influence of the other men in Ellen's family, Sutton won't stand a chance."

Bloody hell, this was the cannon fire Robert had been looking for, the big guns. Robert's fingers covered his mouth. He so wanted to bring Sutton down alone, but to bring him down at all was more important. Robert slipped his arm from Jane's grip and, instead, wrapped it about her shoulders, then nodded at Edward.

~

Five days later, sitting in a winged armchair in the drawing room, Robert listened to the men of Ellen's family, who were spread about the room, discussing their counterattack.

Jane stood behind his seat, gripping its back.

Of course, it would be aboveboard, no setting fires, but Robert's palms were itching again.

The Duke of Pembroke's man of business had investigated Sutton's trading accounts and had identified illegal practices, blackmail, and bribes. Now, Pembroke's man was buying up stock around Sutton's, pulling the same trick Sutton had played on Robert. Meanwhile, Ellen's family was planning the Duke of Sutton's final humiliation.

"Where is it best to face him?" James, the younger of Ellen's sister's husbands, asked.

"At White's, I would say," Richard, the eldest of the group, responded.

Jane's hand pressed on Robert's shoulder. Looking up, he caught her emerald gaze before she looked away. "I want to be there," she

350

said to the room.

"She has a right." Edward backed her up, glancing at Robert.

Robert gave Edward a look which must have appeared sheer steel. Robert didn't want Sutton anywhere near her.

He reached up and covered her hand.

"Leave it to us," he answered, looking up at her.

Her eyes shone with challenge. "I am the one who has been his victim."

"But no longer, with my father-in-law's influence and ours combined. How do you wish to play it, Barrington?" It was Richard who spoke. Robert looked back at him, having watched Jane do the same, and felt Jane's fingers stir beneath his own, but he caught her hand and lifted it, then used his grip to encourage her to come about the chair so he could see her more easily. "Jane, sweetheart, it is better if you stay out of it. We have no idea how Sutton will react."

"He will be angry. If he lashes out—" David Stewart, the Earl of Preston, husband to Ellen's second sister, contributed.

"If he lashes out, I shall get out of his way. You will all be there," Jane said to the room before looking back at Robert. "You cannot deny me a part in this."

Robert sighed, his fingers still gripping hers. "Jane, please have some sense?"

"Let me be there, Robert."

He knew why she asked. The others did not.

She wanted to keep an eye on him, to protect him. She was still scared he'd do something rash, and terrified of Sutton doing something worse. It had not helped when, after the fire, Ellen had confessed that Robert had killed the man who'd abused *her*. Though it had been in self-defence, it had still fuelled Jane's fear.

She didn't trust Robert's temper, she'd said, and she definitely didn't trust Sutton.

351

He could understand. His endurance was erratic, and she'd put up with the Dukes of Sutton's games for two generations. She was afraid because she loved him. Robert had ceased being offended by it. He loved her more for it. But they would be best placed to corner Sutton in White's or the House of Lords, and neither place would admit Jane.

"There is a ball at the Devonshires' a week hence. That would give us a chance to prepare, and a public venue, if you wish to be included, Lady Barrington?" James smiled at Jane, offering her consolation.

Robert sighed. "The Devonshires' ball it is then."

"Sutton won't know what hit him. I doubt he realised the association between our families when he attacked you. I am sure he had a shock at the Rochester ball. He probably knows his game is over, and that is why he resorted to violence. But we'll give him no more opportunity for that," Richard concluded.

Robert shifted in his chair. The thought of paying Sutton back for all Jane had suffered was stimulating. "So, you will let me know who we have on our side? Why do we not establish a meeting at White's the day before the ball? If one of you can propose my re-establishment, then we shall have Sutton riled. And tell your associates not to let him know where they stand until the ball. I do not want him to get wind of this beforehand. I want the pleasure of seeing the shock on his face when he registers his influence no longer reaches to Jane."

The men stood.

Robert did, too, smiling. He knew, with the influence of Ellen's family, half of the House of Lords or more would stand on his side.

Jane hovered beside him as each of Ellen's family shook his hand and took their leave.

He was looking forward to the Devonshires' ball. He only wished he'd thought to resort to the use of Pembroke's power before. Had he taken that tack when Pembroke had approached him in White's, this would have already been settled, and Jane could have avoided the torment of the last few weeks.

His goodbyes complete, his fingers caught hold of Jane's as Edward stepped towards him.

"I'll follow them out if there is nothing more you wish to discuss. Ellen will be waiting for me at the Pulteney, but if you need anything, or if you would rather we stayed here, you need only ask."

Robert nodded and gave Edward a smile of gratitude. "You've done enough. We're grateful."

"We are." Jane let go of Robert's hand and reached to hug his brother. "Thank you."

"It's nothing." Edward hugged her in return. "We'll call tomorrow."

Once they'd separated, Jane walked with Edward to the drawing room door and said goodbye and thank you again.

When the door clicked shut, Jane turned back.

Robert smiled, seeking to be conciliatory. He knew he'd scared the woman witless the other night. Since then, she'd hovered about him, all overprotective.

"It does not feel right to leave it all to Ellen's family. They have no obligation to me," he said.

"It would appear to me they care for you, Robert, as Edward's brother, and they are only talking sense when they tell you to leave it to them. I am very grateful they've offered to help." She crossed the drawing room towards him as she spoke.

"But?" he prompted, hearing hesitation.

Ebony lashes veiled her gaze.

"Spit it out, woman. What thought are you withholding?"

Her eyelashes flickered back up. She had stopped two feet away. "I want to believe they are right, but no one has ever had the upper hand over the Suttons."

"There is always a first time, Jane. But that is why you want to be there, isn't it? Because you fear it will descend into violence. He cannot attack me before an audience, sweetheart, and I promise, I will not attack him. There is no need to worry. They will pen him in and bring him down."

Jane stepped forward, took his hand, and held it to her cheek. "I hope you're right."

"Darling, I know I am." He hugged her. "I am not going to allow Sutton to continue harassing us. This will end it. I wish now I had appealed to Pembroke before."

The need to protect her was overwhelming. His memory fell back to the sixteen-year-old girl, so full of life. He wanted to give her the opportunity to be that person again.

Chapter Twenty-two

Robert had Jane's small hand gripped in his as they walked the edge of the dance floor, weaving in and out of the crush of guests. No one had noticed the moment a certain number of the most influential of the *ton* had simultaneously left the room. Or the Duke of Pembroke himself, open a discussion with the Duke of Sutton and lead him from the ballroom out on to the terrace.

If all was going to plan, Ellen's father had led Sutton to Devonshire's library under the excuse of talking business. Of course, Sutton would already know Pembroke had been buying up shares around his investments, whether he suspected the reason, they didn't know, but to date, to mislead the man, Pembroke had also laid a generous offer on the table for Sutton's stock. Little did Sutton know the proverbial rug was about to be pulled from beneath his feet.

Robert would still rather not have Jane in attendance, but she'd refused to be persuaded otherwise.

Looking at her now, he saw her face was set in a determined expression. Yet beneath it, she was terrified of facing Sutton, but not so much that she would risk letting Robert face Sutton alone. *Foolish woman.*

Glancing across the room, Robert met Edward's gaze as he parted from Ellen.

Edward nodded to identify that Sutton was in place with Ellen's brothers-in-law and their peers.

They'd brought three dozen of the highest Lords to their side. A dozen were here to face Sutton with their claims. Aside from Sutton's behaviour towards Jane, they'd uncovered numerous cases of underhanded dealings affecting many of those who'd come to their side. It seemed Sutton was better at making enemies than he was at making friends. Uniting with Pembroke and his sons-in-law had given these men the opportunity for revenge, too. Like Robert, they would not have succeeded alone.

Leaving the pomp, noise, and glitter of Devonshire's ball behind, Robert led Jane out through the French doors.

The cold night, and perhaps fear, too, made her shiver. The balmy nights of summer were long gone. In her short-sleeved evening dress and shawl, she must feel it more than he did.

"You're cold?" he whispered.

"I'll manage." She drew her shawl from her bent elbows up and over her shoulders with one hand, while her other kept a tight hold of his.

They walked the length of the terrace in silence. No one else was in view. The others must have already entered Devonshire's library. Jane's heels struck the paving in pace with his as they walked, and the sound resonated above the distant music and conversation from the ballroom. The night was drab and dark. The only light to guide their path spilled from the second set of French doors which stood open to the night air at the far end of the terrace.

"A cartel?" he overheard Sutton say as they approached the open doors leading into the library. The chilly autumn breeze caught the curtain, whipping it out in front of them, concealing him and Jane from Sutton's view. Yet Robert had already seen Sutton standing before the hearth beside the Duke of Pembroke, a drink in hand, observing the rest of the group with speculation.

Did Sutton recognise his enemies and suspect what was planned? "That is an idea I would support," Sutton continued, his words compliant, but his tone hesitant and wary.

"There is one more member we are awaiting," Pembroke continued.

Robert looked at Jane. This was their cue. Smiling, he squeezed her hand. She smiled in return, such a gentle, vulnerable look, it wrenched his heart. How the hell could the Suttons have treated a woman of her quality with such a lack of respect? She was worth ten dozen of them. Giving him a little nod in assent, she acknowledged she was ready to face the villain.

"Barrington," Pembroke intoned as Robert stepped into the room, keeping a tight hold on Jane's hand.

She hung back behind his shoulder as Sutton stared, hiding his emotions, although Robert could see the mental calculation running behind the fixed look on Sutton's face.

"The fact is, Your Grace," Robert began, unable to hold back the callous smile which lifted his lips, "this cartel of which the Duke of Pembroke speaks has been established solely to *exclude* you, not to *include* you."

Sutton glared, the muscle of his jaw flickering with controlled anger in response. "What is this?" Sutton looked about the group, scanning each face. "I thought we had gathered to discuss business?"

"We have, and you are it." Robert's voice was deliberately cold. "We have had enough of your games, Sutton, your illegitimate practices that many of us can testify to. If you would rather we address this in a court and make it public, so be it. *Or*, you can accept our terms and withdraw."

Sutton's eyes narrowed. "*Your terms?*" He looked at Pembroke.

"You owe many of us here large sums. Our terms are that you pay back everything you have manipulated from others, excluding my wife's inheritance. She does not care about your father's fortune. Keep it. In return, we shall not press charges within a court. Your choice, Sutton. Public humiliation or repayment of the money you have blackmailed and forced from us, and if any of us hear of any further enforced deals, we break the agreement and present the evidence to a court." Of course, Sutton could easily comprehend their stipulations. It was blackmail, after all.

Again, Sutton looked about the group, but then his eyes fixed on Jane.

Robert felt her fingers leave his, blocking any temptation he may have had to pull her closer.

Instead, she stepped forward, her eyes levelled on Sutton's, while all others in the room watched her.

Robert's hand reached involuntarily to her waist. His instinct to protect her was just as strong as hers to protect him.

"You bitch!" Sutton's eyes flashed with unguarded hatred as his gaze set on Jane and his words sought to wound. Then he shot a look about the room, challenging each and every man. "If you are doing this because of her, she is just a whore. She stole my inheritance with her calculated wiles. She is not worth your effort!"

Jane's chin tilted up, expressing defiance as one of her hands pushed Robert's away from her waist. Her other lifted, palm outstretched, to silence the influential men in the room.

Robert's chest swelled, his heart overflowing, not stirred by a desire to protect, but with immense pride in her strength.

"You and I both know how false that statement is, Your Grace." Her voice was strong and assured. "So much so, I refuse to even protest against it. No one is here because of me. They are here because this time *you* have gone too far. No matter what you believe, you cannot just do as you please to the disadvantage of others. This, Your Grace, is your reprisal. You must face the result of your own actions. You are accountable, Joshua, not I."

"As the lady states, it is *your* behaviour which is in question, Sutton. I have seen nothing inappropriate in Lady Barrington's. There is no call to insult her when it is we who have approached you," the Duke of Pembroke concluded.

Nods and echoes of agreement rose about the room.

Sutton sneered at Pembroke then at Jane. "Then why is she here?"

"Because Lady Barrington has been an equal victim in this." Richard, the Marquess of Wiltshire stepped forward. "She rightly wished to be a part of the meeting, and any further slander or actions against Lord and Lady Barrington will equally incur our information being sent to the courts."

Robert watched Sutton drain his glass and set it down on the mantel. The tension had gone from his body. "Very well." The man faced the room, his gaze passing over those gathered. They had bound him fully. Sutton could make no further move against Jane. "It seems you have won then, Jane." His eyes fixed on her. "Lord Barrington." His eyes lifted to Robert's as his hand reached inside his coat.

Robert held the bastard's gaze. If Jane had refused to bow to his intimidation then Robert was hardly likely to bend. *Give us what you have, Sutton.*

The man drew a pistol and held it in Robert's direction.

The room broke into an uproar as Sutton aimed at Robert's head and the scene slipped into slow motion.

Jane spun and braced herself across his body, as though she could protect him from the shot.

Edward moved, too, leaping across to knock Sutton's hand aside. The shot went wide, hitting the cornice in the corner of the room and sending down a shower of plaster. Others followed Edward's movement, falling on to Sutton and knocking him to the floor.

When the commotion ended, Robert's arm was about his wife,

holding her secure and Sutton was pinned beneath several eminent lords, while Edward's knee was across Sutton's outstretched arm. Richard kicked the gun from Sutton's hand.

"They could hang you for this, Sutton. I'll call for a magistrate." Devonshire stood at the open French door behind Robert, and the terrace was filling up with guests who'd heard the pistol fire.

"At least we can be certain he will be no more trouble." Sutton's gun dangled from Richard's finger by the trigger.

"He had his choice. He made it," Edward added, one hand now also pressing Sutton's cheek to the floor.

"I have always thought you mad. You have only proven it by making such a foolish attempt at murder. Give it up, man. Your game is lost." The Duke of Pembroke looked down on Sutton, who writhed on the floor, angry and fighting against his restraint.

"This is the fault of that bitch. I told you she is a whore, prostituting herself for Barrington's aid."

Jane hugged Robert harder, her face buried into his neck.

"No one is listening to him, Jane. Ignore it," he whispered to her ear.

But her unwavering strength and courage shone through, and she lifted her head as he felt her spine stiffen.

He smiled.

"Thank you," she whispered, pressing a discreet kiss on his cheek.

The Duchess of Devonshire stepped through the French door. "Lady Barrington? Do come away. There are many of us who wish to apologise for believing the Duke of Sutton's nonsense. Leave this to the men."

Jane drew away from Robert, but her eyes said she did not wish to leave him.

"Go. He can do no more harm."

Her emerald gaze shone with the uncertainty he knew she

would only show him.

Curling one finger beneath her chin, he kissed her lips swiftly. "You'll do, girl," he said before the Duchess of Devonshire led her away.

Jane found herself at the centre of a mass of feminine attention as the details of what had occurred spread throughout the gathering. Many came to the drawing room, where Lady Devonshire had secured Jane, to offer their condolence, support, and commiseration for her earlier suffering.

Of course, many declared they had known there was something not quite right about the Dukes of Sutton and wished they had made a complaint against them earlier, or that they had come to the country to offer Jane support. But Jane knew these comments to be nothing but pretension. If the *ton* had cared for anything beyond their own ends, they would not have wished, *but done.*

However, she suffered their hollow professions of concern and accepted Lady Devonshire's offer of tea in good grace while wishing desperately that Violet was still in town. Yet Jane was glad of Ellen's company and looked from one woman to another, accepting condolences, though her eyes regularly turned to the door.

When, finally, she saw the one person she'd been waiting for, she called out, "Robert!" She set her cup aside and rushed to embrace him, like the tide pulled towards the moon.

"All is well, sweetheart," he whispered as she held him. "We have seen the last of him, I hope."

"May we go home?" she answered, looking up into his eyes.

"Home?" he echoed. "Wherever you are is that to me. Come then. At least now, I know you'll be secure there."

She nodded before turning back to the interested group of women. Damn them all. She didn't care who had slept with him. Let them be jealous. He had eyes only for her now, and they had never truly known him anyway, not as she did. Her fingers caught Robert's behind her back. "Thank you for your kindness, Your Grace." She dropped a curtsy to the Duchess of Devonshire.

"Not at all, dear. You are welcome here whenever you wish, and may I call upon you?"

Requests to call upon them were then reiterated about the room. Jane accepted them with aplomb while Robert whispered, "Our afternoons of leisure are at an end then."

She struck his hip with a balled fist behind her dress, offered another curtsy to the Duchess of Devonshire, and said, "Thank you" once more, then looked at her audience, "You're most kind."

"Now, if you will excuse us, I am sure my wife is tired. It is beyond time I took her home to bed." Robert's interjection cut the air, and his fingers gripped her elbow to defend himself from further blows, she assumed.

"Of course, Lord Barrington, do. You must be very fatigued." The Duchess of Devonshire rose. "I will show you out."

Robert's fingers still pressuring Jane's elbow, she followed Lady Devonshire.

"Such an appalling business," the Duchess concluded as they reached the hall. "But at least now, you may sleep in peace, knowing it is at an end."

"Your Grace. Thank you," Robert said when the butler opened the door.

Jane saw James, Robert's groom, in the street below, waiting with the open carriage door in his hand. He helped her in, then her husband's tall, lean, muscular frame slid in beside her.

A few moments later, the horses pulled away and Robert loosened his cravat with one hand while picking up hers with the other and weaving their fingers together. "Thank God we are away. It is *not* sleeping on my mind."

She turned and caught his rakish smile.

"We shall have to retire to the country immediately," he added, "I am not sharing you with them."

She laughed and hugged him. The devil then hauled her on to his lap.

She squealed. "Robert!"

"Robert, indeed! I want you to ride me home." His voice was husky.

"Ride you?"

"I'll tell you how," he whispered to her mouth before he kissed her.

Her heart thumped, the scene with Joshua slipping from her mind. He was pushing boundaries again, and deliberately, to make her forget. "You are wicked."

"And as I've told you before, you love it, my strait-laced *ex*-duchess. Lift your skirts and sit astride me."

Her fingers pressed against his chest, and she held him back a little. "Will you never cease your rakish behaviour, my Lord?"

"Never," he answered. "I've spent too many years fantasising about you, Jane. Now, I have all those years of fantasies to fulfill."

She struck his shoulder with the heel of her hand. "Wretch. You've probably fulfilled them with half the women there tonight."

"But none of them were you. You were the woman I fantasised for. God, I want to make that known. I want to shock the *ton* again. Let them know I love my wife. Shall I ravage you in the midst of the next ball? They already know you love me. You thoroughly glowed in that room when I walked in. Your reputation, my cold, proud, ex-dowager duchess, is in tatters. You'll be the name on every tongue for days."

"Then I shall accept your offer to move back to the country. I have no desire to be renowned as your latest conquest."

His fingers curved beneath her chin. "Then I shall definitely ensure it is made public that it is the other way around. I am

363

yours. Now, give me my husband's due."

"Rogue." She struck his shoulder again in a half-hearted rebuke, but willingly complied, kissing him as she moved to sit astride his hips. She intended to ride him to oblivion. He'd beaten Joshua. He'd done it.

Chapter Twenty-three

Robert watched Jane move about the crowded room. They had settled at Farnborough and fallen into a natural routine. Today, they were holding their first social gathering for family and friends. Unlike in the summer, Jane was truly part of them.

She was circulating, undertaking her duty as his wife. She left Ellen in the company of his friends, the Forths, to speak to the Duchess of Pembroke. Then she glanced across the room at him. He leaned back against a windowsill, his arms folding over his chest, and smiled, giving her a reassuring look, but feeling hungry to be alone with her again. She smiled, too, but then scowled at him, a smile in her eyes.

Robert looked away, biting his lower lip to stop himself from laughing. She'd read his thoughts; she knew what he'd been thinking. Who'd have known he would find her expanding figure so alluring? God, there was something very precious about knowing he'd instigated the bulge clearly visible beneath her day dress. Each time he thought of their child, growing inside her, he felt a sudden wave of awe sweep over him.

He was going to be a father. Not an uncle. *A father*. His and Jane's child was busy forming in there.

"She is good for you."

Robert turned to look at his brother.

Edward smiled and nodded in Jane's direction.

Robert smiled more broadly. "She is more than good for me. She *is* me."

Edward sipped from a glass of champagne, and his eyes strayed to Ellen, who was also visibly with child, before returning to Robert. "I'm sorry. I misjudged you for years. But I still do not see how you kept this thing with Jane from me when we were young."

Robert's lips tilted as he remembered the moment Jane had fallen from her horse and this had begun. "You stayed with friends at times during the holidays. It left us together. When you were here, we passed each other messages in a code Jane developed to tell me where to meet her and when."

"Your early morning rides, when you wanted peace and quiet. Your afternoon walks, when you needed to think. I thought you had outgrown me."

Robert laughed, and Edward turned to put his glass down on the tray of a passing footman. Robert caught Jane's eye, smiled and winked twice, then tilted his head to the right. She narrowed her eyes at him and shook her head, but then, having glanced about to check no one watched, gave him a wicked seductress smile as her finger lifted and rubbed her ear.

He nodded just as Edward turned back.

"Ridiculously," Edward said, "I'd have probably never met Ellen if you and Jane had not gone your separate ways, because you'd never have gone abroad."

"No." Robert stared at his brother. He'd not thought of that, and Ellen was perfect for Edward.

"Uncle Robert!" Mary-Rose barrelled through the French doors, the fresh smell of spring carried with her in her clothes. Bending, Robert captured her as the tot charged into his leg, squealing. He lifted her to his hip as her elder brother, John, raced in behind her. Robert imagined his own children thus, when they came. He was impatient for that day.

"Coward," John accused as he approached, his skin flushed and his chest heaving. Robert saw grass in John's hair and knew, without doubt, Mary-Rose was responsible. John was growing up, and he did not always wish to play her childish games, and Mary-Rose had run to her uncle for safety because she knew Robert was soft on her. There was tension in John's jaw. He rarely lost his temper. He was, in general, a placid lad, but he was in the turbulent years of his life, and he had grown much quieter lately, and more solitary. John lifted his chin with a look too much like His Grace, the Duke of Pembroke, John's grandsire, for comfort.

"She is an imp, Papa. Send her to bed without supper."

Mary-Rose grinned at her brother, unrepentant.

Robert eased the argument by offering to take John riding tomorrow and telling him he might stay with the men after dinner, and then to Mary he offered ice cream in the nursery as her appeasement.

Edward agreed to both of Robert's offers and then took John away to play billiards, leaving Mary-Rose in Robert's arms.

One of Mary-Rose's hands rested on his shoulder, the other touched his cheek then slid to his earlobe. Her small fingers rubbed it.

It was a thing she'd done since a babe. It was a subtle sign she was tired. Her head tipped against his shoulder and he settled her more securely on his forearm. "Uncle Robert?"

"Yes, poppet?"

"Papa said Aunt Jane is expecting a baby like Mama."

"She is, sweetheart, so do not ask either your Mama or Aunt Jane to pick you up." His eyes went to Jane across the room, as he felt warmth bloom in his chest. God, he longed to hold his own child.

His eyes left Jane and looked at the clock on the mantel.

Half an hour later, standing in the rose garden, surrounded by hedges with the start of summer growth, Robert waited, hands in his pockets. The tepid spring air held expectation and budding life, and birdsong rang about the quiet garden. He heard the crunch of light footsteps on the gravel. It was his wife.

When he saw her, the air caught in his lungs, just as it had done that night in London when she'd first returned to public life, dressed in her blacks. Her dress was gripped in a fist to hold her hem away from the damp ground.

She smiled and made a face before saying, "I have no idea why you like to play these silly games. We could have just gone up to bed, and no one would have said a word. Most of our guests have retired in any case."

He smiled, too, with a wicked, wolfish edge he knew she'd spot. "Forgive me. I just can't stop myself from testing to make sure you'll still come."

She stepped into his open arms, looking up at him as he embraced her. "Of course, I shall still come. How could I not?"

"Ooo!" Her palm pressed to her stomach, and he felt concern spin through him as he let her go.

Both her hands were on her stomach. "Oh my goodness!"

His hand braced her arm. "What is it? You should not have hurried."

She laughed. "Oh Robert, it is nothing to be worried over. Feel." She caught hold of his palm and pressed it against her belly.

He felt a sharp little jerk of movement. "What is it?"

"The baby is moving. Ellen told me it would happen, but this is the first time I've felt it. She said sometimes, later, when it grows bigger, you can actually see the shape of a hand or foot."

Robert stretched his fingers out, spreading them across Jane's stomach.

He watched his hand. "I cannot wait to see you," he whispered, then looked up. "Having Edward's family here only makes me more desperate for our own, Jane."

"*Patience*," she whispered.

"Was always something I lacked." He gave her another smile. He'd expended enough. They'd had to endure Ellen's announcement, then Violet's, before Jane had finally followed suit.

It had turned out that Violet's disappearance from London at the time he'd married Jane had been due to an unforeseen circumstance. She'd disappeared into the country to hide her condition, even from Geoff. But Geoff had followed, brought her back and married her. The child had been born only three and a half months later.

Jane had been glad for Violet, but there had also been jealousy. Jane had longed for children; Robert had, too.

It was happening now.

Jane slipped her fingers about Robert's midriff beneath his morning coat and smiled. His head bowed and his mouth claimed hers. They'd not once been at odds since they'd come back to Farnborough.

She broke the kiss, caught up his fingers, and tugged. "Come on, come to bed."

"An offer I cannot refuse," he stated. "But do you think we should?" His gaze dropped to her bulging stomach; he didn't wish to hurt the child.

"Yes, absolutely. Ellen said it does no harm." Stepping backward, she tugged on his hand again. "And if you think I would make my impatient, rake of a husband wait—" she teased.

"I could wait, if I must. Did I not wait long enough for you?"

Lifting one eyebrow, she chided, "That, my Lord, does not persuade, for as I recall, waiting was *not* what you did."

"You injure me. I have said a dozen times I wish that undone."

Jane smiled. She knew how desperately he longed to be able to change the past; he'd made sure she did. Yet he could not.

"A rake, known for deserting woman, with regrets and a tender heart. Who'd have known," she mocked. "Violet will be exclaiming over how domesticated you have become when she arrives tomorrow. I keep telling her you have not changed at all. You are the real Robert. The rakehell was the fraud. I know how much you love me, Robert. I was only teasing."

He nodded, but he still felt emotion welling in his chest, guilt and pain as well as love.

She gripped his nape, pulled him down, and kissed him, cherishing him, he could feel her love. Then she whispered, "Come on," tugging his hand once more and stepping back.

He smiled. "Do you know, I think you're worse than me now, woman."

"That is impossible," she threw back.

Epilogue

A loud wail launched from the chamber along the hall, and, instantly, Robert was on his feet, his heart pounding. He did not even look at Edward, but just ran to Jane's chamber, thrusting the door wide. The scene before him froze him on the spot. Ellen stood before the window, folding a dirty sheet, her dress stained.

His eyes turned to his wife, who lay in the four-poster bed. She was pale, and her eyelids drooped with obvious exhaustion. Her hair was plastered to her brow, damp with sweat, but she smiled broadly as she looked at him.

"A son," she whispered.

His eyes passed to the midwife who was handing Jane a wriggling bundle. As Jane took it, the infant kicked, and the linen slid back, revealing Robert's naked son.

The child opened up his lungs and wailed.

Robert felt his heart stop in silent surrender. He'd never forget this moment, the first sight of his son. Bobbing in a shallow curtsy, the midwife pulled away.

The bed had been straightened and the sheets tucked in about Jane, but as he watched, she drew the babe to her chest, and by some instinct, his son sought and found her breast, nuzzling for her nipple. Then all Robert heard was the sound of sucking.

Emotion welled in his chest.

"Come and see him," Jane urged.

One arm cradling their son, she held the other out to Robert. He barely noticed the other women leaving the room with muted words of congratulations. He was simply too stunned.

"Come and sit on the bed and look at him."

He did, drifting in some odd dream. He kicked off his house shoes and sat beside her, the soft down mattress giving way beneath him. His fingers reached in wonder to touch his son, mentally counting every toe and finger, following every perfect line of every limb, to the mop of black hair atop his head. Robert's finger slipped to the boy's palm and his son's little hand closed tightly.

Robert's heart ached, about to burst. He'd never thought it was possible to feel this happy, so overwhelmingly full of emotion.

His gaze lifting to Jane's, he saw her look at their son. "He's beautiful."

Her head lifted. She had tears in her eyes. "Isn't he? *Henry*." She said the name they'd discussed so often when the boy was still invisible, tucked inside her womb.

He was named for Robert's father, the man who'd been like a father to her, too, more so than her own. If the child had been a girl, she would have been named for his mother.

"He'd be proud of you," Jane continued, speaking to their child. Then she looked up at Robert. "He'd be proud of you both."

Robert arched a brow at that, but it wasn't a moment for old anger.

My son – Henry.

He looked at the tiny boy. When the babe stopped sucking and looked in Robert's direction, he felt his heart lurch again.

Jane covered her breast, then wrapped the sheet back about the wriggling child, and held him out towards Robert. "Hold him."

With wonder and self-doubt, he took the infant, tentatively cradling the child on his forearm.

He'd held small children before, Mary-Rose and little Robbie, but this precious little bundle was his own son. His and Jane's. Every breath Robert took, from this day forward, would be for his family, his wife and his son, and any other children that came along.

Still clasping Robert's finger, the boy's dark grey eyes stared up at him, absorbing everything. Beside them, Jane slid down the bed and rolled to her side, her cheek resting into her palm as her other hand lifted to stroke the child's head.

"Can you believe it?" she said with a dreamy smile, already half asleep. She looked exhausted.

Robert bent and kissed her forehead. Her eyelids lifted as she clearly fought to stay awake.

"Sleep, darling, you've earned a rest. I'll take him to meet his uncle. Besides, you need to build your strength back up. I want a dozen more."

Her lips lifted in a sleepy smile and she whispered, "Not on your life," before nodding off.

~

When Jane woke, Robert was lying beside her, on his side, his head supported on his palm, over his crooked arm. Henry lay on the covers in between them, free of the sheet, and Robert's brown eyes were intently focused on their son. He hadn't even noticed she'd woken.

Robert held Henry's hand, and Jane's joined the embrace, covering it. "Hello, you."

Robert looked at her, and she looked at Henry. "And you, little one." She kissed her son's brow. He smelled delicious.

Robert smiled. "Feel better?"

"Much. But now I am starving. How has he been?"

"Fine, but missing his mama, I think, which is why I brought

373

him back."

She smiled, watching Robert get up. "I like being called that."

Henry gripped her hand. He was so beautiful, so perfect – hers and Robert's – the life they'd both created. The infant's dark eyes turned to her, scanning his new world with a visible thirst for information.

"Henry." She breathed his name as Robert pulled the cord of the servant's bell, presumably to send for some supper. "You are more than precious to your papa and I, little man—"

"Just as precious as you are to me." She looked up as the mattress dipped and Robert knelt back on the bed.

"And you to me," she replied.

"I love you. I'll never be able to say it enough." Robert leaned over Henry and kissed her forehead then pulled back to lie down again, beside their son.

Her fingers touched Robert's cheek. "I love you, too." Her voice was croaky.

Robert turned his head and pressed his lips into her palm. "You know, you're my saviour, Jane, don't you? God knows what would have become of me without you. Certainly not this." His eyes were shining. "My estate would have gone to Edward. I'd never have wed, never have known what this felt like. You're my hero, Jane Marlow. That is what you are."

"Heroine," she corrected.

"No, that's far too tame a word for my Boadicea. You're a bloody hero."

"And you're just in an accommodating mood because I bore you a son."

A knock struck the chamber door. Her maid.

"Just for the record," he said as he moved off the bed again. "Be prepared. I am liable to be in an accommodating mood for the rest of my life. I do hope you won't get bored."

"*Never,*" she breathed with a wicked laugh. "All I longed for before I met you again was a peaceful life."

He smiled.

"Robert, I think we were always meant to be, weren't we? No matter what happened, we would have found each other in the end."

Don't miss the first in this intensely emotional Regency series, *The Illicit Love of a Courtesan*!